A VENOMOUS KISS

"Miz Sunny don't like snakes much," Jube announced.

"Maybe you should sit down, boss," suggested one of the wranglers.

Sunny straightened, shaking her head. "There's no need to make a fuss," she assured, leveling her stare to include everyone but Matt, fearful he still held the deadly menace. Pride kept her from breaking into a run as she headed toward her wagon. Matt grabbed her arm, stopping her hurried flight mid-stride.

"I was starting to believe Miss Sunny Donovan wasn't afraid of anything," he said softly.

"Let go of me." She struggled against his hold and the unfamiliar feelings raging within her. As he released his grip, she searched for an end to this conversation. "I appreciate what you did back there."

"That was a far cry from a heartfelt thank-you, angel," he whispered.

"Don't call me that," she replied as she turned to stare into his midnight blue eyes.

"Fine . . . Sunny," he replied. "Now, about that thank-you. I had something . . . nicer in mind." He smiled teasingly.

She couldn't name what kept her rooted here, and she was further irritated that she found such enjoyment with his sudden playfulness. "What did you want?" she challenged.

He said nothing as he closed his eyes and lowered his lips over hers. . . .

WILD AND FREE

Jackie Stephens

Zebra Books
Kensington Publishing Corp.
http://www.zebrabooks.com

ZEBRA BOOKS are published by

Kensington Publishing Corp.
850 Third Avenue
New York, NY 10022

First Printing: August, 2000
10 9 8 7 6 5 4 3 2 1

Printed in the United States of America

Chapter One

''Drop the gun, mister!''

Matt Lanier's heart skidded to a stop at the soft, throaty demand. *Where in blazes did she come from?*

Looking up, he saw black boots perched on a lower limb of the oak tree. The long, metal barrel of a Colt poked through the concealing foliage—and was aimed straight at his head. Matt swallowed dryly as a sickening wave of terror welled in his belly, then tossed his six-shooter onto the ground beside his hat.

''Hands up, mister. I want them resting on nothing but air.''

He raised his hands as ordered, leaning his head sideways just enough to peer with one eye around the thick, knotty bark. The outlaw he had tracked through the Indian Territory for the last week hadn't moved. Jake Walden sat several yards away astride a bay mare which bore Matt's Rocking L brand and watched as six Comanche braves herded away a good number of cattle in the distance.

My cattle, dammit! And four good horses, too!

Matt recalled every word the sheriff in Ellsworth told him

about Walden's gang. He had mentioned four men, two Indians, and a kid riding with the outlaw—not one thing about a woman! So who was she? And what was she doing here? He jumped at the shrill whistle that suddenly exploded from behind the leaves, then frowned, realizing he had his answer.

Best start making my peace with the good Lord.

Walden reeled the horse around and nudged the mount to a slow walk. Matt took it the woman's signal hadn't been one of alarm, and wisely used the precious seconds afforded him to work on a means of escape. Glancing back up, he saw her boots now dangling inches from his fingers. The gun was nowhere in sight.

Plodding hooves drew closer. Matt's heart pounded furiously. Taking a deep breath, he bent his knees, jumped and grabbed her by the ankles, then yanked hard as his feet returned to the ground with a heavy thud. She let out a loud squeal as she tumbled from the tree. Her knees smacked him in the chest and sent him stumbling backward. He lost his footing, landing hard on his back. A thick braid of hair whipped him across the face as the woman fell on top of him and knocked the air out of his lungs in a loud whoosh. She quickly rolled from his chest. Matt gulped a much needed breath, turned to his side and saw her scramble for her dropped gun. Reaching out, he caught hold of her boot, then cursed when her foot slipped free of the hard leather.

Matt sat up, seized her sock-clad ankle, and pulled her back at the same moment she grabbed for the Colt. She curled her body up and around, then raised her fists. In a situation where his time remaining in life wasn't being counted in seconds, he might have laughed at the little spitfire for thinking she was any match for him—until she kicked him with her free foot and delivered a rock-hard pain to his hip. He swore, grabbed both her legs and pinned them under his, then captured her flailing hands.

"Let her go, or ya'll be wearin' this bullet!"

They stilled at the same time. Matt released her fists. The woman scooted out from under his legs, grabbed her boot off the ground and put it back on, then reached for her gun. Matt rose to his feet.

"Stay put!" the outlaw commanded. The cold metal pressed against the back of his head forced Matt down to the ground.

The woman stood and walked over to where he sat in the grass-covered dirt. Matt's stare raked up long legs, over rounded hips and narrow waist clearly outlined in her tan buckskin pants and loosely tucked shirt. His gaze stopped on the Colt gripped between her slender fingers. She held the weapon with as much confidence as any man he had ever faced, and even without Walden standing behind him, Matt knew he was a dead man.

There had been a time not long ago when he wouldn't have cared whether he lived or died, but things were different now. He was settled, had plans for the future again—or had until Walden had interfered. Damn! He had been so close, worked so hard. Well, if it was his time to go, he would at least enjoy the sight God saw fit to be his last.

He lingered over the generous swell that shaped her thin, white shirt, then lifted his eyes to her softly tanned face, and collided with the prettiest blue eyes he had ever seen. Their soft azure color reminded him of the skies over his ranch, right down to the fierce storm brewing on the horizon of her smoldering depths.

"All right, you snake-bellied varmint, where's Walden?" she snapped.

Matt drew his brows together in confusion. "What the hell are you talking about?"

"You know damn well." Her eyes narrowed with contempt. A thin, white line circled her tightly clenched mouth.

Matt wondered if she was crazy, as well as blind.

"Take a good look, lady, he's standing behind me." Before he could give thought to the shock on her face, something hard struck the back of his head, and everything went black.

* * *

The sun began its daily descent on the horizon, spreading a blanket of warm rays across the prairie which turned the sea of grass nearly translucent. A gentle breeze kicked up and danced slowly in the welcomed fading heat. Closing her eyes, Sunny lifted her face higher. The caressing relief on her cheeks brought a sigh to her lips.

If only all my problems could be solved by the brush of a soft wind.

Her eyes flew open as the left front wheel beneath her pitched upward over the rutted terrain, then slammed back to the ground. Sunny tightened her hold on the reins as the wagon rocked from side to side before settling back to its rhythmic pace. She listened intently, but heard nothing, only the sounds of grinding wood, rubbing leather, and metal bits crashing together as the pair of horses plodded along. Concerned, she shifted her bottom on the hard bench and glanced through the oval canvas opening to her newest problem—the unconscious, dark-headed stranger who hadn't moved or made a sound since they had put him on the makeshift pallet, well over an hour ago.

Sunny chewed on her bottom lip and stared at the heavy growth of beard that darkened the stranger's tanned face. Beaded moisture covered his brow. His tall, muscular form barely fit between the supplies Red Cloud had brought when he had met with her earlier, before his braves came to get the cattle. She frowned, recalling that along with the supplies, Red Cloud had brought news from Fort Sill that Indian Agent Silas Taylor was standing firm on the deadline. She had till the end of the month. Eleven days. No more. If she didn't bring in the two escaped braves riding with Jake Walden by then, the agent would send her younger brother and sister away.

The last thing she needed was another problem. She should be concentrating on what must be done, instead of worrying that this stranger might not be getting enough air. It was not like her to be anxious over a man, especially a white man. Why was *he* any different?

"Any sign of life back there?"

Sunny stopped chewing her lip and turned to the burly cowhand pulling his bay up alongside the wagon. "Not yet. I think you hit him too hard, Shorty."

The cowhand shrugged. "I didn't want to have to deal with him *and* Walden." He spoke through one corner of his mouth and clamped the other side around his half-burnt cheroot. "Course, I wasn't expectin' to find the space behind me empty, either. Ya still thinkin' we were wrong, and he's not in cahoots with the outlaw?"

Sunny nodded. "I saw it in his eyes." Those intense, midnight blue eyes that had sent an unfamiliar heat rushing through her blood, and had the power to distract her still just thinking about them. "He thought *you* were Jake Walden."

"Yeah, but he never got a good look at my face."

Sunny dismissed any concern with a wave of her hand. "No matter. More than likely, he's just passing through. Probably thought he was about to luck into a bundle of reward money. We'll find out his name, and why he's here. Then Jube can feed him and send him on his way."

"Think it'll be that easy, do ya?" One of Shorty's bushy, blond brows arched high on his forehead.

She nodded, though it wasn't what she believed. In truth, Sunny sensed a great deal of trouble ahead with this stranger. But until she knew for sure what threat—if any—he posed, there was no reason to worry her friend.

"Hope you're right."

Sunny stared at Shorty. The hard lines etched in his square jaw enhanced the strong likeness between him and Jake Walden. The resemblance had frightened her when she had first met Shorty, and could still at times stir the memories she tried to keep buried. The cowhand was short and stout like Walden, with broad shoulders, a wide chest, and arms the size of healthy, aged timber. He had the same face and the same blond hair, but that was where the similarities ended. Shorty was calm, cautious, always alert like a well-trained horse. Walden was more like a rabid wolf. For the last two years, she had stayed as far away as she could from the man, let him think she was dead. But now, thanks to Agent Taylor, she was forced to hunt Walden down—face him one more time.

"What did Red Cloud find out?"

Sunny reined in her wandering thoughts. "Not enough. Only that two Kiowa renegades met with Walden, Swift Arrow, and Gray Wolf about a week ago. Not far north from here. He didn't get to talk with Grierson, either. The colonel arranged for the supplies, but he was gone when Red Cloud got there."

Shorty took a long draw on his cheroot, slowly blew out the white, curling smoke, then narrowed his almond-shaped eyes. "So now what, boss?"

"We stick to the plan. Red Cloud will look for those Kiowas and find out what they know. I'll meet with him again in two days."

Shorty nodded, then cocked his head. "Don't take this wrong, Sunny, ya know I trust ya, but are ya still certain this stranger's not ridin' with Walden's gang?"

"Something tells me he's here for another reason." Sunny paused as a queer sense of familiarity settled in the pit of her stomach. Her eyes widened. "Great Spirit. I might know what it is." She looked at the stranger again. Her heart did a confusing skip. Quickly, she turned back to Shorty. "Ride ahead to camp. Tell Maggie what happened. It's possible this is the man she's been telling us about."

Worry sparked in Shorty's eyes. "Dang, I should've thought of that before I hit him."

"There wasn't time," Sunny assured. "We needed to get out of there in case Walden *was* hanging around to ambush us."

Shorty nodded, but she saw the uneasiness linger in his parting stare before he nudged the bay to a faster gait and rode off. Damn! If the man did turn out to be Maggie's friend, Sunny's problems were about to increase tenfold.

She watched Shorty race toward the sloping hill and the valley beyond where she had earlier told the other trail drivers to bed the herd down for the night. With a heavy sigh, she resigned herself to the slower pace of the lumbering wagon. But what she really wanted was to ride with haste and let the wind rip away her concern for this stranger, along with these peculiar feelings his presence evoked in her body. Drawing nearer to camp, she began to question the wisdom of bringing him here, so close to her plan . . . her life.

Sunny tried to brush the worry aside, but her instincts refused to be ignored. She couldn't push away the powerful sensation that her world was about to change . . . because of this man.

Matt barely glimpsed the white expanse before a sharp bolt of pain charged across his head and stabbed the back of his eyes, forcing them closed again. *Where in tarnation am I?* The pounding escalated to a deafening throb. Placing thumb and forefinger at his temples, he rubbed slowly, methodically. His parched throat begged for water. The flesh ripped on his dried mouth when he pried his lips apart.

God, had he taken up drinking again? Surely not. He hadn't had a drink in over three years, not since Denver . . . and the gunfight. Besides, his stomach wasn't churning the way it usually did after a mind-numbing night. So what the hell was wrong with him?

Matt tried to recall his last conscious thought. Nothing. Frustrated, he blew out a heavy sigh, cautiously opened his eyes again, and waited. When no jabbing pain ricocheted through his head, he stared at the canvas sky stretched above, then at his surroundings in the strange wagon. Wooden barrels lined either side, confining him. In a corner at the back, his gaze stopped on a pile of neatly folded clothing. A yellow calico skirt and two white blouses were topped with a silver brush set.

Good Lord, he was with a woman! How on earth had that happened?

The clear image of a blue-eyed beauty sprang from the darkness temporarily ruling his thoughts: a pretty oval face framed with curling blond tendrils, thin nutmeg brows delicately arched, and a cute, pert nose.

Matt sat up on the hard pallet and rubbed the large knot at the base of his skull. Who was she? The last thing he remembered was being alone . . . in Indian Territory!

Matt's heart slammed against his ribs as the memory returned full force. He had come south looking for the stolen herd that had been headed to his ranch in the Wyoming Territory, and for Walden, the piece of scum who had taken them and killed his brother, Danny—the only family he had had left.

Instinctively, Matt reached for his gun, not surprised to find the holster empty. Looking through the opening at the rear of the wagon, he half expected to see Walden and the little spitfire standing outside with their guns drawn. But only evening shadows reigning over the tall, majestic pines and elms filled his vision.

Why hadn't Jake Walden shot him . . . as he had shot Danny? Matt sure wasn't going to hang around and ask. He would be a fool not to take advantage of the outlaw's careless failure to tie him up. It was time to get out of here before someone came to check on him.

Matt scooted across the hard planks toward the back and eyed his black Stetson propped against the wood next to his canteen. The outlaws had found his horse. Good. He would need the swift mount to make his escape. He shoved his hat on his head, then wasting only a few seconds to quench his thirst, crouched low on his feet and listened as the crickets chirped their sporadic, nightly cacophony. Insects fluttered about in anticipation of darkness' cooling respite. A squirrel chattered in a nearby tree. Satisfied nothing but nature stirred,

Matt swung one leg over the wagon end . . . and heard approaching footsteps coming from around the front.

Damn! Tucking his leg back in, he searched the wagon for a weapon. Nothing, unless he wanted to defend himself with a hip flask and a hairbrush. Dropping to his hands and knees, he crawled toward the makeshift pallet. If he pretended to still be unconscious, maybe he could buy himself some more ti—

"Thank the Spirits, you're finally awake."

The woman's strangely whispered words stopped Matt in his tracks. It was hardly the greeting he had expected. She sounded almost . . . relieved. Probably wanted his death to be slow and agonizing, he reasoned. And just what the dickens kind of spirit was she thanking, anyway?

Glancing over his shoulder, he saw the woman he had pulled from the oak tree staring unabashedly at his backside. Their eyes met. He detected a slight flush in her tanned cheeks, but her bright, steady gaze showed no signs of guilt. He lowered his sight down the white cotton-clad arm she hung over the wagon's edge, and immediately recognized the six-shooter gripped in her hand.

Matt swung around and sat down, resting his arms on bent knees. "You planning to kill me with my own gun?"

"What?" Her eyes narrowed in puzzlement, then followed his nod down to the Colt. She looked up and met his stare. "Oh, you mean this. A man can't survive out here without his gun, Mr. Lanier." She slid her fingers to the barrel, spun it around, and handed it to him stock first.

Every muscle in Matt's body tightened. How did she know his name? And why she was doing this? Was it some sort of trick, or was she really as crazy as he had thought earlier?

Matt slowly reached out his hand and circled his fingers around the smooth wood. Their eyes locked again. For a split second he thought she might change her mind, but her hand moved, leaving the full weight of the Colt hanging in his fist.

"What's Walden going to say about this?"

He was taken aback by the heated storm clouds that instantly formed in her eyes. "I don't care what Jake Walden has to say about anything."

Was there something he wasn't remembering? And where was Walden, anyway? "Does the rest of the gang feel that way?"

"How should I—" She stopped. Suspicious humor narrowed her darkened gaze. "I knew it. You *did* think that was Walden. And you think I'm riding with him, don't you?"

Matt's anger grew to threatening proportions at her faint smile. "Aren't you?"

"No."

He cocked a single brow. "I know what I saw. Walden met with those Comanches, and you kept watch from that tree."

"The man you saw wasn't Jake Walden. His name's Shorty Myers."

The dull pounding in Matt's head kicked back up. He didn't believe her. The man he had seen matched up perfectly to the description on the wanted poster in his pocket. "Look, lady, I don't much care for games, so—"

"Is he awake yet, Sunny?" The deep, scratchy voice called out from somewhere to the right of the wagon. Matt recognized the harsh tone belonging to the man who had warned him to stay put earlier. Walden!

"Yea, he's awake," she called out, turning away long enough for Matt to slip his gun behind his bent leg.

The outlaw stepped up beside her, and Matt knew with all certainty this was the same man he had seen with the Comanches. Before, he hadn't gotten a good look at the outlaw's face. Now that he was staring him down, Matt was shocked at his mistake—the man *wasn't* Jake Walden. His broad build and wide, chiseled face strongly resembled the outlaw, even the sandy patch of hair on his head fit the description. Instead of Walden's single blue eye and black leather patch the outlaw was reported to wear though, this fella was looking at him with two good eyes that were brown as dirt. Which meant little Miss Spitfire had told him the truth.

"*This* is Shorty Myers."

Matt ignored the smugness in her voice and stared at the man who looked enough like Walden to be his twin, or at the very least a first cousin.

Shorty nodded his greeting. "Right sorry 'bout hittin' ya so hard, Mr. Lanier. I was just protectin' Sunny. Hope ya won't be holdin' no grudge."

Matt remained silent, assessing the man's large shoulders and round arms straining the cotton material of his faded black shirt. A bright red handkerchief barely reached around his large neck to tie in a knot. Last thing Matt wanted was to tangle with this tree trunk, but he didn't understand a blasted thing that was going on. And their hospitality was more than a little suspicious. Even if they weren't riding with Walden, Matt knew they had some connection to the outlaw. Walden stole his herd, and these two somehow came into possession of some of the cattle . . . then gave them away to the damned Indians!

He had dealt with many a rustler when he rode as a Texas Ranger, but he was having trouble figuring out what these two were after. And why they had kidnapped him. If they were hoping he could buy his freedom, or for that matter pay to have his cattle returned, they were in for a big surprise. He would sure like to know how they found out his name, and why she had given his gun back. For the first time, Matt thought to wonder if it was loaded.

"Well, I reckon it's your choice." Shorty shrugged one broad shoulder and turned to Sunny. "Ya want me to fetch Maggie?" At her nod, the cowhand shoved a worn brown hat on his head and walked away.

Matt met Sunny's glare and saw the flames spark in her eyes. "Maggie said you were blunt and short-tempered, Mr. Lanier, but she didn't mention anything about your downright rudeness."

Matt's tightly held control snapped. "What did you want me to do? Thank him for knocking me out, shoving me into this hot box, and bringing me God knows where? And just who is this woman, Maggie, who thinks she knows so much about me?'' His voice rose with each clipped word until he was shouting. He winced at the renewed throbbing in his head.

Her shoulders dropped slightly in resignation, but the defiance in her eyes clearly showed her refusal to cower. *She's got some backbone.* Much as he hated to admit it, Matt liked that.

''Shorty apologized, but it's your own fault you got hit. You shouldn't have been hiding behind that tree, spying on us.'' Her tone was sharp and even, but lacked any apology of her own, he noted. ''As for Maggie,'' she continued hotly, ''that would be Miss Maggie Hollister, a friend of yours, I believe. And one more thing, *Mr. Lanier,* I'm not deaf, so you don't need to shout.''

Maggie Hollister! Matt's mind raced wildly. Was it possible? Maggie's presence would explain how these cattle thieves knew his name. But what would she be doing way out here mixed up with rustlers? Last he had heard, she was still in Oak Valley, teaching school in the small Texas town she had lived in nearly all her life.

Had she been brought here against her will? Her brother owned a big cattle ranch outside of town. Maybe *she* was being held for ransom.

''What have you done to Maggie!'' he boomed, regretting his outburst when the woman flinched.

''Stop your bellowing. Sunny hasn't done a thing to me. Why don't you come out of there and take in the breeze. Maybe it'll help cool you off.''

He was stunned to hear her voice, and relieved to see her unharmed when she appeared at the back of the wagon. Her rich, auburn hair still curled around her ivory face the way he remembered, and he had almost forgotten her eyes were the same deep emerald as her sister's. ''Maggie.''

''It's been a long time, Matt. How are you?'' Her bright smile tugged at his heart.

He didn't answer right away, but holstered his gun and quickly climbed down. Placing his hands on her narrow shoulders, he stared into her face. "It really is you." He pulled her closer, into a hug. "What are you doing here? Besides saving me one more time," he whispered the last against her ear.

Maggie's warm breath brushed his neck as she chuckled softly. "Matt Lanier, the only thing you've ever needed saving from is that temper of yours." She leaned back and tilted her head to meet his gaze. "It sure is good to see you again."

"You don't sound too surprised."

Maggie shook her head. Her smile faded. "I've been expecting you. I told Sunny you'd come after Danny's killer."

Matt stepped back. "You know about that?"

Maggie nodded. "I'm real sorry, Matt," she told him sadly.

"I know you are." He wiped the tear from her cheek with his finger.

Sunny loudly cleared her throat. Matt looked up, surprised by her fiery blue stare. He dropped his hand to his side, then puzzled over his action. Maggie took a step back, glanced oddly at Sunny, then turned her arched brow at him. Matt tensed, worried she was going to ask what just happened. Since he had no idea, he certainly didn't want to try and explain it.

"I heard about this afternoon. Sunny's a good friend of mine. She didn't mean you any harm."

Matt was relieved Maggie didn't pursue the question evident in her eyes. He stared at her "friend." Was she keeping company with outlaws these days, or was he wrong about Miss Spitfire?

"I suppose that explains why you gave me my gun back, Miss . . . ?"

"Donovan," Sunny supplied, offering her hand.

He removed his hat, nodded. "Miss Donovan "Matt gripped her smaller hand in his longer than he knew was necessary. For the life of him, he couldn't figure out why. It just seemed . . . right.

He smiled at the flush that crept into her cheeks and wondered if she was remembering their earlier struggle. His own unwilling thoughts wandered to the memory of her slender body on his, her blond braid striking his face and arms while she had fought like a wild animal. He pictured her hair loose, the lustrous strands brushing over her shoulders and disappearing down her back. He thought of running his fingers through the heavy mass, then frowned at the heated flow that raced through his veins. He hadn't felt anything for a woman since . . . well, not for a long time. He didn't want to feel anything, either, especially for a little gal with pretty sky eyes he was sure could melt his heart to a puddle if he let them.

"Did you know my brother?" he asked, as curious to hear her response as he was to divert his straying thoughts.

Sunny nodded. Matt wondered at the look of guilt which flashed across her face. Before he could give thought to what else she might be feeling guilty about besides stealing his cattle, she told him.

"I was with Danny when he died."

Chapter Two

"With him?" Matt's midnight stare boldly swept her from head to boots. "Just what the hell were you doing with my brother?"

Sunny curled her hands into tight fists at her sides to keep from slapping the suggestive hint from his face. "I wasn't his camp follower, if that's what you're asking." Heated fury rose in her chest. "We'd met on the trail a few times, nothing more. But that didn't stop me from holding him in my arms, and listening to his dying words."

Matt sucked in a loud breath as though he had been shot. Maggie groaned, and shook her head disapprovingly.

Why had she been so cruel? Sunny wondered. Why did she care what this man thought about her?

"Then . . . thank-you."

The catch in his voice tore at Sunny's heart. A cold, consuming wave washed over her, in harsh reminder that this man's suffering was her fault. Danny's blood stained her hands, an invisible crimson guilt she knew would haunt her heart forever. She should tell him she was sorry. But how could she explain this overreaction of her temper? Great Spirit! She didn't understand it herself.

"You mind telling me what Danny said? Did he mention me?" he quietly asked, drawing Sunny's attention.

She sighed, and met his imploring stare. "You're all he talked about. He made me promise I'd get the herd to his brother. Said it was real important. Then he told me to tell you he was sorry he wasn't going to make it to the end of the dream. He said you'd know what he meant."

Matt nodded, and looked away. A chilling silence hung in the air for several long seconds. Sunny swallowed, then clasped her hands behind her back. When he turned back, his black brows were drawn together, forming a single line above the fire now raging in his eyes.

"I saw the brand on those cattle Shorty gave the Comanches today. They belonged to me." He stroked his chin and regarded her closely. "According to the sheriff in Ellsworth, though, Walden made off with the entire herd. You telling me he's wrong?"

Sunny nodded, then glanced quickly at Maggie, but her friend's expression was unreadable. *Not a good sign.* Worried, she chewed at the inside of her bottom lip. For the last week, Maggie had adamantly voiced her opinion that Matt should be told the truth if he turned up. But Sunny refused, just as strongly. She didn't have the same trusting heart Maggie did, and Sunny knew she couldn't afford to take a chance on being wrong—not with her siblings' future at stake.

Matt dropped his hand to his side. Impatience burned in his eyes. "How many head *did* Walden make off with?"

"None."

"Then, where the hell's my herd?" he ground out.

"Bedded down over that hill." Sunny pointed toward the small rise in the fading western twilight.

Matt didn't bother to look where she pointed, but continued to stare at her with distrust. "Why did Sheriff Dodson tell me they were stolen?"

"I don't kno—"

"Tell him," Maggie insisted. Sunny glared at her friend.

"Tell me what?" Matt's icy stare cut a path between her and Maggie.

Sunny saw Maggie open her mouth, and hurriedly interrupted. "I bet you're hungry, Mr. Lanier. Why don't we get you something to eat . . . and talk about all this later?" Sunny turned to leave.

Matt grabbed her arm, halting her escape. "I'd rather talk about it now."

The heat from his touch frightened her with its intensity. She tried to jerk free, but his grip tightened. She stared at his constraining fingers. Her vision blurred, and she was seeing the hand of another man. Panic seized her heart. "Let go of me!" she shouted, fighting his hold.

Maggie's hand rested lightly on her shoulder, stilling her struggle. "Matt's not going to hurt you, Sunny," she assured in soothing tones.

The pressure on her arm eased, then left. Sunny took a step forward and forced the air back into her lungs. No, he wasn't. No man was ever going to hurt her again . . . or her family. She took a deep breath, then released it. Matt Lanier just wanted answers about his brother—answers he had a right to know. Answers she couldn't truthfully divulge in full, but she knew that didn't give her the right to run away. According to Maggie, Danny had been Matt's only family. Sunny knew if something happened to Gentle Wind and Running Bear, she would want the truth. Matt deserved that much, if for no other reason than because Maggie called him friend. Despite her reservations, deep down she trusted Maggie's judgment.

"Sunny didn't want anyone to know what happened to the herd, so she told the sheriff they were stolen."

But that was not how she planned to explain it! Shocked, Sunny reeled around and searched Maggie's grim expression. Why would her friend betray her like this? What past did she share with this rancher? Sunny hadn't given it much thought, not until Matt had held her friend in his embrace and brushed away her tears . . . and again now. Sunny fully intended to find out—later. First, she had better take care of *this* problem, before it grew any worse.

"Fine, we'll talk now," she told Matt, then shifted her stare to Maggie. "Alone."

Maggie hesitated, green eyes blazing. Sunny expected a fight, but to her immense relief, Maggie only told Matt she would talk with him later, then walked off.

Slowly, Sunny turned and faced the tall rancher. With muscled arms crossed over his broad chest, and a menacing scowl pulling at his lips, his commanding presence made her uncomfortable. She swallowed the sudden dryness in her mouth. "Why don't we sit down."

She barely got the words out before Matt stalked off toward a fallen tree a good distance away from the wagon, leaving her to follow. He waited for her to sit first, then lowered himself onto the log, keeping a respectable distance between them. But not enough distance, Sunny thought, as the light evening breeze carried his scent past her nose: a warm mixture of masculine sweat, and nature's musky smell of woods, air, and grass. Her heart tripped unexpectedly. Her eyes drifted over the hard lines etched in his tense face, and she remembered how they softened when he smiled. Her gaze trailed over his broad shoulders, along the corded muscles outlined beneath his blue cotton shirt, and down the length of powerful arms resting on his bent legs. He held his large hands tightly linked between wide-spread knees, and she could see his anger in the whitened knuckles of his fingers. For some reason, she suddenly didn't want to lie to this man. She recalled the strength in those hands, and remembered how he had been gentle even as they struggled. He could easily have hurt her if he had wanted—then, as well as a moment ago.

Great Spirit! How this man could distract her! He had been gentle because she was a woman, Sunny reminded herself. A woman whose past he knew nothing about. Would he be as kind if he knew the truth?

Why do I even care?

"If you're through with your inspection, Miss Donovan, I'd like some answers?"

Heat flooded her cheeks. She looked away, watching as the sun dipped below the horizon and sent darkness to snake quietly across the prairie. She wished for the night to hurry, to swallow her guilty embarrassment in its black cover. Matt was too perceptive, and much too dangerous. She did not fear him physically, but she definitely feared his ability to make her forget, make her react in ways she didn't understand. She must put a stop to these crazy feelings . . . now!

"I'm real sorry about your brother," she offered sincerely. "He shouldn't have died. None of those men should have."

"Obviously Walden didn't agree, or did someone else kill my brother?" The strain in his voice and the cold, piercing look in his stare tugged hard at her conscience. "Did you lie to Sheriff Dodson about that, too?"

"No," she answered honestly.

"Why don't you quit stalling, Miss Donovan, and tell me what happened?"

Sunny squared her shoulders and raised her head higher. "I was riding with an army wagon carrying payroll to Fort Sill. Not far from where your brother and his men were camped, we hit a rut and broke a wheel. Danny and several others came to help. That's when Walden and his gang attacked. The few trail drivers that weren't killed were wounded."

"What about the army? Why didn't they stop Walden?"

"There was only Captain McGuire."

"What?" Matt shouted. His upper body leaned threateningly closer. "You saying the army sent a payroll shipment with only one soldier to guard it?"

Sunny forced herself not to back away from his pressing anger, to keep her concern from showing in her eyes. What should she say? She couldn't tell him the wagon was a decoy, not without explanations she wasn't willing to give about the phony shipment she had arranged, or her suspicions of how Walden learned about the set-up and showed up miles from where Colonel Grierson and his men waited.

"It wasn't a scheduled shipment. The army thought it would be safe."

"Stupid thinking. I take it Walden got clean away."

His words stung. "Yes."

"With the payroll?"

Sunny shook her head.

"Really?" The moon's early evening glow lit up his suspicious gaze.

She looked away. "I went for help. McGuire stayed with the wounded. Afterward, I hired some cowhands and started rounding up your herd."

"Found these men right there on the trail, did you?"

Sunny turned back to face him and tilted her chin higher. "As a matter of fact, I did."

Matt arched one dark brow, then sat up straight and grumbled something she couldn't make out. He ran long fingers through his black hair, leaving wide furrows in the shiny, moonlit waves, then shot her a look of disgust and turned away. She could tell he didn't believe her. Frustration coursed through her blood. She wished now she *had* lied, rather than corner herself with this much truth.

She watched discreetly as the rancher pulled a cheroot from his shirt pocket and concentrated on the task of lighting the end. Silently, he puffed on the small cigar. An owl hooted softly in the distance, its calm call in direct contrast to her jangling nerves. Sunny clasped her shaking hands together in her lap and stared at the white streams of smoke floating into the air.

"Why'd you steal my herd and pin the crime on Walden?"

Sunny jumped at his harshly spoken words. "I didn't steal your herd."

"Wyoming is north, Miss Donovan. Where the hell are you headed?"

Same place he was—Outlaw Canyon. The remote, desertlike area in the northwest section of the Indian Territory was where Walden was reported to have a hideout. But that was the last thing she wanted him to know. "I sent a wire to Ogallala where Danny was supposed to meet you, but you'd already left."

"So you just forget about that promise you made to my brother?"

"No," she sharply defended. "I fully planned to track you down."

"When?" he snapped. "When it was convenient? When the first snow fell and it was too late to make the trek north?"

"After I took care of other business."

"Business!" His incriminating tone grated over her already frayed nerves. "If I'm correctly reading between the lines here, that business has to do with Jake Walden and the army. Why are you involved?"

"I can't tell you."

"Can't, or won't?" Matt held her with his challenging stare. She remained silent. "Have you also made it your *business* to feed the entire Comanche population with my herd? Tell me, how much of my stock *have* you given away?"

His words hit too close to her heart. Sunny's anger flared. "Whatever was fair for the use of Indian land. Are you opposed to paying for grass for your cattle? And what about safe passage?"

"I don't mind paying for feed. I shouldn't have to pay for safety, especially when I have no reason for being here in the first place. But what I want to know is who the hell determined what was fair payment, you or those savages."

Blood boiled in her veins. "Those *savages,* Mr. Lanier, are people," she replied hotly, heedless of the questioning arch of his dark brows. "Men, women, and children who have as much right to live where they want, and eat when they're hungry, as white folks do."

"Whose side are you on, *Miss Donovan?* Danny's letter said payment meant giving up a dozen head. Those Comanches rode away with ten times that many." His frigid tone only served to fuel her rising temper.

"I'm on the side of right over wrong, *Mr. Lanier.*"

"I assume that's the same side demanding this hefty payment of cattle?"

Sunny stared at his granite expression, then slowly rose to her feet. "You can assume whatever the hell you want. This conversation's over."

Matt watched her leave, and thought about the hurt he had seen in her eyes, even thought about going after her. But what would he say? He was sorry? He wasn't. He had no liking for the Indians. Still, it didn't set well with him to think children were going hungry—even Indian children. On the other hand, they would grow up to be savages, just like their fathers and grandfathers, if something wasn't done to corral their uncivilized ways.

Sunny was right, though. Whatever the future fate of the Indians, the children didn't deserve to starve. He could spare a few head of cattle—provided she hadn't given away many more payments such as today's! He wished now the sun wasn't gone. He had a sudden urge to see just how much of his herd was left. He would be up riding at first light, that was for sure.

And when he was done checking on the herd, he planned to check out a few things about Miss Donovan. She might not be the outlaw he had first thought, but she was definitely mixed up in something. He believed about half of her story, and he aimed to find out the rest. Because of Danny and Maggie, he told himself. But there was a nagging deep inside that suggested his reasons had more to do with the little spitfire herself. He was none too happy about the way his body had responded to her open appraisal. Matt angrily brushed the thought aside. He had learned his lesson about women a long time ago—especially the ones that lied.

Matt's stomach rumbled, interrupting his thoughts with its

loud protest of neglect since early morning. He followed the wafting smell of beans and sourdough biscuits, stopping in the gray shadows outside the glow of a large cooking fire. He recognized none of the eight cowhands relaxing on the ground in a half circle around the campfire. Briefly, he wondered where Maggie and Sunny were, then glanced at Shorty before focusing on the cook with short-cropped, wiry gray hair standing next to the cowhand. The tall, thin black man stood hunched over and dipped a long, wooden spoon into the Dutch oven hanging over the fire. Something about the way his head bobbed in agreement to whatever Shorty said was vaguely familiar to Matt. Before he could give it much thought, the cook looked up.

"Well, lookee who's here, boys." Prominent black eyes, lit with knowing laughter, peered out from beneath bushy, gray brows.

The snatches of conversation around the campfire came to an abrupt stop as the cowhands turned and closely studied him.

"I'll be damned." Matt stepped into the light and continued over to the cook. "Jube Johnson, I didn't expect to find you here." He greeted the black man with a firm handshake and a resounding slap on his thin shoulders.

"Been a mighty long time." Jube's smile slipped.

"A long time," Matt echoed. "How you been doing?"

"Ain't got nothin' worth complainin' about, not whiles I keep workin' for Mr. Will."

"And Elethea?"

"Still pretty as the day I upped and married her twenty years ago. Still just as stubborn, too." Jube's grin widened mischievously. "What about you . . . *Bronco?*"

Hoots of laughter filled the air around him. "I see you've been bragging about suckering me into riding that bull."

Jube didn't alter the slow, circular path his spoon traveled around the huge pot. "Shore do make for a good story after a long day. 'Specially when the man hisself be a comin' round."

The cowhands' laughter grew stronger, but one soft, melodious chuckle stood out from the rest of the deep-throated chortles. Matt spun around, and saw Sunny standing behind the group of men. Bright flames illuminated the smile on her lips and the merriment in her eyes. Matt felt the embarrassing heat rise in his face. Oh, hell, even he had to laugh at himself when he thought back to what a cocky, short-tempered cuss he had been in those days.

He had accepted the cook's challenge because of his damned pride—the curse of the young and foolish—and to impress Maggie's older sister, Ashley. But he learned right quick he should have kept his mouth shut when Jube said there wasn't a man alive who could stay on the huge, motley bull for longer than a couple seconds. He didn't know much about cattle, but he had busted a fair number of wild mustangs growing up on his own and figured it couldn't be much different. All too soon, he found out his line of thinking was painfully stupid. Afterward, he completely understood why none of the other, more experienced hands had taken Jube's challenge. Not only had he lost an entire month of his Ranger's pay to the cook, but he wasn't able to sit his saddle for two days. To top it all off, he had been dubbed Bronco—obviously for life.

"That's probably the best story you've got, Jube."

"Dang close to it." The cook bent one knee, slapped the side of his thigh with the palm of his hand, and let out a loud whoop. "Never will forget watchin' your backside hit the dirt."

"I doubt you'll let me forget it, either." Matt responded good-naturedly. "Now, dish me up some of that grub. I'm hungry enough to eat a whole damn cow."

"I bet you are." Jube nodded, his good humor slowly fading. "Just heard about you scufflin' the dirt, fightin' with Miz Sunny."

The laughing banter among the cowhands died a sudden death. Matt took quick note of their hard, narrowing expressions and realized this was the first they had heard about his tussle. He wondered what Jube was trying to start. The old cook was known for stirring up tension, especially if it involved a bet he was aiming to win.

"She shouldn't have threatened to shoot me."

"Miz Sunny don't threaten without reason." Jube's smile was gone, his mouth thinned with displeasure.

Matt grew uncomfortable beneath the cook's pressing stare. It was obvious to him the story of this afternoon had been recounted with every intention of making him out to be the bad guy. But what about the fact he had been knocked unconscious and, truth be told, was probably lucky to still be alive?

He glared at Shorty, then turned his stare to Sunny. "I came here looking for answers, and my herd."

"And I can guess how you went 'bout lookin' for 'em, too," Jube admonished, releasing his hold on the wooden handle and shaking his finger at Matt's chest. "Always was a hot head."

Matt watched the unattended spoon circle the pot of beans and fall against the side, then turned his sight to Jube's slim, bony digit. The cowhands rose to their feet, hands to their guns. What the hell had he walked into? Matt wondered. And why did Miss Donovan need so much damned protection?

"Go easy on him, Jube." Sunny pushed her way through the wall of wranglers. "It's fair to say we both had some misunderstandings to work out."

"No doubt cuz he's so dang pigheaded," Jube scolded with another shake of his finger. "Now, you gonna eat, Bronco, or stand here causin' a big ruckus?"

Matt opened his mouth to argue that he wasn't the one who started this ruckus, but the thunderous stares of Shorty and the others made him think twice.

Sunny stepped forward and crossed her arms over her chest. "That's enough, Jube, just feed the man."

She turned, faced the others and pointed at two cowhands, telling them to be ready to take next watch at midnight. Then, she picked out two more and assigned them to last watch. The men soon wandered off after her sharp comment to use their time in less strenuous activities and get some shut-eye while they could. Without so much as a glance in Matt's direction, she walked away.

''Ain't you gonna eat somethin'?'' Jube called out.

''Maybe later,'' she answered back over her shoulder.

Matt watched her determined stride carry her from the circle of light. He was amazed at how easily the men responded to her orders. There was no question they respected her. He had never met such a strong-willed female. She exuded confidence with that stubborn tilt to her chin. And her body filled out a pair of pants and plain white shirt better than should be lawful. Without giving much thought to what he was doing, Matt took off after her.

''Hold up there, angel.'' The endearment slipped easily from his lips, confusing him. He grabbed her arm and instantly felt the small muscles bunch beneath his fingers. Even before she spun around, he knew her eyes would be ablaze. She didn't disappoint him.

''I have things to tend to, Mr. Lanier,'' she snapped, jerking free of his hold. ''Why don't you go eat, or sleep . . . or something.''

Remembering her fierce reaction when he had grabbed her earlier—and Maggie's strange comment—Matt let his hand drop to his side instead of reaching for her again. ''I'm not one of the hands you can order around, Miss Donovan.''

''No, you're not. If you were, you'd be fired—or dead—for calling me angel.''

He wasn't happy about that little slip either, and was still trying to figure out where in tarnation it came from. ''It won't happen again,'' he assured, as much to himself as to her. ''I'll be taking these men, and my herd, and heading for my ranch tomorrow. I doubt our paths will cross again.''

Dammit! That was not at all what he planned. He wasn't going anywhere until he took care of Jake Walden. Blasted spitfire had a way of riling his temper to the unthinking level. He hadn't had a woman rattle him like this in long time.

''You . . . can't,'' she choked on the whispered words.

Matt cocked a curious brow at the brief shock that cracked her determined expression. "And why not?"

She straightened her shoulders, tilting her chin up higher. "I made a promise to your brother. I don't go back on my word."

"Very admirable, but not necessary. I'll get my own herd up north." Matt crossed his arms over his chest in a show of authority.

"Well, it's your herd." She shrugged. "Guess there's not much I can say, except good luck." Her sweet smile stirred an unfamiliar cord in his pulse, even as her light, abrasive sarcasm placed him further on guard. She was up to something. He sensed it.

"I reckon I can get this herd to Wyoming as good as you."

She straightened her stance and deepened her smile. "You'll have to do better."

Matt narrowed his stare. "What do you mean?"

"In case you forgot"—she planted her fists on gently curved hips and let her smile drop—"*I* rounded up these men, paid them to drive your herd. They take orders from me, no one else."

Matt's anger escalated. "I'd say we're even," he grated in a low voice. "The Indians have food, and I have an outfit to take my herd north. If you want to keep giving orders, Miss Donovan, I guess you'll have to come along."

What on earth was he doing? The last thing he wanted was to spend more time with this infuriating woman. She turned and stormed off, but not before he saw an odd panic flash in her eyes.

Matt's traitorous gaze enjoyed the natural sway of her stride, slightly more pronounced now at her hurried steps. He had never been one to approve of a woman wearing britches, but as he ran his sight slowly down her long, coltish legs, he was unable to find any fault with the curve-hugging pants—until he watched a cowhand tip his hat politely as Sunny passed, then tuck his head down and stare back over his shoulder.

Matt balled his hands at his sides and fought the strong urge to break something. That wrangler's nose was top on his list. Second on the list was his own. Maybe it would knock some damn sense into him. What the hell was he doing getting riled up over a woman? A woman he didn't even know.

"Ain't got all night," Jube hollered out, pulling his attention. "Best get to decidin' if'n you want this grub or not, Bronco."

As he sauntered back toward the campfire, Matt silently reaffirmed his belief that women and trouble went together like a matched pair of gloves. By the time he grabbed the plate of beans from Jube's outstretched hand and sat down, he had pushed the blond spitfire from his mind, with a harsh reminder he had had enough of both trouble—and women—to last him a lifetime.

Pale light drifted through the open door, along with the drunken, boisterous laughter from the men playing poker around the crudely fashioned table inside. Swift Arrow sat cross-legged on the porch, pressed his shirtless back against the mud wall, and stared ahead into the night. He had decided earlier not to join the game and was trying hard not to change his mind now. But he knew the captain would come soon, and he wanted to know if the officer brought news of Sunny.

Walden wanted this white woman, and Swift Arrow was curious to know why. The outlaw refused to say, even threatened death to the next one who dared ask.

He stared at the outlaw through hooded eyes. Walden propped his chair back against the door frame and sat with arms crossed over his chest. His eye was closed. The long scowl pulling at his mouth assured Swift Arrow the man did not sleep, but was only growing more impatient at the soldier's late arrival.

The sound of an owl's screech suddenly ripped through the night. Swift Arrow opened his eyes full at the signal. "Gray Wolf comes, with the captain."

"'Bout damned time!" Jake roared, letting the chair fall to all four legs with a resounding thud as he stood.

Swift Arrow rose to his feet and stood beside the outlaw. His nostrils flared at the smell of fire water being passed among the others. He licked his lips and tried to ignore the craving in his throat, his gut. He turned his attention to the average-build officer who dismounted and marched up the steps onto the porch. One side of his pocked face appeared ghostly white in the moonlight, the other shadowed in darkness. The soldier removed his hat. Dark brown curls swirled the man's head in a tangled mess that lifted and swayed in the light wind blowing through the canyon.

"What are you doing here, Cyrus?" Jake demanded.

"I need to talk to you . . . about Sunny."

Swift Arrow quickly looked at Gray Wolf, standing back in the shadows with the horses. He could not see his friend's face clearly, but saw the brave slightly shake his head. Either the news was not good for the woman, or the brave did not know what had brought the soldier this far north.

"We'll talk in private." Jake stepped off the porch, motioned for the officer to follow, then headed out behind the hideout.

Seconds later, Swift Arrow stepped off the opposite end of the porch and stealthily made his way to the corral. Crouching low, he hid among the moonlit shadows of the secured horses, well within earshot of the two men leaning with arms looped over the top of the wooden pen.

"Something's up," the officer said. "Grierson ordered troops up here to sit and wait."

"For what?" Walden growled.

The officer shrugged, and edged his hands around the brim of his dark blue helmet. "Didn't say. We're to stay put for five days. If we don't hear from Sunny, half the men are to head southeast and look for her."

"Did the colonel say anything about lookin' for a cattle drive?"

"Yea, how'd you know?"

"Doesn't matter. Did you find out why Sunny's looking for me?"

"Has something to do with two half-breed brats. A boy and a girl. I don't know the details, though. Grierson's keeping tight-lipped. Even that damned agent isn't talking. There's a rumor going around the fort, though, that it has something to do with Swift Arrow and Gray Wolf. Some kind of an exchange."

Swift Arrow flinched, and startled the sorrel next to him. The mare danced sideways and set the other horses to stirring.

"What was that?" the officer whispered, looking anxiously around. Walden straightened and cautiously searched the area with his sweeping stare.

Swift Arrow held his breath and crouched lower among the restless horses. He clamped his lips together when a hoof pressed down hard on his foot, his thin moccasin no defense for the crushing weight. Seconds passed with only the light wind and the howl of a distant wolf to break the silence. The horses settled.

"It's nothing," Jake assured, and leaned back against the railing.

Swift Arrow slowly released the air from his lungs and nudged the horse's foot from his.

"Any chance you can bring me those Injun brats?"

"No, Grierson's got them staying at his house."

Jake pulled away from the fence and turned to face the officer. "What about the other half of your men, Cyrus?"

"They'll leave next week to meet up with the paymaster from Fort Dodge and give escort to the fort. Grierson's not taking any chances this time."

"You just make sure there's a damn distraction when the time comes. I'll take care of the payroll. Keep your men away from the canyon. I'll be headin' out tomorrow."

"You going after the gold?" The officer straightened and placed his hat on his head.

"Don't worry 'bout the damn gold, Cyrus. You'll get your cut."

The two men walked away. Swift Arrow slipped from the corral and was standing on the porch when the officer mounted his horse. Walden climbed the steps, walked past him, and headed for the doorway.

"Listen up, boys," Walden yelled, bringing the slurred shouts and rowdiness to a silent halt. "We're ridin' out at first light." He turned and looked straight at Swift Arrow. "Till then, no one leaves."

Swift Arrow met the outlaw's stare with an empty one of his own, letting nothing of what he had overheard show. But he didn't hide his smile after Walden looked away first, then stepped off the porch and disappeared into the darkness.

Chapter Three

Lustrous grays and pinks proclaimed their brilliance across the early morning sky, promising another hot, humid day. Sunny tipped the brim of her hat, shielding her eyes from the glare. Nature's contentment was evident in the birds' soft songs, the squirrels' fussing chatters, and the cattle bawling in the distance, a blatant contradiction to her furiously pounding heart as she approached Jube's cook wagon . . . and the men seated around the dying campfire. To her relief, Matt was not one of the three wolfing down what remained of Jube's hotcakes and dried fruit. She wanted no more confrontations with the rancher until she could find Maggie.

She had searched well into the night before finally admitting her friend didn't want to be found, then went to bed only to toss and turn with worry. At daybreak when there was still no sign of Maggie, Sunny's anxiety escalated. Her friend's words, "we'll talk later," echoed in her head. Had Maggie spent the *entire* night talking with Matt Lanier? And how much had she told him?

Bidding the cowhands a brief good morning as she passed,

Sunny continued on to the cook wagon. Jube was packing up his supplies, slamming closed the wall of wooden drawers stacked at the back of the wagon. He reached for the tin pot sitting on the flat work surface lowered at the end. "Ya want this last bit o' brew, Miz Sunny?"

She nodded, reached for a cup, and waited while he poured. Sipping the hot liquid, she watched in silence as Jube secured his utensils and staples, preparing to pull out for the nooning spot. She knew she couldn't wait much longer, but she didn't want to rouse Jube's curiosity either. Last thing she needed was him stirring up another bet among the men.

"You seen Maggie this morning? Or Mr. Lanier?" she inquired, proud of the calm tone which hid the riotous concern warring within.

"Miz Maggie ain't been 'round. But Matt was up 'fore me. He ground the coffee while I whipped up the hoecakes. Left a short while ago, with the peppe'mint from the Arbuckle's bag." Jube's lips spread into a wide grin. "And Shorty a glarin' at him every step."

Sunny smiled, well imagining Shorty's indignation. Grinding Jube's coffee was a privilege, because every cowhand knew at the bottom of a bag of Arbuckle's coffee beans was a peppermint stick. Candy on the long, dusty trail was a real treat for a cowhand, and one Shorty was willing to fight for, if necessary. But he wouldn't dare challenge Matt, because the bottom line was this rancher *did* own the herd they were driving.

Jube issued a loud grunt as he hefted the large Dutch oven into the wagon. Glancing sideways, he grinned at her. "Matt left here a grumblin' somethin' 'bout ya sleepin' the day away."

Sunny narrowed her eyes as she realized Jube was purposely trying to get her riled. *Darn! He must already have a bet going.* So what was it this time? she wondered. The dark gleam in his eyes combined with his taunting comment led her to believe it had something to do with Matt.

After last evening, probably who's going to be in charge.

Had he bet for her or against her this time? If the interfering rancher wasn't friends with the cook, she wouldn't have had any doubts. Sunny didn't like being unsure about anything, but it irked her to realize that insecurity stretched far enough to include one of Jube's silly bets . . . or Matt Lanier.

"Did Mr. Lanier say where he was going, back to Wyoming, maybe?"

Jube cocked one gray brow and smiled.

"What's so funny?" she snapped.

"You, Miz Sunny. I ain't never seen ya get testy over a man 'fore."

Sunny set the cup down hard on the wagon, sloshing the dark liquid onto the wood, then planted her fists on her hips. "What do you mean *testy*? I just asked a simple question."

"Backed it right up with some o' that female testiness, too." The cook straightened, his black eyes beaming with mischief. "I reco'nize the tone, cuz my Elethea does the same thing. Course now, she does it cuz she loves me."

Was Jube suggesting she cared about Matt Lanier? Sunny swallowed the constricting knot in her throat. That was ridiculous. She had just met the man. Her pulse pounded in her ears. It was crazy. Jube was crazy. Matt meant nothing to her but trouble. The cook was only up to his old tricks. This had something to do with a bet. She was sure.

With a loud huff, she turned away. "Any of you seen Mr. Lanier this morning?" she called out to the cowhands.

"Yes, ma'am, saw him earlier," Pete answered around a mouthful of food. The heir to a large plantation before the war, he was now a seasoned cowhand with sun-toughened skin, nut brown hair, and hazel eyes, but still carried a trace of his once slow southern drawl. He swallowed, then stood. "Up on the farthest ridge with Shorty. Looked like they were gonna start stringing out the herd."

Sunny nodded, and smiled her thanks. Good. She could at least trust Shorty not to tell Matt anything, or to start trouble. He shared no past with the rancher, and with any luck wouldn't be feeling obliged to answer a bunch of questions after the peppermint incident. But Jube was another matter, and so was her friend. "By any chance, did you see Maggie with them?"

"Here come Miss Maggie."

Sunny turned around to look where Pete pointed and saw Maggie walking from the river toward camp. Dressed in a black split riding skirt and white blouse, her auburn curls glistened damply in the morning light. Sunny headed out to meet her, but as she approached, so did Manuel Lopez, the outfit's horse wrangler. In his short, leather-clad fingers, he held the reins to Sunny's bareback palomino and a chestnut with a saddle cinched around its middle.

"I bring the horses, Señorita Hollister."

"Thank you, Manuel." Maggie took the reins and handed Sunny the single lead to the hackamore around Molly's golden muzzle. "I thought I'd ride with you today, so we can talk."

Sunny nodded, then tensed. Maggie hated riding. Wagons and buggies were more to her comfort. This didn't look good. But if they were going to disagree about Matt again, she saw the wisdom in her friend's decision to do so where they wouldn't be overheard. "I'll have Gordy drive my wagon. We'll follow." Grabbing a handful of Molly's long white mane, she swung herself onto the mare's back.

Keeping to a steady gait, they rode alongside the wagon, Maggie making easy conversation with the young cowhand. Sunny just wanted to hurry up and get away from camp, before they ran into Matt. She barely waited until they were out of sight, then drew back on Molly's rope, pulling the mare up to a walk. Maggie did the same. They rode in silence until the wagon gained some distance ahead.

"Before you say anything," Maggie started, a heavy dose of irritation coating her voice, "I didn't talk to Matt last night."

Relief was slow to wash over Sunny. Something didn't feel right. "Why?"

"I didn't want to talk to him, or you, until I had a chance to think about things."

Sunny didn't like the disturbing look in Maggie's narrowed

green stare. It made her wary, and sad. Was she about to lose a friend? She had so few, and Maggie was the dearest. She owed much to the schoolteacher who had helped ensure her adjustment and education back to the white man's world. But she owed far more to Gentle Wind and Running Bear, and she could let nothing stand in the way of their freedom.

"What did you need to think about? More importantly, why did you tell Matt about my lie to Sheriff Dodson?"

"I've told you all along I believe Matt should know the truth."

"And you know my reasons for wanting to keep things quiet, or does our friendship no longer matter now that this man has come?"

Maggie gasped. Her face turned a faint scarlet. "How could you even think such a thing. I would never break my promise to you, Sunny."

Sunny reached out a hand and touched her friend's arm. "I'm sorry. I shouldn't have doubted you."

Maggie sighed, and shook her head slightly. "Matt's a good friend, too. I still believe he needs to know about the danger."

"As long as Walden doesn't know anything, there is no danger."

"What if Walden *does* know, just like he knew about your other plan? If something goes wrong, you may need Matt's help."

"Nothing's going wrong this time."

"Matt *can* be trusted."

Sunny couldn't take that chance. It was bad enough his brother was dead. She didn't need Matt's blood on her hands, as well. "I don't know this man, and I can't share your trust."

"I've known Matt a long time," Maggie argued.

"Then why, until two weeks ago, have I never heard you speak his name? For that matter, why hasn't anyone at the Circle H ever talked about him?"

Deep pain sprang into Maggie's eyes and surprised Sunny with its glowing intensity.

"When Matt left Texas five years ago, none of us at the ranch thought to see him again."

"Why?"

"He was engaged to my sister. The night before their wedding, she ran off with one of the cowhands. I found her note the next morning."

A ripple of shock surged through Sunny's veins. Maggie and her brother, Will, rarely talked about their older sister, and they had never mentioned anything about an engagement—broken or otherwise. The only thing she really knew about Ashley Hollister was that she died almost four years ago, along with the babe she gave birth.

"Matt was already waiting at the church by the time I got to town. He took the news pretty hard. Stirred up quite a fuss."

It was on the tip of Sunny's tongue to ask for more details, but she didn't. It was obvious by the veins standing out in ridges on Maggie's temples, and the sudden squaring of her shoulders, she wouldn't discuss it. Sunny knew all too well the strength it took to fight off the past, and couldn't bring herself to pressure her friend just to satisfy her own curiosity.

"Matt would help you if I asked him," Maggie said with conviction, but Sunny was far from convinced.

"Without wanting answers?"

Maggie shook her head.

"And once he had those answers, would he be willing to risk his life for two half-breed children?"

Maggie's shoulders slumped. "I don't know." The confidence in her voice a moment ago was gone. "Matt lost his parents and sisters during a Kiowa raid."

Sunny's stomach tightened into a hard ball, and sadness twisted around her heart. "Then, I think we both know the answer to my question. It's best if we just stick to the plan."

Maggie closed her eyes and reluctantly nodded her agreement.

"I do need another favor from you, though."

"What?" Slowly, she opened her eyes. Sunny sighed with

relief at the familiar, steady gaze of support Maggie leveled at her.

"Matt's threatening to leave with the herd today. I want you to stop him. I've already told him I won't let the men go, but he doesn't strike me as a man who'll listen if he's set on another course."

Maggie shifted, and sat up straighter in her saddle. "You're right about that, but I've had success before at talking him out of things. I'll see what I can do this time."

Matt reined his solid black mount to a stop a good distance away from the herd and stared at the line of longhorns strung for miles over the flat plains. To his untrained eye, the cattle looked to be in good condition after being driven clean across the Indian Territory. Danny could have told him for sure. He had been counting on his brother to teach him a few things about these blasted longhorns, but it looked like he would have to learn on his own now. The prospect weighed heavily on his mind and soul. He had allowed himself to take a chance again, to dream, and just like before, everything had come crashing down around him—this time with Danny's death.

God, how he missed his brother. He had no one now. No one to share in his hopes, his plans. He was alone. The reality settled uncomfortably in his heart, right alongside the sad realization that after years spent making his own way, he was once again at someone else's mercy for his future.

Sunny had him over a barrel where the cattle were concerned, and he didn't like it one damn bit! Unlike her, he knew he wouldn't be lucky enough to find a group of trail drivers looking for work in the middle of the Indian Territory—not that he had the funds to pay them if he did. When Danny's letter came suggesting they partner up in this cattle venture, Matt didn't hesitate to give his entire savings to his brother. He was just thrilled Danny wanted to come north and work at building the dream they once shared with their pa to have a thriving family ranch—a legacy that could be handed from generation to generation. It was that single hope, that driving determination, that led his folks to load up all their belongings, their four children, and head west. They had gotten as far as Texas before the Kiowas attacked.

Matt shook his head, clearing his thoughts. His family was gone, and so was the dream. But the ironclad contract he had with the army still loomed. He had recouped a good portion of his investment by guaranteeing to supply beef to the surrounding forts this coming winter and managed to buy himself a three-month extension on the mortgage payment coming due on his horse ranch. But if he didn't get this herd to Wyoming, in good condition to survive the winter, the banker would demand immediate payment. He had worked hard over the last three years building the two-story, white clapboard house, barns, and corrals on his thousand-acre spread—too hard to lose it all.

He had ridden out first thing this morning half expecting to find the herd thin and tired, and was relieved to discover just the opposite. According to the cowhands—the few willing to engage in conversation with him—he had Sunny to thank. Of course, he also had Miss Spitfire to thank for bringing the herd here in the first place, and still wasn't sure he believed the men didn't know why Sunny had taken this lengthy route. It was easier to believe she had paid them for their silence along with their trail pay. But whether or not that was true, he couldn't deny the respect he heard in their voices when they talked about her ability as trail boss.

Matt pulled a fresh cheroot and match from his pocket. Lighting the end, he took a long draw and slowly released the white smoke to curl into the air, then shifted his sight to Shorty, riding point on the right forward corner of the lead cow. Matt's gut instinct told him Sunny's little side trip had something to do with Jake Walden and that Shorty knew all about it. But what? Why? The cowhand wasn't saying anything. In fact, he had been rather curt, bordering on rude most of the morning.

Matt really didn't care why, either. He was more concerned with getting answers, not making friends. He already had a friend who could tell him what he wanted to know—if he could ever find her.

He had searched everywhere for Maggie after choking down his dinner the night before and had finally been forced to admit the painful truth—she was avoiding him. He suspected he had Sunny to thank for that, as well.

With gloved fingers, Matt knocked the fire off the barely smoked cheroot and slipped it back into his pocket next to the peppermint stick. Then he rode out to join the herd, drawing up alongside the stocky cowhand.

"Where's Sunny? Doesn't she ride with the herd?" He shouted over the noise of the cattle.

Shorty shifted his unlit cigar stub to one side of his mouth. "Nope. She mostly rides ahead, scoutin' out the trail."

Matt sat up with a start. "Alone?"

Shorty stared at him hard, challenging. "Yeah, alone. I reckon she'll be at the noonin' spot."

What the hell had he done to anger the cowhand? Matt wondered. He couldn't think of a thing. "What about Maggie?"

"She rides with Jube, or follows him in Sunny's wagon. They're pushin' the trail up ahead a ways."

Matt thanked the cowhand for that bit of information, then spurred Thunder to a gallop. A short while later, he caught up with the cook's wagon, only to find Jube riding alone.

"I thought Maggie would be with you."

"She rode out with Miz Sunny 'fore you and the boys started pullin' out the herd."

"They rode out alone?" Frustration mixed with fear tinged his voice. "What the hell's wrong with everyone around here?"

"Ain't nothin' I can see. What's got ya a shoutin' at the world?"

"Two women riding out alone—in Indian Territory. Don't you think that's a little bit reckless, not to mention dangerous? Yet no one seems to give a damn. Last night, though, they were all ready to gun me down, thinking I'd hurt their precious little boss. And what about Maggie? Aren't you the least bit worried about her? You always used to be. I swear, Jube, call me stupid, but I'm having trouble understanding what's going on around here."

Jube shook his head and chuckled. "Well, Bronco, first off, they wasn't alone. Gordy went with 'em, driving Miz Sunny's wagon. Second, Miz Sunny's friends with most the Indians around these parts, so I reckon they're as safe as they'd be anywheres."

"Why doesn't that surprise me," Matt grumbled. "She's very generous to her 'friends,' especially with other people's property."

"What ya gettin' at, Bronco?"

"Just that it's easy to make friends when you're giving them beef to string up in their village, but it doesn't guarantee loyalty, or safety."

Jube's thin face grew taut, his black eyes darkened, narrowed. "I don't know if you've ever gone hungry, boy, but I have. I know what it feels like havin' your belly gnaw at ya, listenin' to the cries of the child'ens, and not have nary a scrap in the cupboard." A haunting pain clouded the old man's eyes. "When a man—any man—can't feed his family, well, that can make him mighty desperate, make him do things that ain't so right. Times are desperate 'round these parts. Miz Sunny's just tryin' to help."

Matt felt thoroughly chastised and knew he deserved it. He had been twelve twenty years ago when his folks were killed and he was left with the responsibility of his eight-year-old brother. Many times he and Danny had gone without food. Many times he had been forced to do unsavory things to survive. He wouldn't feel right putting another child—any child—in that situation, especially when he *could* help. Besides, he hadn't ridden up here to start a fight with Jube.

"You're right, I'm just being ornery. I apologize. Sunny's

done fine by the Indians, done a good job with the herd, too. But tell me something; why's Maggie on this drive?''

''I reckon ya'll have to ask her yourself, Bronco.''

''When I find her, I will.'' Jube cocked one bushy gray brow, and Matt quickly reined in his surliness, knowing he would get no answers from the old cook by being rude. ''So what about you, Jube? How'd you wind up out here?''

''Me and the boys were comin' back from a drive to Abilene when Miz Sunny waylaid us.''

The spitfire had told him the truth. Matt was surprised, wary, too. ''Will doesn't know his men are here?'' He remembered Will Hollister as being a sound businessman and a stickler about keeping his wranglers in line.

''Mr. Will knows.'' Jube's thin body swayed with the rocking motion of the wagon. ''Miz Sunny sent word back to him, 'bout your brother and all.''

Matt frowned. ''I'm surprised Will would hire a woman, let alone give her free rein to order his men around.''

Jube leaned his head back and roared with laughter. Matt stared, puzzled over what the man found so funny. ''Ya shoulda heard the hollerin' match them two had 'bout her a workin' the trails. We could hear 'em plumb over to the bunkhouse.''

''Did she come to the Circle H looking for a job?''

''Lordy no, boy. Will found her one day, 'bout two years ago, whilst he was out roundin' in strays. Up near Bear Creek, I believe.''

''If I remember right, Comanches used to make camp by that creek. What was she doing up there?''

''Don't know. She'd been shot real bad. When he brung her back to the ranch, my Elethea didn't give her much hope o' makin' it through the night, let alone survivin' at all.''

Matt lifted his brow, surprised. ''Who shot her?''

''Don't know. She don't talk none 'bout it.''

''Why didn't she leave when she got better? Didn't she want to go home?''

"It took Miz Sunny a mighty long time to get better, there bein' other problems and all."

"What kind of problems?" Matt probed, his curiosity fully piqued.

"Look, Bronco, I ain't one to go 'round gossipin'. Ya be wantin' answers, ya best talk to Miz Sunny."

Fine, he would just do that! But when they reached the spot for the noon break, neither Sunny nor Maggie was anywhere around. Matt cooled his heels for an hour, waiting, and was about to ride back out when the men started to come in with the herd, and Maggie finally rode into camp.

"Where's Sunny?"

Maggie shot him a furtive look at his none-too-gentle tone, but said nothing until he assisted her from the horse.

"We split up a little while ago. She rode on ahead to scout out a camp for tonight. I rode in with Gordy." She nodded toward the lean, young hand who finished setting the brake on Sunny's wagon, then jumped easily to the ground. The same cowhand he had wanted to punch last night.

Matt turned his sight, surprised at the increased anger raging through his blood. He grabbed Maggie's arm. "I guess you're stuck answering my questions, then." He moved forward, halting on his second step when Maggie refused to budge.

"I've got some things to say, all right. Starting with a reminder that you don't intimidate me." She glared at his hold on her wrist, then looked back at him with her unflinching stare.

Matt quickly released her arm, greatly bothered by the depth of his misguided anger, bothered even more by the fierce jealousy that had stabbed him in the gut when he recognized that cowhand. He thought he had left all that behind five years ago.

"Why don't we eat under that tree over there, where we'll have some privacy." She pointed to a tall pine with wide, heavy branches. Matt nodded, and left to get the food.

Carrying two full plates of beans, fried meat, and biscuits, he made his way past the cowhands, laughing and joking while they ate, and over to where Maggie sat alone on the blanket she had spread in the shaded grass.

"Thanks." She took the tin from his hand, then waited until he settled himself opposite her. "I tried to find you last year," she told him softly.

Matt stared. He had thought they were going to talk about Sunny. What was this? "Why?"

"I heard what happened in Denver."

Matt frowned, as much at her comment as the telling heat that rose in his face. "Denver was years ago."

"I only found out then."

"How?"

"Will hired on a new cowhand. He happened to be there when the shooting took place. He was just recounting a story. He didn't know any of us at the Circle H knew you. Why'd you do it, Matt?"

He searched her questioning eyes for condemnation, thankful when he saw none. Maggie was a good friend—definitely nothing like her sister—and the only woman he had met who was smart enough to read through his loud barking and know he would never lay a hand on a female, no matter how mad she made him. Maggie wasn't afraid to stand up to him, challenge him, and neither, he realized, was a certain little spitfire he had recently met. Matt mentally pushed aside the unwanted thoughts of Sunny.

"I won't lie to you. I saw Garrison across that poker table, and I let my temper get the better of me. I provoked him into that fight, hoping he'd draw first so I could kill him. He did. But I didn't break my promise, Maggie. I didn't take revenge for Ashley's lie, or for the fact he ran off with her and never bothered to marry her. I was still angry over what he did to you," Matt told her honestly.

"I suspected as much," she whispered. Her hand lifted, crossed the distance between them, and gently stroked his unshaven cheek.

He took her hand in his, uncomfortable with her gesture. He

had suspected long ago Maggie had feelings for him . . . feelings he couldn't return then, or now. They were friends, nothing more. He hoped she still understood. Matt gently patted her hand and looked deep into her eyes. "Let's leave the past where it belongs, Maggie. We helped each other through some bad times, did each other favors. That needs to be the end of it."

Maggie leaned forward and pressed her lips softly to his cheek. "I agree."

"Good." Matt pulled back, releasing her hand. "So, Miss Hollister, what brings you on this cattle drive?"

She cocked her head. "Would you believe I just needed to get away from teaching for a while?"

"No more than I'd believe you came because you like cattle. So, what are you doing here, Maggie?" Matt finished on a more serious note.

She sighed, looking away, then back at him with troubled eyes. "Helping Sunny go after Jake Walden."

A tightness formed in Matt's chest and threatened to choke the very air from his lungs. He sat back and crossed his arms over his chest. "Why is she after Walden?"

Maggie frowned. "Personal reasons that I'm not at liberty to explain. But I can tell you that Sunny learned everything she knows about trail driving from Will, and she'll make sure your herd gets to Wyoming in good condition."

"Is Walden the reason she panicked when I said I was taking the herd today?"

Maggie nodded, but offered no explanation.

Matt blew out an exasperated sigh. "Dammit, Maggie! Tell me what's going on?"

She sat back and squared her shoulders. "I can't. I promised."

Matt ran his fingers through his hair to keep from grabbing her and trying to throttle some sense into her. But he knew Maggie would never go back on her word. It was the reason he still counted her as a friend when so many others had gone by the wayside throughout his life. "Are you in danger?" he demanded.

She hesitated, and Matt wondered if she was thinking of lying to him. "A little. Not as much as Sunny."

"What on earth would make you two risk your lives against this outlaw? And why would Will let you get involved?"

"Matt, you don't understand—"

"Damn right I don't understand!" he shouted, unmoved by the torn emotions he saw warring in her eyes.

Maggie sighed, reached over and lightly touched his arm. "Will's as much behind Sunny freeing her brother and sister as I am."

Matt sat up, instantly alert. "That murderer has her brother and sister?"

"He doesn't actually have the children, but . . . Matt, please, I promised Sunny I wouldn't say anything. This is her problem. She knows what she's doing. You'll just have to trust me."

He saw the desperation in her eyes, in the furrows that creased her smooth, narrow brow, and hated seeing her so worried. But he hated this secrecy even more. "Does anyone else know what Sunny's up to?"

She hesitated, then nodded. "Besides me and Will, only Shorty and Colonel Grierson, the post commander at Fort Sill."

"So she is involved with the army somehow?"

"Yes."

"And my herd?" he questioned sternly.

"It's only a temporary cover. She needs for things to stay as they are, just for a few more days. After that, you can take the herd, and the men, and leave."

Matt turned away from Maggie's pleading stare. His gut was telling him Sunny didn't know a blasted thing about what she was walking into. He had no intentions of going anywhere in a few days, either. He wasn't about to leave Maggie, or Sunny, behind to ride into danger alone—and with Jake Walden involved, he knew danger was a given.

What could the outlaw possibly have to do with Sunny freeing her brother and sister? Free them from what? And why would the army be involved, yet send a woman to do their fighting? Maybe Sunny was spying. That would certainly explain the mystery surrounding the little spitfire and the need for secrecy. No, spies didn't risk their cover worrying whether the Indians had food or not. It just didn't make any sense. What was she up to? Whatever it was, Matt realized he wouldn't feel right purposely ruining her chance to save her family. Family was important and, he knew from past experience, sometimes the only reason a person had for going on with life.

"All right, we'll play it your way . . . for now." He heard Maggie's sigh and looked into her relieved face, wishing he felt as confident. "But if things start to get dangerous, you're gonna tell me exactly what's going on, or I'm pulling the herd out and taking you with me. Agreed?"

Maggie quickly nodded.

Chapter Four

Will Hollister reined his sorrel mare to a halt in front of the porch, which wrapped around the sides of his sprawling ranch house, and saw his wife, Rebecca, hurry out the front door. She stopped at the top of the steps and wiped her hands on the white apron stretched over her enlarged abdomen, round and heavy with child. Will could see the worry in her anxious brown eyes, and wished like hell he had better news.

"What did you find out about Maggie and Sunny?" she asked breathlessly.

He dismounted, climbed the four steps to the porch, and pulled her into his embrace. "Nothing. The wire said Grierson's not due back at the fort until later this week."

Rebecca stepped from his light hold and looked up at him with a distressed stare. "What do you think has happened?"

Will removed his hat and ran his hands along the worn felt edge. "I don't know, Becky. I just don't know."

"You have to find them."

He stiffened. "I'm not leaving you."

"Something's wrong. I can feel it." Her bottom lip trembled.

"What if Matt found them? You remember how stubborn and hotheaded he can be. What if he got in the way and ruined Sunny's plans? They could all be dead by now."

Her soft-spoken directness did more to grate on Will's already frayed nerves than if she had shouted at him, but in the four years they had been married, he had never once heard her raise her voice. She did her yelling with her eyes, and right now, her cinnamon, gold-flecked gaze was screaming at him to somehow fix this mess. But how, dammit? There was nothing he could do, short of agreeing with everything she had just said.

"Please, Will, you have to find them."

"I'm not leaving you. For Pete's sake, Becky, you're about to give birth to my child. How can you expect me to go running off at a time like this?"

"Maggie and Sunny need you," she quietly insisted.

"*You* need me, Becky. I won't lea—"

She pressed a finger to his lips, cutting off his protest. "The baby's not due for another month. You'll be back in plenty of time."

Will gently removed her slender digit and released a heavy sigh as he cradled her hand in his larger one. "What if something happens? What if the baby comes early?"

"I'll send the foreman to town for the doctor. Besides, Elethea will be here."

Will pondered her response. He knew she was right. He had to go. Still, it was the hardest decision he had ever had to make, and he prayed he would never be torn like this again. The very thought of leaving his wife at this crucial time fairly ripped his heart in two, and if not for Elethea's presence, he doubted he could make himself go. But his wife would be in good hands, he knew. He had seen the elderly black woman work miracles before, and knew she would do everything in her power to keep his family safe.

He stared into his wife's brave, tender face. "All right, I'll go. But you promise me two things."

Rebecca sighed her relief. "Anything."

"You do whatever Elethea tells you."

"I will. And the other?"

"Don't have this baby till I get back."

She smiled. "I'll do my best."

Kissing her soundly, Will draped his arm around her shoulders as they walked inside to pack his saddlebags.

Sunny sat astride Molly's warm, bare back and ran leather-clad fingers through the mare's white mane. She glanced over the motley-colored longhorns strung in a line across the plains' grassy hills, then focused on Shorty, a dark silhouette against the sun's bright afternoon glare. As he rode closer toward her, she pushed aside the consuming thoughts of Matt that had plagued her all afternoon.

The cowhand drew his bay up alongside while transferring the lit cigar in his mouth to one side. "Pete said you wanted to see me."

Sunny nodded. "Have you seen Mr. Lanier this afternoon?"

"Nope." Smoke rushed out from between Shorty's parted lips. "He left a short while after we broke the noon camp. Ain't seen hide nor hair of him since."

That was pretty much what she had learned from Maggie earlier. Her friend also told her about the conversation she had had with Matt. Sunny was relieved the rancher agreed for now to leave things as they were, but it didn't lessen her concern over his whereabouts.

What if he had gone after Walden? She had wanted him to leave—that much was true—but not there! If he didn't turn up soon, she would have to go look for him.

Early this afternoon, she had found a small clearing two miles west and five sets of unshod hoofprints confirming Walden's meeting with the Kiowa renegades Red Cloud had told her about. The prints were several days old, but with no recent rain to wash them away, she easily determined two riders had headed south, the other three west. The only thing west of here was the trail the white man traveled, called the Santa Fe . . . and Outlaw Canyon. She hoped Matt hadn't found the tracks as well and headed for Walden's hideout.

"Tell Hank and Web to bed the herd down in the clearing east of Beaver Creek. About a quarter mile up the trail, there's a good section of bunch grass. They can water the herd downstream from where Jube's already made camp," she instructed.

The cowhand's brown eyes narrowed to mere slits. "Why we stoppin' so early? We got at least two more hours of daylight."

"I want to rest the herd, then drive them west again in the morning for a ways."

"We're gettin' close?"

Sunny nodded.

"How ya gonna explain headin' that way to Mr. Lanier?"

"I'm not."

Shorty's thick brows arched high. He cocked his head to one side. "I agree he don't know a whole lot 'bout cows, but don't you think he knows the difference between north and west?"

Sunny shrugged. That was the least of her concerns. "I'm trail boss at the moment. He can rant and rave all he wants, won't change anything."

Shorty eyed her skeptically, but offered no further opinion. "How long before we ride for Outlaw Canyon?"

"Three days."

"Good. I'm itchin' to get this over with."

"You having a change of heart?" she asked, careful to keep the quickening tension clear from her voice.

"Nope, just worried about this damned deadline."

The deadline. Agent Taylor's ticking clock. Sunny's stomach contracted as tight as a fist. She had less than two weeks left; nothing could go wrong.

"Thanks for helping, Shorty." She reached over and touched the cowhand's arm, then hid her smile when she saw a faint blush creep into his leathered cheeks before he abruptly looked away.

"No need to be a thankin' me. If your friends didn't believe in ya, Sunny, we wouldn't be helpin'."

Tears pooled in her eyes, and she blinked them away. Friends. Two years ago, she had none. Now she had several—the Hollisters, Jube and Elethea, Shorty, and a few of the other cowhands at the Circle H. Times like this, the lie she had told everyone about her real family nagged at her conscience. But she couldn't tell them the truth. Not then. Not now.

Shorty patted her hand lightly, then tipped his hat and rode off.

Sunny held her palomino back and watched him go. It wasn't until the last of the long string of trail-weary cattle came into view and she saw Gordy bringing up the rear alone, that she realized she had been watching for Matt. Where had that man gone?

She spurred Molly forward into the swirl of dust kicked up by thousands of hooves and reined to a stop beside the youngest member of her hand-picked crew. Gordy was three years younger than she, and at eighteen still a bit shy and anxious to please. But he could drive cattle as well as any seasoned wrangler, and he loved doing it.

"Howdy, boss." He pulled the red handkerchief down from his nose and mouth, then tipped his hat politely.

"Have any trouble today?"

"Not a bit. Word come down the line we're stoppin' early. That true?"

She nodded. "We could all use the extra rest."

"Won't hear me complainin'. This heat's enough to drain the juice right out of a man."

"It's plenty miserable, that's for sure. By any chance, did you see Mr. Lanier this afternoon?"

"No, ma'am." His hazel eyes danced with anticipation. "You want me to go lookin' for him?"

Sunny couldn't even work up a smile at Gordy's eager, lopsided grin. "No, he'll turn up on his own soon enough. Jube should be ready to start dishing up grub as soon as you boys get the herd settled. I'll see you at camp.''

''Shore thing, boss.'' Gordy jerked the red cloth over his face and spurred his horse forward to catch up with the trailing herd.

Sunny headed for Beaver Creek. Guiding Molly through the heavy stand of redbuds and pines, she ground tied the mare within easy reach of the stream, then using the privacy offered, washed the day's heavy layer of dust from her body. The cool water slowly eased the tension in her taut nerves, but it did nothing to stem her uneasiness over Matt's disappearance. Frustrated that she couldn't stop thinking about the man, she swam to the bank and stepped out of the water. By the time she had dried herself and dressed in a clean pair of soft buckskin pants and pale blue shirt, her mood had switched from worry to downright irritation.

She grabbed Molly's reins and led the horse back to camp. After leaving the mare with Manuel and the rest of the remuda, she headed straight for her wagon in search of Maggie.

''Have you seen Matt?'' Sunny called through the back canvas.

Maggie stuck her head out, apprehension etched on her face. ''No. You haven't either?

Sunny shook her head, her vexation soaring. ''Maybe he decided to go home.''

''I doubt it.'' Maggie regarded her with a look of uneasy puzzlement. ''He was mad enough to spit bullets because I wouldn't tell him any details, but he held his temper better than I expected.''

''So where do you think he went?''

''I would have bet money he went looking for you.''

''Too bad he didn't find me,'' she grumbled. Honestly, the man was *worse* than trouble. She knew in her heart he hadn't left. She prayed he hadn't gone after Walden. And frankly, she was tired of letting her annoyance with the man get the better of her. He was beginning to occupy way too many of her thoughts.

"Well, it's not like he's going to get lost. He'll turn up sometime."

"You're right," Maggie chuckled. "He's too stubborn to do anything else." She climbed down out of the wagon and smoothed the front of her high-buttoned white blouse and yellow calico skirt. "You ready? Jube said he was fixing up something real special for supper."

Sunny nodded. "I hope he found some berries. I haven't had his cobbler in a long time."

"Me either. Come on."

Night hovered like a thief as hastening clouds gleamed on the horizon, their large, puffy banks shaded cerise to deep gray. Darkness swept down, beginning its leisurely promise. Sunny spooned the last of the sweet berry pie into her mouth and slowly rose to her feet.

"Jube, you've outdone yourself. That's got to be the best blackberry cobbler you've ever made."

The cook grinned. There were murmurs of agreement behind her from the cowhands and Maggie.

Sunny walked past Jube's large cooking fire and made her way to the chuckwagon standing several yards away.

"Too bad Bronco ain't here to have some."

Sunny detected a slight tinge of regard for the rancher's safety in Jube's lowered tone. She set her empty plate on the flat work surface at the back of the wagon and turned to face Jube. "Any idea where he might be?"

The cook stared past her, his jaw gripped tightly. His eyes narrowed, grew alarmed. She realized the cowhands had put aside their tins and were pulling their guns. Her eyes flitted to Maggie's ghostly, pale face.

"Don't move, Sunny." Jube bit out the warning strong and firm.

What on earth was wrong? she wondered, her eyes darting from side to side in a frantic search. "Jube, what is it?" Before he answered, she heard a faint rustling in the short grass, coming from behind—toward her feet! The small hairs on the back of her neck rose. The eerie sensation of a crawling spider shivered up her back. Then out of nowhere the singing sound of metal sliced through the air, and a loud thwack resounded as the knife struck its target.

Sunny clutched at her racing heart and spun around. Matt held the headless snake in his upraised hand, shoulder-high, and still the copperhead's thick body curled on the ground. She shuddered, tried not to recall the haunting memory that always made her skin crawl. But her mind went black, the nightmare flashed bright, and her high-pitched scream rang out across the camp. She fled backward, her feet rising high off the ground in fear of stepping on a mate somewhere. Her heel caught, and she tripped, screaming again as she began to fall. Strong hands grabbed her shoulders from behind.

"Whoa there, now. You're gonna hurt yourself, or start a stampede." Shorty pushed her back to a standing position and helped steady her.

Maggie rushed to her side and took hold of her arm. "Are you all right?"

"Uh . . . yeah . . . um . . . I . . . I'm . . . fine." Sunny gently brushed away Maggie's grip and looked over her shoulder at Shorty. The cowhand dropped his hands to his sides. "Thanks," she whispered, wishing she could stop the hot flush that rose in her cheeks, wishing her friends didn't look so worried. She turned back, then quickly averted her gaze to one side, avoiding the sight of the snake as much as the puzzled concern blazing in Matt's eyes.

"Miz Sunny don't like snakes much," Jube announced, in what Sunny could only imagine was his way of trying to get past this awkward moment.

"Maybe you should sit down, boss," Web suggested.

Sunny looked at the tall, lanky wrangler who waved toward the log he had been sitting on just moments before.

"Maybe you should, just for a minute," Pete added, taking a step forward in readiness to assist.

Sunny straightened, shaking her head. "I'm fine, really." The cowhands weren't used to seeing her flustered, and appeared uncomfortable with her sudden vulnerable state, but no more than she. Sunny hated this feeling, hated losing control. She took a deep breath, wiping her sweaty palms on her pant legs. "There's no need to make a fuss," she assured, leveling her stare to include Maggie, the eight wranglers, and Jube—everyone but Matt, mainly because she didn't want to know if he still held the deadly menace.

Quickly, Sunny excused herself, then kept her pace to a fast, controlled walk when what she really wanted to do was run like the wind and reach her wagon as fast as possible. Dust-scattering steps rapidly approached from behind. She sensed instantly it was Matt. Heated embarrassment forced her to keep going; pride kept her from breaking into a run. He grabbed her arm, stopping her hurried flight mid-stride. She turned around sharply.

"What do you want? I said I was fine." He was standing closer than she had expected, and her words bounced off the wide, muscular chest nearly pressed against her nose.

"Then, why are you still trembling?" His deep-throated gentleness took her by surprise.

Her breath lodged in her throat. Looking up, she met his dark, searching stare. His hand slid down her arm and tightened around her shaking fingers.

"I was starting to believe Miss Sunny Donovan wasn't afraid of anything. Guess I was wrong." His tender gaze softened the mocking note in his voice.

A warm flush crept into her cheeks. Her heart fluttered, then pounded its rapid beat in her ears. Suddenly, she couldn't concentrate with him standing so near. Blood surged hotly up her arm from his touch, then flowed downward to settle in the pit of her stomach.

What was happening to her? What kind of spell was he weaving? No other man had made her react with such intensity, not even her beloved White Bear—her fierce, brave warrior she had lost to a soldier's bullet during the army raid that had torn her family apart. She didn't want to feel anything for this white man. Certainly not a strange, warm glow she did not understand.

"I don't much care for snakes. So what?" she snapped.

"So stop the tough britches act, and tell me why you were ready to run for the hills back there."

Sunny looked away. When she tried to step back, his hand tightened around hers. "Let go of me." Anger rose in her, a much more comfortable reaction than the unfamiliar feelings she had been fighting. She struggled against his hold.

He refused to let go. "As soon as I'm sure you're all right."

"I'm fine!"

Matt shook his head. "You're shaking."

She pulled, fought to break contact with him, then felt a moment of disappointment when he released his grip. Great Spirit! What was wrong with her? Feeling more confused than ever, she frantically searched for something to say that would bring an end to this conversation.

"I . . . I appreciate what you did back there." She waved her hand in the direction of Jube's wagon. "Now, let it be."

Sunny turned, and ran the rest of the way to her wagon. Standing at the back, one hand gripped on the wooden edge, the other clutched over her pounding heart, she lost herself in the confusing rush of emotions which whirled inside her like a winter wind. When strong male fingers grabbed her shoulder, she instinctively clenched her fists and opened her mouth to scream. A large, warm palm quickly stifled her protest. Then he leaned closer, and Matt's distinctive, woodsy scent drifted past her nose. The hand at her shoulder slid down, circled her body under her breasts, and pinned her arms to her sides.

The firm, but gentle contact sent tingles shooting through her, tightening her nipples. She froze with fear at her body's instant reaction to his touch.

Why couldn't the man just leave her alone?

"That was a far cry from a heartfelt thank-you, angel." His whispered words brushed warmly across her ear, her cheek. The faint scent of peppermint drifted past her nose. She stiffened. His hand fell away from her mouth as did the arm that held her.

Slowly, she turned to face him and searched his eyes, doubting the caring interest in his midnight blue depths. "Don't call me that."

Boldly, his gaze raked over her, tingling her nerves. "What would you prefer? Honey? Darling? Sweetheart?"

"I'd prefer Sunny. But for you, Miss Donovan will be fine."

Matt chuckled, and it took every bit of her self-imposed will not to join in.

"Fine . . . Sunny." The soft flame that rose in his eyes when he said her name nearly took her breath away again. "Now, about that thank-you." He smiled teasingly.

"What did you want?" she challenged, irritated that she found such enjoyment with his sudden playfulness.

"Oh, I had something . . . nicer in mind. Something sweeter."

"Thank you," she cooed demurely, and batted her eyes twice, just the way she had seen the single women behave toward the soldiers when Maggie had dragged her to a dance at Fort Sill several months back. "How was that?"

"Not your style, angel." His hooded stare dropped to her lips. "But that wasn't what I meant."

She couldn't name what kept her rooted here. She had felt nothing for any man since losing White Bear. Why now? Why Matt? The insecure feeling scared her, but not enough to make her gain control of her next response. "And just what did you mean?"

He said nothing as he closed his eyes and lowered his lips over hers. Sunny was powerless to stop him and, letting her eyes fall shut, leaned closer to his solid frame. His mouth was gentle, firm, warm against her flesh. His whiskers rubbed lightly against her cheek. A rage of heat flowed through her limbs, met with a rush, then pooled low in her belly. Just as quickly he pulled away, and she felt a sharp coldness sweep through her. Confused, she let her instincts take over, curling her right hand into a tight fist. She drew back, then connected hard with Matt's gut. Her eyes flew open as a breath of warm air blew across her face. She watched him turn and walk away, his head held high, and his shoulders slightly hunched.

Sunny wanted to get away, needed to think and figure out these strange, unsettling desires coursing through her. She spun around, ready to flee, and saw Maggie standing in the evening's gray shadows, her eyes widened with shock, her mouth agape.

Chapter Five

What the hell had he been thinking?

Matt threw another round, flat stone into the creek. It skimmed across the surface of the water, then sank. He had thought to tease her a little, then give her the rest of the peppermint stick in his pocket, not kiss her. But standing so close to her, he hadn't been able to stop himself. He couldn't recall a single time in his entire life he had ever wanted to kiss a woman so bad—not even Ashley Hollister. Matt tossed another rock and watched as it bounced once, twice, three times in the shimmering moonlight before sinking to the bottom of the shallow stream. So what was it about Sunny that drew him like a moth to the firelight?

She was stubborn. She was a spitfire and, from what he had been able to determine so far, nothing but trouble. Yet, he found himself irresistibly drawn to her. Seeing her genuine fear over that snake, and the internal battle she had fought to pretend otherwise, he had wanted to comfort her, protect her. Held spellbound by those fiery blue eyes when he had dared to follow her to the wagon, he couldn't have stopped himself from kissing her any more than he had been able to stop the light tripping of his heart at their teasing exchange. And he was at a loss to understand why.

Recalling the brief contact of his lips on hers, Matt realized he had gotten just what he deserved. The power behind her punch had taken him by surprise. He never would have guessed that little gal could pack such a wallop. *She's probably had plenty of practice fighting off unwanted advances.*

Had his kiss been unwanted, though? Had he only imagined the light pressure he had felt in her response, or the warmth of her flesh against his? And if she had hated his kiss so much, then why did she wait until it was over to hit him? Damn, that woman was confusing and mysterious, and downright dangerous, he was starting to think—not to mention the last thing he needed, or wanted, in his life.

All these years he had been content to pay for his female companionship when the need arose. He would do best to stick to that. Besides, he had enough to deal with just trying to save the Rocking L, and the herd. He had no time for commitments outside of his ranch. He sure as hell wasn't ready to trust another female, either. Not with his heart, or his future.

He threw another stone into the creek. It sank with a single loud plop. *Liar!* his thoughts scoffed. He was trusting Sunny, wasn't he? Because he had no choice. If he didn't deliver on the promised supply of beef, he would have to go back to gambling in order to save his new ranch. After Denver, he had vowed never to pick up a deck of cards again, or a bottle of whiskey. Much as it grated on his male pride, he didn't have any choice right now but to trust Sunny.

As for the brief kiss they had shared, well . . . that had been a mistake. A mistake he wasn't going to repeat. For the rest of the time he would be forced to endure her presence; until this "business" of hers was over and they got to Wyoming, he had best remember what was at stake and keep his thoughts as far away as possible from *that* woman.

As though in defiance, her image suddenly appeared in the

moonlit reflection of the water. Matt blinked several times, but sky blue eyes continued to mock him. His irritation mounted. Reaching down, he scooped up a handful of rocks, picked out the biggest one, and threw it into the center of the milky, reflecting pool. The image swirled and spread wide, but refused to be shattered.

"Dammit!" he grumbled. Approaching footsteps and the soft swish of petticoats jerked his attention. Matt dropped the rest of the rocks in his hand and spun around. "Maggie, what are you doing here?"

She stopped, frowning as she planted small fists on her rounded hips. "I was looking for you. I saw you kiss Sunny."

He detected a hint of condemnation in her tone and, raking his fingers through his hair, groaned aloud. "I don't want to talk about that," he warned.

"Funny, Sunny didn't either."

Maggie's disapproving stare only added to his own frustration. The last thing he needed right now was a tongue-lashing for his behavior, even though he knew it was his due.

"She took off like a skittish colt. I came down here hoping to find her."

"I haven't seen her," Matt defended, his eyes anxiously searching the trees that lined the creek's edge.

"Did you want to?"

"No."

"I thought not." Maggie's hard tone ground his search to a skidding halt.

He glared at her, then opened his mouth to explain he had been trying to avoid the blond problem, for both their sakes, but quickly changed his mind. Judging by the green fire that blazed in her eyes, he realized Maggie probably wouldn't believe him anyway. It was obvious she had already formed her own conclusions.

"Don't worry. You're the only one I found," she spat.

Matt cocked his head. "Why are you so mad? It was just a kiss."

"I have no doubt it meant nothing to you."

"It didn't mean anything to Sunny either, or she wouldn't have hit me."

Maggie shook her head. "You're wrong. That's the first time I've seen her let a man get that close."

"Maybe you don't know her as well as you think."

The heat in her eyes intensified. "I know you both. Very well."

"Meaning what?" he growled.

"I remember quite well what you said that last night I saw you, about never loving again. Don't play with Sunny's emotions, Matt. She's suffered enough. And the last thing she needs is for you to try to break through that wall she's built just because she's a challenge."

Was that what he had done? Had he kissed her because she presented a challenge to him? Like Ashley? No, he had kissed her because her fear had torn at his heart, because he had felt a strong, primitive need to protect her. In that brief moment, he had felt more for that little spitfire than he had ever felt for any woman . . . and it scared the hell out of him.

"I have no intentions of hurting your friend."

"Good. Then, I can assume there won't be a repeat performance of that kiss?"

His brows cocked skeptically. "Have you appointed yourself her protector? Because I can assure you, she doesn't need one."

Maggie huffed. "You're impossible. I'd hoped the years had changed you, softened your heart some. I see I'm wrong. Maybe I'm also wrong to call you a friend, as well."

Matt sucked in his breath. He had gone too far. His anger was with himself, not this woman, this friend who had nearly died in the accident he had caused. She had forgiven him, but he had never forgiven himself, and never would. Besides, he didn't have many friends, and he certainly didn't need to estrange the few he did.

"I'm sorry."

"For what? Being an overbearing ogre? Or for kissing Sunny?"

"Both," he answered honestly.

Maggie dropped her hands from her hips and let her stiffened shoulders relax, but the gleam in her hot stare warned Matt that she was far from forgiving him so easily.

In spite of his decision not to think about Sunny, he found himself intrigued by Maggie's reference to the little spitfire's past. "You said Sunny has suffered. I take it that means more than just being shot. Did someone break her heart?"

"How did you know she'd been shot?"

"Jube told me."

"He had no right," Maggie fumed.

"I asked. But don't worry, he didn't tell me much of anything else. That's why I'm asking you. Tell me what happened," he prodded.

Uncertainty plagued Maggie's stare, then quickly vanished. Without a word, she stepped forward, took his hand, and led him by the water's edge to a cleared spot beneath a large pine. He sat down beside her on a bed of fallen needles that cushioned the hard, packed dirt. With controlled patience, he leaned back against the bark of the pine and waited while she nervously arranged her yellow skirt around her.

Finally, she looked up at him, her face pale in the moon's soft illumination. "You know I'd never break a confidence, but there are some things I can tell you to help you understand better. Still, Sunny wouldn't be pleased, so promise me that what is said will go no farther than between us."

Matt nodded his agreement, and wondered why Maggie's hands shook in her lap. What was she about to say that caused her so much torment?

"Sunny's . . . betrothed died the same day she was shot. Her mother and father, as well."

Matt sat up straight, his insides reeling with shock. He thought of his own family's death, understood the pain she had no doubt experienced. "Who killed them?"

"Sunny never would say, but my guess is the army."

"Why would the army shoot them?" Matt asked, stunned at her accusation.

"The army needs little reason to raid an Indian village."

"Indian village! What the hell are you saying, Maggie? That Sunny's part Indian?"

Maggie shook her head, and sighed. "Sunny and her ma lived with the Comanches for many years."

"They were captives?" Matt arched a questioning brow.

"Sunny doesn't talk much about her past, but no, they weren't always regarded as captives. Two years ago, the army raided a Comanche village up near Bear Creek. A few days later, Will found Sunny unconscious and barely alive. Her wounds were badly infected. Elethea stayed with her day and night for nearly a week and, thank God, managed to save her life." Maggie stared out across the creek. "I don't know who was more surprised that she lived . . . her, or us." A small chuckle escaped her lips. "Grateful as she was, though, she didn't waste any time trying to leave. The third time she got up and started her wounds to bleeding again, Elethea actually tied her to the bed to keep her there."

"Where was she planning to go?"

Maggie shrugged one shoulder. "Sunny remembered very little English back then, and there wasn't anyone at the ranch who knew more than a word or two of Comanche. We found out later she was trying to leave and go find her brother and sister."

Matt blew out a heavy sigh, sat back against the tree, and let her words sink in slowly. Water rushed along the flowing stream, in matching speed to his thoughts. He recalled Jube's comment about there being a problem with Sunny's recovery and realized now the old cook had meant more than just her wounds. Was Sunny still tied to the Comanches somehow? Was that why she defended them and worried about their hunger?

"What happened to her brother and sister?"

"Sunny finally found them about six months ago. They're

on the reservation at Fort Sill now, but she's trying to get them back.''

''Why doesn't she just leave with them?''

Maggie lifted her head higher. ''Because they're half Comanche.''

''Half-breeds!'' Matt ground out through clenched teeth.

''Children!'' Maggie reprimanded just as sternly. ''Sunny's sister just turned twelve. Her brother's only nine.''

Practically the same ages he and Danny had been when their parents and sisters had been brutally taken from them, Matt thought. But half-breeds? Suddenly, he wasn't so sure he was willing to risk his herd under those conditions. The Indians killed his family. He had no reason to help, no reason to risk *his* future—what was left of it.

''Just what does Sunny have to do to get her brother and sister back?''

Maggie shook her head. ''I can't tell you any more.''

Matt leaned forward and narrowed his gaze. ''It has something to do with Walden, doesn't it?''

''Yes, but—'' She waved one hand nervously in the air. ''It's more . . . involved than that.''

It sure as hell was! Involved enough for Danny to get killed so she could try to free these two half-breeds. He swallowed the bitter realization, felt its sour taste settle heavily in the pit of his stomach. Maggie's hand stopped moving and rested lightly on his arm.

''Danny's death wasn't Sunny's fault. Walden didn't *have* to kill anyone.''

Matt nodded, not surprised she had so easily read his thoughts. It wasn't the first time. He knew Maggie was right. Walden was the one to blame . . . for the killing, anyway. But Sunny was guilty as well. Guilty of being desperate enough to take his herd, then threaten to leave him stranded with them if he didn't do as she wanted. Desperate enough to risk her own life, and the life of anyone willing to help. And for what? To be with two half-breed children—who obviously meant a great deal to her if she would go to such lengths. Were her crimes really any different than his own years ago? He had been forced to steal, and lie . . . but he had done it because he had no choice. He had Danny to consider. Maybe he was being too hard on the little spitfire. From what Maggie had hinted at so far, it didn't sound like Sunny had much choice in the matter, either.

"Will you tell me what she's trying to do?"

"No," Maggie answered softly. "I've only told you this much because I wanted you to understand why Sunny doesn't need distractions right now, or worse, to foolishly fall in love with you."

Matt couldn't stop the chuckle that escaped his lips. "I don't think you have to worry about that last part. She hates me. Besides, I don't plan on ever getting married, remember?"

Maggie nodded. "That was my whole point in bringing up this conversation."

Matt let her stinging words pass. "Tell me something."

"If I can."

"That man Sunny planned to marry, was he an Indian?"

"Yes. His name was White Bear."

Matt's heart lurched painfully. Why the hell had he asked? Why did he care? "How did you get involved in all this, Maggie?"

Her mouth curled up slightly at the corners, her eyes sparkling in the moon's soft glow. "Sunny and I spent a great deal of time together. I taught her how to read and write, and to live among her own race again. She taught me things about the Comanches. I came to Fort Sill because she asked me to help the other Indians, and to begin her siblings' teaching while she took care of getting them freed."

"And when that happens, then what?"

Maggie's cold glare gave him a start. "That's not your problem."

"Is it yours?" He cocked a single brow, puzzled at her sudden icy behavior.

She blew out an angry breath. "Is there a point to this? As long as your herd gets to Wyoming safely, what do you care?"

"We're friends, Maggie. I care what happens to you."

"Well, don't," she snapped. "I can take care of myself."

She stood before Matt realized what she was about. He jumped to his feet, but wasn't quick enough to stop her from walking away. Dumbstruck, he could only stare at her retreating form and wonder what he had said to make her so angry.

Women! How many times did he have to keep reminding himself they were nothing but trouble? Matt shook his head, then reached down and grabbed his hat before heading back to camp.

Sunny stayed within the darker shadows along the stream and walked on silent steps, just as White Bear had taught her when at age twelve she had begged the young brave, four years her senior, to secretly teach her the skills of the Comanche warrior. Even now, she could still recall her stepfather's anger at the discovery. Chief Black Eagle had forbid her to leave the camp for weeks afterward, and threatened punishment to White Bear if he taught her any more. Her Comanche grandmother, Walks-in-Stream, had also scolded her unmercifully, and forced her to spend many days cooking and fetching water with the rest of the young girls. Only her mother had understood Sunny's essential craving, her need to know she could defend herself. It had been the only time Sarah Donovan had gone against Black Eagle's wishes. Because he had been already half in love with Sunny, White Bear had ignored the threat of severe punishment and agreed to Sarah's pleading to continue teaching her daughter the skills. It had not been easy slipping away, taking the horses, hiding her own cache of weapons from Black Eagle's ever-watchful eye. But they had managed, persisted, and she had learned well.

The smoky clouds stretched across the night sky in a wide, patchy mass. A tightly clustered section slipped over the full moon and plunged the land into pitch-black. She cut through the trees, feeling her steps carefully. The clouds moved on as she reached the edge of the sparse woods.

Moonlight bathed the grassy valley and the restless herd milling about. Their uneasiness mirrored her own mood. This time of night the cattle usually rested and weren't ready to eat again for another hour or more. Had something spooked them? A stampede in the dark would be disastrous.

As though reading her thoughts, Gordy began softly singing a love ballad while he guided his horse aimlessly through the herd. His low, soothing voice had an instant calming effect on the jittery longhorns. Sunny heard Pete's low drawl join in. Before long the cattle began to lie down, dotting the prairie with their large, bulky forms. She released a heavy sigh, but her relief was short-lived as her mind drifted away from the threat of a stampede and settled back on Matt.

Why had he kissed her? Why had she let him? White Bear was the only man she would ever love. She should have hit Matt much sooner. But his mouth had been so warm on hers, so soft, and her body had melted like wax to a flame. Sunny traced her lips with one finger. She should never have let it happen. She certainly wasn't happy about being caught by Maggie. She definitely shouldn't be standing here wishing he would do it again.

Damn Matt Lanier and his confusing interference, she silently seethed. Her first impression had been right. The man was nothing but trouble. And he was threatening her very future.

The sharp crack of a branch snapping beneath booted feet broke the stillness. Sunny spun around, her hand gripped on the Colt holstered around her hips. She saw the bright red tip of a cheroot, then Shorty's wide, somber face before the moon slipped behind another slow-moving cloud.

"Didn't mean to scare ya," Shorty whispered. "Couldn't make out who it was standin' under this tree, and thought I'd best come check it out. I was just leavin'."

"No need." She waited for him to join her. "The herd's a

little restless. Could be a storm brewing, or it could be trouble. Tell Web to post extra guards tonight."

"I'm way ahead of ya. This close to Outlaw Canyon, I figure we need to be ready for anything."

"Good."

"Um . . . I think there's somethin' you need to know."

"What?" Sunny held her breath. Her body tensed. What now? Her nerves drew as taut as a bowstring when she saw Shorty remove the lit cheroot from his lips.

"Jube's got a bet goin' with the men."

She relaxed, a small chuckle escaping her throat. "I'd already guessed as much. This have to do with who's going to be in charge, me or Matt?"

"Nope. He couldn't get anyone to bet against you on that one." His grin was evident in the revealing white teeth against the black of the night. "This one's got to do with the sparks that keep flying between you and Mr. Lanier."

Sunny frowned, planting her hands on her hips. "What are you talking about?"

Shorty stuck the cigar between his lips and turned from her stare. "Jube's bettin' the two of you are gonna fall in love before this drive's over."

"You're kidding!" Sunny straightened her stance, crossed her arms, and smiled. "I hope you got in on a chunk of that action. Could be the first time the old cook's ever lost."

"I don't know, Sunny. Ya shoulda seen the look on Mr. Lanier's face when you spooked the way you did over that snake. I ain't never seen a man get so white. Scared him plumb to death, ya did."

"That's hardly enough for Jube to make such a ridiculous bet."

"I think it's got more to do with the way Mr. Lanier tore off after ya. Or it could be 'cause he kissed ya."

"How do you know that?" The moon peeked again, and she saw Shorty shift his stance uncomfortably, the cheroot firmly planted in its usual spot at the corner of his mouth.

"Well, um . . . me and Jube followed him. But only to protect ya."

"And Maggie?"

"She was concerned ya might still be upset."

"Great! So the whole camp knows?" Sunny was glad for the darkness that slipped over them again, hiding the heated flush that crept into her cheeks.

"He didn't tell the men. They find out you let Matt get that close to ya, ain't no one would have taken him up on the wager."

"Including you?"

"Now, Sunny, ya know I ain't a bettin' man," he hedged, much to her growing consternation.

"Well, you tell Jube I'm putting fifty dollars on that bet. Double or nothing. And that I'll be the first one standing in line to collect when this drive's over."

"Ya goin' all the way to Wyoming after we get done with Walden and them braves?"

"I wasn't planning on it." She tilted her chin stubbornly. "But I'm not about to miss seeing that miserly cook lose his first bet."

Sunny walked with Shorty back to camp. After bidding him good night, she headed for her wagon, her thoughts full of the rash, outspoken commitment she had made to complete the drive to Wyoming, and the even more confusing feeling in her heart that her decision was the right one. Surely it had nothing to do with Matt. The unwelcome suggestion sparked her anger. Of course it had nothing to do with Matt Lanier. She hardly liked the man—tolerated him even less.

Huffing her irritation, Sunny rounded the corner of the wagon, and ran straight into Matt's solid wall of a chest. She sucked in a sharp breath and stumbled back. He grabbed her upper arms, steadied her.

"You okay?"

She looked up and nodded. His warm eyes and handsome, lightly bearded face heated her insides and set her pulse racing.

His firm mouth curled on the edge of laughter. She really needed to quit thinking so much about the man!

"Damn, but you're dangerous, angel." He smiled, then released her and bent to retrieve his fallen hat. The moon's soft glow highlighted the furrows in his dark hair. It took Sunny a second to realize she had reached over to touch the shiny black mass. She gasped, and quickly jerked her wayward hand behind her back.

"What are you doing here?" she asked, harsher than she had intended, and saw one of Matt's brows arch high.

"I wanted to talk to you."

"It's late, and I'm really not in the mood." Sunny made to step around him, but Matt blocked her path.

"This won't take long."

"Don't you ever take no for an answer?"

Matt shoved his hat on his head, then crossed his arms over his chest. "Don't you ever confront a problem head-on, instead of running off to avoid it?"

"You'll get no argument out of me that you're a definite problem," she snapped.

"I wouldn't be a problem at the moment if you'd just shut up and let me say what I came to say." he shouted.

"Would you two find somewhere else to argue; I'm trying to get some rest." Maggie's sleep-husky voice came from the other side of the canvas.

"Sorry," they answered at the same time, then glared at each other.

Matt grabbed her hand and dragged her along as he stormed off toward the creek. She tried to twist free of his hold, but he refused to let go. Not wanting to raise an unnecessary alarm by putting up a loud fuss, she whispered her heated curses at him, using every vile white man's term she knew, then switched to several others in her more familiar Comanche tongue. But he only ignored her and lengthened his stride so it was harder for her to keep up. When he stopped with no warning, Sunny collided with his back. Her breasts flattened against his hard muscles. He pulled her arm around his middle and prevented her from moving away. Startling heat coursed through her at the intimate contact and spurred her to action, doubling her efforts to free herself.

"Let go of me," she hissed. To her surprise, he did. She stumbled backward and fell, landing hard on her bottom.

Matt spun around and stared down at her. "Don't you ever say please?" He reached a hand out to help her up. She ignored it and got to her feet without his assistance, then brushed the dirt from the seat of her pants.

"I tried a few times. It never worked for me."

"Probably because you didn't try hard enough."

Anger flaring, Sunny stilled her movements and stared up at Matt. "How would you know? You don't know the first thing about me, or what I've had to go through. But I can assure you, Mr. Lanier, outside of Oak Valley and the Circle H, that pleasant little platitude you think should come dripping like sugar from my mouth hasn't done a damn thing to help me."

Matt regarded her with his unflinching stare and placed his hands on his lean hips. "You're right, I've got no call to judge you. And I didn't come looking to start a fight, either."

Sunny planted her fists on her hips. "So why did you come? To tell me where you went this afternoon?"

Matt frowned. "No, but since you asked so nicely, I'll tell you. I just needed some time to think, that's all. Now, I came to find you so I could apologize, and I'd just as soon get on with it."

"Apology accepted," she snapped, dropping her hands to her sides.

"Don't you even want to know what for?"

"I can guess." She assumed it had to do with the kiss and wasn't at all sure that she wanted to hear it said aloud.

"There's already been enough misunderstanding between us. I'd just as soon spell it out, if you don't mind."

Strangely, she did, but said nothing.

''I shouldn't have kissed you. And you don't need to worry; it won't happen again.''

A slicing pain seared through her heart at his words. When she dared to look at him, her breath lodged in her throat at his softened midnight gaze. He looked as though he wanted to kiss her now . . . and to her utter amazement, she wished he would. ''I'm sorry I hit you.''

''I deserved it.''

Silence hung heavily between them. Sunny shifted her feet in the dirt. Matt stared at the clouds floating above.

Finally, he looked down at her, his expression closed to her scrutinizing gaze. ''Well, that's all I had to say. Night, Sunny.''

''Good night, Matt.'' His name slipped from her lips, catching her unaware.

Matt turned back, staring at her in puzzlement. Why had she picked this moment to use his given name for the first time? Sunny had no answer, and to her immense relief, Matt walked away without asking for one.

Chapter Six

Matt leaned against the cook wagon and sipped at a cup of Jube's strong morning brew. Every so often, one of the six cowhands seated around the fire would glance at him, then share a look of secrecy with the others, and follow it up with a passel of snickering. For the most part, Matt paid them little attention. He knew exactly what was up. Jube was keeping unusually quiet and more than once shook his long, wooden spoon to hush the men. *This has something to do with a bet.* And since he hadn't heard anything about it, Matt figured he was the target again. Well, Jube could try, but he wasn't falling into any trap *this* time.

He rubbed at the itching whiskers along his jaw, then tipped his hat brim and stared at the ominous gray clouds blanketing the early morning sky. The threat of rain hung heavily in the already rising temperature. He was in no mood for delays. After spending a sleepless night thinking about little Miss Spitfire, he was more than ready to saddle up and get this blasted herd to his ranch—as fast as possible.

Matt wished he hadn't gone looking for Sunny last night to

apologize. When she had bumped into him, he had had a hard time letting go, and realized he liked the warm feel of her in his hands more than he should. Then he had promised not to kiss her again, but when she said his name, he had almost pulled her into his arms and done just that. He needed to get back to Wyoming, and away from the distracting spitfire. She was taking up way too many of his thoughts.

"There you are."

Matt jumped, and warm coffee sloshed from the cup, staining the front of his shirt.

Maggie came around from behind and smiled up at him. "Sorry, didn't mean to startle you."

Matt set the cup down on the wagon, picked up one of Jube's towels, and dabbed at the brown circle on his shirt pocket. "My fault. Should've been paying more attention," he grumbled.

Maggie eyed him quizzically. "Something on your mind?"

"Nothing I care to discuss." Matt glanced down at his shirt and rubbed at the stain uselessly again before putting the towel down. When he looked at Maggie, he could tell by her knowing stare and frown she knew exactly what, rather who, had been on his mind. "Were you looking for me?"

If she had come to issue more warnings about Sunny, he hoped he would be able to hold his temper.

"I wanted to tell you goodbye."

"What?" Matt straightened. "Where are you going?"

"If the weather holds, I'm leaving for Fort Sill right after we make the noon camp. I didn't want to take a chance on missing you then."

"Why are you going back to the fort?"

"I never intended to stay gone this long. I'm sure Running Bear and Gentle Wind are worried."

Matt arched his brow. "Running Bear and Gentle Wind?"

"Sunny's brother and sister."

Matt nodded. *Of course the half-breed children would have Indian names.* "Who's going with you?" His tone dared her to even think of suggesting she would make the trip alone.

Maggie smiled, reached up and touched his whiskered jaw. "You sound like Will, always worried about me." Her hand dropped. "I'll be fine. Gordy's riding with me. He'll catch up with the herd in a few days."

Matt nodded, knowing there was nothing he could say about her decision, or her commitment to Sunny and her siblings. He gathered her into a tight hug, then loosely held her in his arms as he leaned back and looked down into her face. "Well, it was sure good seeing you again, Maggie. Maybe you'd like to come to Wyoming sometime? To visit."

"I'd like that very much." She smiled, then lifted her lips to his cheek.

Matt dropped his arms to his sides, and stepped back. A movement over Maggie's left shoulder caught his attention. He glanced up in time to see Sunny turn and run behind the wagon.

Sunny hurried around to the other side of the cook wagon and stopped. Her heart raced as fast and wild as the shock still rippling through her limbs at seeing Maggie in Matt's arms and watching them kiss. She hoped they hadn't seen her. It was bad enough walking up on them; she certainly didn't want to discuss what she saw. Although . . . she was definitely curious and, oddly, disappointed. That last realization caught Sunny by surprise, and she frowned. Why did she care who Matt kissed? It was none of her concern.

Then, what was this aching feeling in the pit of her stomach? It was emptiness, because she hadn't eaten. Nothing more.

She would go eat and talk with the cowhands about the day's work as she had been headed to do when she came upon Matt and Maggie—just as soon as they left. She didn't want to run into them. Well, she didn't want to run into Matt, anyway.

Sunny tapped her foot impatiently and chewed on her bottom lip. Had she given them enough time to leave yet? Bending in half, Sunny peered underneath the cook wagon, relieved when she saw no sign of Maggie's skirt or Matt's denim-clad legs.

''Lose something?''

Gasping, Sunny straightened and whirled around. Matt stood with one hip casually resting against the back wheel, his arms loosely crossed over his broad chest. The sight of his firm, smiling lips and handsome face heated her blood to a fiery glow. She swallowed the constricting lump in her throat. ''How . . . long have you been there?''

Teasing light danced in the depths of his darkened gaze. ''Almost as long as you.''

''Why didn't you say anything?''

He shrugged. The smile on his lips deepened. ''I got distracted.'' He cocked his head slightly. ''By a most enjoyable view.''

Twin spots of heat sprang into her cheeks. Had he really been standing there staring at her backside? The thought pleased her, until she remembered he had been kissing Maggie just moments ago. He had told her when they had first met he wasn't a man who liked playing games. She wondered if that was true. Sunny glared at him through lowered lashes. ''Did you want something, Mr. Lanier?''

His smile faded. He pushed away from the wagon and stepped closer. ''Last night it was Matt. What happened?''

''Last night I was tired. And now I'm hungry. If you'll excuse me.'' Before she could move, his warm fingers gripped her shoulder in a light, but firm hold.

''Why did you take off like that when you saw me and Maggie?''

Great Spirit! Matt *had* seen her. She peeked around his shoulder to see if Maggie stood behind, then met his observing stare.

''Maggie went back to the wagon. She didn't see you.''

Sunny released a small sigh of relief. Good! One problem avoided. Of course, there was still the problem of Matt. A problem that seemed to escalate every time she was around the man.

''Now, are you going to answer my question?'' His tone

brooked no argument as to the number of choices she had—one.

The sight of him with Maggie flashed in her mind. An angry, confusing pain stabbed at her heart. She tilted her chin at him. "I saw the two of you were . . . occupied, and I didn't want to interrupt." To her chagrin, she heard the hurt tone in her voice, and by Matt's curious stare, she knew he had as well.

"She was saying goodbye. We hugged, and she kissed me on the cheek. I'd hardly call that 'occupied,' and certainly no reason for you to walk off like a hurt puppy with its tail tucked between its legs."

Shock flew through her. "You . . . I saw . . . cheek?" His words sank in fully. She furrowed her brow and planted her hands on her hips. "Who are you calling a hurt puppy?"

"You, Miss Tough Britches." He touched a finger under her chin and tilted her head back. A warm smile graced his lips, but the laughter was gone from his eyes, replaced with a hunger as fierce as the threatening clouds overhead. "I didn't kiss Maggie. But if I don't leave right now, I *am* going to kiss you." He dropped his hand, then turned and walked away.

Stunned, Sunny watched him go. He wanted to kiss her again! Her feet itched to follow after him; her hands craved to halt his retreat. But what could she possibly hope to gain by going after him? She must forget this foolishness, forget these crazy feelings. She must forget about Matt Lanier!

She turned, hurried around the wagon, then slowed her pace as she crossed the last several yards over to the campfire.

"Where'd Bronco go?" Jube asked with a knowing smile as she approached.

Sunny felt the heat rise to her cheeks. How much had Jube heard? she wondered, thankful that the cowhands were engaged in their own conversation and paying her no attention.

"How should I know?" She frowned at Jube, then grabbed the offered tin of food from his hand and stomped over to join the men. Pushing her thoughts of Matt aside, she discussed the pending threat of the storm with the cowhands, then laughed at their jokes while she finished eating.

"Last chance for coffee!" Jube hollered out, holding the pot in his upraised hand.

Pete and Lefty grabbed their tin cups off the ground and jumped to their feet.

"Ya want some more, Sunny?" Pete asked, his hand proffered to take her cup.

She smiled, and shook her head, then turned her attention to Web and Shorty. "Have the men start stringing out the herd. I want to be ready to pull out soon and maybe get a mile or two in before the rains come."

The two cowhands nodded and rose to their feet. Three others did the same. Sunny watched as they headed toward the remuda where Manuel was already cutting out the horses the men had chosen to ride today, surprised when Matt appeared and fell into step beside them. Sunny swept her stare over his muscular, denim-clad legs, lean hips, and broad shoulders as he sauntered along with the others. Jube cleared his throat. She turned her head slightly and found the cook standing off to the side grinning big at her.

Sunny stood and brushed the dirt from her pants. "What are you looking so smug about, Jube?"

"Not a thing, Miz Sunny. Is there any reason you're gettin' so testy again? Wouldn't have to do with Bronco, would it?"

"No," she snapped, remembering Jube's silly bet about her and the rancher. Turning on one boot heel, she stomped off.

"Ya goin' to check and see if'n Miz Maggie's about ready to pull out?" Jube called after her, teasing humor still laced in his tone.

"Yeah," she yelled back, not missing a step. She really needed to rid herself of this attraction she had for Matt. Granted, he was a handsome man, and probably had a lot of women looking at him, but she didn't have to be one of them. And there was no way she was going to let Jube win *this* bet!

She found Maggie at the wagon and passed along Jube's

message, then headed back across camp toward the remuda. Still a good distance away, she noticed Matt engaged in a heated discussion with Manuel. The rancher held the reins to his saddled black mount and squared off with the much shorter Mexican wrangler who held the single lead rope to her palomino. Frowning, she hurried her steps.

"Is there a problem?" she asked as she approached. Both men turned to face her, but it was Manuel who spoke first.

"This gringo insists I put a saddle on Molly."

"And this wrangler's trying to tell me you don't ride with one. How is that?"

Sunny couldn't stop the giggle that bubbled from her throat at the source of their argument. Matt arched his brow and stared down his handsomely arrogant nose at her. She couldn't resist having a little fun with him.

"Quite easy, actually, Mr. Lanier. Watch." She stepped closer, grabbed a handful of the mare's long mane and swung herself up onto the palomino's bare back. She smiled at Matt's gawking expression and took the rope from Manuel's hold. "I like to travel light. Saddles aren't a necessity," she offered by way of explanation, then reeled Molly around and spurred her mount to a steady gait.

As she rode away, she heard Manuel's laughter ringing in the air. She wasn't the least bit surprised at the hoofbeats pounding behind her seconds later, or when Matt drew up alongside. Still in a teasing mood, she nudged Molly a little faster and pulled ahead.

"Would you stop, dammit!" he shouted. She refused to spare even a glance in his direction. He was in the process of grumbling a string of curses about her stubbornness when the next thing she knew, she was lifted from Molly's back by a strong arm and dragged sideways to sit in front of him. The hard leather saddle horn bit into her hip.

"What are you doing!" she yelled, squirming to break the contact of his body against hers. But she only succeeded in pressing herself closer to the heat radiating through his denims and blue cotton shirt and found she liked the feel way too much.

Matt pulled back on the reins until the horse stopped. She jerked her head up, catching his nose with the edge of her hat brim. He swore, then grabbed her hat and tossed it to the ground. "I told you to stop," he grated.

"You might try saying *please* next time," she retorted.

Matt threw his head back and let out a great peal of laughter. The rich, baritone sound sent a shiver of delight up her spine. Sunny couldn't stop the smile forming on her lips and lifted a hand to cover her mouth. He looked down at her with warm blue eyes.

"Point taken, angel."

Sunny sucked in her breath at the endearment. The warmth vanished from Matt's eyes. She looked away, and only then saw the curious, frowning stares of Manuel and three other cowhands watching them. She wondered if they would be changing their bet with Jube at the nooning camp now.

"I was planning to ride out with you today."

His comment grabbed her full attention. She drew her brows together and stared up at him. "Why?" she asked curtly.

He cocked his head, staring hard with his probing gaze. "Is there a reason you don't want me around?"

Plenty of reasons, not the least of which was the way his body felt next to hers. "No, it's just that I'm staying with the herd today, because of the storm. Now, will you let me down before we draw an even bigger crowd?"

His eyes narrowed, then registered his irritation as he focused on the four men watching in the distance. Without a word, he took hold of her arm and helped her slide from his horse. As she walked over and retrieved her hat off the ground, Matt nudged the black gelding to where Molly stood waiting patiently, chewing on a mouthful of prairie grass. Grabbing up the mare's lead rope, he returned. Sunny swung herself onto Molly's back.

"How long did you live with the Comanches?"

Her lips parted with surprise; her heart pounded against her ribs. "How did you know I lived with the Comanches?"

"Maggie."

Sunny narrowed her gaze. "What else did Maggie tell you?"

"Nothing for you to get your feathers ruffled over."

"I think I would be a better judge of that."

"Tell you what"—Matt tilted his head back and peered down his nose at her—"ride with me. We'll talk. You answer my questions, and I'll answer yours. Deal?"

Sunny hesitated, knowing if she agreed, his questions could lead her down a path of memories and secrets she would rather not travel. But the burning curiosity to find out what else Matt had learned overpowered her worry. She nodded, then nudged Molly to a slow walk. Matt followed alongside.

"I lived with the Comanches for ten years. What else did Maggie say about my life with the Indians?"

"She told me about Running Bear and Gentle Wind."

Sunny stiffened. "What about them?"

He lifted one brow. "Sorry, my turn. Were you happy living there?"

"Yes. Now, what about Running Bear and Gentle Wind?"

"She told me they're your brother and sister and you're trying very hard to get them back."

Sunny's stomach contracted into a tight ball. "Did she tell you how?"

Matt shook his head, reached in his pocket and pulled out a fresh cheroot, then a match. "She told me about White Bear, though."

Her gasp mingled with the sound of his striking match, and she was thankful he showed no signs of hearing it. She turned away and stared at the blackish gray clouds thickening on the horizon, moving ever closer. The cattle lumbered along in the distance, and she watched as several of the more skittish raised their heads, sniffing at the pending threat.

"Were you in love with him?"

Sunny shifted her seat, brushing Molly's mane absently with nervous fingers. "I don't think that's any of your concern."

"Maybe not, but I'd like to know." His curious but gentle tone touched a cord in her heart she had never felt before and couldn't explain.

She lowered her head slightly, using the hat's brim to hide her stare as she glanced sideways at the rancher. "Were you in love with Maggie's sister?" She saw him stiffen, then pull the cheroot from his mouth.

"Let's talk about something else," he ground out harshly.

She frowned, disappointed he didn't answer. But not enough to pursue the subject any further, knowing he would demand answers about White Bear in return. "Why don't we not talk at all?"

"Because I enjoy your company." His voice was soft and deep. "You're quite an interesting woman."

Her pulse beat faster. He thought her interesting? Her heart pounded furiously. Why did his words send this pleasing flow through her?

"Is that a compliment, Mr. Lanier?"

He issued a small chuckle and smiled. "Yes, but if you have to ask, I guess I need to do better next time."

Great Spirit, how this man confused her! How was it he could make her so angry one second, and consume her with such a powerful, gladdened warmth the next? Sunny forced her confusion aside and drew in a deep, cleansing breath, then slowly released it. She repeated the process, glad when her heartbeat returned to normal, and relieved to have control of her emotions once again. She couldn't recall having this much trouble before.

"How long have you been ranching, Mr. Lanier?" she asked, latching on to the first safe ground of conversation that came to mind.

Matt blew out a mouthful of white smoke, then knocked the fire from the end of the partially burnt cigar and returned it to his pocket. "I bought my land three years ago. Decided to raise horses."

"And where did you get these horses?"

"Started out catching and breaking wild mustangs to sell to the army. Kept out some of the better ones, and built up a pretty good herd. Then I bought a couple of good quality stallions, and now I breed my own stock."

Low, rumbling thunder sounded overhead. Sunny cast a quick look up at the darkening sky, then at the cattle. They moved along steadily.

She glanced over at Matt, sweeping her gaze across the clear-cut lines of his profile. "And now you plan to raise cattle, too?"

Matt shrugged. "Got a good number contracted out as beef to the army. Rest of them, well, I'm going to see how they winter in this colder weather up north first. Then next spring, I'll decide whether to stay in the cattle business."

"Sounds like a wise plan." Had this been his plan before or after Danny's death? Was that what he had ridden off by himself to think about yesterday? Guilt jabbed anew at her heart, and she couldn't bring herself to ask.

A streak of lightning suddenly bolted across the sky, followed by a loud boom renting the air seconds behind it. Loud, panicked bawling filled the air, but the cattle stayed at their same steady pace.

"I need to talk with Shorty and Web. You want to ride along?" Sunny was amazed at how easily the offer rolled from her tongue, how comfortable it sounded.

"Sure." The corners of his mouth lifted in a smile. His dark blue gaze warmed her blood. "But it's my turn to ask questions next time."

Sunny smiled, but made no promises before she spurred Molly ahead. The wind kicked up and nearly ripped the hat from her head. She anchored it down with one hand, then tightened her grip with the other around the rope and a handful of the mare's mane to better steady her seat.

The two point riders flanked either side of the lead steer, a mouse-colored longhorn with large black spots juxtaposed in marked contrast along its hind quarters and sharp horns that spanned nearly three feet each. Lightning flashed, and thunder rolled closer across the sky. The longhorn's black eyes widened, and his frightened bawl blended with the others.

She drew up alongside Shorty and slowed Molly to match his bay's gait. Matt rode in beside her.

"You going to let them run?" she asked the cowhand, shouting to be heard above the deafening bawls.

Shorty nodded his response.

"I'll ride flank," she yelled out. She reined Molly out away from the cattle, then pulled her back to a stop. Matt's light tap on her arm turned her attention. "Why do you want them to run?" he called out loudly. "Won't they scatter?"

She shook her head. "We'll keep them together till they tire out, or until the storm passes."

Lightning cracked overhead. Thunder grumbled low across the sky, growing louder until it exploded with enough force to shake the ground beneath them. Hundreds of cattle bawled their fright; then the herd broke into a run, a color-splotched streamer racing along the prairie.

Sunny reached for the handkerchief around her neck and jerked it over her mouth and nose to ward off the swirl of dust which filled the air. Matt did the same with his, and she couldn't help but think how even more dangerously handsome he looked with just his warm blue eyes peering at her. She motioned for him to follow, then spurred Molly down the line of fleeing cattle.

They worked together, riding up and down as they guarded several hundred yards of the long line of frantic cattle. Matt never once questioned her shouted orders at him or the other men. When a mother cow and her calf bolted from the fleeing herd, Matt spurred his horse after the pair. She smiled when the cow got away from him, listening to his heated swearing as it carried on the wind. He finally managed to guide the errant pair back into the running herd. His stare sought hers, and she could tell he was well pleased with his success.

Sunny reined Molly hard to the right, barely dodging a sharp horn as a cow charged past. Matt started to ride toward her, but she shook her head that it wasn't necessary and waved him on back to the herd. The cattle ran for a good thirty minutes and started to slow not long after the lightning and thunder subsided. Then the dark sky opened and released the heavy deluge that had bulged at the edges of the low-hanging clouds all morning. The weary herd lumbered along at a much slower pace. The rains bogged the trail. It was mid-afternoon before the drive reached the nooning spot at a south section of the Cimarron River, and Sunny called a halt for the day.

Jube had hot coffee and plenty of food waiting. By the time everyone ate their fill, it was late into the afternoon, and widening patches of vivid blue sky broke through the fading clouds. The sun offered a comfortable, languid warmth, and a welcome relief after the rough morning.

It was too late in the day for Maggie to leave for Fort Sill, and Sunny had her friend keep her company while she took a much needed bath in the river. When they got back to camp, the men decided it was their turn. Jube was taking a nap under his wagon. Maggie spread a blanket on the damp grass near the low burning cook fire and opened up a book.

Restless, Sunny rode out to the herd and offered to ride watch for either Pete or Gordy, so one of them could join the men in their swim. They both declined, saying they would just as soon take this watch and later get a good night's sleep. She rode back to camp, brushed the mare down before turning her in with the rest of the remuda, then slowly made her way to where Maggie sat reading. She heard the men's loud whoops and hollers above the loud splashing and easily distinguished Matt's deep laughter from the others.

"Sounds like they're having a good time."

"Ummm . . . huh." Maggie didn't even bother to glance up from her book.

Sunny frowned as she dug the toe of her boot into the dirt. "Feel like taking a walk?"

Maggie briefly looked up. "No."

Sunny stared in the direction of the river. More splashing, more shouts. Matt's rich laughter. She blew out a long sigh and shifted her feet. Her frown deepened. "How long does it take to get clean?"

"They're doing what you told them, relaxing. You should give it a try."

Sunny turned at Maggie's perturbed tone and saw the irritation in her friend's glare. "I am relaxed. Just bored."

"I have another book in—"

"No, thank you," Sunny huffed. She read for one reason, to learn. It was a mystery to her what enjoyment Maggie found in those silly dime novels.

Maggie went back to reading her book. Another round of raucous laughter drowned out the birds chirping in the trees. Sunny looked toward the river again. "Let's go see what they're doing."

"What!" Maggie's head snapped up.

"Let's go see what they're doing," she repeated, excitement building in her veins.

"Are you crazy? We can't go over there!"

"Sure we can. We'll take a fast look, see what they're up to, then leave. They won't even know we're there."

Maggie closed the book with a soft thud. Her sharp green glare cut straight to Sunny. "Does this have anything to do with that story you told me? About wanting to sneak off with the other girls in your village and watch the boys at bathing time?"

Sunny stuck her chin out and crossed her arms. "I should've gone with my friends that morning. But I couldn't risk getting into more trouble with Black Eagle. He was still furious over finding out I planned to ride in the buffalo hunt."

"With good reason. You were thirteen."

Sunny shrugged. "You coming with me or not?"

Maggie's eyes widened. "I most certainly am not!"

"Then, don't expect me to give you a detailed accounting." She arched her brows, then smiled and turned to go.

"Wait." Maggie stood and shook out her skirts. "If you insist on doing this, then I should be there to make sure you don't get into trouble."

"Concerned about my etiquette?"

"Always." Maggie grinned.

Minutes later, she wished she had never goaded Maggie into tagging along. The schoolteacher was as quiet in the brush as a captured animal. Sunny looked back over her shoulder, raised her finger against her lips for the third time, and motioned sternly at her friend to keep the noise down. For her effort, she received a scowl and a glare, then another whispered protest that they should not be here.

Sunny thanked the Great Spirit when Maggie refused to go any farther, and soundlessly covered the last few feet alone. She stopped behind a patch of tall, heavy brush. She heard a muffled voice, but couldn't make out the words. Then suddenly the men busted out laughing. Matt's rich sound was the only one that held her attention. Her heart pounded wildly, and her fingers shook as she pushed aside a small section of the greenery. Bending slightly, she peeked through.

The men stood in the shoulder-high water, tossing about a bar of soap. At one end of the calm pool was a wide outcropping of flat rocks which hung over a steep drop in the river and overlooked a deeper pool below. Sunny glanced over the cowhands and stopped on Matt's dark head. His hair was slicked straight back. The wet, black strands stuck to the back of his neck and sparkled with droplets that danced in the sun's rays. She listened to their playful banter and watched as they splashed water at each other like kids. Then Hank dared Matt to dive off the rocks, and he readily agreed. Sunny wasn't surprised. He didn't strike her as a man who would turn from many challenges.

Using his hands, he plowed through the water toward one

of the flat rocks. Inch by inch, the water line on his body dropped lower. Sunny sucked in her breath at the first sight of his bare, darkly matted chest. Her eyes followed the thick patch of black curls as they tapered to a thin line down the center of his well-muscled stomach. He stopped. The shadowed water barely covered his hips. The top of one sinewy, hair-covered thigh broke through the surface as Matt placed his foot on the rock, then hauled himself out of the water, turning slightly so his strong, firm back faced her. His glistening skin held her stare. Her gaze dropped, devouring the smooth flesh of his tanned, masculine form. Tough, lean, his body was beautifully proportioned. She forgot to breathe as he raised his arms over his head and stood proudly in the sun's yellow glow, as one with nature's backdrop of green trees and blue sky.

Heat flushed her skin, then cooled and scattered goose bumps along her limbs. She closed her eyes, then just as quickly opened them. Her heart beat a furious tempo. Her palms grew sweaty. She knew she should be ashamed. She had certainly gotten more than her curiosity aroused. Even now, she told herself the best thing would be to turn and go, but her feet refused to move. Then Matt dove off the rock, and all she could see was his long, sturdy legs disappearing into the water. Seconds later, his head broke the surface, and a sigh escaped her dry mouth. The rest of the men began to draw closer to the rocks, hooting and hollering their appreciation. Sunny let the leaves fall naturally back in place and stepped away from the brush—right into Maggie's back!

The schoolteacher let out a startled gasp. Sunny froze, listened, then released a grateful sigh when the men continued with their fun. She grabbed Maggie by the arm and made a hasty retreat back to the campsite.

''So, what did you see?'' Maggie asked. Bright curiosity shone in her usually prim and proper green eyes.

Sunny was reluctant to discuss the sight of Matt standing on that rock, with the sun beaming down on his tanned, well-formed body. "It was just like you said. They were having fun, and relaxing."

Maggie puffed up with indignation. "Nothing else? You didn't see anything?"

Sunny shook her head.

Maggie stared at her skeptically. "I think next time I'll just have a look myself." She snatched up her book and the blanket and stormed off toward the wagon.

Bright moonlight spilled from the cloudless sky. A light breeze bathed the late summer evening in mild pleasantness. Sunny slowed her steps as she approached Jube's cook fire and saw several of the cowhands standing around Matt and a squat, makeshift table. The rancher towered above the rest of the men, and there was something different about his powerful presence that Sunny was at a loss to explain. Matt looked, caught her staring, then nudged aside a couple of the men and sauntered away from the group.

"Aw, come on, Mr. Lanier, "Web called out. "You sure you don't want to sit in on a hand or two? We heard you used to be purty good."

"I'm positive. You boys go right ahead."

Dressed in snug denims, a black shirt, and with his hat planted firmly on his head, Matt's determined stride carried him closer to Sunny. Ever since this afternoon, the sight of his splendid naked image had hung at the edge of her every thought, and returned full force now.

"Hi." He stood before her, and she realized what was different. He had shaved. Gone were the heavy, dark whiskers. Firelight reflected the glimmering shadows of his strong, handsome face, bronzed by the wind and sun. Soft lines defined the narrowing of his smooth, rugged jaw and firm, sensual lips smiling warmly down at her.

She swallowed. "I . . . was looking for you."

"I'm glad. Why?"

Her mouth went dry. She swallowed again.

Suddenly, a terrified, high-pitched scream rang out from the edge of camp, and Gordy came running from the dark, shadowy woods toward them.

He skidded to a stop, his breathing labored. "We . . . got . . . trouble, Sunny."

She glanced down and saw the red stain seeping through his right sleeve just above his wrist. Sunny's thoughts immediately sprang to Walden. She reached for her gun, but Matt's hand covered hers before she could slip it from the holster.

"What kind of trouble?" Matt asked.

"Pete and me found an Indian girl, hidin' down by the river."

Sunny's stomach constricted into a hard knot as her heart leapt into her throat.

Chapter Seven

Sunny jerked her hand from Matt's hold and, ignoring his shout to wait, ran to the tree-lined edge bordering the river. Seconds later, Matt's fingers settled on her shoulder, firmly grounding her to the spot.

"You men spread out, search the area," he ordered. "And be careful, it could be a trap."

"No!" Sunny spun around to face Matt and the cowhands who had followed her hurried flight. She angrily brushed his hand from her shoulder. "It's not a trap," she snapped, glaring at the tall rancher before shifting her stare to Gordy. "Where is she?"

Gordy shook his head. "Pete must still be havin' a time with her. She was fightin' like a wildcat, even bit me." He held up his bleeding arm.

"Stop your blasted kickin'!"

Sunny turned at Pete's hollered demand. He emerged from the shadowy darkness of the woods into the moonlight with a girl slung over his right shoulder. Her brown dress was hiked up to her knees, and Pete had both arms looped around her slim bronze legs to keep them still; but there was no protection from the fists beating on his back.

"Put her down, Pete!" Sunny sharply commanded. "She's my sister."

"Your . . . sister?" Pete stammered, then quickly set the girl down on her feet.

"Morning Sky!" Gentle Wind ran into Sunny's embrace.

Sunny blinked away her tears and gently pushed her sister back, gazing into her round, dirt-smudged face. Her long, black hair was badly tangled and not much cleaner than her cheeks. One shoulder of the loose-fitting brown dress was ripped at the seam and exposed a small cut, now covered with dried blood. "Are you hurt?"

Gentle Wind shook her head. Her bottom lip trembled; then suddenly she burst into sobs.

Sunny cradled the girl's head against her chest. "Shhh . . . it's all right, little one. You're safe." She soothed her with more whispered assurances, held her closer, and stroked the matted hair along her narrow back.

Gentle Wind's tears slowly subsided. She lifted a hand and brushed at her eyes, then stepped back, but refused to let go of Sunny's hand. "I have . . . been . . . looking for you, Morning Sky."

"Why? What's happened?"

"What's going on?"

Sunny turned at the interruption and saw Maggie hurrying over, saw as well the men watching with questioning stares. She had forgotten about the cowhands. And about Matt. He stood off to the side with his arms crossed. Moonlight glinted in his unreadable gaze.

Maggie stopped. "What's all th—oh, my God," she gasped, as her hand flew to her breast. "Gentle Wind?" She stepped closer.

"Stay away from me!"

Shocked, Sunny stared at her sister, further confused by the taut, angry lines in her bronze cheeks. "Gentle Wind, what is wrong with you?"

"It's her fault." She pointed an accusing finger at Maggie.

Sunny looked from her sister to Maggie's hurt, perplexed stare, then back. "What are you talking about? She has done nothing but be our friend."

Gentle Wind's eyes narrowed. "Agent Taylor is sending us to that school far away because our *friend* did not come back."

"What?" Shocked, Sunny straightened and stepped back. A strong, supporting hand gripped her arm. She looked up, surprised to find Matt standing beside her, his dark eyes filled with questions. Of course he would want to know what Gentle Wind was talking about. She glanced at the cowhands and realized they were just as curious. Sunny tried to pull away, but Matt tightened his grip.

Gentle Wind stepped closer and kicked him in the leg with the toe of her black kid boot. "Let go of Morning Sky!" she demanded in her childish voice.

Sunny gasped. Maggie and some of the cowhands chuckled low. Matt kept his hand firmly on her arm and looked at Gentle Wind. To Sunny's astonishment, one corner of his mouth lifted in the beginnings of a smile. After a few seconds, he dropped his hand to his side.

Gentle Wind made to kick him again, but Sunny stepped in front of Matt and blocked her aim. "Stop it. He wasn't hurting me."

Her sister's glare spoke her doubts, but she made no further moves. Sunny looked up at Matt. "I'm sor—"

"No need," he whispered. His hovering smile faded. "You were looking for me earlier. If there's something we need to talk about, I'll wait up for you."

Sunny shook her head, then briefly speculated over the disappointment that flashed in his eyes. "I need to stay with Gentle Wind. We can talk later. Tomorrow."

Matt nodded his understanding, then left, urging the cowhands along with him as he went.

"Who is that man? Why do you let him touch you?" Gentle Wind asked harshly.

Sunny saw Matt glance back over his shoulder, and knew he had heard, but evening's gray shadows kept her from seeing his reaction. She turned and faced Gentle Wind. "We'll talk about that later."

"Why don't I get Jube's medical supplies," Maggie offered. "I'll meet you at the wagon."

Sunny nodded her thanks, then took hold of Gentle Wind's hand and led her toward the wagon. Maggie arrived a few minutes later with the supplies, two leftover biscuits, some strips of hardtack, and half a peppermint stick she told them was from Matt. Sunny was surprised at the rancher's kindness, especially after Gentle Wind had kicked him. Knowing how his family had died, and seeing his anger at the number of cattle she had given to the Comanches, she suspected he had no fondness for the Indians. He obviously had a soft spot for children, though. The thought made her feel strangely glad.

Gentle Wind sat on a blanket Maggie spread on the ground beside the wagon and ate the food ravenously. She sucked on the peppermint while Sunny cleaned and bandaged the cut on her shoulder by the soft glow of the lantern Maggie held.

"Feel better?" Sunny asked, as she repacked Jube's supplies in the wooden box. Gentle Wind nodded. "Good. Now, I want you to explain what you meant about Agent Taylor sending you away. And where is Running Bear?"

Gentle Wind pulled the candy stick from her mouth. Watery sadness filled her eyes. Alarm raced through Sunny, and she glanced nervously at Maggie, finding no reassurance in her friend's worried stare.

"Our *moneta* got very sick, and the colonel took us to his house. The army doctor tends him there."

Running Bear was ill! Panic welled in Sunny's throat, nearly choking off her breath. "What is wrong with him?"

"A fever of some kind. But I saw him before I left to find you, and he was doing better."

"How long ago?" Sunny queried anxiously.

"Four days."

Sunny arched her brows, her eyes widened. "How did you get this far on foot in such a short time?"

Gentle Wind looked down. "You will be mad if I tell you."

"No, I won't." The edge of impatience crept into her voice.

Gentle Wind's doubts were mirrored in the wide-eyed, wary gaze she lifted. "I stole an army horse."

"You did what!" Sunny sat up straight.

"Why, Gentle Wind?" Maggie asked in a much calmer voice, for which Sunny was grateful.

Losing her temper wouldn't change anything—the damage was already done. Sunny knew Agent Taylor would not easily overlook this serious offense. Colonel Grierson might, though, depending on the reason.

Why had her sister done this?

Sunny sighed. Because Gentle Wind was still a child and didn't fully understand the repercussions her actions could cause. But the girl knew better than to be rude like she had been to Maggie earlier, and Sunny could tell by the heated glare in her brown eyes that she was about to do it again.

"Maggie wants to help. Whatever Agent Taylor has done, she's not responsible."

"But she didn't come back," Gentle Wind argued. "And Agent Taylor told the colonel that we had to have schooling. He said if Maggie wouldn't see to it as she promised, we had to be sent away at the end of *this* week, whether Running Bear is well or not."

"I'm sorry, Sunny." Maggie's eyes darkened with sudden regret. "I shouldn't have stayed and waited for Matt."

Sunny shook her head. "He's your friend. And I trust Colonel Grierson to keep his promise. He'll see that Taylor sticks to our bargain until the deadline next week." She shifted her gaze back to Gentle Wind, then reached out and took one of the girl's hands in both of hers. "And I understand that you got scared. But there's no need. You won't be sent away. I gave you my promise. And you cannot go about stealing horses, Gentle Wind,'' she gently reprimanded.

''But, I had to come and find you,'' she argued, near whining.

Sunny sighed, and patted her hand comfortingly. ''I know. But tomorrow you will go back to the fort with Maggie.

''No! I want to stay with you, Morning Sky.''

''You can't.'' A sharp pain sliced her heart at the tears that welled in Gentle Wind's eyes. ''I'll return to the fort soon, and this will all be over. You must be brave, little one. You must go back. Our *moneta* needs you.''

''What about Agent Taylor saying we must go away?''

''I won't let that happen,'' Maggie assured. ''I promise you.''

''Colonel Grierson won't either,'' Sunny added.

''But Colonel Grierson has been gone from the fort for almost a week. What if he does not come back in time?''

Grierson was gone? Where? Sunny hid her concern at this news and wiped away the tear running down the side of the girl's small, lightly freckled nose.

''He won't let us down,'' she stated with confidence. Whatever had taken the colonel away from the fort, Sunny was sure he wouldn't go back on his word. They were friends. ''Neither will Maggie. They'll make sure you and Running Bear stay safe until I return.''

Gentle Wind looked between the two women, sighed, and slowly nodded her agreement.

''Now, tell me where you left the army's horse so—''

''I don't have him anymore,'' Gentle Wind informed her.

Sunny stifled a groan. Stolen, and now missing army property. Could it get any worse? ''What happened to him?''

''He ran off while I was hiding from the soldiers.''

''What . . . soldiers?'' she stammered, realizing it could get a great deal worse, and possibly just had.

''Captain McGuire and his troop. I saw them two days ago.''

Sunny could tell by Maggie's tightened jaw and wide eyes that her friend was just as surprised . . . and disturbed. ''Where?''

"Crossing the Canadian River."

"Do you know which way they headed?"

"North, same as me," Gentle Wind told her. "But more west. I never saw them again after I started following the cattle tracks."

Sunny swallowed. Her heart hammered against her chest. Grierson promised her McGuire wouldn't be anywhere near Outlaw Canyon. What had gone wrong?

"Is there anything else we should know?" Sunny almost hated to ask, but had no choice. She had to know. One slip, one wrong move, was *one* too many to risk when dealing with Jake Walden.

Gentle Wind shook her head. Sunny noticed her sister's eyes start to grow heavy. She stood, and gently tugged the girl to her feet.

"Come, let's get you cleaned up. Then you need to get some rest."

A blanket of stars twinkled their brilliance against the black satin sky. The full moon rode high, lighting Sunny's path as she walked from the river. The time was late; but daylight was still hours away, and she was far too restless to think of sleep. She paused at the wagon and looked through the back opening at Gentle Wind sleeping peacefully beside Maggie.

Sunny's relief that Gentle Wind hadn't been seriously hurt was immense, but did not drown out the slight anger she felt at her sister's risky journey. The girl didn't understand the damage her disappearance could cause, or the numerous perils she could have encountered. It was a miracle she had made it all this way with no more than minor scratches. Sunny closed her eyes, and lifted a prayer of thanks to the Great Spirit, along with a plea for Running Bear's speedy recovery.

She looked one last time at Gentle Wind and wondered how Agent Taylor would use the girl's disobedience to his own advantage. Sunny had no doubt the manipulative agent would find a way, and was sure it would somehow concern the release of the children. Sunny shook her head. Gentle Wind should never have come, but she understood her sister's fears, her desperation, which closely mirrored her own. They only had each other now, and they had been separated far too long.

Knowing sleep wouldn't come easily tonight, not with so much weighing on her mind, Sunny sighed and turned to go. On her way toward the glowing embers of Jube's cook fire, she stopped and spoke with two cowhands riding out to take the midnight watch, then quietly passed the other men asleep on their bedrolls in the darkness of the camp. Jube sat alone by the fire, sipping at a cup of coffee. He looked up as Sunny approached.

"How's that little one a doin'?"

"She'll be fine. She's more tired than anything else." Sunny sat down on the log beside the cook.

"Lucky thing she found us." Jube took a sip of coffee, then smiled and cocked one bushy gray brow. "Or maybe luck had nothin' to do with it. I see a lot of ya in that girl, Miz Sunny. She's a fighter."

Sunny matched his smile with one of her own, but offered no comment.

"Whatcha doin' up so late?"

Sunny shook her head. "Just restless. I thought maybe Matt might still be up." Where had that come from? she wondered. Matt hadn't consciously been on her mind for hours.

"Ain't seen him for a good hour or more. Prob'ly done turned in for the night, which is what I'm fixin' to do." He stood and stretched his tall frame, then pointed at the tin pot warming in the coals. "There's more coffee if'n ya want some. See ya in the mornin'."

Jube took two steps, then stopped and turned back. "Plumb near forgot I been wantin' to ask ya somethin'."

"What?" Sunny looked up.

"Shorty right? Ya wanna go double or nothin' on that fifty-dollar bet?"

She nodded, and grinned. "Darn right I do, and I'll be the first in line to collect, too."

Jube cocked his head. "Ya talkin' like I'm gonna lose?"

"You don't stand a chance, old man." Sunny chuckled, ignoring the guileful smile that spread Jube's wide, ashen lips. "I can't wait to tell Will you finally lost a bet. And a good chunk of that money you've been taking in over the years."

"I reckon we'll just have to see about that, now, won't we? Way I see it, I got a lot more to gain here, than lose."

"Jube, you got more chance of winning a fight with Elethea, than you do of winning this ridiculous bet that Matt and me are going to fall in love. I can barely tolerate the man. He likes me even less. I think you've dug yourself a big hole this time."

"That's cuz ya ain't seen the way he watches ya, like I have."

"You telling me suspicion and lack of trust are the pathway to love? Because that's how he looks at me, Jube."

"It ain't none of that lightin' up those eyes like fire, 'specially when he thinks no one is a lookin'. He's smitten, all right. I'm a guessin' he just don't know it yet."

Sunny narrowed her stare and studied Jube's now serious face. Her heart pounded. Was he telling her the truth? Did Matt's eyes really light up? Or was the old cook just bluffing, hoping to get her to up the ante? Her good sense stepped in, chose the latter, and quickly overrode any foolish notions about Matt before they could take further root.

"You better hope he doesn't find out. About the bet, I mean. Matt may decide to throw his money in the pot and get you back for that bull incident. If you're not careful, he'll be expanding that ranch of his with *your* money."

"You're a forgettin' one thing, Miz Sunny," he commented with a trace of laughter in his voice.

"Oh?"

"I only bets on a sure thing."

"Until now," Sunny countered with a smile.

Matt rounded the end of the chuckwagon and heard Jube's

hearty laughter ring out. Immediately, his eyes turned to Sunny's radiant smile. His insides warmed as he recalled the taste of her lips. Irritated at the sudden path his thoughts traveled, he shook his head to clear the unwanted reminder.

"What's so funny?" he inquired as he walked over to the fire.

Jube spun sharply around, his laughter dying. Sunny jumped to her feet, startled. Matt saw the color rise in her smooth, golden cheeks, then shifted his gaze to the cook's guilty expression.

"Never mind. Something tells me I wouldn't find it as funny," he snapped.

"Don't be gettin' your britches in an uproar," Jube scolded. "Me and Miz Sunny was just havin' us a little talk 'tween friends. Nothin' for ya to get heated about. Fact is, she came over here a lookin' for ya."

Matt glanced from one to the other, wanting to believe what Jube said was true. He couldn't, not fully, but decided it really didn't matter. Whatever little Miss Spitfire had to say about him wouldn't change the fact that once this drive was over, he would never see her again. So Jube was right; he didn't have any reason to get all worked up.

"Why don't ya take Miz Sunny for a walk, down by the river," Jube suggested. "These tired ol' bones is a headin' for some rest." The cook bid them good night and left.

Matt didn't miss the look of disapproval Sunny gave Jube's retreating back. "You want to go for a walk?"

She looked at him with hesitant eyes, and he was surprised when she nodded her agreement. His heart jumped into his throat.

Dammit! He was worse than a schoolboy in the throes of a first crush. Quickly, he quelled his reaction and waved a hand for her to precede him.

Minutes later, they were walking side by side in the moon's soft white glow down the narrow path to the river. "How's your sister?" he asked.

"She'll be fine. A few cuts and bruises. Nothing serious.

She'll return to the fort with Maggie tomorrow.'' She looked up at him. ''Thanks for not getting mad at her . . . and for the candy.''

Matt shrugged away any importance to his gesture. ''She's just a kid. I knew she was only worried about you. Danny used to jump to my defense, whether it was necessary or not. Couple of times, I ended up *having* to get into a big scrap with some boys, thanks to my brother.''

Sunny's smile sent the blood pumping through his veins. He tried unsuccessfully to stem the heated flow.

''Why did she . . . come here?'' He had been about to ask why she had run away from the reservation, but decided against the accusatory remark at the last second, sensing it would only displease Sunny.

She sighed, her mouth thinned with worry. ''She wanted me to know our brother has taken ill.''

He tensed, surprised at the spark of concern that tripped through him. ''How serious?''

Sunny's eyes shimmered with unshed tears, and Matt's heart compressed in his chest. ''Gentle Wind says he's developed a fever that is so bad, Colonel Grierson felt the need to take Running Bear to his home. The army doctor is caring for him.''

They stopped beside the water's edge.

''I'm sorry.'' Matt reached for her hand as a single tear slid down her cheek. To his amazement, she offered no resistance. He held her warm palm against his and rubbed the top of her fingers lightly with his thumb. ''Will you go to him?''

Sunny shook her head. ''Maggie will check on him as soon as she gets back. And Colonel Grierson is a friend. I know he'll take good care of Running Bear.''

Her eyes sought his. Sadness mingled with fear in her azure stare. He wanted nothing more right then than to comfort her, hold her in his arms. Take away the pain he had seen hovering ever-present in the shining depths of her eyes since he had first met her. He stroked her hand with his thumb. Why did this woman affect him so strongly? He had spent the last five years hardening his heart to this very feeling. He had gotten used to the cold, dead emptiness that had been Ashley's unknown parting gift. But Sunny was starting to do things to his insides that had him feeling like a tangled-up rope. And her eyes . . . well, her eyes just seemed to touch his soul when she looked at him, and melt his heart to mush—like now.

He pulled his thoughts up short. What the hell was wrong with him? He had no business feeling anything for this woman, or her half-breed siblings.

"What was it you wanted to talk about?" His tone was harsher than he had meant, and he saw Sunny flinch, then stiffen.

She pulled her hand from his, and he fought the urge to grab it back. Her eyes, darkened with anger, made him suddenly wary. The way she tilted her chin warned him of a forthcoming battle. *Damn!* The last thing he had wanted was to get into an argument with her.

"I wanted to tell you that Shorty and me will be leaving day after tomorrow, and you can take your herd on to Wyoming," she told him with grave calmness. Matt's body tensed; his nerve endings tingled. "With Gordy leaving to take Maggie back to the fort, the drive will be a little short-handed, but Web and Pete have both bossed drives before. There shouldn't be any trouble. Shorty'll be back in about a week, Gordy before that. Pete's a good one to send out scouting for a campsite if you don't want to do it yourself. They know the trail to Ogallala; from there you can guide the rest of the way."

Well, she has it all tied up in a nice, neat package. Sounded to him as though she had rehearsed it several times before presenting it, too. And he had made quick note of the fact that she had mentioned nothing about returning herself.

"Are you going after Jake Walden?" He spoke low, his voice edged with steel.

"That's not your concern." A silken thread of warning in her tone raised Matt's anger a notch.

"You're wrong, lady." His blood simmered, barely below

the surface. "That outlaw killed my brother. I don't aim to leave this territory till justice is done."

"Rest assured, Matt, justice will be done, no matter how Walden meets his end."

"Since I intend to make sure that happens, I think I'll just head out with you."

Fiery flames sparked in her eyes and burned daggers into his. "This is my problem. *My family.* I will take care of it."

He fully understood the kind of pride that drove a person to vengeance. It was what had brought him to the Indian Territory in the first place, and caused him to kill that man in Denver. Thanks to Maggie, he knew Walden was somehow involved with Sunny's effort to free her siblings, so he had understood her comment about family, though he wasn't sure she realized her own slip yet. But what chance in hell did she have against that murdering outlaw? Matt had been in gunfights before—more than he cared to remember. He knew how to win, even when the odds were stacked against him. This little spitfire might be able to handle a gun with ease, and pack a darn good wallop, but she was no match for the likes of Jake Walden—even with Shorty riding along. There was no way Matt was staying behind. He had his own agenda. And he argued with himself that it didn't have a blasted thing to do with Sunny, or the fact she was riding into danger.

"Danny was *my* family. I'm going."

"I don't recall issuing an invitation for your company," Sunny remarked heatedly.

"And I don't recall asking your permission."

"What about your precious herd?"

Matt raised a mocking brow. "I haven't been much help so far. I doubt I'll be missed. Besides, I have your assurance the cowhands are more than capable of driving this herd, and that we'll see Wyoming well before winter. So, there's no reason I can't tag along and finish what I set out to do."

"There's *one* good reason." She turned to face him fully

and planted her fists on her shapely hips. "You'll get in the way and wind up dead."

"You're so sure you won't meet the same fate?"

"Quite sure."

His hands itched to grab her up, shake some sense into her. His heart constricted with fear for her safety. She acted so tough, but he had caught the brief look of doubt that swept across her face. "You're a stubborn fool, Sunny."

"And you're a pigheaded jack—"

With no thought of consequences, he gripped her by the shoulders and pulled her to him, cutting off her insult with his mouth. She struggled against his hold; he drew her closer. There was no tenderness as his lips captured hers, only a raw, powerful need that flared like lightning and caught him by surprise. The first taste of her sweet lips sent a swirl of liquid heat into his stomach . . . and lower. With savage intensity, he moved his mouth over hers, surprised to feel her slow response. It was all the invitation he needed. With his tongue, he traced the softness of her shapely lips. Her lips parted beneath his touch, and he slipped into the warm recesses of her mouth. She trembled beneath his touch. A warning bell went off in his head, breaking through the sudden desire threatening to burn out of control in him.

Slowly, he drew back and gazed into her flushed face. A myriad of emotions flashed across the horizon of her sky blue eyes, and he waited, half expecting her to hit him as she had done the last time.

"Why did you do that?"

He dropped his hands from her shoulders. *That is a damn good question!* And he wished like hell he had an answer.

"You didn't want me to stop?" He opted for flippancy to hide his own confusion. It didn't work.

She stepped back, crossed her arms over her chest, and glared at him. "You know that's not what I mean."

He raked his fingers through his hair as a gamut of perplexing emotions warred within him, none of which he could explain to himself, let alone her. "It seemed like the best way to shut you up," he answered with a shrug.

Her blue eyes clouded with tortured disbelief, and he could have kicked himself for being so insensitive. That wasn't at all why he had kissed her, but he doubted she would believe him now.

"I suppose you also thought that would change my mind about you riding with me and Shorty," she snapped. "Well, you can forget it. You want to go after Walden, fine. But you'll do it alone. And don't get in my way."

Matt stared at her retreating form as she hurried back up the path toward camp. Now what the hell was he going to do?

Sunny sat beside the river, thoughtfully watching darkness fade to the lighter gray of dawn. Her head pounded from the warring emotions that had raged in her mind, keeping her awake most of the night. She was still furious at Matt's arrogant attitude, and more than a little worried he would make good on his threat to go after Walden.

Damn! Double damn! She didn't need another complication to her plans. And she didn't have time to waste trying to keep Matt Lanier alive. If it hadn't been for Maggie and Gentle Wind, she would have roused Shorty last night and left right then. A smile touched her lips. It would have served the rancher right to wake up and find her gone.

She lifted a finger to her mouth, remembering the heat of Matt's kiss and the tingles that had shot through her at his touch. He had taken her completely by surprise. Why else would she have responded? The sudden rapid beat of her heart contradicted the excuse.

No man had ever invaded her mouth in that fashion before, not even her beloved White Bear. Had Matt done this because it was a white man's custom, or to shock her? she wondered. She wanted to ask Maggie if it was normal for a man to put his tongue into a woman's mouth. But how could she? Her friend would jump to all sorts of conclusions if she knew about the kiss, and Sunny wasn't up to a barrage of questions. Especially ones she didn't have answers for—like why he had done it, and why she had liked it so much. Even more disturbing, why she wouldn't mind if it happened again.

"I've been looking for you."

Sunny jumped at the unexpected interruption. Her hand flew to her breast, and her heart raced like a herd of wild ponies. "Gentle Wind, you scared me."

"What is wrong, Morning Sky?" The girl's black brows drew together to form a single line above her curious stare.

"Nothing." Slowly, Sunny climbed to her feet.

"I do not believe you."

"Why?"

"You have the instincts and training of a warrior. Yet, you did not hear me come. Something must be heavy on your mind."

Gentle Wind was too smart, Sunny mused. And *she* needed to get a better handle on her emotions.

"The only thing on my mind is your safe return to the fort . . . and Running Bear's recovery." Sunny stepped forward and placed her arm around the girl's shoulders. Gentle Wind slid her arm around Sunny's waist.

Sunny forced a smile to her lips, so as not to worry the girl. "Jube should have breakfast about done. You hungry?"

Gentle Wind cautiously nodded. "Will . . . there be enough?"

"There will be plenty." Sunny frowned. She had a suspicion why her sister asked. "Have our people not received the government rations yet?"

"No. But the cattle you sent back with Red Cloud helped. And the colonel makes sure me and Running Bear do not go hungry."

"He is a good man." But that did not excuse the missing food and clothing allotments that were becoming a regular habit. *More of the white man's lies.* She made a mental note to discuss this infraction with Colonel Grierson, again.

The sun peeked on the horizon as Sunny led her sister by the hand through camp. Warm, brilliant white rays spread over the prairie, awakening the territory to a new day. Light chased away the grayish night skies and left a soft powder blue cover in its wake.

Laughter, the sound of metal forks against tin plates, and the smell of frying meat grew stronger as they drew near the chuckwagon. Sunny scanned the faces of the men seated on the ground, and stopped on Matt. As though sensing her scrutiny, he looked up and met her stare. Setting his half-eaten plate of food on the ground, he rose to his feet. Sunny quickly looked away and hurried her steps toward Jube, but Matt stepped into her path, forcing her to stop. Gentle Wind looked up with worried eyes. She whispered a soft reassurance to the nervous girl.

''I want to talk to you.'' Matt's voice rang with command.

Sunny was sure this had to do with their conversation about Jake Walden. Lifting her chin, she boldly met his gaze and started to tell him there was nothing more to discuss, but a loud blast of gunfire suddenly rent the distant sky.

Chapter Eight

"Sunny! Sunny, where are you going?" Matt shouted into the iron-handed quiet which briefly fell over the camp. She had ordered her sister to stay put before taking off, but said nothing to him. If she replied now, he didn't hear over the frightened bawls that immediately broke the silence.

He started after her, following her hurried flight past the men who had jumped to their feet and stood with guns drawn, their breakfast forgotten. She ran toward the grassy hill which bordered the north side of the valley where the cattle were confined.

Another blast of gunfire erupted, followed by two more rounds, then nothing but frantic cries from the herd.

Sunny stopped, and squatted, placing one gloved palm flat against the earth. Matt skidded to a halt behind her. Quickly, he surveyed the area with a sweeping stare, his gun aimed from the hip, cocked and ready. Nothing. No one moved. Not even the cowhands.

What the hell are they waiting for?

He looked down at Sunny. "What are you doing?" He yelled

to be heard above the cattle's terrified cries. The ground began to vibrate beneath his boots. Her reply was lost in the noise. He leaned closer. "What?"

She sprang up and clipped the bottom of his chin with the top of her head, sending him staggering two steps. Irritated that she didn't even spare him a glance as she ran back, Matt swore under his breath and took off after her, arriving a split second behind.

"Jube, they're stampeding this way. Get Gentle Wind out of camp. See if you can find Maggie. Hurry!"

Jube grabbed Gentle Wind's hand and ran toward the north end of camp. Sunny turned, and Matt grabbed her shoulder before she could run off again.

"How do you know that?"

"I felt it."

"Just by touching the ground?" He made no effort to hide his harsh disbelief.

Sunny nodded sharply. "There's no time to stand here arguing with you." She jerked from his grasp and hurried over to where the men stood. "Hank, you and Jackson keep the herd out of the river. Turn the leader east. I'll head him off, and we can cut them back into the valley. Lefty, you and Gordy find out who was shooting, and watch your backsides."

The hands rushed for the horses Manuel already had saddled and readied for the day.

Matt grabbed Sunny's arm and stopped her from following. "We don't have any idea how many guns are out there. You could be sending these men to their deaths back in that valley."

She glared at him with her blazing blue stare. "And we could get trampled to death right here. Now, if you don't want your herd running back to Texas, either mount up and help or get out of my way!"

The earth shook from the force of the stampede. A swirl of dust started to rise above the valley walls. Matt slid his hand down her arm and gripped her gloved fingers, then broke into a run. She gained her pace quickly and to his surprise soon matched him stride for stride. When they reached the horses, she swung herself onto the palomino's back before Matt had a chance to holster his gun and stick his foot in the stirrup. The first wave of longhorns crested the grassy hillside as Matt spurred Thunder out of camp after Sunny. The sound of crumbling tin and breaking wood soon added a damning note to the cacophony of bawls and thundering hooves which filled the air.

More delays. Matt dismissed the concern. He would deal with it later.

Bending low against the palomino's neck, Sunny raced toward the east slope. Her hat was gone, and her long braid bounced against her back in dancing rhythm with the mare's swift gait. She dug her knees into the horse's sides and gripped the palomino's mane with both hands. A wave of fear rippled through him. For her own safety, as well as his peace of mind, he wished like hell she would ride with a blasted saddle!

Sunny reined to a stop at the top of the hill. Matt halted Thunder beside her and looked around the outer rim of the valley. Thousands of crazed longhorns ran wild and spilled over the north side. The cowhands rode hard, chasing and directing the cattle over the rise after the leader. They were having a difficult time of it, too, from what he could tell. He saw two riderless horses fleeing among the frightened cattle. A deep, hollow pit formed in his stomach at the sight.

Matt turned to say something to Sunny. She was gone! He twisted farther around in the saddle and spotted her heading back down the slope. Torn between his worry for her and his instinct to find whoever had started all this, Matt fingered the handle of his gun nervously.

A brown, corkscrew-horned cow broke through the trees, followed by hundreds of wild-eyed cattle. Sunny rode straight in their path. Matt spurred Thunder into a hard run down the hill. She veered to the right, then jerked her mare around and came at the leader from the side. Matt swore under his breath and urged the gelding faster. *What the hell is she doing?* He thought for sure they were going to collide, but at the last second, the cow turned and ran, side by side with, and dangerously close to, the little palomino. The herd followed, with the cowhands spread out trying to keep them in a line.

As Sunny and the stampede's leader raced by, Matt reined Thunder around and rode in as close as he dared with the running herd. She topped the hill and disappeared on the other side. He followed a good distance behind, but as he rode down into the valley, he couldn't spot her through the thick layer of dust coating the air and blurring his vision. His attention turned to keeping the cattle running together, and trying not to get his leg torn with a horn. A large, motley cow darted out in front of him. Matt reined Thunder hard to the left and ran after the errant animal. As he was running the cow into the herd, he realized they had reached the other end of the valley and were circling back.

The shouts, the bawls, the banging horns . . . Matt's head pounded with the deafening noise. But his thoughts were all on Sunny. He finally saw her, and his heart nearly stopped, then kicked up with a force as wild as the crazed animals. She started to force the leader back into the still-running herd. The animal refused to go and turned to the left. Sunny's mare didn't miss a step, but turned and followed. She tried again, and this time the leader went. He watched her ride into the frantic longhorns, so close to the deadly horns he feared they would rip her in two. Then he lost sight of her as he followed with the cattle back around, then around again. Soon the valley was filled with the circling herd, and the longhorns had nowhere to go. The animals slowed to their lumbering walk, then stopped. It was over. Before long, some of the cattle started to graze as though nothing had happened.

Matt scanned the herd, frantically searching for Sunny. He saw her walking her foam-flecked mare through the much calmer cattle, and relief washed over him.

The little spitfire sure proved her mettle. She had handled the stampede with confident authority, letting no one go off half-cocked into danger, including him. He was impressed, and quite proud. Then anger slowly set in. She had no business scaring the hell out of him risking her life that way.

Matt stared at the loose strands of hair ripped from her thick braid and wildly framing her face. She had ridden the mare flat out, neck to neck with the lead cow, and every second he feared she would slip from the horse's bare back. Her pale blue shirt clung to her skin, clearly outlining her slender shape. A vision of her forcing the stampede's leader back into the herd formed in his mind. She had come within inches of the cow's deadly horns. His temper mounted. They were a bunch of damn cows. She should never have taken the risk. He should never have let her.

Matt spurred Thunder and rode toward where she worked her way out of the herd. She reined to a stop after riding clear of the grazing longhorns. He drew the gelding up beside her and tried not to let her pretty flushed face make him forget his anger. Before Matt could say anything, Web came riding up from the opposite side and jerked his horse to a halt.

"We lost a few head, boss," the cowhand reported. "Ain't sure how many. We're workin' the edges. Once we get 'em bunched, we'll start a count."

"Good. Get me a number as soon as possible," Sunny ordered.

"Any idea who fired those shots?" Matt asked.

Web shook his head. "Pete and Shorty went to check it out right after the first shot. Ain't seen 'em come back yet."

Matt thought about those two horses he had seen, but said nothing. *Better to deal with one trouble at a time.*

Web rode off, and Matt turned his attention, and his anger, to Sunny. "What the hell were you trying to do out there? Get yourself killed?"

"If I'd known you were going to be so ungrateful, I'd have just let your stupid herd drown in the river." Heated azure eyes glared at him and pricked at his conscience.

"I'm sorry. I shouldn't have jumped at you. But you got no

business running after cattle like that.'' He crossed his arms over his chest.

She leaned closer over the horse's neck. ''Should I have tried ringing the dinner bell to see if they'd come back? And what are you upset about anyway? Milling a herd's the best way to stop a stampede. I didn't do anything different than any cowhand would have done.''

''Then, why didn't you let one of the cowhands chase after the leader?''

Sunny arched a thin, nutmeg brow at him. ''Were you worried about me?''

''Hell yes, I was worried,'' he snapped.

''Why?''

''I—'' He what? He liked the spitfire, there was no denying that. But how could he tell her his heart nearly stopped for good when he thought about her getting hurt . . . or worse? How could he explain the wrenching fear that gripped him when he had lost sight of her amid the dust and cattle? She would think he was crazy. He *was* crazy. He didn't have time to get involved with a woman. He didn't *want* to get involved with a woman, especially one carting around as many troubles as this one had.

''Never mind, it doesn't matter.'' She waved a dismissive hand and gathered the mare's lead rope in her fingers.

''It does matter,'' he ground out roughly.

''All right, so why were you worried?'' She cocked her head.

''I didn't want you getting hurt.'' He should just tell her the truth, Matt thought. What would it hurt to tell her he liked her?

''Well, I appreciate your concern.'' She smiled at him, and he suddenly decided he would tell her.

''Sunny, I—''

''Sunny!'' Gordy hailed, and quickly reined his lathered roan in front of them.

''What's wrong?'' she asked, frowning strangely at Matt before turning her attention to the cowhand.

Matt could tell by the kid's pale face and wide green eyes that the cowhand was bringing bad news.

"It ain't good, Sunny. Me and Hank didn't find the shooter, but—" His voice broke off; he swallowed.

"Spit it out, boy," Matt urged in a low voice.

Gordy looked from one to the other, then shifted uncomfortably in his saddle. "We found Pete and Shorty. Pete's been shot up pretty bad. And Shorty . . . well, um . . . Shorty's dead. Took a bullet through the heart."

"D-dead?" Sunny's voice quavered. Her lip trembled.

Matt's gut twisted into a tight ball. He suspected something bad had happened when he had seen those riderless horses. He wished like hell he had been wrong this time.

" 'Fraid that ain't all." Sweat beaded thickly on the cowhand's forehead. "Hank found an Indian brave. Someone shot him in the back. He's alive, but barely."

Sunny gasped. "No." Her eyes darted about nervously. "Where is he?"

Matt watched her chew on her bottom lip as though she were trying to suck it right off. Why would news of *this* Indian upset her? he wondered.

"Lefty went to fetch your wagon. Hank sent me to tell you they'd be bringing Pete and the Indian into camp shortly."

Sunny straightened, her face void of any expression. "Spread the word I don't want anyone going after the shooter. Understood?" Gordy nodded. "From here on out, Mr. Lanier will be bossin' this drive. You boys take your orders from him. Got that?"

Gordy quickly shut his gaping mouth and acknowledged the command with a slight tip of his dirt-covered hat, then rode off to carry out her instructions.

Matt quickly recovered from his own shock at her words. "What the hell's going on here, Sunny?"

"Not now," she snapped.

Before Matt could utter a word, she kicked the little mare

in the flanks and raced toward camp. He blew out an exasperated breath as he sat and watched her go.

Swift Arrow stood with arms crossed and stared at the prairie. Pines, grass. No riders. Why didn't Jake and the others return? The morning was half gone; they should have been back by now.

"Sit down, Swift Arrow, you're making me nervous."

"Why?" Swift Arrow made no move to look at Rusty. There was no reason. He knew the young red-hair who boasted too much was doing the same thing he had done all morning—chew the pungent tobacco leaves and make irritating noises with his mouth every time he spit into the dirt. And Hooker's fifteen-year-old brother, Luke, still sat against the tree and read from an open book propped on his knees.

"You been standin' in that same spot for thirty minutes, and I ain't seen you flinch a muscle. Hell, I wasn't even sure you were still breathin'."

Rusty spit louder. Swift Arrow clenched his teeth tighter and stared ahead. Something moved in the distance. He narrowed his gaze. Horses. Riders. They were back. "Walden and the others return."

Rusty grunted and rose to his feet. Luke closed his book, looking about with anxious brown eyes. Swift Arrow watched the kid from the corner of his eye. The lanky boy didn't belong here. He was no warrior, had no heart for raiding or killing. Swift Arrow wasn't sure the kid could even shoot a gun, since he had never seen anything more in the boy's hands than the white man's printed words.

Pounding hooves drew closer. Jake spurred the lathered gray horse to a hard run as he and the three other riders approached. The outlaw hauled back hard on the reins at the last second. The gray stopped, reared up on its hind legs, then slammed its front hooves back to the ground a few feet from where Swift Arrow stood. The others reined their horses to a stop with less force and show. Swift Arrow wasn't particularly fond of Hooker, Cal, or Stu, but he at least gave them credit for understanding the importance and value of a horse, as the Comanche did. Jake had no such concern. In the three months Swift Arrow had been riding with the gang, he had seen Walden run two good ponies to their deaths. The gray looked to be next.

Swift Arrow slowly unfolded his arms. He touched the gray's warm, wet muzzle, looked into the gelding's crazed black eyes, then at Walden. The outlaw's clear blue stare was just as wild as the horse's, and Swift Arrow felt a sudden tightening in his stomach. "Why does Gray Wolf not return with you?"

" 'Fraid your friend wasn't feeling up to the ride back," Jake sneered.

Swift Arrow narrowed his stare to mere slits. His unease deepened and twisted the knot in his stomach. "Why?" He eased his left hand toward the knife sheathed at his waist, cursing himself for not retrieving the rifle he had propped against the tree behind him before Walden got here.

Jake reached for his gun. "Don't do it, Swift Arrow." He pulled the hammer back. It clicked loudly into place.

"What are you doin', Jake?" Hooker nudged his roan closer.

Jake lifted a long, crooked finger to the black patch over his left eye. "Something I've been waitin' a long time for. Now get those hands up where I can see 'em, Injun."

Swift Arrow didn't move. He had known after the soldier's visit it would come to this, but he had not counted on it being so soon.

"This ain't a choice, Injun!" Jake barked.

Swift Arrow slowly took his hand away from the knife and lifted his arms.

"Hooker, you and Rusty tie him up, and throw him on his horse." No one moved. "Now!" Jake yelled.

Hooker jumped from his horse. Rusty grabbed Swift Arrow's arms and pulled them behind the Indian's back.

"Get his knife, you fool!" Jake ordered.

Rusty removed Swift Arrow's knife from its sheath.

Swift Arrow stared at the gang leader, hatred burning inside him like fire. ''Why not just kill me now?'' he challenged.

A sinister smile curved the outlaw's lips. ''I got plans for you.'' Jake shifted his stare to the others. ''All right, boys, let's ride. We got work to do.''

Sunny's heart pounded furiously as she slowed the mare to a trot and rode through camp. Crumpled tin was scattered about everywhere, trampled into the grass and dirt. The cook wagon sat awkwardly on the ground, one back wheel gone, splintered beyond recognition. Broken crates spilled out, littering the ground with their food supply. She passed two cowhands already sifting through the rubble, but didn't stop as she made her way toward the wagon rolling into the far end of camp.

The supply barrels had been unloaded from her wagon and stood lined up in the dirt. As she drew nearer, she saw Jube climb through the back, his medical box tucked under his arm. Maggie followed. Sunny searched the area for Gentle Wind and found her standing in the pale shadow of the pines. Her eyes were as round as a frightened fawn's, but there was no outward sign that she was physically hurt. Sunny breathed a heavy sigh of relief and turned Molly toward the trees. She stopped only long enough to help Gentle Wind up onto the horse, then quickly rode back to the wagon. Dismounting, she told Gentle Wind to watch the mare. A knot of apprehension gripped Sunny's stomach as she hurried to the wagon. She had to know.

Swallowing, Sunny peered through the opening and saw Maggie leaning over the Indian, blocking his face. She climbed into the wagon and moved slowly in the crowded confines toward the brave. He was lying on his stomach with his head turned to expose only half of his square, bronze face. Her shoulders slumped with relief. She released a sigh and gave her silent thanks to the Great Spirit that it was not Swift Arrow lying there. Then quickly added her prayers for this warrior's recovery.

She recognized Gray Wolf, though he was not from her Penateka tribe, but Kwahadi Comanche. She had seen him once almost a year ago when she had met with the fiery, young renegade chief Quanah Parker during her search for Running Bear and Gentle Wind. Gray Wolf had been arrested and brought to the fort for killing a family of settlers, and no doubt would hang for the crime upon his return to the fort. She understood his pride and honor as a warrior to defend his people, and knew he would want to die proudly—not from a coward's bullet to the back. Damn Jake Walden!

Her heart ached for the young brave, but she was growing weary of all the fighting, and the killing. Chief Black Eagle had been right—it was time for the Indians to find peace with the white man. She had to make Swift Arrow see that it was their only hope of survival now, and she prayed she could save him from the same fate that awaited Gray Wolf. Colonel Grierson had said nothing about Swift Arrow's part in the deaths of those settlers, but the brave *was* a renegade—a crime in itself. And he had been with Gray Wolf when the soldiers arrested them. Her stomach churned at the possibility of her childhood friend's involvement. If guilty, she understood his reasoning, though she no longer believed that was the way to settle this fight. But could she watch him hang? Even for the sake of her siblings?

"How bad is it?" she asked quietly.

Maggie shook her head. "It's not good. The bullet is still in him, and from the way he's bleeding, I'm not sure he's going to make it."

Sunny followed her friend's stare down to the blood-soaked bandage pressed against his bronze flesh. Fear knotted her insides, twisted her heart. She met Maggie's worried gaze, knowing they shared the same concern. If the brave died, would the agent still honor the agreement? Sunny had no answer.

She moved closer to the front where Jube tended after Pete, and looked down at the cowhand's barely opened eyes.

"They came . . . out . . ." He choked.

Guilt stabbed at her heart. Sunny touched a hand to the man's trembling arm. "Don't try to talk. I know there was nothing you men could do." She knew exactly where to lay the blame—with herself, and Jake Walden. "You just worry about getting yourself well."

Pete thanked her with his pain-filled stare, then closed his eyes. Sunny turned to Jube. "Is he gonna make it?" she whispered.

Jube shook his head in doubt. "The bullet to his shoulder went clean through. He wasn't so lucky with the one to his gut."

"Think he can last long enough to reach the doctor at Fort Sill?"

Jube shook his head again, then lifted one shoulder in a slight shrug that was far from reassuring. "I sure wish my Elethea was here."

Sunny nodded, then implored the cook with her eyes not to give up.

This bargain she had made with Agent Taylor was taking too deadly a toll. Except for Shorty, these men didn't have any idea what they were doing so far from the trail. They hadn't asked questions, either. They had followed her orders because they trusted her, and she had led them into danger. Now Shorty was dead—Walden's latest casualty. Pete and Gray Wolf were close to becoming the next. But no more. She would risk no more lives. From now on, what had to be done, she would do alone. She would find Swift Arrow. She would be with Running Bear and Gentle Wind. And it didn't matter anymore that she had to go through Jake Walden to make it happen. The man had been a sharp thorn in her side for as long as she could remember. Too long. It was time she did something about it.

"Jube, I want you to gather up what supplies Maggie's going

to need until they can get to the fort. I'll tell Gordy to make ready to pull out as soon as possible."

Jube nodded. Sunny turned, and purposefully avoided Maggie's stare as she crawled to the back and climbed down. There was no time to argue about her decision, and she knew that was exactly what her friend would do. She found Gordy and explained the situation, then made her way to where Gentle Wind sat waiting on one of the supply barrels. She took the girl's trembling hands in her own.

"There's no need to be scared anymore, little one." She made to gather the girl in her arms, but Gentle Wind pushed back.

"I wasn't scared. It was like watching the buffalo run."

Sunny saw excitement dancing in the girl's round, brown eyes, and found herself remembering, longing for the days when their people roamed free. It wasn't fair. The Indians didn't deserve to have their lands taken away, their livelihoods destroyed. Their families killed. But the white man was greedy and took what he wanted. Looking down into Gentle Wind's soft, bronze face, Sunny's own greed tightened her heart. This time, she, too, would get what she wanted. No matter what, no matter who tried to stand in her way.

She placed her hands on the girl's slender shoulders. "Those were happy times. I miss them, as well."

"I remember the last hunt. White Bear was angry that you refused to stay behind and wait with the rest of the women and children."

Sunny smiled at the recollection. White Bear had already laid claim to her by then, and feared for her safety. But she had refused to stay behind. He was the bravest warrior in their tribe, and he had taught her everything she knew. Even Chief Black Eagle had given his consent for her to go on the hunt. That was not the first time her young brave had cursed the day he had agreed to teach her the warrior skills, she recalled with a smile. "Yes, but he was not so angry when I brought down two buffalo on that hunt and proved his skill as teacher."

"You were very brave, Morning Sky. You made Black Eagle proud, our *pia* as well."

Sunny recalled the smile on their mother's face that day and forced back the tears which welled in her eyes and threatened to spill over. "And now you must be brave, little one. Preparations are being made for Maggie and Gordy to take the wounded men to the fort as soon as possible. You will go with them."

Gentle Wind frowned. "Did that brave fire those first shots?"

"No." There was no doubt in her mind who had fired first, or why Gray Wolf was left behind.

"Is he one of the braves you've been searching for?"

Sunny nodded.

"Will he die?"

"I don't know," she told the girl honestly. "Maggie will do everything she can to see that doesn't happen."

Silence hung heavy for several seconds; then Gentle Wind pulled from her grasp and turned away. "I would rather stay with you, Morning Sky."

"That's not possible. You'll be safe with Maggie."

Gentle Wind spun back around. "What about the agent?"

"We have struck a bargain. With the return of Gray Wolf, Colonel Grierson will have more leverage to force the agent to stick to our agreement. And Maggie has given her word she will see that no harm comes to you, or Running Bear. Trust her, Gentle Wind. And do everything she tells you."

The young girl hesitated. Tears glistened in her brown eyes as she slowly nodded. "I will miss you, Morning Sky. Promise to return soon."

Sunny gathered her sister into a tight embrace. "I promise."

Together they walked over to the wagon. Sunny saw Maggie off to the side with Jube, their heads bent together as the cook gave last minute instructions for tending the wounded. She glanced away, studying the activity around the wrecked camp, and not for the first time wondered about Matt. She was surprised he hadn't followed her, his ever-demanding tone shouting at her for an answer of one sort or another. But as she scanned the bustling campsite, she realized he wasn't there. She pushed aside her concern about Matt when she saw Gordy hurrying over.

"Everything's ready, boss. We can pull out whenever you say."

"Gentle Wind can ride up front with you."

"I'll take right good care of her." Gordy smiled.

"Thanks." Sunny couldn't smile back. "Keep a close eye out for trouble, and skirt the trail around to the east for a ways. I'm sure the ones who started the stampede are long gone, but it won't hurt to be extra careful."

Sunny hugged her sister tightly and whispered reassurances they would be together again soon, then brushed away the flow of tears from the girl's smooth, youthful cheeks. Stepping back, she handed her over to the cowhand and watched as Gordy led Gentle Wind to the front of the wagon. Sunny rubbed away her own tears, then started over to tell Maggie it was time to leave, but the schoolteacher saw her coming and met her halfway.

"You're not going after Walden alone, are you?"

Sunny knew by the challenge in Maggie's tone that her friend was going to protest strongly to her answer. She decided to avoid the inevitable. "Everyone's ready; You got what you need from Jube?" Maggie planted her hands on her hips and nodded. Sunny rushed on. "Then, you need to get gone. It's not yet noon. Gordy should be able to make good time to the fort. Shouldn't take more than two days."

Maggie stood her ground. "Shorty's dead, Sunny. What are you going to do?"

"What I came to do. Now, it's time to go."

"You need help," Maggie pleaded. "At least wait until we make it to the fort and I tell Colonel Grierson about the attack and McGuire being up here."

She shook her head. "There isn't time. No doubt, thanks to McGuire, Walden now knows what I'm after. Gray Wolf is proof of that." She saw the agreement in her friend's eyes.

"He'll hightail back to Outlaw Canyon and wait for me to come for Swift Arrow. As long as I know what he's up to, I'll be fine."

"And if you don't know? Sunny, you can't . . . do this alone." Maggie's protest was broken by the catch in her voice.

Sunny straightened, and crossed her arms in front. "You're wrong, my friend. I can, and I will."

"You're the one who's wrong."

Sunny spun around at Matt's deep, sharp voice. He stood facing her across a span of several feet, fists pressed against lean hips, his jaw rigid. Beneath the brim of his hat, his hard stare bore into her face.

"You can't go after Walden by yourself. And you won't."

Chapter Nine

Well, what do you know, Matt thought. *The little spitfire is speechless, and she isn't walking away from me, either.* But Matt knew he hadn't won this easily. There was going to be a battle all right, and judging by those stormy, blue eyes of hers, he didn't have much longer to wait.

"That's *not* your decision to make, Mr. Lanier." Her tone was low and smooth, but Matt wasn't fooled in the least. She was mad. And darn pretty in the process, he had to admit.

He crossed his arms over his chest and shrugged one shoulder. "I've already made it."

She stared at him through lowered lashes, and there was a perceptible tilt of her head, but to his astonishment, she remained silent.

"Besides, you're a woman." He couldn't resist sweeping his gaze over her for emphasis and saw her body stiffen. *That got her feathers riled up.* He had himself a little more heated up than he'd intended, as well, but it sure wasn't anger straining his manhood after staring at her shapely curves. "And despite the fact that you seem to know what you're doing with that gun you carry, and you got some fight in you, you're no match in strength for Jake Walden."

"I don't plan to battle him hand to hand, so there shouldn't be a problem."

"I'm sure you weren't aiming to fight me, either. But look what happened when I yanked you from that tree. Wasn't for Shorty, who knows how that might have turned out."

She bristled visibly at his undeniable argument.

"Since I'm going after Walden anyway, it only makes sense that the two of us should hook up together and do the job. Don't you agree?"

"Yes." Maggie stated.

"No!" Sunny turned and glared at her friend, then looked back at him. "I don't agree. Besides, you have the drive to worry about. Remember?"

Matt cocked his head to one side. "You told Gordy to have the men report to me. They did. I put Hank and Web in charge of leading the drive."

Sunny stared at him through long, pale lashes. "Why?"

Matt shrugged lightly at her wary inquiry. "Someone has to be boss while we go after Walden. You trust these men. I figure I can, too. If they reach Ogallala before we get back, I told Hank to send a wire to Cheyenne. I mapped out the trail west to head the herd on. They'll meet up with one of my ranch hands before they get too far."

"You've wasted your time, Mr. Lanier. I'm not going to change my mind."

"Sunny, don't be stubborn," Maggie begged. "You need Matt's help."

Sunny turned around and faced her friend. "No. I've already gotten enough people killed. I won't risk any more."

"I take my own risks. Make my own decisions." Matt drew her attention back to him. "Walden's the reason I came to the territory. That hasn't changed. I'm going after that murdering outlaw, with or without you."

"Let Matt help," Maggie implored, her hands clutching at

Sunny's arm. "You can trust him, Sunny. You need him. You know you do."

Matt saw Sunny's hesitation in the blue gaze she darted between him and Maggie. Beneath her wavering uncertainty, he also saw a calculating determination that put him instantly on guard.

"If I agree, will you get in that wagon and leave for the fort? Now?"

Maggie nodded quickly.

"Fine." Sunny turned to face him. "We'll ride together."

Matt didn't trust her motivation. She had made the decision too fast, and way too easily. And if he had learned anything these past few days, there was nothing easy about Miss Sunny Donovan. The spitfire was up to something. He sensed it. He also had a strong, unexplainable need to figure out what it was and stop her before that stubborn pride of hers got her killed.

After pushing hard toward Dodge for the last hour, they slowed beneath the blazing yellow ball hanging mid-sky to let the horses walk and cool down in the afternoon heat. Sunny rode silently alongside Matt and watched the white, puffy clouds, in brilliant contrast to the azure expanse, float lazily overhead.

Matt's tight-lipped anger evidenced his continued displeasure with her decision that they would ride to Dodge and arrange for the necessary supplies to be sent back to the drive. He had argued before and after Shorty's brief, but proper burial that it was a waste of time, that one of the hands could go. But Sunny stood firm. She had no intention of riding to Outlaw Canyon with Matt, and she knew it would be easier to lose him in the small town, than out on the flat, open plains. She had wanted the delay for another reason, as well. She knew Walden was expecting her, and a day or two of cooling his heels would no doubt put the man on edge and hopefully make him careless. She would need every advantage when she confronted the outlaw, especially at night—alone.

Sunny covertly shifted her stare to Matt. After tomorrow, she knew he would be angry with her again, but at least she wouldn't be subject to that bout, because by then she would be gone. And as long as she got to Walden first, Matt Lanier would remain safe, and alive.

She watched as Matt inhaled in a long draw from his cheroot, then released thick, white smoke rings, one at a time. The circles grew wider and thinned before disappearing into the air. Watching his sensually formed mouth, she almost envied the smoke. Sunny swallowed, and forced herself not to think about how soft his lips had been on hers.

"Wanna see it again?"

"Wh . . . what?" Sunny stammered, turning her gaze fully to Matt.

He turned his head. One corner of his mouth lifted in a mocking smile. "You were watching that smoke with some great fascination. Or maybe it's just me you like looking at."

Heat rose to her cheeks at his unsubtle suggestion. He peered at her intently. She looked away from the vague passionate light that passed between them. "I've seen men smoke before, Mr. Lanier. And you're not much different looking than any other white man," she lied. He was the best-looking man she had ever laid eyes on, Indian or white.

He threw a hand over his chest. "Ouch! You're hard on a man's pride."

She smiled, her eyes darting to his virile presence in spite of her earlier resolve not to let this man get to her. "I doubt your pride has ever suffered."

His teasing smile slipped, replaced with a tense frown. "You're wrong about that, ma'am." He looked forward and took another draw on the cigar.

Sunny realized she had been careless with her words. Was he thinking about Maggie's sister leaving him at the altar? she wondered. Or about Maggie?

"I've learned a woman can bruise a man right smart if he's not careful."

"And how many women have 'bruised' you, Mr. Lanier?" she dared to ask.

His stare slid back to her. Sunny watched his gaze darken, then narrow. His voice was low, controlled. "Only one. But she did a damn fine job. And I don't aim to go through anything like that again."

Was he warning her? Had her undeniable attraction to him been that obvious? She should tell him he had nothing to worry about. Whether she was fascinatingly drawn to him or not, it changed nothing. She had to find Swift Arrow and free her brother and sister. Afterward, she would raise her siblings on her own. Her future was planned. So why didn't she just tell him that?

"I'm assuming you know about Ashley from Maggie."

Sunny nodded.

"What else did Maggie tell you about me?" he demanded in a cool tone.

When she didn't answer, his hand snaked across the distance that separated them and circled her arm. His fingers pressed against her sleeve and sent a jolt of heat through her startled, tingling flesh.

"Tell me," he grated impatiently.

Sunny lowered her eyes from his angry, heated stare to his hand, then back. The sudden anxious concern that blazed in his eyes sent off a warning bell. There was something he didn't want her to know. What? Whatever it was, judging by his hard, concerned look, Maggie knew about it. Or maybe it involved Maggie. Was this somehow connected with the secretive past neither her friend nor this rancher wanted to talk about? In the last few days, she had learned Matt was a man who liked to deal in cold, hard facts. If she were honest with him, would he drop that hard, protective shell he kept on the past?

"Maggie's told me more than once, you're a man to be trusted. She considers you a very good friend. Other than that, nothing."

His hand slipped free of her arm. He straightened in his saddle, gauged her face with a wary eye, then visibly relaxed.

"What is it you're hiding, Matt?" she whispered daringly, not surprised to see the lines in his jaw etch deep again.

"I'm not 'hiding' anything." He looked away and took another draw on the near burned-out cheroot. "Most folks carry around a part of their past they're not real proud of and don't like to have brought up. Including you, I'd bet."

A cold chill snaked up Sunny's back. Walden's image jumped into her thoughts. She shook the mental picture away and forced the surging memories back to the dark recesses of her mind. "Fine, we won't talk about the past."

Matt snubbed out the small cigar against the hard leather of his saddle, then tossed the butt to the ground and slowly arched his brow at her. "Let's talk about the present, then. Why didn't you want any of the cowhands to go look for the person who started that stampede and shot Shorty and Pete?"

"Because I already knew it was Walden."

"Before or after you knew he dropped that Indian off as his calling card?"

He had obviously heard more of her conversation with Maggie than she had realized. Sunny glanced nervously away and stared at the flat grassy sea that covered the prairie for miles. Her mare jumped as a rabbit darted across their path, and Sunny pressed her knees closer to the horse's sides to hold her seat. Molly settled back into her slow gait.

"I had my suspicions. Gray Wolf confirmed them."

"Would you care to fill me in on what we're riding into?"

Sunny's muscles tensed. "I didn't ask you to come along. And you don't have to stay."

"I'll take that as a no, but I'm staying anyway," he ground out roughly.

They rode in silence for a ways, long enough for Sunny's nerves to stretch near to breaking, and she gave a small start when Matt spoke.

"Why don't you tell me some more about your life with the

Comanches.'' His voice was low and smooth as silk, and caused her pulse to pound faster as blood raced through her veins.

Sunny met his probing stare and was confused by the genuine interest she saw reflected in his gaze. ''Seems to me you know quite enough already.'' Too much, she silently added, turning away.

''I don't know a darn thing about you,'' he scoffed lightly. ''Except that you're stubborn, and smart. I think it was that flanker, Lefty, who said, you've got some 'right good sense 'boutcha.' '' His approving smile made her feel proud, and strangely faint. ''I know everyone trusts you. Especially Maggie. And I know you lived with the Comanches a good part of your life.''

''There's nothing else to tell.''

He chuckled. ''I don't believe that, angel.'' Matt's soft-spoken endearment caused her breath to lodge in her throat. ''I'd say there's a whole store of stuff I don't know.''

She swallowed, and regained her breath, then looked away from her feigned interest in the stand of trees on the distant horizon and turned a challenging stare to Matt. ''I could say the same about you.''

He shrugged his agreement. ''Your sister calls you Morning Sky. It's nice. It fits you.''

Sunny's heart tripped unexpectedly, then stopped. Did he just pay her another compliment? Warmed blood surged through her veins.

''Is Sunny your given name?'' he asked. ''Your white man's name, I mean.''

She nodded. Tender memories of her mother sprang into her thoughts, and she was unable to stop herself from telling him more. ''It was my grandmother's name. I never knew her, but Mama always talked about her a great deal.''

''What about your pa?''

Sunny stiffened, and quickly glanced away. Outwardly, she held herself straight, proud, but inside, her body and mind warred in chaotic confusion over the conflicting emotions that threatened to weaken her toward this man. She could not trust Matt Lanier. She would not. No one must know her past. Sunny closed her eyes and prayed for strength to fight her pulling attraction to this man.

Imposing an iron control on her wavering confusion and building affection, she looked back at the rancher. "The horses have walked enough, and we've got a lot of miles to cover before dark if we plan to reach Dodge tomorrow."

Sunny nudged the mare with the heels of her boots, urging the palomino into a fast canter. She rode away, leaving Matt's startled, heated protest hanging in the air behind her.

Lifting the hem of her calico dress, Maggie dabbed at the beaded moisture collected above her lip. With one hand she undid the first two buttons of her sweat-dampened blouse, then fanned herself with the cumbersome skirt. The afternoon heat was stifling in the airless wagon, and taking its toll.

Pete lay at one end of the rough-swaying wagon. His eyes were closed, but his soft moans suggested a painful, half-conscious state. Gray Wolf slept quietly on the other side. She had been surprised earlier to look over at the Indian and find him watching her through hooded eyes. She managed to get him to swallow a couple sips of water before he had turned his head and drifted back into unconsciousness.

The smell of blood and sweat filled her every breath and threatened to make her nauseous. She checked the men's bandages again, a fresh wave of concern washing through her at the blood-soaked sight. Gray Wolf never stirred as she applied a fresh dressing. She had started to remove the red, soggy cloth from Pete's gut when the wagon suddenly hit a hole in the arduously bumpy trail and sent her toppling on the cowhand's lower half. Pete groaned. His eyes snapped open and met hers. Maggie scrambled back onto her knees, apologizing profusely. Careful not to cause him further pain, she pressed a clean bandage to his wound, but the white circle around his thinned mouth, and his tightly closed lids, told the depth of his suffering. She decided to have Gordy stop while she mixed another dose of the powdered pain medicine Jube had sent along.

Maggie neared the front of the wagon at the same moment Gordy suddenly whipped the horses into a run and turned sharply to the right. She grabbed hold of the white canvas overhead to steady herself as they bounced from side to side over the uneven terrain.

"What's going on?" she called out.

"Trouble comin', ma'am," Gordy hollered back. "Two men ridin'—"

A shot rang out, cutting off Gordy's words. Gentle Wind screamed. Pete groaned roughly behind her. Gray Wolf's eyes opened and sought hers. Maggie thought she saw a look of warning in his brown stare before they settled closed again. The horses picked up speed, pulling the unsteady wagon at a dangerous pace. It was all Maggie could do to keep herself from falling on the wounded men.

"Gordy?" she called out.

"He's been shot, Maggie." Gentle Wind's high, panicky voice sailed through the canvas opening. "Men are after us."

Dear God!

"Grab the reins, Gentle Wind. I'm coming." Maggie sank to her knees, then crawled back to where Pete lay. Taking the gun from his holster, she stood, hunching over to keep from hitting her head on the wooden canvas supports, then haltingly made her way toward the front end of the wagon . . . and the defenseless girl. She reached a hand through the oval opening and grabbed at the flat wooden bench. A splinter ran under her skin along her palm. She swallowed the pained sob that filled her throat. Her searching fingers made contact with the heavy cotton of Gentle Wind's skirt, just as the wagon bucked over a deep rut. Her tentative hold gave way, and she flew hard against the wooden side. The gun sailed from her fingers, hit the boards with a thud, then slid to the back. She struggled upright, but fell before she found her footing. Gentle Wind screamed again.

Dear God! She had to get to the girl.

Determined, Maggie got to her feet and started forward. The horses suddenly turned to the left, forcing the wagon to rock precariously on two wheels. She lost her balance and landed flat on her back. The air rushed from her lungs, leaving her momentarily helpless. She closed her eyes and sucked in a much needed breath, then rolled over and pushed herself up to her hands and knees.

"Hurry, Maggie! They're gaining."

The wagon lurched treacherously side to side, threatening to throw Maggie off balance again. She looked around frantically for a weapon, then remembered the gun Sunny had given her, tucked safely in her small valise. Relieved to see her bag not far away, she crawled toward it.

"Don't touch that horse!"

Maggie's heart skipped a full beat at Gentle Wind's frightening words. The wagon began to slow, then gradually came to a stop. Just as she started to open the catch on the bag, she heard Gentle Wind's daring shouts, and froze. The young girl's terrified voice was abruptly cut off. Maggie heard sounds of a struggle, growing muffled as though moving away from the wagon. Then silence. With shaking fingers, she undid the clasp.

"Don't move, schoolteacher."

Maggie's head snapped up, her eyes fixed on the fierce green stare that matched the deadly tone to the attacker's warning. The kid was barely old enough to be called a man, she thought, judging his smooth, freckled face and red hair that stuck out wildly from beneath his worn hat. But the gun he aimed at her gave him the definite advantage.

"Who are you? What do you want?" Her concern for Gentle Wind mounted, but Maggie forced herself to remain calm She would be no good to the girl dead. She couldn't help wondering if Gordy had already met that fate.

"There's been a change in plans." The kid snarled, then

eased his mouth into a smile that sent shivers running down her spine. "Get down," he grated, his smile disappearing. "Now!"

Maggie swallowed back the fear that gripped her and darted a quick glance between the wounded men. Gray Wolf lay lifeless. Pete was silent now, his eyes still closed.

"Hurry it up. I ain't got all day," the kid growled.

Maggie risked a look through the front canvas opening, hoping to see Gentle Wind. Nothing but emptiness greeted her. She made her way to the back of the wagon and climbed down. Standing as tall as her small stature allowed, she planted her fists on her hips and glared up at the kid still sitting his horse. "What do you want?"

He swung down from his saddle and strolled to within inches of her. "You're purty brave, ain't ya, schoolteacher?" A thin layer of trail dust coated his clothes and face. His stale whiskey breath nearly made her gag. "Feisty, too. I like that. Now, move," he ordered, giving her a rough shove on the shoulder that made her stumble backward.

Gaining her footing, Maggie turned and stepped to the front of the wagon. Then she stopped and looked up, doing her best to ignore the metal barrel of his gun poking into her spine. Refusing to let him see her fear, and her growing panic, she searched the wooden seat, but found no sign of Gentle Wind or Gordy. Her gaze rested briefly on the blood-splattered end of the narrow bench—Gordy's end—then frantically scanned the surrounding area. Where was Gentle Wind? Dread filled her stomach as the full realization of their danger became clear.

Her captor rammed the barrel into her back. "Keep walkin'."

Frigid fear washed through her. Who were these men? And what heinous acts did they plan?

She did as ordered. When she cleared sight of the horses, Maggie glanced quickly to her left, and missed her next step. She stared at Gentle Wind's limp form lying crumbled on the ground. *Dear Lord, please don't let the girl be dead.* An older, heavily whiskered man stood above the unconscious girl. Maggie stopped, then gasped, drawing the brown-haired man's attention.

"Don't fret." His slow grin didn't reach the cold darkness of his eyes. "She ain't dead. Jake wants the both of ya alive."

"Ja . . . Jake," Maggie stammered. Stark, icy panic seeped into every fiber of her being. "You mean Jake Walden?"

"That's right," the kid mouthed laughingly against her ear. "You've been given a personal invite to come a callin'. Me and Cal, we was sent to fetch ya."

"What about the girl?" Maggie asked cautiously. Her mind whirled with alarming thoughts and horrible possibilities. She couldn't let Walden get his hands on Gentle Wind.

"She gets to come along, too." The kid's nauseating breath assailed her nose. "But first, Cal and me got us an itch we need takin' care of. And you're just the one to help scratch it."

"I'd rather die." Her voice was shakier than she would have liked, and she tried to stand taller, bolder. The kid put a hand to her shoulder, his long, grimy fingers biting into her flesh. She sucked in an audible breath as a disturbing quake raked through her.

"Well now, that ain't possible. Not yet. But if'n it's pain ya want, I can oblige ya with a little rough pleasure. How 'bout ya, Cal?"

The bearded man nodded, and grinned lasciviously. "Sure thing, schoolteacher."

Maggie's body turned colder. She knew exactly what they planned to do. The color drained from her face as she realized she was helpless to stop them, but she refused to give up. She would fight them as long as she could. And, if they so much as laid a single filthy finger on Gentle Wind, she vowed to find a way to kill them.

"Move." The kid jammed the gun sharply into her back, catching her off guard and causing her to stagger forward several steps. He shoved her again, and she stumbled, then fell hard against the ground. Her hair spilled from her neat bun and covered her averted face.

"Looks like she's all ready and eager, don't it, Rusty?"

She heard Cal's sinister chuckle from across the way. The kid joined in above her with his own jeering laugh. The warmed earth seared her cheek. Small, round rocks littered the hard ground and pressed into her body.

With a sinking dread, Maggie listened to Cal's approaching steps. She struggled to regain her breath and keep her mind clear. She had to think—to find some way out of this . . . before Gentle Wind got hurt. She feared these men would finish their filthy lust with her and then turn to the girl's fresh, young body. And she had no idea what Walden would do. But whatever the outlaw planned, she had no doubt he would try to use the girl against Sunny.

A hand grabbed at the back of her blouse, pulling her roughly to her feet. She was pinned between both men and faced the older of the two.

"Ya like games, teacher? Cuz, we're gonna play us one." Cal grinned, and waved his gun in her face. "Ya just pretend this is your classroom and me and Rusty are your students." He swept his eyes over her body and pressed the gun into her stomach. Maggie stood motionless. "You can start the teachin' by takin' your clothes off."

"I will not." Her eyes filled with unshed tears that belied her boldness. She refused to let the moisture spill out, sensing they would take great pleasure in her fear.

"Your choice." Cal shrugged. For a second, Maggie thought he was going to turn away, but before she took her next breath, his grimy hand reached out, grabbed the collar of her blouse, and ripped it down the front. Rusty let out a loud whoop behind her.

Maggie froze as Cal trailed the tip of his gun along the lace edge of her cotton chemise. "Now, schoolteacher, you wanna do the rest? Or you want me to finish it for ya?"

From somewhere deep inside her, anger fought its way past

the fear. She would not let this happen. A well-spring of strength surged up within her, coursing through her very being. Maggie spit in Cal's face, then turned slightly and started to run. She got no farther than her first step before Rusty shoved her face first into the dirt.

"Stupid bitch! You're gonna pay for that," Cal retorted hotly.

Before she could move, her skirt was jerked up and thrown over her head, plunging her into suffocating darkness. A pair of hands pinned her shoulders to the ground. She kicked her legs wildly and tried to twist free of the hard grasp. The heavy weight of a man's body sank down on the back of her thighs. Hands groped at her thin undergarments. Hot tears spilled out and trailed along her cheeks. She prayed they would finish quickly, and swore she would not let them touch the girl—even if it meant offering herself again. From under the darkness, she felt a tug and heard the sound of cotton ripping. The outlaw shifted his seat down to her calves, and the sun's late afternoon rays beat down and touched her bared legs.

"She's ours now." Rusty's young, excited voice reached her ears and gave her a new surge of strength.

Maggie struggled to roll over, tried to kick at his probing hands with her legs, but she was no match for their masculine power. She told herself not to think about what was happening. Told herself to focus on anything other than the feel of their verminous hands making her flesh crawl. She tried, but she couldn't. A piercing pressure stabbed her lower region as the kid tried to enter her, and Maggie struggled again to force him off. It was no use. Tears coursed like rivers down her face at the hopelessness of her situation. Then suddenly, two shots rang out in rapid succession.

The sun's final descent tinged the prairie with varying shades of salmon-colored streaks, touched with a brassy glow, as it slipped below the horizon and chased the day away. A small stream gurgled nearby, and the current flowed rapidly across its rock-lined bed. The smell of roasting rabbit filled the air and assailed Sunny's nose. Her stomach rumbled low, reminding her that in all the confusion of the day she had had no chance to eat anything but a couple strips of dried beef.

Sunny looked up from the campfire and watched Matt in the distance with the horses. She couldn't help but admire his easy manner as he rubbed the pair down with fresh grass and hobbled them for the night, all the while speaking to the mounts in hushed words she couldn't discern. She wasn't fooled, though. She could tell by the lines that ran deep in his tightened jaw he was still angry.

They had spoken little as the afternoon slipped past. Well, she had, anyway. Matt had had plenty to say when he finally caught up with her after she rode off at his question about her pa. He made short order of letting her know his anger, telling her she acted childish every time she took off like that. Then he threatened her with a much deserved spanking if she tried it again. At that point her own anger escalated. She pulled her gun and suggested he would be a fool to try. The heated stare he sent her gave her pause to wonder if he intended to prove her wrong at that very moment—just enough pause that Matt was able to snatch her gun from her fingers. He rode off after that, leaving her alone and somewhat vulnerable, but she suspected he wasn't far away. Or so she thought. When his absence became prolonged, she started to grow a little concerned. More so when she heard a single shot fired. But shortly after that, he'd returned, carrying a dead rabbit.

To her relief, he had asked no more questions and demanded no more answers. She had done enough battling for one day, mostly with herself over why she hadn't just told him what everyone else thought to be the truth about her father—that he was dead.

She had spent a good deal of time contemplating her feelings for Matt, as well, and realized her heart was dangerously engaged in a fiery game where this man was concerned. A fire she feared would fan itself out of control if she wasn't careful. She knew she had to stop herself from caring, but she couldn't. Matt drew responses from her, both inside and out, that she had never experienced before, not even with White Bear. For the first time in a good number of years, she found herself unable to restrain her feelings, and her responses. Her emotions where this man was concerned had somehow slipped beyond her authority. She felt almost like that helpless little girl she had once been, so long ago. And she didn't like the feeling at all.

Matt's soft whistling penetrated her musings and alerted her to his approach. She looked up, her gaze colliding with his shuttered stare. He smiled at her then, a genuine, angerless smile that sent warm blood rushing to her cheeks.

"Smells good." Matt tossed his hat down on his bedroll and stretched out on the ground, using his saddle as a backrest.

Sunny stared at the length of him across the fire and felt a heated tingling in the pit of her stomach. She must be too close to the flame, she reasoned. Of the fire, she further amended, lowering her gaze from Matt's disturbing presence. She scooted back a little. "It's just about done. You want some coffee?"

"Thanks." Matt sat up, reaching for the cup as she leaned over and handed it to him. Their fingers brushed ever so lightly and sent a white-hot jolt up her arm. The tin fell as Sunny jerked her hand back before Matt had a good grip. The cup hit the ground with a deadening thud, splashing hot liquid on Matt's pant leg. He let out a soft expletive, then pulled the denim material away from his skin.

"I'm so sorry." Sunny's hand flew to her mouth.

"It's all right, angel. I'm getting used to suffering pain of one sort or another around you." He looked at her with tender, smiling eyes. His lips parted to reveal even, white teeth. "You definitely keep a man on his toes. And tied up with curiosity, too.''

Sunny didn't know what to say. His teasing smile rocked her senses. She realized she much preferred his anger, which kept her at a distance, as opposed to this understanding playfulness which threatened to bowl her over and weaken her defenses further.

She stood. ''Supper's done. Help yourself. I'll be back in a few minutes.''

Matt watched her walk into the darkened shadows and disappear in the small stand of oaks and redbud trees. He realized he had scared her off again, but how? He hadn't yelled at her. Hell, he had even worked off most of his anger over this afternoon while rubbing down the horses, and decided he wouldn't badger her with a bunch of questions for a while. So what had he done this time to make her take off like a skittish colt?

Damned if he could figure it out, or her. She was a complicated woman. And he didn't have time for any more complications. So why didn't he just walk away?

A part of him wanted to, but he was afraid if he left now, his heart would stay behind and worry about what happened to her. Matt shook his head. What in tarnation was wrong with him? He had no trouble keeping to himself before, especially after Ashley. But with Sunny it was different. Try as he might, he couldn't bring himself to let the spitfire face Walden alone, and he knew without a doubt she would try.

Shaking off the unwilling concern he had for the little blonde, Matt cut off a large chunk of blackened meat and took a bite. Quickly, he spit it out into the fire and glared at the remaining hunk he held between his fingers. It was charred on the outside. He flipped it over to reveal the still-pink meat inside. He hoped to hell she was better at catching outlaws than she was at cooking.

Matt put the meat back on the fire and opened a can of beans to heat. His attention was instantly distracted by a rustling in the brush, then Sunny's sharp gasp and small squeal. He jumped to his feet and reached for his gun as she came running from the cover of the sparse trees. He barely made out her mumbled curse about some damn snake, and bit back the relieved smile that threatened his lips.

"More coffee?" he asked innocently as she reached the circle of their small fire.

"No," she snapped.

He forced down the laughter that hung back in his throat at her wide-eyed expression. Gazing into her sparkling blue pools, he wondered if she had any idea how she affected him. Or how much he wanted to protect her. God, how was it possible that he had become so smitten with this blond angel in such a short time? "If you need to go again, I'll be happy to escort you," he offered sincerely.

"That won't be necessary," she told him with a grim expression. "I'm sure I looked the fool running from the trees like that. But I assure you, I can take care of myself."

So brave, he thought. But who was she trying to convince—him or herself? "Did you tell that to the snake, as well?"

She chuckled softly. The low, melodious sound washed over him like warm honey. Then she smiled at him, and his blood pounded in his ears.

"There wasn't time," she quipped, lowering herself down onto her bedroll.

He shared a moment of laughter with her and, as much as he wanted to, decided not to press for any details about her fear at the moment. He wasn't in the mood for any kind of argument that might ensue from the discussion, or lack thereof on her part. He had spent his anger enough for one day, and right now, he was content just to enjoy her company for a while.

"You're not eating." She nodded toward the rabbit carcass suspended above the low flame.

"No offense," he responded politely. "But, it was a little too rare for my taste."

"None taken," Sunny assured with a soft chuckle that made Matt's pulse kick up speed and his heart slam against his ribs. "I'm not a very good cook, though my Comanche grandmother, Walks-in-Stream, spent many hours trying to correct that fault. So did my mother."

"You weren't an attentive student, I take it." Matt arched a brow curiously. He wanted to ignore the pain that sliced through him at the reminder that she once lived with Indians. The same race of savages that had killed his family and taken so many other innocent lives on their wagon train that morning so long ago. He wanted to, but he couldn't.

"I was interested in learning other things."

"Such as?" Matt prompted.

"Such as useful skills. Like hunting, tracking, and being able to defend myself."

"And how did your mother feel about that?"

"My mother cared about two things in her life. Her husband, Chief Black Eagle, and my happiness."

"How could you be happy living with those savages?" The question was out before Matt could stop it. He saw her tense, readying for battle. He hated the Indians, but right now he wished like hell his own anger hadn't gotten the best of him.

"The Comanches are my family," she defended strongly, her eyes narrowing. "I would be with them now if it were possible."

Behind the temper flashing in the blue depths of her eyes, he glimpsed her unspoken love for the Comanches. A vision of his folks and his two younger sisters being killed and viciously scalped flashed across his mind. Something inside him snapped. "Did they teach you to kill folks, as well. Women? Innocent children?" he ground out dangerously low.

"I've never taken a person's life. White or Indian. Can you say the same?" she challenged.

Matt stared hard, his insides churning like a raging river. He couldn't lie to her, but he didn't want her to know the truth, either. He had killed many men riding as a Ranger—white-

and red-skinned both. But that cowhand in Denver was the first and only time he had killed for revenge.

Abruptly Matt rose to his feet. He slapped his hat on top of his head and looked past Sunny as he spoke. "I'm gonna check the horses one last time. That meat should be done in a few minutes. I suggest you eat and turn in. We got a lot of ground to cover tomorrow."

Chapter Ten

Immediately following the two surprising blasts of gunfire, everything had grown ghostly quiet. After what seemed an eternity in which nothing stirred, Maggie pushed back the cotton material covering her head. The smell of blood and death permeated the air. Lifting one hand, she brushed her hair away from her face, then raised her head and saw the two outlaws lying dead on the ground. A sob of relief escaped her lips; then just as quickly, terror struck her heart. Who had killed them? She rose to her knees and frantically searched for her rescuer, wondering if she had been spared only to have someone else attack. She saw no one but Gentle Wind's unconscious form.

She rushed to the girl's side. An ugly purple bruise already darkened Gentle Wind's bronze cheek. A trickle of blood eased from her nose and trailed down around her partially opened mouth. To Maggie's deep mollification, Gentle Wind's breathing was strong, rhythmic. The girl would no doubt be sore, but at least showed no outward signs of suffering, or permanent harm.

She headed toward the wagon and, drawing near, saw Pete

slumped facedown on the wooden seat, a gun dangling loosely from his pale fingers. Climbing onto the wagon, she touched her palm to his back, grateful to feel the slow rise and fall of his weak but sure breaths. Blood pooled beneath him, and she knew he had jeopardized his own thin hold on life to save her.

Maggie struggled to get him back in the wagon and on the pallet, then tended to his freshly opened wound. Next, she roused Gentle Wind and helped the frightened girl back into the wagon before making a quick search of the surrounding area for Gordy. She found his body not far from where the wagon had been forced to stop, and wept at his untimely demise. Lifting her eyes heavenward, she asked God's forgiveness for not giving the young cowhand a proper burial. But time was of the essence. She feared Jake Walden wouldn't be far behind the two outlaws he had sent. Quickly, she left the deadly scene, praying for a safe, swift journey to Fort Sill.

As the afternoon gave way to night, she made a cold camp in the cover of the dense woods, a good ways off the trail. Before darkness fully settled, she changed the wounded men's dressings again. Afterward, she coaxed some water down their throats, wishing she could risk a fire to fix a warm broth, then fed Gentle Wind a light meal of beef strips and leftover biscuits. It had taken her almost an hour after that to calm the restless girl enough to get her to go to sleep.

Now Maggie stood alone in the darkness, staring at the thousands of winking stars lighting up the midnight sky. Crying softly, she gazed past the glowing half-moon to the darkened heavens and gave her heartfelt thanks again for being saved from the afternoon's terrifying ordeal. Her thoughts turned to the three helpless lives depending on her to keep them safe, and to Sunny, who was counting on her to reach Fort Sill with the urgent message for Colonel Grierson about McGuire.

Her worries jumped back to those two outlaws who had tried to rape her. Then unwillingly farther into her memory to another man who had had his way with her years ago. She had trusted that man, but he had hurt her physically anyway, then scarred her emotionally when he had proposed . . . to another woman. Maggie shook her painful thoughts aside. She must stay alert. Jake Walden could be anywhere, watching. Waiting.

She climbed onto the wagon's seat, the now ever-present gun held tightly in her grasp, and settled in for the all-night vigil she intended to keep. All too soon, though, the adrenaline that had seen her through the near rape and aftermath began to dissipate. Her eyes grew heavy. She tried to keep them open, but eventually her own weariness took hold, and she was powerless to fight the sleep that overcame her.

She awoke with a start to find Gentle Wind looking down at her with concerned brown eyes. "You wanted to get an early start," the girl reminded.

Maggie was surprised to see the somber gray morning already, and greatly relieved they were still safe. She nodded, then sat up straight and rubbed at the knotted muscles in her back. "We must try to reach the fort today."

Gentle Wind helped as Maggie changed the men's bandages and made ready to pull out. They rode in silence as the morning dawned and the sun rose high into the blue, cloudless sky. Try as she might, Maggie couldn't shake off the uneasy feeling that trouble lurked close at hand. For the first time since agreeing to help Sunny, she thought about her brother's stringent disapproval of her decision. Will had understood Sunny's need, her drive to reunite with her family, but he hadn't believed Maggie needed to become this involved in the plan, or that she should give up her job at the Oak Valley school to teach Indian children. But she was a grown woman, and her brother soon realized there was little he could do to stop her. Maggie wondered if she should have listened, if she would ever see her brother again.

Her uneasiness grew. She tightened her grip on Pete's gun and patted the folds of her skirt where she had hidden the Colt Sunny had given her.

The prairie grass swayed gently in the warm breeze. Few birds called out to one another in the growing heat. She watched a rabbit scurry across their path, then listened beyond the jingle of the harness, the grinding sounds of the wagon as it rolled along. Everything appeared normal.

The road ahead curved around a stand of cottonwoods. Deep, black shadows hovered beneath the dense, wide-spread foliage. Her sense of pending doom increased. She whipped the horses to a slightly faster gait and glanced over at Gentle Wind. The girl's round, worried eyes shifted nervously from side to side. Slender bronze fingers gripped the edge of the bench.

"It's all right, Gentle Wind," she falsely assured. "I just want to get past the trees as quickly as possible." That much was true.

As soon as the wagon rounded the bend, Maggie saw the stranger blocking the road ahead. He squatted, and appeared to be inspecting his horse's right front hoof.

Maggie tensed, and swallowed back her surging fear. "Get in the back, Gentle Wind."

The girl lifted her drab, brown skirt and scrambled over the seat. Maggie cocked the gun in her lap and slowly pulled back on the leather reins. The man stood and turned as she brought the wagon to a stop, still a good distance away.

Maggie lifted the heavy Colt, gripping the smoothly worn handle with both hands. "Get out of my way, mister."

"Whoa there, ma'am." He pushed back the wide brim of his dusty felt hat as his hands snaked into the air above his head.

Maggie stared at his crooked hawk nose and craggy face. "I said, get out of my way. Now."

"I ain't lookin' for no trouble, ma'am. My horse went lame is all."

Maggie didn't trust the sincere smile on his dust-coated lips. "I'm sorry about your horse, mister, but I'm in a hurry. So I'd be much obliged if you'd move out of the road."

" 'Fraid he can't do that."

Maggie jumped at the deep-throated voice that rose up from the side of the wagon, but didn't look down. Instead, she steadied her gun and kept her eyes focused on the stranger in the road. When he dropped his hands and reached for his gun, she pulled the trigger. Her shot went wild. Before she could squeeze off another round, the man at her side fired. The bullet ricocheted off her revolver, ripping the gun from her fingers. She faltered sideways from the impact and clutched her hands to her arms in a futile effort to ward off the pain searing through her limbs.

Straightening, Maggie glanced down into a wide, chiseled face that reminded her strongly of Shorty. The black, leather patch over his left eye confirmed her already growing suspicion. Jake Walden! Maggie met his single blue stare. Shock rippled through her at the familiar azure color; then fear blocked out all thought. Nervously, she ran her fingers along the folds of her skirt, settling on the handle of the gun hidden beneath. "You bastard," she hissed.

"Spare me your opinions, schoolteacher." His evil grin was more frightening than the gun he aimed at her. "Don't try anything stupid, either, or I'll kill the girl."

An icy chill seeped into her bloodstream. Maggie quickly twisted herself around and stared into the back of the wagon. Gentle Wind's fearful brown gaze met hers and tore at Maggie's heart. The boy who held Gentle Wind with one arm snugly wrapped around her narrow shoulders and covered her mouth with a trembling hand was at least six years away from being a man. And if the worried expression on his face was any indication, he was more than a little uncomfortable with the present situation. Maggie tightened her hold on the hidden gun and wondered about the consequences of trying to use it.

Could she risk it? Should she?

The renegade Comanche watched from the cover of the darkly shadowed woods and thought how foolishly brave the woman behaved. She did not stand a chance against the white outlaws, especially the one-eyed man. But his concern was more for the young Comanche girl he had seen disappear beneath the canvas covering. He had watched the boy slip into the wagon from behind, and knew by the dark-haired woman's anxious stare when she looked inside that the girl was in danger.

He wanted to strike now, but knew that would not be wise. There were other men who rode with the outlaw. Men he did not see, yet knew could be hidden as he was . . . waiting. With practiced patience, he watched and listened.

"Get down, lady," Jake Walden ordered.

"Wait!" the man in the road hollered out. A distinctive click echoed in the still air. The scar-faced man started toward the wagon. "What you got under that skirt?"

"We ain't got time for that, Hooker," Walden warned.

"We best take time, or are you forgettin' about findin' Cal and Rusty dead? She's fingerin' somethin' under there, and it ain't just her leg."

The woman screamed as Walden pulled her roughly from the wagon. She hit the ground on her side and rolled onto her back. The renegade raised a surprised brow when she lifted another gun she had managed to bring down with her. A split second later, Hooker swung his foot out and kicked it from her hand. She reached for the gun, but Walden stepped forward, effectively covering it with his boot.

The one-eyed outlaw jerked the woman to her feet and dragged her to a waiting horse. Burning hatred ate at the renegade as Hooker reached into the back of the wagon and hauled the Comanche girl out. Her weak struggles were no match against the outlaw's strength as he forced her onto his horse and climbed up behind. More movement caught the renegade's eye. He stared with intense interest as a fourth outlaw rode out of the woods, leading a horse with an Indian tied up and thrown belly first on the mount's back. The renegade couldn't see the brave's face; but in his heart he knew the Comanche's identity, and his anger and hatred grew.

When the group was well out of sight, he silently stepped from the trees into the sunlight. Knife held ready, his stance slightly crouched, he circled the wagon. Nothing but the skittish horses stirred as he passed around to the back. With learned caution, he peered inside.

The white man barely breathed. The renegade looked over to the other man, startled to see he was Comanche, and noted the brave's breaths came no easier than the white man's. Judging by their blood-soaked bandages, he doubted either one would live long. Even though he didn't know the wounded brave, he briefly considered trying to help one of his own. But there were others who needed him more: the Indian slung over that pony, and the young girl whose face he had only glimpsed, but whose features were forever drawn into his memory—Gentle Wind.

There was also his revenge. He would not let the one-eyed man get away, not this time.

The renegade gave the brave a final glance, offered a prayer to the Great Spirit for the Indian's journey to the after world, then turned away. As he mounted his pony, he wondered about the identity of the woman Walden had captured. He had heard from a band of Kiowas there was a white man, Hollister, looking for a dark-haired schoolteacher. Was it possible she was this woman? If so, he knew he could count on trouble to follow closely on his trail. He would need to be very careful.

A bell jingled overhead, announcing Matt's entry into the local mercantile.

"Afternoon, mister." A balding, portly man paused from his sweeping and crossed his arms over the top of the broomstick. "Can I help ya?"

"I'm looking for a woman." Matt barely glanced at the stoutly proprietor as he searched the vacant store.

The man chuckled. "You'll be wantin' Miss Rose's place, down the street a piece."

Matt smiled at the man's misunderstanding. "No, I'm looking for a specific woman. A blonde, about so high." He lifted his right hand even with his shoulder. "She was wearing pants and a blue shirt. Said she was coming to buy a dress."

The proprietor looked thoughtful for a moment, then shook his head. "Ain't seen no one fits that description. Haven't sold any ready-made dresses in more than a week, either."

Matt frowned. "Are there any other stores in town?"

"Yeah, you can try McCarty's Drug Store over on Front Street. He sells ready-made dresses."

"Much obliged." Matt tipped his hat as he opened the door, setting the bell to an annoying clang again. He stepped off the wooden walkway, crossed the wide, dirt road, then turned left at the corner.

He noted the bank of gray clouds building in the western sky. Pushing ahead of it was the telltale smell of moisture, a warning of what was to come. Matt wanted to be out of Dodge and a good ways down the trail before the rains hit. He rounded the corner onto Front Street and scanned the crowded walkway for Sunny as he made his way down the road.

Damn that woman! Where the hell was she?

They had gotten to town shortly before noon, purchased the needed replacement supplies, and arranged drayage back to the drive. After that, the strained silence that had surrounded them through their morning ride to Dodge returned. When Sunny told him she needed to buy a dress, he had kept his suspicious questions quiet. Truth be told, he had welcomed a brief respite from her company.

Matt knew full well Sunny had been expecting an apology, and he knew he owed her one. Hell, he had jumped all over her about walking away to avoid a question; then he had gone and done the same blasted thing. Damned if he could bring himself to say he was sorry, though. His past was none of her business. He had told Maggie the truth about killing Garrison, because she deserved to know. He had no plans to tell anyone else. But the apology weighed heavily on his heart and fueled his anger with himself for letting Sunny get close to sparking a fire to his dead and buried emotions. He had needed to clear his thoughts, get his focus back.

An hour later, after a bath, shave, and haircut, he was feeling much better, more relaxed and confident now that his emotions were once again under control. But that all changed when the time to meet Sunny came and passed, stretching into fifteen minutes, then half an hour. By the time he set out to find her, his muscles were tense, his mood ignitable. And he hated the fact he couldn't help being worried about her.

Matt opened the door to McCarty's Drug Store, thankful there was no bell to rattle his already jangled nerves. A minute later, he walked back out, no more enlightened than when he had gone in. He looked up and down the street, stepped off the walk into the dirt road, and strode purposely southward. He crossed over the railroad tracks and headed for Ham Bell's livery stable, situated a piece north of the Arkansas River.

He found the young stable hand raking out the stall where Sunny's mare had been. "Have you seen the woman I rode in with? Her horse was in that stall." Irritation made his tone sharp.

The boy, all of about ten, stopped raking and turned wide, frightened eyes to Matt. "Ye . . . yessir," he stammered. "She um . . . rode out 'bout an hour ago."

"An hour ago!" Matt's voice thundered down at the sandy-haired youngster.

"Ye . . . yes . . . sir." The boy's head bobbed up and down, his eyes shimmering beneath watery pools.

Remorse washed over Matt. What was he doing taking his anger out on this kid? It wasn't the boy's fault Sunny left, or that he was worried she had decided to do something foolish like go after Walden alone. "Sorry I yelled at you, kid. You say she left a while ago?"

The boy nodded, then swiped at his eyes with his hands. "She wasn't wearin' pants no more, though, sir." The youngster swallowed, sending his Adam's apple sliding along his throat. "She had on a blue dress."

Well, at least she didn't lie about getting one. Small consolation, though. She was still gone. "Any idea where she got that dress?"

The boy nodded. "She asked me where she could get one, and I . . . um . . . well, she's small like my ma, and . . . we need the money real bad, mister . . . so . . . um . . . well, she bought one of my ma's dresses."

Matt wasn't the least bit surprised at Sunny's kindness, but it didn't make him any less angry that she had left. He reached into his pocket and pulled out a silver half-dollar.

"Thanks for the information." He tossed the shiny coin, and smiled when the boy caught it easily in his thin, dirty fingers. "There's another one for you after you fetch me my horse. The black gelding." The boy flinched and stepped back. Matt frowned. What now?

"I . . . um . . . can't, sir."

"Why not?" Matt held his mounting anger in check so as not to further frighten the boy.

The kid visibly shook anyway, then swallowed hard and slammed his fist over the coin. "The lady, she . . . um . . . took your horse with her . . . sir."

Will Hollister reined his horse up a short distance from the deserted wagon. He had found Grierson the day before on a reconnaissance south of the fort, and the colonel had sent along one of his soldiers to help with the search. The private pulled up alongside him.

"Have a look in the back, Anderson. I'll keep watch, case we're not alone here."

The private nodded, and reeled his mount around. Will nudged his gray toward the front of the wagon, all the while scanning the surrounding area with careful eyes. He rounded the pair of still-harnessed bays and glanced down. Pulling back on the reins, he stared hard at the disturbed dirt.

It looked to him like someone had rolled around in that spot.

He studied the ground some more, then followed the small footprints leading away from the wagon. He noted a larger pair imbedded in the dirt next to them.

"Mr. Hollister, you best come see this."

Will's gaze shifted toward the private's urgent voice. Gently, he prodded his horse and rode to the back, then dismounted. Sauntering over, he looked through the wide, oval opening. His stare slid over the motionless Indian and settled on the other wounded man.

"Pete?" he whispered incredulously. Will climbed into the wagon and made his way over to the cowhand. He pulled his leather glove from one hand and pressed his fingers against Pete's neck. A sigh of relief escaped him when he found the ranch hand's weakened pulse. Will turned his attention to the private. "He's alive." When he looked back. Pete's eyes slowly opened.

"Hi . . . boss." the cowhand's words were barely audible.

Will leaned closer. "What happened, Pete?"

"Out . . . laws. Ridin' . . . with Walden. Got . . . Mag—" Pete started to cough; his hand lifted weakly to his gut.

Will glanced down and saw fresh blood seeping between the wounded man's fingers. He slipped his stare back to Pete's. "Don't try to talk any more. Just rest. I'll see to it you get help as quick as possible."

Pete slowly lowered his head in a nod, then closed his eyes. Will paused beside the Indian, felt for a heartbeat and found one, then climbed down from the wagon.

"Anderson, I want you to take these men back to Fort Sill."

"But Colonel Grierson ordered me to stay with you, sir."

"They need a doctor, fast." Will tugged his glove back on his hand and swung himself into his saddle. He stared down at the private. "Find Grierson, and tell him I'm going after Jake Walden. Also, make sure he knows about that wounded Indian. It's possible he's one of the braves Sunny's been looking for."

The private's face expressed a dazed confusion, his dark

brows furrowed together as one. "Sunny? Braves? I don't understand."

"Don't worry, Grierson will." Will lifted the leather reins, preparing to leave. The private stopped him.

"What should I tell the colonel about your destination? Or when you'll be returning, sir?"

Will sat silent for a moment, then turned and looked down at the blue-clad soldier. "I don't have an answer for you, Anderson, or the colonel. Just make sure you do everything you can to keep these men alive." Will nodded toward the wagon. "Between the two of them, Grierson should be able to find out exactly what he needs to know."

Will laid the reins against the gray's neck and sent the gelding northwest, the same direction he had spotted the trail of hoofprints headed after he had followed the smaller set of prints—footprints he now knew belonged to Maggie.

Judging by the sun, he figured he could ride another two hours before darkness settled full. He would rest then, and later head out by moonlight—just like he had been doing since he had left the Circle H and his beautiful Rebecca. With a sigh, he sent up a silent prayer for the continued good health of his wife and child, and a desperate plea for the good Lord to keep his sister safe.

Chapter Eleven

The stream lay nestled among a dense stand of pecan trees interspersed with ash and elm. Haws and persimmon bushes sprouted in the undergrowth. Wild berries grew along the sandy banks, shaded by large jutting rocks which lined one side and stretched across to form a natural dam. Sunny watered the horses and hobbled them to graze. She built a protective lean-to, made a small fire close by, then placed a rabbit to roast over the low flame.

As the final hour of daylight filtered through the gunmetal gray clouds and heavy foliage, Sunny sat beside the water and finished a handful of sweet, juicy berries. She stared at the long shadows dancing in the moisture-laden breeze, but the imminent rain was the farthest thing from her mind. Since last evening, she had done little else but think about Matt.

He had the gall to tell her she was acting like a child, but he had done the same thing. Had he walked off because she had come too close to the truth? Had Matt killed someone? Was that the secret he shared with Maggie? Sunny frowned.

Whatever past Matt and Maggie shared was of no matter. She needed to stop thinking so much about Matt Lanier.

Sunny knew she must look to the future, and there was no room there for her disturbing interest in the rancher. But that didn't stop her heart from becoming an instant traitor to rational thought every time she looked into his midnight blue stare. With every warm gaze, every smile, every soft endearment whispered into her ear, Matt chipped away at her deeply buried emotions. And he ignited new sensations with his touch, his kisses, that left her confused and afraid, and yearning for more. She walked a thin line where love was concerned, and Matt was tugging on her heartstrings with great force. She didn't want to feel anything for the man, but it was too late. She could no longer deny Matt meant something to her, but she refused to delve into those feelings. He was a white man, and had no liking for the Indians. To admit she loved him would be like turning her back on her family—on the Comanches. She could never do that. Besides, she would be a fool to further complicate her life with a man who infuriated her almost every time he spoke. She had made her decision—the right decision—the minute she rode out of Dodge alone. So why wouldn't her heart listen?

Sunny knew Matt would try to find her, if for no other reason than to retrieve his horse. She suspected he wasn't a man who let go of things easily. But she had needed some time to make her escape and decided she could use the mount for Swift Arrow when they fled Outlaw Canyon. And provided Maggie got that message to Colonel Grierson about McGuire, by the time Matt reached the hideout, the outlaws would be on their way to jail. She would return the horse then, and Matt could rejoin the herd and ride to his ranch in Wyoming alive and safe.

It was done. Settled. It was for the best.

So why did her heart ache at the thought of never seeing him again?

Sunny sighed and shook her head in frustration. She desperately needed to clear her mind of Matt and prepare for the battle ahead with Walden. Standing, she unfastened the buttons of the dress and shrugged out of the garment. Next, she removed her boots, pants, and shortened cotton chemise. Sunny closed her eyes and faced the last of the sun's offering, her thoughts slipping back to the days of her warrior training. She touched the small medicine bag hanging around her neck and called upon her guardian spirit for courage and strength. Then she stepped into the cool stream.

Matt reined his newly acquired dun to a stop beside a narrow opening in the woods and scrubs running parallel with the main road. The stable boy had said Sunny headed south across the Arkansas River when she left, but Matt knew better than to think she would stick to the well-traveled path. He had searched all afternoon for her tracks, but so far had found no sign of her, or the noticeable chip in Thunder's left back hoof.

Narrowing his gaze, he stared down at the roughly scattered branches and leaves covering the small entrance into the dark, shadowing trees. They appeared undisturbed. His gut told him otherwise. He recalled Sunny's words about choosing hunting and tracking over cooking lessons, and knew she had probably learned how to cover her trail well. But he had tracked down a fair number of Comanches in Texas. As long as he paid attention, and quit being distracted by his worry over the blasted spitfire, he knew he would find her.

Matt swung out of his saddle and knelt down for a closer inspection of nature's haphazard display. With a gloved hand, he brushed the leaves aside, revealing nothing but dirt. He pushed back a few more and saw the faint edge of something suspicious. Clearing a larger spot, Matt uncovered a fresh pile of horse droppings, broken and pressed into the dirt. The signs of ingested oats was enough suggestion that the horse had been recently stabled for him to investigate further.

He stood, grabbed the dun's reins, and led the horse down

the barely visible path. A good distance into the woods, he found Thunder's first print. Matt smiled at his success and admired Sunny's ingenuity. She was definitely a survivor, like him. One more reason he couldn't seem to get her out of his mind for longer than a few seconds.

Up ahead he heard the flow of a steady stream. Tying the dun's reins to a tree limb, he proceeded alone to the creek's edge. Sandy banks cushioned his footsteps, and varying sizes of rocks helped hide his approach. He paused at the sound of gentle splashing which came from above and just beyond the small waterfall formed over the rock dam. Matt tossed his hat onto the ground, then climbed up the sloping side of an oversized chunk of granite. Pressing flat against the warm, hard surface, he peered cautiously over the top.

The sun's diminishing rays reflected soft and hazy, surrounding the widely formed pool in its pale glow. Spellbound, Matt stared at slender, glistening arms dipping repeatedly into the smooth surface as Sunny swam gracefully along the top. Her loose blond hair, darkened several shades from wetness, fanned over her back like a protective blanket. Her long legs kissed the top of the water as she kicked with frequent rhythm.

Matt's breath lodged in his throat. God help him, he knew he should look away. For a second he even pictured his mother's disapproving stare, but for the life of him, he couldn't tear his gaze from this beautiful, golden splendor. Hot flames of desire swept through him, surprising in their consuming strength.

He watched every heart-stopping move as she swam the length of the shadowy water area. She stopped close to the side, turned, and started across again. Halfway she slowed, rolled over, and rested back to float. His manhood strained against the tight confines of his pants. Matt stared, mesmerized by the burnished-tipped globes peeking teasingly through the glassy surface. His heart raced like a steam engine. His mouth went dry as he devoured her body with his gaze, drinking in every inch of her beauty.

A nagging sense of chivalry knocked once again at his conscience. Matt cursed silently, then slammed another barrier across that door. Sunny, this lovely, golden angel, was more beautiful than anything he had ever seen, and right now all he could think about was how much he wanted her.

A slow movement parted the water in slithering waves and snagged his attention. Matt narrowed his gaze, looking beyond where Sunny innocently swam, and felt his heart slam to a stop. With urgent speed, he reached for the gun strapped around his hips, knowing he was about to get caught in his impromptu spying, and not giving a damn. Sunny was in trouble.

Matt took careful aim at the large, dark head of the water moccasin, then eased his finger back against the trigger until the gun exploded with a loud crack. He swore viciously when the bullet hit slightly left of its intended target.

Sunny came upright, saw the snake, and thrashed wildly about trying to escape. Her panicked efforts blocked Matt from getting a clear second shot. Her back faced him, but he could mentally picture the fear on her face. Any second, he expected to hear her ear-piercing scream. She made no sound, but suddenly disappeared beneath the churning surface. Matt wasted no time and fired off another round, relieved when the snake's head fragmented into tiny pieces.

Holstering his gun, he searched the empty pool, concern mounting as seconds ticked by and Sunny didn't resurface. Matt climbed to the top of the rock, stood, and called out her name. Sunny's head broke through the glimmering top, and her hands instantly clawed at the water. She opened her mouth, issued a pitiful, choked scream, then quickly sank below again. He saw her suck in water as she went under. Ripping his gunbelt from his waist, he dove fully clothed into the stream after her.

He groped the underwater darkness until his lungs burned, but surfaced empty-handed, cursing his failure. Matt gulped in air, heard the slap of hands beating at the water, and twisted around. Sunny fought to stay above, her eyes wide with uncontrollable fear. He swam toward her, his fingers brushing against her hair as she slipped into the blackness below. Grabbing a handful of the heavy strands, he pulled her struggling body up into his arms. She coughed harshly, spewed water from her throat. She fought his hold, wrapped her arms around his head, and pushed him under despite his efforts. Matt kicked his feet hard, driving them upward. He spit out the water he had taken in before it could choke him.

"Sunny." He coughed, panted. "Stop!" He fought the building pain in his leg muscles as much as her frenzied attempts to drown him. Matt pried her arms from his head and captured both slender wrists in one hand, pinning them behind her back. He leaned close to her ear. "The snake's dead," he said firmly, hoping to break through her consuming fear. "You're safe."

"No!" She wrenched her body. Matt pumped his legs faster to keep them afloat.

"I swear it, angel. You're safe. It's dead."

Her eyes darted frantically. She thrashed, and screamed again. "No, they're not! I feel them . . . around my legs!"

Matt released her wrists and put his arms tightly around her waist, pulling her close. Her heart pounded against his chest. His own heart ached to comfort her, release her from this nightmare she relived. But first he had to calm her down before she drowned them both. His calf and thigh muscles burned, and he didn't know how much longer he could tread the water.

"Ssh . . . Sunny . . . honey . . . it's all right," he whispered through his labored breathing. "There's nothing . . . there. You're safe. I'm not going to let anything hurt you . . . I promise."

She stilled in his embrace. He pressed her trembling body closer.

"Matt?" Her voice was weak, strained.

"Yeah, it's me, angel." His mouth brushed against her earlobe; his hand smoothed the hair back from her face. She sighed, and relaxed in his hold. Keeping one arm snugly around her waist, he swam toward the bank.

When Matt could touch the sandy bottom, he stood and walked until he was satisfied the water level was sufficient for

Sunny's smaller height. Then he gently set her away from him, lifting his eyes from the shadowed liquid that properly covered her. Reluctantly, he dropped his arms to his sides.

"Are you all right now, angel?"

She nodded, then looked up at him.

Matt saw the diminishing fear in her eye's sky blue depths, her gratitude for his understanding and assistance . . . and something else he couldn't readily identify. Admiration? Desire? No, Sunny didn't want him—in her plan or her life. She had made that clear from the start, reinforced it when she left Dodge without him. But like a lovesick kid, his heart rushed foolishly ahead anyway. God knew he didn't want to care for her. It was too late, though. The love he had fought from the moment he looked into her eyes was too strong to ignore. It came knocking with full strength as he had plundered the underwater depths, fearing he wouldn't find her in time. The thought of losing her nearly tore his heart in two—even now. Unconsciously, he lifted a hand to her cheek and tenderly stroked the smooth satin of her skin.

She stepped closer and reached up to cover his hand with her own, stilling his exploration of her face. "Thank you," she whispered, meeting his stare with her darkened gaze.

Matt followed the journey of her long, wet lashes as they closed over her eyes, let his gaze wander over the faint spattering of freckles that bridged her nose and blended with the honey smoothness of her face. He watched in disbelief as her mouth drew nearer, then lowered his head and tenderly captured her invitation. He kissed her slowly, then traced his tongue over the soft fullness of her warm, moist lips. She moaned, and parted her mouth at his gentle nudging. Matt explored the warm recesses of her mouth and was rewarded with a flow of ecstasy he had never known before when her tongue matched his every stroke. He started to reach for her, to pull her into his embrace, but memories of her naked body gliding smoothly across the water returned to trouble him. Clearly, he recalled his envy of the blue liquid molding her flesh, sliding gracefully between her golden thighs, and remembered how badly he wanted her. His desire, his need, was only stronger now. But he could not act on those feelings. He would not take advantage of her vulnerability, and he wanted, needed, far more than her gratitude.

With great restraint, Matt broke the kiss and pulled back. "Wait here," he whispered.

Sunny watched Matt leave the pool and stop long enough to remove his boots before hurrying over to her lean-to. He wasted only a second removing his soggy, black leather vest, then snatched up the blanket neatly folded at the end of her bedroll. She sighed, trying to recall a single time she had ever felt this safe with any man. She couldn't. He had come to her rescue, and hadn't laughed at her vulnerability, but guided her tenderly, protectively through the fear. The emotions she had tried so hard to push aside earlier with her swim came flooding back. He was a man unlike any she had ever known, and his promise not to let anything happen to her still echoed in her head. She believed him, trusted him to keep his word. Why, she didn't know. It just felt . . . right, in her heart.

Kissing him felt right as well, and she had no strength to stop his seeking mouth. Even now, she still wished to go on losing herself in the secure, warm sensations Matt evoked. She wanted to feel his kiss again, feel the heat he built inside her with even the smallest of his touches. Her body felt empty, cold, without him.

Matt stepped into the water up to his ankles and stopped. With a single sharp snap, the blanket opened full. He bunched one end in his hands, keeping the wool clear of the water. "You need to come out before you catch a chill." He turned his head and closed his eyes. "Don't worry, I promise not to look."

She smiled, touched by his thoughtfulness, and strangely irritated as well. Didn't the man have the least bit of curiosity about seeing her unclothed? Even White Bear, her stoic brave, had often whispered in her ear how eager he was to become man and wife and take his time learning her body. But Matt didn't look as though he were having any trouble at all closing off his sight, she fumed as she stepped from the stream. Turning around, she jerked the covering from his hands and drew it down over her shoulders. She barely had the folds closed when Matt swept her into his arms and carried her toward the camp.

"What are you doing?" She instantly regretted her shrewish tone that clearly did more than just hint at her bruised feelings.

Matt arched one quizzical brow and looked down at her. "After saving your pretty hide, I thought I was being a gentleman and seeing to your comfort." He knelt, placed her gently on the pallet, then gazed at her with such intensity, it took her breath away. "Is there something else you'd rather I be doing?" One corner of his mouth lifted in a slight grin.

"I . . ." She shivered. Matt tightened the blanket around her. His concern melted her defenses. His tender, darkened gaze made her light-headed and turned her limbs to liquid fire.

"Are you getting warm, angel?"

Her heart hammered in her ears, a delightful vibration racing through her. Sunny nodded, not trusting herself to speak.

He turned from her, dragged his fingers through his hair, and breathed deeply. He stood, and she instantly wanted to draw him back to go on drinking in the comfort of his nearness, to feel this heat only he could arouse in her.

"Sunny, I'm sorry." He pulled his hands behind his back and stared down at her with tortured eyes. "I didn't mean to take advantage and attack you like some lecherous bear back there."

He looked no older than her brother, standing there with his head hunched between his tensed shoulders, waiting with hesitant expectancy. Sunny couldn't stop her smile. "Maybe it's me who should apologize. I more or less invited that bear."

Matt straightened, relaxed, then stared at her gleaming interest. "In that case, I'd say neither of us have anything to be sorry about. And just so you know, ma'am, I'd take you up on that same invite anytime."

Hot, tingling excitement shot through her. A boldness she didn't even know she possessed claimed her thoughts, her words. "Even if it came right now?"

Matt knelt before her, cupping her chin in his hand. "As long as you understand it won't stop this time with one kiss. Do you?"

Oh, she knew full well. The question was, could she give her love, her body, knowing she had no future with this man? He would offer her nothing because of her Comanche ties, which was fine since she had nothing to give him in return, for the same reason. But she wanted Matt, wanted to give in to her attraction . . . her desire. She wanted to experience the full outcome of these sensations he created, to learn the joys only he could teach her. Did she dare? More than anything, she wanted him safe from Walden. In that aspect, nothing had changed. But could she give herself to Matt as she so longed to do and still walk away from him when morning came?

"Never mind." Matt touched his forehead to hers. "Your silence is answer enough. For now." He dropped a light kiss on the tip of her nose, then stood and strolled off toward the rock damn.

Sunny stared after him. She wanted to call him back, ached to feel his arms around her again, his lips moving over hers.

The emptiness returned, as did the cold that sliced through her body. She was a coward. For all her bold words, her belief in her strength, her courage, her ability, she was nothing but a blasted coward where Matt was concerned. She could have what she wanted, what she desired; all she had to do was open her mouth. Sunny sighed. Deep inside, she knew she had made the right choice . . . for both of them. But that didn't stop her heart from racing and her body from craving his touch.

Matt climbed to the top of a rock. Sunny stared, puzzled at his action. He bent and retrieved his gunbelt, then scooted down and disappeared. Until this moment, she had given no thought to Matt's most fortunate arrival. As she continued to stare at the empty rock, she started to wonder just when he had gotten here . . . and how long he had been watching her.

Surprisingly, the thought of his spying on her swim was more exhilarating than irritating. Perhaps he enjoyed her body more than his abrupt halt to their kiss in the water suggested. And besides, why should she be mad? Wasn't she just as guilty of indulging in a little peek herself when Matt had gone swimming with the cowhands? Still, she planned to confront him about his actions, if only to tease him for a while. She would be wise to do so clothed, however. Fate had tempted her enough for one day.

She swore softly when she found only her clean, white cotton shirt and fresh underthings in the saddlebag, and remembered leaving the rest of her clothing on the water's bank where she had dropped them. Sunny quickly donned her undergarments and shirt, then headed for the stream. She stepped into her pants and bent to retrieve the rest of her things.

"I swear, angel. I've never seen a woman look as good as you in a pair of pants, nor one that can char a rabbit any blacker."

Sunny gasped, and spun around. She had not heard his approach, but there he was squatting beside the fire, grinning as he held the skewered, burnt carcass in his upraised hand. He wore dry denims and a blue shirt. His feet were bare. An average-size dun, still saddled, was tied to a tree in the near distance.

"Yeah, well, I bet it's done on the inside this time."

Matt chuckled. "We can hope."

Sunny stepped away from the stream. "Tell me something, Matt."

"What?"

"How'd you find me?" She dropped her clothes onto the bedroll and sat down facing him.

"It wasn't easy. You're quite good, but I learned a thing or two about tracking as a Ranger." Matt took his knife, peeled back the burnt hide, cut a chunk of the meat, then handed it to her. "I almost rode right by your clever coverage of that trail off the main road. After that, I finally picked up Thunder's print."

Sunny nodded. "That chip in his hoof was becoming a pain to hide." She bit into the meat, surprised that it was only slightly overcooked. She chewed slowly and watched Matt do the same with the piece he popped into his mouth. She swallowed, and with a demure stare looked up at him. "And how long did you watch me swim before that snake showed up?"

Matt's jaw stopped moving. He swallowed. Sunny quickly hid her smile at the telling flush that crept into his cheeks. He stood and walked closer, then sat down next to her on the pallet.

"Long enough," he admitted, taking her hand into his stronger one, gazing at her with such tenderness her breath lodged in her throat. "I don't aim to say I'm sorry either. I'd only be lying. You're the most beautiful woman I've ever met, Sunny, and I enjoyed every second I watched you."

A tremor shot through her body, and her palms grew moist. Sunny inhaled a deep breath, then released it slowly. "You mean that?" she whispered.

"Every word."

Sunny was awed and pleasantly pleased at the sincerity in his low tone. With his free hand, he cupped her face. His smoldering eyes held her captive more than his fingers.

"Now, will you answer something for me, angel?"

Sunny hesitated. Fiery heat coursed through her limbs, pooled in her womanly core, and blocked out all thought save this man. She ran her tongue along her mouth, lightly chewed on her bottom lip, and nodded.

He leaned closer. "Why'd you steal my horse?"

Chapter Twelve

Blood coursed through Matt's veins like an invigorated river. His heart turned over in response to Sunny's innocent, sensual motion of wetting her lips.

She pulled back, blinked. "What?"

The surprised flush rising in her cheeks wasn't helping, either. He wanted to kiss her. Matt could tell she wanted it, too. But he had promised himself not to take advantage, and no matter how hot these waves of desire sweeping through his belly grew, he wouldn't alter that decision. Before this past week, he would have taken a grateful woman up on whatever she offered—if he so chose—then easily walked away. With Sunny, he didn't want to think about leaving.

"Why'd you steal Thunder."

Defiance sprang quickly into her eyes. Miss Spitfire was back.

"I didn't. I only borrowed your horse. I would've returned him."

"I believe that. I want to know why you took him." When she turned from him and started to rise, Matt caught her arm.

Matt's doubts could have filled an entire valley and, he knew, would only start a fight with his determined spitfire, so he kept them to himself. Just as he kept silent at her comment concerning Walden's fate. But there was one thing he couldn't keep quiet about.

"Did you love White Bear?"

Sunny gaped at him in stunned silence. Matt felt the heat rise to his cheeks and looked down. *I shouldn't have asked, again.* Wasn't *he* the one who hadn't wanted to talk about past loves before? He shook his head. "I'm sorry. That's none of my business."

"It's all right." Her voice was low, with no hint of anger.

Matt looked up at her, then wished he hadn't. The sorrow etched deep in her eyes made his heart stop as a painful lump formed in his throat.

"I loved White Bear once, in another lifetime. But he's gone, and as the days go by, I grow more content with the white man's ways. Now my future is with Running Bear and Gentle Wind." She paused, hesitated as though there was something more she wanted to say, but only sat quietly.

Matt wanted to ask her what that future was exactly, but stopped himself. Whatever it was, it didn't include him. Only her siblings.

"Do you still want to help?"

Matt smiled at the way she tilted her chin, so proud, so brave. She really believed her plan to capture Walden would work. Matt's tightened gut was screaming they would be lucky to get out of Outlaw Canyon alive. "More than ever, angel."

"Thank you." Welcome relief showed in her eyes, in her sigh, in the hand she started to reach out to him. Quickly, she pulled back. "We should eat and get some rest. I want to get an early start in the morning."

Matt smiled, relieved to see the fear gone from her eyes, replaced by the trust she had bestowed on him, and pleased to see the fire back in her gaze telling him his little spitfire had returned with full strength. God, how she could make his blood simmer with desire.

"You intend on giving orders the whole way?"

She cocked her head and smiled back. "You intend to follow them?"

"Hard to say." He crossed the distance between them with his hands and took hold of both of hers. "You order me to keep you safe, there's no problem, angel. You tell me to stay away from you"—he looked deep into her eyes—"my ears just might go deaf."

Matt couldn't stop himself from leaning forward and pressing his lips to hers. He traced the fullness of her soft flesh, parted his mouth to capture her sigh, savored the feel of her warm breath mingling as one with his. She tasted faintly of berries, and hungrily he devoured her mouth, drinking in her sweetness. She kissed him with a reckless abandon he didn't expect, then slid closer and settled onto his lap. Every gentlemanly intention he had hightailed it right out the back door of his mind. All he could think about as he closely embraced her slender, trembling body was how good, how right, she felt in his arms.

Maggie's eyes opened wide as she felt herself begin to fall. Jerking upright on the horse, she reached for the saddle horn. The leather tie binding her wrists together cut into her flesh, and blood oozed warm and sticky onto her palm. She didn't remember falling asleep, but the pain searing her tightened neck muscles confirmed she had dozed off, at least for a bit. She glanced up at the heavy clouds which hid the moon and coated the prairie in blackness.

Was Walden planning to ride all night?

She was in dire need of a break from this saddle, more specifically a concealing bush where she could tend to the personal matter of nature's call. The sun still rode high on the horizon the last time the outlaws had stopped to rest and water the horses, but she hadn't been given an opportunity to be alone then, especially with Gentle Wind.

What would Jake Walden say if she just turned around and demanded that he stop? she wondered. Shoot her? Beat her? Rape her? Then what? No, it wasn't worth the risk, not with Gentle Wind to consider.

Maggie sighed, and turned her sight to Hooker's gray, shadowy figure riding ahead. Gentle Wind rode in front of him, hidden by his larger form. She prayed the girl was holding up, maybe even finding some way to rest. She looked to the Indian thrown over the back of the horse beside her. The brave hadn't made even the slightest whimper through the entire ride, but twice she had caught him looking up at her. She couldn't see his face in the darkness and wondered if he was awake now or asleep.

"Hold up there, Hooker," Walden called out from behind. "We'll rest here for a couple hours."

The horses came to a stop amid a stand of pines. Hooker dismounted, then reached up and pulled Gentle Wind down and pushed the girl into a stumbling walk. Maggie twisted around in the saddle, her stare following Gentle Wind as the outlaw shoved her past and over to where Walden, Stu, and the boy waited in the smoky shadows. The girl never looked up. Maggie's heart ached to give comfort to Gentle Wind and hated that there was nothing she could do.

Strong hands suddenly gripped her waist, yanked her roughly from the mount, and released her to fall to the ground. Maggie bit her tongue to keep from crying out as a rock jabbed painfully into her backside. She looked up at Hooker, started to spit out a retort, then thought better of it. Trouble flowed in plenty at the moment, without her stirring up any more.

"Best be gettin' up, schoolteacher. Ya ain't got but a few minutes to see to your business," Walden snarled.

Maggie stood. "What about the girl?"

"She stays here, to make sure ya don't forget to come back." Walden circled Gentle Wind's arm with his hand. Maggie stepped forward and instantly saw the young girl wince as the outlaw tightened his hold.

Quickly, Maggie turned and ran into the darkness. Moments later, she walked back toward the small fire Hooker worked at keeping lit, all traces of her recent tears brushed away. She looked around for Gentle Wind, but saw the girl nowhere. A sudden dread washed over her, and she stared at Hooker. He looked up. She shuddered, her body instinctively shying away from the eerie shadows the firelight cast on his craggy face and the smirk on his evil, grinning lips.

"Worried, schoolteacher?" His smile deepened, and the look he shared with Stu made her want to tremble anew.

Maggie forced herself not to move or show her fear. "No. I came back. He has no reason to hurt her."

Hooker shared another devilish grin with Stu. "Don't be too sure." He stared back up at her. "But for now, the girl just couldn't hold it any longer."

Hooker stood and approached. Grabbing her by the arm, he led her toward a tall pine where the Indian sat tied to its trunk. His head hung low on his chest; his eyes were closed. Maggie wondered if Swift Arrow was truly asleep. Hooker forced her to sit opposite the brave and secured her to the tree with a length of rope he looped around the bark and the unmoving Indian. Then he left, sauntering back to the campfire.

Less than a minute later, Walden stepped into the fire's glow, dragging an exhausted Gentle Wind in his grasp. The boy followed, and steadied Gentle Wind with a hand to her shoulder when Walden let go and she staggered. Maggie was surprised at the warm look she turned to the boy, and relieved that Gentle Wind appeared unharmed. Walden tied the girl's hands behind her back; then Hooker spread out a blanket and motioned for her to lie down. The poor girl looked to be asleep the moment she fell to the ground. Walden bound Gentle Wind's feet together and tied the loose end of the rope around his wrist.

Maggie released a heavy sigh and leaned her head back against the hard bark.

"Why are you with Gentle Wind?"

Maggie lifted her head at the roughly whispered words and tried unsuccessfully to see around the pine. "Swift Arrow?"

"You know my name? How is that? Who are you?"

Maggie looked back at Walden and Hooker. They spread out their bedrolls and laid in. She turned her head to the other side and spoke in low tones. "I am a friend of Morning Sky's."

"Morning Sky is dead," his deep voice ground out harshly.

"No, she's very much alive. Her name is Sunny."

"Sunny? The same woman who seeks me and Gray Wolf for the exchange of a boy and girl?"

"You know of that?"

"Walden knows."

"Dear God."

"Yes, lady, you would do well to pray to your God."

"Wh—"

"Hush. Rest. We'll talk later."

"Bu—" A sudden stir pulled Maggie's attention. Walden sat up on his bedroll, looked straight at her, and cocked his gun.

The renegade froze. He looked to the woman and the brave. They appeared to be sleeping now, but he had seen them conversing only moments ago. He was sure it concerned Gentle Wind. Had the outlaw heard?

The renegade stared at the sleeping girl, surrounded by the three outlaws and the boy. She was so small, so fragile . . . like her sister had once been. He pulled the curved knife from between his teeth and sheathed it in the beaded case hanging at his side. He had been ready to sneak in and kill the outlaws quickly. But Walden was up, alert now. He would have to wait . . . just a little while longer.

* * *

An odd hissing sound pervaded Sunny's light sleep. Instantly alert, she opened her eyes and sat up. Light rain splattered the roof of the brush shelter. The fire cracked and popped, sizzled as raindrops fell through the flames and hit the red-hot embers. She looked at Matt stretched out on his bedroll beside the campfire. He stirred, pulling his hat down over his face and the blanket higher on his shoulders.

"Matt?"

"What?" There was no denying the edge in his voice.

"Come sleep in here, out of the rain."

He sat up, assessed her with narrowed eyes, but said nothing. Sunny wondered if he would reject her offer of a dry spot. Was he concerned she wouldn't behave? Granted, when he had kissed her earlier, held her in his arms, she had been ready to abandon herself completely to the feelings he awoke. Then he had suddenly pushed her from his embrace and bluntly agreed with her earlier suggestion—they did need to get some sleep. Matt had added to her confusion by tracing her lips softly with his finger and running a troubled gaze over her face before leaving to make his bed by the fire. His tender action had helped ease the hurt of his unexplained withdrawal, but only a little.

Without a word, Matt threw off his blanket, gathered up his bedroll, and crossed the short distance which separated them. He spread the bedding as best he could in the narrow space beside her and sat down. "Night." He lay back, placed his hands behind his head, and closed his eyes.

"Well, you're welcome!" The waspish retort sailed from her lips before she could stop it. Great Spirit, what was wrong with her?

Matt opened one eye. "You want me in here, or not?"

She looked away and stared through the open-ended shelter at the campfire. The flames struggled to stay lit in the slow drizzle. "Yes, it's fine," she finally answered on a long sigh.

"Something bothering you, Sunny?"

"No," she lied. Stifling a groan, she lowered herself down onto the blanket and turned her back toward Matt. His presence was overpowering in the small confines that left them separated by only a few feet. She could hear his every breath, feel his warmth radiating across the short distance. Her heart pounded faster.

Why did she have no strength to stop this traitorous weakness he inspired? Why could this man make her defenses soft with just a word, her insides hot with a single look? If he weren't so handsome, so gentle and understanding, maybe her heart wouldn't beat so fast in his presence. If she didn't trust him, didn't believe he honestly wanted to help and protect her, maybe she could forget this path her emotions had unwillingly chosen to travel the moment Matt came into her life. But his tenderness and his powerful male appeal were proving more than she could resist. He touched her deep inside like no one ever before. He had reached into a part of her she hadn't even known existed and set in motion all this confusion, this heated wanting.

Did Matt feel this same heat? Did he want her as well? Sunny knew he felt something for her, heard it in his whiskey-smooth tone whenever he called her angel, saw it in his darkly passionate gaze when he looked at her and thought she didn't notice. But Matt agreed only to help, nothing more. He had offered no future beyond Outlaw Canyon. She would be a fool to even contemplate such a fanciful thought. The distance between their worlds was too wide for them to cross, and Matt hadn't indicated any interest in bridging the gap. So why wouldn't her heart listen? Why couldn't she stop wishing that he would take her in his arms again, kiss her until she lost all reason but the need to know his passion, and have him awaken her own.

What was wrong with her? White Bear had kissed her when she would slip out from the tipi to meet him in the cover of night, but never like Matt. Her brave had even touched her breasts once, but his hands never heated her body with such consuming intensity. Nor had his kisses, his very nearness, sent her heart racing like the wild ponies, while at the same time making her yearn to be possessed, branded, tamed by desire.

Sunny groaned.

"You're fidgeting like a kid at Sunday morning sermon. What's wrong?" There was mild irritation in his voice, and a strong note of concern.

Why did the man have to sound like he cared? He sure wasn't making it any easier for her.

"I can't get comfortable." She squirmed, shifted more onto her side, brought her legs up, then straightened them back out.

"Try being still."

Maybe she could if he would go away. Her right arm, trapped beneath her side, tingled with pending numbness. Sunny raised up to free the limb. "Ouch! Damn!"

"Now what?"

"My hair's caught."

"On what? You need some help?"

"No!"

Matt coming to her aid would only make things worse. Sunny was sure of it. She yanked at the long strands trapped under her shoulder, then sat up, staring at the low, flickering flames which struggled to relight now that the rain had ceased. She shifted her gaze and found Matt on his side, propped up on one elbow, watching her.

"Something's got you worked up. What is it?"

Oh, if she could only tell him, but that wouldn't be wise. She had tested the limits of her willpower once already tonight, only to be rejected. Much as it pained her to admit it, she knew Matt had done the right thing.

Sunny pulled her knees to her chest and wrapped her arms around her legs. "I'm just having trouble falling asleep, that's all."

"Feel like talking?"

"No." What would they talk about? The fact that she couldn't stop thinking about him? Couldn't stop wanting him?

He moved so quietly she didn't know he was beside her until

he draped his arm around her shoulder. His thigh pressed against her hip; his rock-hard strength sent warm tingles shooting through her. In spite of what good sense suggested, she couldn't deny the comfort he offered and relaxed in his embrace. Resting her head on his solid chest, she listened to his heart beat a rapid tempo in her ear. His shirt smelled clean and carried a light trace of the natural musky scent that belonged solely to him. It took every ounce of her being to resist the urge to touch him, let her fingers seek out every line, every muscle, of his firmly chiseled body which had been burned into her mind since that day at the river.

Was she going mad? There were so many other things she should be thinking about. Swift Arrow—Running Bear and Gentle Wind—her forthcoming reunion with Jake Walden.

"Sunny, if you're worried about going after Walden, that's understandable. Anyone would be." His low, encouraging words tugged at her conscience.

She should be worrying about the outlaw, but Jake Walden was the last thing she wanted occupying her thoughts.

"You're not. You have more courage and strength than many braves I know. I don't believe you're afraid of anything, or anyone."

"That's not true." Matt lightly rested the bottom of his chin against the top of her head. His soft sigh breezed through her hair. "There's a certain blue-eyed angel that makes me as skittish as a newborn colt when I'm around her."

She tried to chuckle, but it came out more like a croak. "I think you mean a mad rooster. I've seen nothing of this nervous affliction." Sunny wished her heart wasn't so evident in her words, but realized she had no control to stop her spiraling emotions.

Matt gripped her shoulders in his strong hands and turned her gently to face him, staring deep into her eyes. "Then, you're not looking close enough, angel. You tie me up in knots all the time with your constant stubbornness, your pretty smiles, and your beautiful blue eyes. Trying to stay away from you, keep my hands off you, is the hardest thing I've ever done.''

Sunny's heart pounded and felt as though it threatened to leap from her chest. Great Spirit, how she wanted to believe what he said, how she wished his feelings could compare to what raged inside her at his nearness. Until now, she hadn't realized how much she had longed for this moment . . . this man. It was as though she had been waiting all her life for him, and more than anything she wanted to grab this chance with Matt, let herself feel safe, whole in his arms. But did she dare? The only promise in their future was that after Outlaw Canyon they would go their separate ways. A deep sadness washed over her at the thought; then a strange sensation pricked at her heart, telling her this moment with Matt would never come again.

''Then, don't try,'' she boldly whispered, making her decision. ''Kiss me instead.''

Gentle fingers bit into her shoulders. His jaw drew taut. ''I meant what I said earlier, Sunny. This won't stop with kissing.''

''I don't want it to.''

Lightning illuminated the darkness, and thunder rumbled overhead nearly drowning out Matt's deep groan. His lips crashed down on hers, hard, searching. He assailed her mouth, sending tiny heated jolts surging through her breasts, her stomach, lower. His strong arms circled her waist, gently pulling her atop him as he carried her down onto the blanket.

Sunny slid her hands along his wide shoulders, marveling at the feel of her breasts flattened against the hard muscles which rode across Matt's chest. Through the barrier of their clothing, her nipples peaked into hard nubs, responding to his powerful heat. His fingers journeyed over her back, her hips, then slipped beneath her clothing, scorching her flesh in their sensuous quest. She lost her breath at the first contact of his hands on her breasts, moaned her pleasure at the feel of her fullness in his palms. Heat, slow and sensual, licked through Sunny's limbs as Matt ravished her lips with a fevered kiss, stroked her burning flesh, crushed her harder against the full evidence of his desire. She wound her hands in the soft tangle of his hair, matching every velvet stroke of his tongue with her own.

Matt was amazed at how perfect she felt in his arms, how soft and warm her skin was beneath his hands. She kissed him with enough fiery passion to make him forget all his good intentions, make him forget everything but having her. He rolled Sunny under him, then stared into her gaze, softened to a deep azure in the fire's waning light, and deftly worked the buttons loose down her shirt. Shifting to his side, he freed her of the hindering garment. Her thin chemise followed. He trailed his finger along the strip of thin leather around her neck, then lifted the small pouch nestled between her pale golden globes. She stopped him when he started to remove it.

"No," she whispered softly, her eyes serious.

"Why?"

"It is my *puha,* my power. I must keep it close, or my guardian spirit will not grant me courage and strength on this quest to Outlaw Canyon."

Matt lowered the bag against her warm flesh and ran one finger along the outer edge of her firm breast. Her polished brown nubs hardened under his gaze. Another bolt of lightning flashed. He lightly touched the half-moon scar of puckered flesh on her left shoulder, then looked into her eyes and removed his hand from her soft skin when he saw the apprehension in her stare. She had asked him to kiss her, brushed aside his warning of where this all was headed. Was she having a change of heart? He propped his head in one hand and ran the other along her silky hairline, her cheek. "Do you want me to stop?"

She shook her head, then closed her eyes. Matt swallowed, unsure what to do. An unfamiliar insecurity surprised him. He realized it had been a long time since he had done more than just get down to business with a woman. He tried to recall a time when he ever wanted to please a woman as much as he wanted to please Sunny, and couldn't. Suddenly, Matt was afraid to touch her—afraid she might change her mind and it would be too late for him to stop—afraid she wouldn't stop him and he would move too fast for his beautiful little spitfire. His heart skipped a beat at the realization of how important it was to him that Sunny find this experience pleasurable. He had never worried before, not even with Ashley. But what really came as a surprise was the significant importance to him that she have no regrets afterward.

"Are you sure, Sunny?"

Slowly, Sunny opened her eyes and looked at him. His open concern struck a cord deep in her heart. A maelstrom of fresh, raw emotions gripped her. He was always thinking of her, worrying about her. It was one of the things she loved about him. There was no denying she wanted him, needed him, and no matter what happened tomorrow, next week, she would always have this memory of Matt.

"Very sure." She lifted a hand to the exposed part of his neck above his shirt.

Raw excitement coursed through him at the confidence in her smoldering gaze, at her words, her touch. Lightning split the sky; thunder roared in equal force to the pounding of his heart.

"Have you . . . did you and White Bear—" A low growl issued from his throat as Sunny quickly shook her head. He kissed her deeply, plowed his hands into the long, thick strands of her hair. She fumbled with the buttons on his shirt, freed them, then tentatively rested her fingers on his chest.

He captured her hand and encouraged her curiosity. Sunny was surprised at the softness of the black curls that covered his smooth flesh and lined the middle of his tightly muscled stomach. Her hands glided over his hard torso, along his broad shoulders. He slid his pant-clad thigh along the top of hers. His manhood pressed into her hip, surprising her with his male warmth which throbbed through their garments and heated her flesh. Responding to the seduction of his passion, she arched her back, gasping as her naked breasts brushed against his hair-roughened chest.

"My turn, angel." His fervent demand made her light-headed and fueled her flaming desire.

"Please." She moaned her delight when his large, heated palm covered her breast and gently stroked, kneaded, drove her nearly wild wanting more. He dropped a kiss to her shoulder, then lower . . . lower, until his lips closed over one nipple. Currents of fiery pleasure swept through her limbs as he worshipped her with lavish wonderment, first one breast, then the other. She clutched at his shoulders. His hand floated featherlike over her nakedness, then along her pant-clad hip and over her thigh, stopping at the juncture of her legs. Tremors shook her stomach, and liquid heat moistened her core.

He released her nipple and ravished her lips with his while his hands quickly unfastened her pants. His mouth left hers and marked a path over her breasts, down her ribs, her stomach, nipping, tasting until she moaned from the pleasure. Her skin cooled when he sat back, then flamed with renewed passion as he eased the buckskins over her hips and down her legs, lightly touching the scar on her thigh.

He shrugged out of his shirt, wrestled with his pants, then turned and knelt before her. The storm's wrath lit up the prairie night and illuminated Matt in its brief beauty. In that split second, she saw his full desire and experienced a moment of uncertainty. He was so big, so strong. But then he was beside her, so firm and muscled against her softness, so gentle with his touches, and he quickly chased her worry away, replacing it with a consuming hunger she had never known before.

Sunny writhed beneath him and drove Matt to a passion-filled frenzy that made him want to forget slow and take her now. Drawing in a deep breath, he forced himself to think only of her need. Languidly, he retraced his path along her body and claimed her breast with his lips. He caressed her supple curves with one hand, drew the other across her soft tuft of hair. She arched herself into his palm and sent his blood pounding through his veins, his desire straining for release. He ran one finger lightly across her warm, heated entrance and found her swollen, wet, ready for him.

Matt kissed her lips, taking her cry of startled wonder into his mouth as his fingers slipped inside her slick, sweet core. Sunny groaned, relaxed, then convulsed tightly around him as he stroked, in and out. He felt her pleasure build like wildfire in his hands, racing full speed toward a high precipice.

"That's it, angel," he whispered in her ear. She bucked against him. Her short nails dug into his shoulders. Ruthlessly, he urged her on. "Don't stop, honey. Let me feel your pleasure. Let me love you, Sunny." Matt reveled in her cries of passion, in her liquid fire that greeted his touch.

She screamed his name as the stars behind her eyes exploded into a blinding white light, as waves of hot pleasure coursed gloriously through her. Sunny thought her heart would pound a hole in her chest. She gasped for breath and slowly opened her eyes. Matt was beside her, his face so close. His tantalizing smile sent a new surge of excitement rippling under her skin.

"That . . . was—"

He kissed her, ran his hand through her lower curls, and laid his palm flat on her stomach. A delightful shiver raced through her, overwhelming her with a craving so strong she was helpless against it. "Is there more?"

"Definitely more, angel." His lips were as soft as the words he breathed against her mouth. He moved to cover her with his hard body, fitting every smooth, muscled part of him neatly into her smaller curves. He aroused her to a new height of excitement with his sweet words and his sure, knowing touch. Then, gently, he nudged her legs apart and pressed his manhood to the wet folds of her feminine core.

He brought his arms around her, held her close. "It'll hurt for only a second," he softly assured. "Then never again. I swear it, angel."

Matt lowered his hands to her hips, eased himself slowly inside to her virginal barrier, then with one strong thrust buried himself deep into her. Sunny went rigid at the first pain and dug her nails into his back. Thunder rumbled across the night, shook the ground under them, but didn't completely drown out her moan. His conscience pricked at his aching heart. He would have given anything not to cause her this pain.

He soothed her with tender words, caressed her with his hands, until she relaxed. Then he took his time, wanting to please her, loving the feel of her wild, passionate body squirming beneath him, her hands gliding down his back, her long, satiny legs locking behind his hips, pulling him closer. He lost himself in the intoxicating warmth of her soft flesh. Withdrawing almost completely, he plunged inside her velvet tightness again.

Sunny arched her hips, wanting to reach the sweet-hot pleasure hovering near the edge. He had promised her short pain. He had told the truth, but he said nothing about this heat, this burning conflagration that was pushing her to soar as high as Matt could take her . . . higher . . . higher. The tremors began, the fire reached its peak, and everything exploded inside her in that same glorious white haze.

Matt was stunned at the powerful release he felt, and growled his pleasure as he spilled himself inside her, then collapsed on top of her, breathing hard. He stroked the damp tendrils of her hair, rained kisses along her smooth jaw. When their labored breaths slowed to near normal, he grew fearful his weight was too much for her smaller body and rolled to his side, pulling her with him.

She touched his face with trembling fingers. "I never knew . . . that was—"

"Beyond words." He brushed his lips along her cheek, then trailed a line to her ear and thrilled at the feel of her pounding heart beating a steady rhythm close to his own. "And it'll only get better."

"If it gets any better, I don't think I'll survive."

Her soft breaths cooled his moistened skin. Her fingers gliding over his sweat-dampened back ignited a new fire.

"Sure you will, angel." Matt grinned, running his finger down the side of her neck, between her breasts. "And I'd be more than happy to prove it to you."

Thunder clapped, or was that her heart, Sunny wondered. The rains came, pelting the ground around them, smothering the fire in a final sizzling breath, and blocked the world from her thoughts as a heavy grayness slowly settled over their camp.

"I'm ready when you are."

His face was close enough for her to see his surprised look, even in the shadows surrounding them. She smiled, and he kissed her, then proceeded to lead her on a journey she had never dreamed possible.

Chapter Thirteen

Something was wrong. Matt wasn't sure how, or even what exactly, had caused the problem, but he could definitely pinpoint the exact moment when. The minute Sunny opened her eyes this morning, his passionate little spitfire was gone, as were the sweet words and silky touches he had enjoyed . . . and, by God, wouldn't mind enjoying again. Of course, that wasn't about to happen—not as long as Sunny kept up this silent brooding.

He stared at her stiff back as she rode astride the palomino, keeping just far enough ahead to make conversation impossible. In such a rush to break camp, she hadn't taken time to braid her hair, and it fell in golden waves beneath her brown felt hat. His assessing gaze stopped at her narrow waist neatly outlined in the smooth buckskin pants and white shirt, then moved to the single leather holster strapped around her shapely hips, which swayed in perfect rhythm with the mare's stride. Matt swallowed, remembering the feel of her warm skin.

He had tried to talk to her about last night while she rushed him through a cup of coffee, and later tried to kiss her when he brought her horse. Sunny put a stop to both right quick. But it wasn't anger he had seen in her eyes—thankfully, not regret, either—it was sadness, and it was tearing him up trying to figure out why.

Last night was unlike any he had ever known. She had touched his heart with her sweet, trusting abandon and excited cries of pleasure, touched his very soul as no other woman before. The last thing he had wanted was to make her sad, or have her avoid him as though he had some contagious ailment.

Had she expected something more from him? Some profession of his feelings? God knew he had come close to blurting out his love for her more than once during the long, passion-filled night. He wasn't sure what held him back more—the fear she would find his declaration only another burden to bear or the reality of their future. Sunny longed for a life he couldn't give her, a life that no longer existed, and he knew she was set on a course destined to take her from him forever. It was going to hurt like hell to watch her ride away after Outlaw Canyon—far worse than Ashley's rejection.

He had wanted to settle down with Ashley. He put his trust in her, made plans for the future, even went so far as to overlook the fact she wasn't a virgin when he bedded her the first time, because she was so beautiful, and he wanted her so damn bad. When the fickle Miss Ashley Hollister later ran off, breaking his heart and his trust, it took him a long time to accept the fact that he got exactly what he deserved for making the mistake of thinking with the lower half of his anatomy. But Matt realized what he thought he felt for Ashley couldn't begin to measure up against the feelings he had for his little spitfire. He loved Sunny with a depth he never dreamed possible. She was caring, giving, stubborn and tough as a mule at times, and so obviously devoted to her family—all the things his former betrothed wasn't—and he wanted her all right, with an intense longing he had never experienced around Ashley. He had never really loved Ashley, though. No, his heart had waited all these years to love another woman . . . this woman. For the first time in his life, Matt realized, he had made love to a woman for all the right reasons, and he had done it with the full understanding that sadness and hurt awaited him in the end. But by God, he certainly didn't want Sunny to feel those painful emotions.

Matt pulled a fresh cheroot and match from his shirt pocket. He sparked the flame and started to touch it to the cigar hanging from his mouth, but never got the chance as the dun trailing alongside chose that moment to nip at Thunder's hindquarter again. The black horse sidestepped, swung its massive head around, and bit Matt's leg.

"Sonofa—" His curse blew the flame out. He pulled his leg back before Thunder could take another bite and reined the gelding hard against the neck. The little dun took advantage of his loosened grip and jerked her reins free. The feisty mare ran a short distance to the side, stopped, then lowered her head and tore up a mouthful of the short bunch grass that coated their trail.

"Trouble there, Bronco?"

The first thing he noticed was the faint smile on her lips. The second was that her humor didn't reach her troubled gaze. She sat facing him, forearms loosely crossed over the palomino's neck, the end of the single hackamore rope dangling from her fingers. She didn't ride with a damn saddle. Hell, she didn't even use a bridle! He had both and still couldn't control this pair. Of course, if he could get his mind off her for longer than a second, the horses' constant dispute this morning wouldn't have escalated.

"So now you're talking to me?" He knew his frustration was evident, but it was nothing compared to the temptation he fought to climb out of his saddle, take her in his arms, and erase whatever haunted her stare.

"Just checking to see if you're hurt."

"Why?"

"Despite what you think, I do care."

"You'd know what I think if you'd bothered to talk to me this morning." Matt tossed the burnt match to the ground and put the cheroot back in his pocket, then needing something to do with his hands, grabbed Thunder's reins.

She sighed. "What was there to say, Matt?"

His mouth went dry. *How about I love you,* he wanted to tell her, but didn't. He knew it wasn't what she wanted to hear. "For starters, I want to know if you're okay."

She looked up, down, everywhere but at him, then sighed again. "Is anyone ever okay after something happens to change their life?"

Matt wasn't sure which way to step with that loaded question. Was she having regrets after all? Was her sadness from a loss of something she could never regain? Did she hate him for taking her innocence? Suddenly, he hated himself. "Sunny, I—"

She lifted one hand palm outward, and shook her head. Her tortured blue stare tore at his heart, his conscience. "Please don't say it. If there's any blame for what happened, it's mine. I all but threw myself at you." She reached up and pulled the wide, brown brim of her hat lower, blocking her eyes from his sight.

"Into willing arms, I assure you, angel."

"Please," she choked. "Don't call me that."

Her words were like bullets searing his chest. His heart missed its next beat, and a sudden fire burned a hole in his gut. Matt took a deep breath, then slowly released it. He told himself he should have expected this. As much as he wished she would jump into his arms with a great big smile on her pretty face and beg him to take her to Wyoming, he had known all along it wasn't going to happen. But dammit, he hadn't expected her to pull away from him so soon, or for the pain to settle in so fast with such slamming force.

He nodded once in response to her demanded request, hoping he could keep his word, but there was something he aimed to get clear before she cut him out of her life for good. "I don't want you thinking I was about to apologize for last night. I wasn't. I'm only sorry that I hurt you, and that you're having a change of heart about what happened."

Her head snapped up higher. "I already told you, you didn't hurt me . . . and I haven't had a change of anything. I wanted to be with you last night. I very much enjoyed . . ." She paused, seeming to gather her thoughts. Matt thought he detected a faint blush in her cheeks before she tucked her head down from his view. "What we shared . . . well, it . . . what I mean is . . . well . . . it was perfect. Thank you. I didn't know I was capable of trusting someone so . . . completely. It was nice."

She trusted him. Matt's heart soared. "You can always trust me, ang—Sunny."

She nodded, then looked back up at him. "That's why I thought it only fair to tell you, part of my reason for going after Jake Walden is to kill him myself."

Fear ground his heart to a skidding stop. "If anyone kills Jake Walden, it'll be me."

She lifted her chin in that proud familiar tilt, and Matt braced himself for a fight. "I understand you want revenge for Danny—"

"I want justice, and if it comes to a showdown, you're going to stay the hell out of the way where you won't get hurt."

"It's been a long time coming."

Matt wasn't sure what caught his attention first, her low tone, or the look she leveled at him from beneath her hat brim. Her tempered stare was as fierce as any Comanche warrior's he had ever faced, and one he had never seen from her before.

"Walden's finally going to pay for everything he's done, and it will be by my hand, not yours."

He forgot the argument over the outlaw's demise and concentrated on Sunny's unyielding demeanor, her clenched jaw, the faraway glaze in her stormy eyes. He recognized the signs, had seen them mirrored in himself when he had met up again with that cowhand. Sunny's words hinted at a past with Jake Walden. He wanted to know what that past was and what the outlaw had done to make his little spitfire this determined to kill.

"What happened, Sunny? What did that piece of scum do to you?"

She stiffened, and shook her head. "I don't want to talk about it."

Matt anticipated her next move and spurred Thunder at the same moment she reeled her mare around. His swifter mount had no trouble catching the smaller horse. Matt leaned to the left and looped one arm around Sunny's waist. She pummeled his hand with her fists as he hauled her from the mare and sat her in front of him. Then she switched and pounded at his chest while screaming at him in a mixture of English and Comanche. He didn't need to understand all of what she said to know he wasn't being compared to anything favorable. Matt dodged her hat as it sailed from her head; but the movement left him off balance, and when Sunny sucker punched him in the gut, he started to fall. Releasing Thunder's reins, he grabbed her flailing fists and pulled her down with him. He hit the ground hard, the air rushing from his lungs. Sunny kicked at his legs and struggled in his hold. He sucked in a quick breath, rolled and pinned her beneath him in the grass.

"Tell me what he did," he demanded.

She snarled, and tried to squirm out from under him. Matt tightened his hold on her wrists, held them above her head, and looked deep into her heated stare. "Tell me!" he ground out between clenched teeth.

"Let go of me!" She twisted, bucked, tried to push him off with her legs, but her smaller weight was no match.

"Answer me!"

"No!"

"Yes!"

A fierce, strangled cry ripped from her throat. She fought harder, working her knee free and making every attempt to plant it firmly in his groin. "Get off me, you bastard! You're hurting me . . . just like *he* always did!"

She stilled instantly, and Matt couldn't have let go any faster if he had held hot coals in his hands. He sat back, staring at the surprise on her face. It was obvious she hadn't meant to tell him that. He sure as hell hadn't expected to hear it. "I'm not like Jake Walden, Sunny. The last thing I'd ever do is hurt you. I just want to know what he did."

She closed her eyes, sighing long and heavy. "It's none of your business." Her weary voice contradicted the fight in her words.

His heart fairly crumbled into painful pieces as he reached a finger to the corner of her eye. "That's where you're wrong." Matt choked back his own threatening tears and brushed away each droplet of hers that slipped free. "I'll make it top on my list to take care of whatever makes you cry—if you'll let me, trust me enough."

"I can't," her voice was barely above a whisper.

"Sure you can, angel."

She shook her head, but the fact that she didn't resist when he pulled her into his embrace gave him hope. Tenderly, he stroked her hair. Matt pressed her trembling body closer, tightened his arms around her as she curled herself against him. God, she felt so helpless in his arms, but he knew she wasn't. Sunny had enough spunk for ten people, and it hurt to see her run and cower from this memory. She was as tough as a warrior, his beautiful spitfire. But somehow Jake Walden had broken that spirit, caused her pain, and was still doing it now. Matt's reason for wanting the outlaw dead doubled.

"You can tell me anything." He tucked her head under his chin, drawing her closer still, wanting her to feel safe. "And sometimes, honey, memories that hurt deep are often the ones which need talking about the most."

She said nothing for a long time, and it tore Matt up inside thinking she didn't trust him after all—not the way he wanted her to.

"Did you learn that from experience?" Her low, tear-smothered voice twisted his gut.

"Yeah, I did, with the help of a good friend."

She sighed. "Are you my friend, Matt?"

He swallowed the sudden lump in his throat. Whether or not she wanted his love, she would always have his heart. He would do anything for her, and if all she wanted from him was a friend, then that was all he would be—no matter if it killed him. "Always."

She sighed again, her warm breath slipping through the loose opening between his shirt buttons and heating his skin. He closed his eyes and tried not to remember her willing and wild in his arms, tried not to think about the fast approaching day when she would walk out of his life forever.

"Talk to me, Sunny," he coaxed in a hushed tone. "Tell me how Jake Walden hurt you."

"He killed my mother." She shuddered in his embrace. A cold fist closed over Matt's heart.

"What happened?"

She took a deep breath, then slowly released it. "Two years ago, Walden was an Indian scout for the army."

Matt was surprised at how calm she sounded, how in control. He might have believed it if he didn't feel her shaking in his arms.

"One morning he led the troops to our village. The same morning I planned to wed White Bear."

She squirmed in his arms, and only then did Matt realize how tight his grip had become at the mention of the brave's name. He immediately loosened his hold.

Sunny looked at him strangely, then continued. "I was bathing alone at the river and heard the shots from the soldiers' guns. Gentle Wind and Running Bear had come with me and were off playing in the woods. I found them, made them hide in a tree, and promised to return. Then I left and ran back to camp, only to watch helplessly as the army killed my friends . . . my family . . . all fleeing for their lives. That's when I saw Walden throw my mother to the ground, hit her in the face with his fist . . . then shoot her. There was nothing I could do." She sat up and stared off with the same fierce look Matt had seen earlier.

"But I tried. I ran into the fighting, picked up a dead soldier's gun. Walden saw me. We fired at the same time."

"He shot you?" Matt gripped her shoulders and turned her to face him.

She nodded. "Twice."

"The scars on your shoulder and thigh?"

"Yes."

Matt shook his head, raked his fingers through his hair. "Why would he shoot? I thought the army was supposed to rescue white captives."

"Their orders were to kill anyone who fled or fought back. Besides, we weren't captives, Matt."

Matt nodded, regretting his slip. He knew his little spitfire was as much Comanche as if she had been born one. Now he had an even better understanding of why. His hatred of the Indians stemmed from their senseless attack on the wagon train, the senseless killing of the innocent. Listening to what Sunny had witnessed, he realized what the soldiers and Walden had done to the Comanches was no better, and her hatred no different. Sunny's family and friends hadn't deserved to die, any more than his own that long-ago day. And Sunny certainly hadn't, but he knew she easily could have that day. Matt tried to pull her back into his hold, but this time she did resist.

"Black Eagle is the man I will always call Father, and the Comanches will always be my family. I was happy then, safe."

Her eyes sparkled with memories, and that bothered Matt. He had never seen a single hint of that light in her gaze, and he hated the resentment which rose in him toward the Indians responsible for putting it there. He wanted to be the one to make her feel safe, make her eyes shine with love.

"How did you get away?" he asked.

She closed her eyes. "I don't know. I remember running, then nothing until I woke up at the Circle H."

Matt raised his hand and pressed his palm lightly against her cheek. "You're lucky Will found you."

Sunny nodded.

"What happened to Running Bear and Gentle Wind?"

She opened her eyes, but didn't pull from his touch. "They hid until the soldiers were gone, and escaped with Black Eagle's brother and a few others to one of our allies' camps. But a year later, they were captured when that village was raided. The prisoners were being held at a fort in south Texas. With Colonel Grierson's help, I arranged to have them returned to their families on the reservation, and in return convinced the Indians to stop stealing the army stock . . . at least for the time being. Agent Taylor was grateful for a peaceful solution to the problem."

"Grateful enough he gave you reason to believe he would let your brother and sister go free, is that right?" Things were beginning to make more sense to him now.

"Yes, but now I'm concerned if Gray Wolf dies before Maggie gets him to the fort, Taylor won't honor the bargain. Even when Swift Arrow returns."

"That bas—" Matt blew out an exasperated breath. It was obvious to him Taylor was using Sunny's love for her family to his own advantage and would no doubt continue to do so. Matt's temper soared to the edge. No one was going to do that to his little spitfire. He had no control over Gray Wolf's fate, but he could sure as hell see that the agent got Swift Arrow back alive, and stuck to the damn bargain. Setting Sunny from him, Matt got to his feet and pulled her up.

"What are you doing?" Her thin brows arched with confusion.

He kissed her soundly on the lips, cutting off her startled gasp, then grabbed hold of her hand and tugged her along. "Come on, we've got an outlaw to catch, and another brave to find. We best get at it."

Sunny stepped from the stream and hurried to dry herself. Matt would be back from hunting up their supper any time now, and she hadn't even started a fire. She slipped a short, clean chemise over her head, then gathered her wet hair between her hands and twisted the excess water from the long strands. Finishing, she reached down for the blue dress folded neatly on the rock, pausing when her fingers touched the cotton material.

Maybe this isn't such a good idea. When she had snatched the garment out of her saddlebag instead of her last clean pair of pants, it had seemed sensible. Now she wasn't so sure.

She held the full length of the long-sleeved dress out before her and stared at the light blue flowers and green stems against the darker blue background. It should have the word guilt woven into its fabric, she thought. She had bought the dress to ease her guilt over lying to Matt about needing one. And now she was feeling guilty about wearing it. Was Matt going to think she was wearing it for him? Would he think she was inviting him into her bed tonight? Was she?

No!

Sunny adjusted the bulky material in her hands and slipped the dress over her head. She *was* being sensible. Nothing more. Bending over, she slipped the soft moccasins on her feet, then retrieved her comb and crossed the several yards to where they had made camp. Quickly, she gathered wood and started a fire, then carefully spread her bedroll on one side of the small blaze, and Matt's on the other. The sun was not far from being gone by the time she finished, and she was surprised Matt hadn't returned. Sitting on her side of the fire, Sunny combed the tangles from her hair and waited for him.

Her eyes kept darting across the flame to the empty bedroll. Her thoughts jumped back to the night before, and her hand paused in mid-stroke. Matt had been wonderful, so patient, so tender. Throughout the glorious hours spent in his arms, he had gently urged her, playfully coaxed her, to new sensations, new heights of passion. He had made her feel safe . . . and special . . . and loved.

Matt didn't love her, though, Sunny knew that. She jerked the comb through the thick strands. He wasn't going to saddle himself with a woman like her. A woman who was more Comanche than white in her heart, and came with two half-breed children in tow. Knowing his strong dislike of the Indians, she was still surprised he had been so kind to Gentle Wind.

She stared at his bedroll. But Matt was a kind man, though she sensed he purposefully kept it hidden underneath his often displayed temper. He was strong and passionate. He was everything she wanted . . . and everything she couldn't have.

Sunny sighed, tugged hard on the comb, then swore at the pain which tore at her head as it caught on another tangle. She needed to stop thinking about him, needed to stop wishing and wanting. She had made her decision last night. Now she had to go on—without him. After Outlaw Canyon, Matt would leave, and she would try to forget how much she wanted to lie in his arms, have him love her again.

She had decided this morning, it would be best to start that forgetting process now, before she got in any deeper and Matt became too buried in her heart to ever forget. But after spending the night in his arms, trusting him in ways she never dreamed possible, she had wanted him to at least know her true intentions about Jake Walden. It was only fair. He *was* risking his life to help her, and her siblings.

She hadn't expected him to be persistent enough to chase her down to find out her reasons for wanting the outlaw dead, though. And she hadn't expected his sudden burst of determination when she had told him her concerns about Taylor honoring the bargain. She realized she should have expected it. Matt was a man who got answers, then took action.

From their first conversation, he had dogged her with questions, and it hadn't taken her long to figure out he wasn't a man who liked being told no. He wasn't a man who liked being lied to, either. Sunny frowned, pulling the comb one last time through her hair. She hadn't *really* lied this afternoon, though.

Jake Walden did lead the raid on the village, and he *did* kill her mother. But Matt had asked what Walden did to *her,* and she had answered his curiosity, not his question. For a single second, she had wanted to tell him, wanted to believe in her trust in him, wanted to believe he would understand. He wouldn't, though, not unless she explained the rest of the truth about her past with the outlaw. And *that* truth would die with Jake Walden. She would see to it. Matt would never know . . . no one would.

Sunny stared at his blanket opposite the fire, then at the sun three quarters gone on the horizon. Where was he? What if he had been hurt? Her heart stopped, gripped in jabbing pain before guilt wormed its way into the center. If anything happened to Matt, it would be her fault, and how would she ever live with herself? She pulled her knees up close to her breasts and looped her arms around her skirt.

Matt sucked in a quick breath and halted his steps. He looked at the campsite, at the woman dressed in blue. Had he lost his bearings? Had he wandered into someone else's camp? He stared at the cascade of blond hair shimmering in daylight's final glow. The same hair he had run his fingers through last night. The same hair she had draped over his nakedness throughout their hours of lovemaking.

But what is Sunny doing in a dress? He had been surprised she bought the thing in the first place, but he never thought she would actually wear it.

Matt loudly cleared his throat. She spun around on the blanket, tangled in the skirt, and landed half-sprawled across the wool, her blue eyes wide with fright. Only then did he see the gun she had been reaching for, and made a mental note not to sneak up on her too often.

"You scared me," she whispered breathlessly.

Matt smiled. "We're even, then. I thought I was walking into the wrong camp." He gestured with one hand toward the dress, and she blushed. He couldn't recall a prettier sight.

She regained her seat on the blanket and adjusted the skirt around her. Her back faced the setting sun, and the warm glow settled around her like a halo, turning her golden hair to a translucent white fire. Matt forced himself not to run, not to grab her up in his arms and make love to her right then.

He led Thunder the rest of the way into the small clearing, ground tied the gelding beside Sunny's mare, then carried the skinned rabbit over to the fire. "You don't mind if I do the cooking tonight, do you?" he teased. Her blush deepened, and he thought for sure his grin would wrap around and meet behind his head.

He had hoped her mood would improve while he was gone, and was glad to see it had. She had hardly said three words to him all afternoon, but he hadn't gotten the impression she was mad, or that she regretted telling him about the raid and her ma. He just figured she needed some time to herself. He knew firsthand that riding back through memories could sometimes be a rough trip, especially when the memory was a tragic one. He also knew that afterward, a person often needed some time to work things through on his own. But knowing it still hadn't made the afternoon easy for him. A thousand times he had wanted to stop, take her in his arms, make sure she was all right. A thousand times he had told himself to leave her alone, give her some space, some time. He was glad now that he had. She looked wonderful, radiant . . . happy.

She held her hand out toward the skinned rabbit. "It's a small fire. I can at least get the meal started, and if you hurry, you should be back in time to save it from burning."

Matt chuckled, but didn't hand her the rabbit. Instead, he took her hand in his free one and helped her up. She stood close to him, and her sweet fragrance of wildflowers sent his pulse racing. As she smiled up at him, his breath lodged in his throat. She reached for the small carcass, but he pulled it away. "You're all clean; I'll do this."

Before she could protest, he reached down for a long stick and skewered the rabbit. She did take it from him then and bent at the waist to secure the meat over the fire. The snug dress pulled tighter over her narrow waist and shoulders. Her full, rounded breasts filled the tiny-buttoned bodice better than anything he had ever seen. Matt swallowed, sweeping his gaze down the blue cotton dotted with flowers that reminded him of bluebonnets littering the Texas prairie in spring. The hem was higher in back because of her stance, giving him a generous sight of trim ankles and slender calves. His pulse beat faster. He stared at the shapely curves of her backside. The bulge in his pants grew tighter, hotter. The simple calico looked good on her, not the least bit out of place on her slender body. He wondered how quickly he could get her out of it.

She glanced sideways and caught his stare. He felt the heat rise to his face as her lips lifted in a smile. "I thought you were going to see to your horse."

"On my way." He turned to go, took a couple steps and stopped. He looked back over his shoulder at her. "In case I forgot to mention it, you look beautiful in that dress, angel."

A faint pink tinged her cheeks again. "Thank you." She tucked her head shyly, and Matt couldn't stop the smile from spreading across his lips again. He should pay her compliments more often, he thought.

Matt quickly unsaddled Thunder and rubbed the horse down with fresh grass before heading to the creek to wash. He whistled a tune as he sauntered back to their campsite, and once again lost his breath at the first sight of Sunny. He stood and watched her for several long minutes as she sat on her bedroll and deftly worked at securing her thick mane of hair into a braid. A twinge of disappointment flashed through Matt. He realized he preferred her hair loose, free and wild . . . like Sunny.

The sun was gone, and darkness settled in slow, deepening shadows. The fire's glow turned her skin a healthy, golden sheen. Matt wanted to run his fingers along the smooth flesh exposed above her modestly low-cut gown, up the column of her slender neck. His manhood swelled and strained against his pants. Matt shook his head, then breathed deeply.

He needed to stop thinking so much about her, or he would walk right over there and take her by the fire, and he couldn't do that. She might be talking to him, even smiling at him, but he had no idea whether she would let him touch her ever again. She hadn't this morning. She hadn't this afternoon, either, when they had stopped to rest the horses and he had tried to put his arm around her. He had never forced himself on a woman—ever—and he wasn't about to start now.

He smelled the strong coffee brewing over the fire and curled his nose slightly. He should tell her he liked his coffee the same way he liked his meat—cooked through, but not overdone. A frown pulled at his lips. No, he wouldn't say anything. In a few days, Sunny would be gone, and he would be back to fixing his own coffee—for the rest of his life. Matt pushed the thought from his mind. He wouldn't think about that, either. Tonight, he didn't want to think about anything—not Walden, not the braves, not her siblings who would take her away from him. They would reach Outlaw Canyon sometime tomorrow. Tonight was all the time they had left alone together, and he wasn't going to waste it wondering and wishing. There would be plenty of time for that *after* Sunny was gone. Tonight, he wanted to be with her, hopefully make love to her, but he wouldn't push.

Not wanting to startle her as he had done before, Matt took up whistling the same tune and made sure to make plenty of noise as he approached. She finished tying her hair with a short leather strip, but didn't turn his way. He stepped up beside her and knelt. "Well, the outside's not black. That's a good sign."

The smile she gave him seemed forced, and puzzled him. What had happened to her good mood? Matt turned his attention to the rabbit, then frowned at the bedroll he spotted on the other side of the fire.

Well, at least I know now how the night's going to end. All right, he could handle this. He would be fine. Rather, he would be just as soon as the pain eased and his heart started beating again.

He reached for the coffeepot and swore when the hot handle singed his fingers.

"Here, let me." Sunny got to her knees and tugged loose a section of her skirt, then held it in her hand as she reached for the pot. Her arm brushed against his and sent a jolt of heat shooting through him.

Matt shifted away from the contact. If he was supposed to sleep on the other side, he best get over there . . . before he lost all control. She poured the pitch-black liquid into the cup and handed it to him. He thanked her and stood.

"Where are you going?" The quick surprise in her voice kept him from moving. The smoldering fire in her blue gaze made him nearly drop his cup.

"I thought you might be more comfortable if I sat on the other side." He sure as hell knew he would be, especially if that was where she expected him to sleep.

"I thought so, too." She narrowed her stare at him, then smiled. "But I've changed my mind."

Matt folded himself down on the blanket so fast, he dumped the hot coffee right into his lap.

Chapter Fourteen

"Damnation!" Matt tossed the tin aside and jumped to his feet.

"Are you all right?" Sunny stood and reached for the top button of his pants. His large hand settled over both of hers.

"What are doing?" he rasped.

Sunny looked up into in his taut face. "Seeing if you're hurt, what do you think?"

"I *think* you better let me do that," he whispered. A savage inner fire glowed in the midnight depths of his gaze.

Concerned that Matt had been hurt, she hadn't thought about her actions. Now that he had brought it to her attention, Sunny gasped. In one quick movement, she dropped her hands and stepped back, then turned. Great Spirit! What was wrong with her?

She had been so worried when he hadn't returned, then greatly relieved and stupidly giddy when he had. She still couldn't believe how she had blushed when he looked at her with such desire and told her she was beautiful. And now she was trying to take his clothes off! She had promised herself to stay away from him, away from the temptation of what she couldn't have. But she had felt so cold when he stood to go, and desperate to feel safe in his strength, his warmth. She had merely called him back in her mind, not intending to speak the words aloud. Now that she had, her heart did not want to take them back. She wanted to be with Matt, wanted one more night of memories with him before he was gone from her forever.

He touched her shoulder. Fire raced down her arm. She reached up and covered his hand with hers.

"What's wrong?" His breath warmed her ear.

How could she tell him what she wanted? How did a woman go about inviting a man into her bed? She couldn't just say the words. What if he told her no? Uncertainty plagued her. Maybe this was a sign she shouldn't give in to this wanting. She should be strong. "Nothing, I—"

"I know you better than that, angel." He gently turned her to face him.

She tried to look just at the buttons on his black shirt, but he forced her chin up with his finger. His eyes held concern, warmth, desire . . . all for her. Hot waves swept into her stomach and pooled lower.

"Something's on your mind. What is it?"

Sunny swallowed. She didn't want to be strong, not tonight. Her body ached for his touch; her heart ached for the love he could show her. She tried to tell him, but her voice failed. She tried again, then frowned at the strange odor wafting past her nose.

Matt sniffed the air, an odd puzzlement crossing his face. Sunny turned at the same time he did, and saw the rabbit ablaze.

"Not again," she groaned. She stepped forward and reached down to grab the stick. Matt's hand at her shoulder stopped her.

"I'll do it. I don't want you to get burned." He pulled the rabbit from the fire and dropped it, stick and all, in the dirt, then rolled the carcass with his boot until the flame went out.

Sunny stared at the dirt-covered clump of blackened meat

and wasn't sure what she wanted to do more—laugh at another of her attempts to cook for Matt, or cry over the interruption to the moment.

He stood with his arms crossed, shaking his head and softly chuckling down at the rabbit. "A man could starve around you, angel." His darkened gaze roved over her in slow appraisal, igniting her body anew as heat surged through her blood. His eyes met hers. "But, you're enough of a distraction to make me forget a whole lot more than cooking dinner."

He stared at her with an intense longing that made her forget to breathe, made her forget everything but the need to be in his arms.

"What else do I make you forget?" she asked in a hushed whisper, feeling suddenly daring.

"For starters, when you look at me like you are right now, you make me forget my bedroll's on the other side of that fire."

He lowered his gaze to her breasts. A surge of tingling excitement rippled through her, tightening her nipples and setting her heart to a fierce pounding. Sunny took a step closer, letting the tips of her breasts rest lightly against his crossed arms. She heard him suck in his breath and smiled at the undeniable passion in his stare.

"What else?" she whispered.

Matt uncrossed his arms and placed his hands on her shoulders. "You make me forget there's a tomorrow."

He brought his lips down on hers in a searing, searching exploration that made her senses spin; then he pulled her to him. Sunny snaked her hands over his shoulders, wound her arms around his neck, eagerly deepening their kiss with her own probing quest. Matt's hands moved slowly along her back, over her hips, scorching her flesh through the cotton with his touch. She plowed her hands through his hair. He grabbed her hips and pressed her closer to him, closer against his swollen manhood.

His mouth left hers and trailed hot kisses down her neck.

She could feel his uneven breathing brush her skin and marveled at the knowledge that she could take his breath away as easily as he did hers. He followed the neckline of her dress with his lips, kissing her heated flesh, sending a rush of liquid desire raging through her blood. His hands floated feather-light around her waist, along her sides.

Matt reluctantly tore his lips from her soft, sweet-smelling flesh and searched her gaze, thrilled at the welcome desire which met his stare. He didn't know why she had changed her mind, but she chased away any further doubts he had by cupping his face in her small hands and bringing her mouth to his in a giving touch that reached him deep in his soul.

Fire surged through his veins. He captured her breasts through the thin material. Her nipples hardened against his palms. She groaned as he stroked her full mounds, trembled when he rubbed her hard buds between his fingers, and kissed him with a sweet fierceness that made him want to get lost in her forever.

Matt reached for the top button on her dress and forced himself to work the fastenings open slowly instead of ripping the garment from her as had been his first thought. He tore his mouth from her sensuously distracting lips and looked into her eyes as his hands slipped inside the waist of the opened dress. She stared at him through long lashes, and he watched her eyes darken with unbridled desire when his fingers slid upward along the thin chemise and gently brushed the sides of her breasts. He didn't stop, but worked his way to her shoulders and slowly eased the bodice from her body, then over her hips until it pooled in a blue puddle around her ankles. Bending down on one knee, he eased the soft moccasins from her feet, then stood.

Sunny stilled his hands before he lifted her chemise, and with her gaze on his in passion's accord, she undid the buttons of his shirt, then let her hands wander at their leisure over his chest before slipping the garment from his shoulders. She brought her fingers to the top of his pants, and paused.

Matt knew by the teasing glint in her eyes, she was thinking how he had halted her attempt before, and covering her hands with his, he brought his mouth close to hers. "Don't even think of stopping," he growled.

She smiled. "I wouldn't dream of it."

He felt the buttons give, felt her hands burn his skin as she pushed the denim over his hips and down his thighs. She stared at his hard shaft, brushed her fingers against the tip. Matt groaned, closed his eyes as she slowly ran her palm along his full erection, and nearly lost himself when she closed her hand around him. He captured her wrist.

"I'm sorry," she whispered, and tried to pull back.

Matt's eyes flew open. "Don't be sorry; that felt good." His voice was hoarse. "Too good to finish things just yet."

He sat on the blanket, pulling her down with him, then quickly removed his boots and pants. Sunny sat in front of him, boldly raking her gaze over his body. Matt felt a pride unlike any he had ever known at her pleased appraisal. He reached over and took hold of her chemise at her hips. She raised her arms, easing the way as he lifted the soft, white material up over her head. Matt's breath lodged in his throat at the first sight of her naked in the fire's glow. Her skin gleamed like spun honey, and he devoured every inch of her with his eyes; her beautiful round breasts and pebbled brown nubs, her slender waist and flat stomach, her triangle of dark blond hair.

Matt rose to his knees and took her long braid in his hands. Untying the thin leather strip, he loosened the heavy mass from its confines, letting it fall in shiny, fire-lit waves around her shoulders. Then he leaned his body closer over her, not stopping his forward motion until he gently forced her back onto the blanket.

He slid one warm palm up her thigh, fingered the scar on her leg with his gentle touch, then brought his lips down and kissed the spot where she had been shot. Sunny thought she would cry at the tenderness of his gesture. Then he moved his hand over her hip and along her stomach. She closed her eyes and arched her back as his hand closed over her breast. His fingers stroked her to a fire as hot as the one burning beside them. She moaned her ecstasy as his tongue teased her nipples, and his mouth suckled at first one breast then the other.

Matt slowly ran his hands over her body, searching for spots to pleasure her, thrilling in her writhing cries at each one he discovered. His lips followed the path his hands traveled, and tasted the sweet nectar of her desire. Her moans deepened, grew more urgent; then her hands lightly gripped his shoulders, urging him up to her. Matt slid his body along the top of hers, kissing his way to her lips. As he entered her velvety warmth, his heart soared with love. Her body melted against his, flesh against flesh. She matched him stroke for stroke, wild and passionate in his arms. He urged her on with coaxing words, touches, loving her cries of exquisite pleasure which filled his ears. And when he could stand it no longer, he spilled his seed into her, crying her name out to the heavens in pure, blinding bliss.

She panted beneath him, her breathing as labored as his own. Matt tried to roll his weight from her, but Sunny locked her arms around his back, refusing to let him go. He braced himself with elbows planted on either side of her head and looked down into her face.

''Thank you,'' she whispered, her half-closed eyes hazy with contentment.

He kissed the tip of her nose. ''It was definitely *my* pleasure, angel.''

''Not all of it.'' She smiled lazily, then all at once opened her eyes wide.

Matt drew his brows together. A sudden panic gripped his heart. ''What's wrong?''

''I'm starving, and I just remembered the rabbit.'' She frowned. ''Now we have nothing to eat.''

Matt smiled, greatly relieved her only concern was food. ''Well, you're in luck. Jube gave me some extra canned food and dried fruit. Told me to put it in my saddlebags in case of an emergency." He raised a teasing brow at her. "By any chance has he seen you cook?"

Sunny grinned. "Once."

The renegade halted his trail-weary pony in the shadow of the tall pine, careful to stay out of the moon's bright glow. He searched the dark, flat plains as far as his vision could reach. Nothing. Had they stopped to camp, and he had somehow passed them up? He scanned the night for signs of smoke, sniffed the air. Nothing. How could he have lost them?

He nudged his pony forward, staying within the shadows. It was too dark to look for tracks, even with the moon riding high in the star-covered sky. But he didn't need the light of day to know this was the way to the outlaw's hideout. He had traveled it before when he had followed the soldier. He also knew the canyon was still some hours away. Surely the outlaw didn't plan to ride straight through, not burdened with the woman and child.

"Stop right there, Injun," the gruff voice demanded.

The loud click of several rifles being cocked sounded on three sides of him. His first thought was to run, but the only side open to him was the moonlit prairie. The renegade pulled back on the rope, halting his pony.

"Let me see those hands," the same gruff-voiced soldier ordered.

He slowly raised his arms into the air. The sound of numerous hooves moved closer, crunching the fallen pine needles underfoot. The renegade watched as one soldier walked his horse into the moonlight in front of him, then around to the side. Other soldiers drew in closer until he was completely surrounded. He shifted his stare slowly. Everywhere he looked, he faced the barrel of a soldier's gun.

"Sanders, get the Injun's knife. Mackenzie, bring the rope and tie his hands."

Two soldiers left the circle and rode up to him on either

side. One pulled his knife from the sheath at his waist; the other bound his wrists together behind him.

"All right, boys, let's go. We got a long ride back to camp."

Maggie slowly opened her eyes and eased her head up. Thousands of sharp, needle-prick sensations shot through her neck and shoulders. Her back was stiff, unresponsive, and ached from being hunched over. She realized she had somehow managed to fall asleep during the night. But how she managed to stay on the horse was a mystery to her.

She forced herself upright, groaning with every slow inch gained as pain shot up into her shoulders and down into her numb bottom. She bit her lips against the straining ache in her arm when she raised a hand and rubbed at her eyes. The insides of her thighs burned from constant shifting against the saddle.

And still this blasted horse keeps moving.

Walden had pushed them on through the night, stopping twice to rest the horses. Maggie stared at the gray morning sky and prayed they were almost to their destination. She couldn't take another day in this saddle. She doubted she would last another hour. And what about Gentle Wind?

She hadn't seen the poor girl since the first time Walden called a rest. After that, he had made the girl ride with him in the rear of their procession, instead of with Hooker up ahead. Maggie glanced down at the Indian trussed up on the horse beside her. The second time Walden stopped, Gentle Wind had been kept from her, but Swift Arrow had managed to whisper a few words to her, not very encouraging words either, she recalled.

He had told her not to fight whatever Walden said or did, or the outlaw would kill her.

Maggie slowly rolled her head, trying to work loose the sore muscles in her neck. The saddle creaked and groaned with each of the mare's steps. She shifted her seat, hoping to ease the searing pain in her legs, but only managed to find new spots of sore, stiff muscles. There wasn't a single part of her body she could feel that didn't hurt.

Morning dawned, and with it Maggie got her first look at Outlaw Canyon. Hooker led the way as they entered a narrow, barren valley bordered by tall, rocky ravines on both sides. At the end of the desertlike stretch, he took a path off to the right. Maggie lost her bearings as they wound their way through trees and brush, then across another short section of dirt and rocks. Hooker stopped in front of a shabby-looking soddie. Her mare came to a halt behind him, and so did the horse carrying Swift Arrow.

Walden rode up alongside, and Maggie shifted her attention quickly to Gentle Wind. The girl was asleep, slumped over in the outlaw's arms, her head lolling against his shoulder. The young boy, Luke, came riding up behind Walden and was the first to dismount.

Maggie was surprised when the boy walked over to the outlaw and raised his arms. "Let me have the girl. I'll take her inside."

Walden handed Gentle Wind over without a word, then dismounted. Maggie watched Luke carry Gentle Wind inside the dark hideout, then turned to Walden.

"Where's he taking her?"

"Don't worry about it, schoolteacher," Walden snapped. "Now, get down."

She started to swing her leg over, but was suddenly grabbed around the waist by large hands and yanked out of the saddle, then dumped on her backside in the dirt.

"You need to learn to move faster, schoolteacher," Walden snarled down at her. "Get up!"

Maggie thought about Swift Arrow's words and bit her tongue, scrambling to her feet as quickly as her sore muscles would move. The outlaw grabbed her by the arm and pulled her along with him up the steps to the porch. At the doorway, he stopped and turned. "Stu, tie Swift Arrow up out back. Hooker, you come with me."

An icy fear crawled up Maggie's spine. Dear God, what were they going to do to her? To Gentle Wind?

Little sunlight shone through the soddie's lone window, and it took Maggie a few seconds to adjust her sight to the dim shadows inside. She searched the room for Gentle Wind and spotted her huddled in a corner. The girl was awake now and staring back with widened eyes. Luke sat beside her, his blond head bent close to the girl's darker one as he whispered something. Maggie couldn't hear what he said, but Gentle Wind looked from her to the gang's leader and back with round, fearful eyes.

Walden released his hold on her arm. Maggie stepped toward the girl. Walden shoved her between her shoulders and sent her staggering forward until she stumbled and fell onto the hard dirt floor. She heard Gentle Wind's low cry of alarm and prayed the young girl wouldn't do anything foolish to get herself hurt. Matt wasn't the type to hit a child, or anyone, but if Gentle Wind attempted to kick Walden or his men, Maggie knew the girl's fate would not be a simple smile of understanding and a peppermint stick later. She had to get to her and make sure Gentle Wind kept silent.

Maggie pressed her palms against the packed dirt and started to rise to her feet. Hands grabbed her collar and roughly jerked her upright. Glancing over her shoulder, she saw Hooker standing behind her, his warm, stale breath brushing across her face, singeing her nostrils with its pungent odor. Walden circled the crude wooden table, the only furnishing Maggie could see in the tiny room, and stopped in front of her. His face was a contortion of tight lines and burning anger, his only eye as clear and cold as a winter stream. Maggie swallowed.

"All right, schoolteacher, I want some answers." The venom in his voice was even more sinister than the hatred in his stare, and Maggie felt a wave of terror wash through her blood. "Tell me what Sunny's planning."

"I don't know what you're talk—"

Walden's hand came around with the speed of a snake striking and backhanded her across the mouth. Maggie cried out as her head snapped hard to the right, and would have fallen if Hooker hadn't still been holding onto her shirt. She tasted blood in her mouth and felt the swelling throb in her lips.

"Don't lie to me, schoolteacher!" Walden snarled close to her face. "Tell me what Sunny's planning."

"She's pla . . . planning to come after you." Maggie's voice quavered. Her body shook. She took a deep breath to steady herself and kept reminding herself not to let Walden see how afraid she was, not to let Gentle Wind see.

"When?" Walden snapped.

"I'm not sure." Maggie cringed when Walden raised his hand again, but this time he didn't strike her.

"Who's she bringing with her?"

Maggie didn't answer. Walden's fist crashed against her temple. This time Hooker didn't steady her, and Maggie fell sideways against the table. The hard wood cut into her hip and side. Walden pushed her, and she rolled off onto the floor, landing hard on her bottom. She winced against the pain shooting through her body and briefly closed her eyes, praying for strength, praying for Gentle Wind's safety and her own.

Walden spat into the dirt at her feet. "Now, you start answering my questions with the truth, schoolteacher, or the girl's going to be next."

Maggie opened her eyes and stared up at the outlaw. She had never seen such evil hatred in a man's eyes before. She had never feared for her life more, but her only concern was Gentle Wind.

"No one. She's coming alone."

The outlaw's blond brows drew together, and slowly he nodded. Maggie hid her relief at his obvious acceptance of her lie. "What about Grierson?"

A spark of defiance rose in her. She squared her stiff shoulders. "What about him?"

"Were you taking a message to him at the fort?"

"No."

"You're lyin', bitch!" Walden walked over, grabbed Gentle Wind's arm, and jerked her to her feet.

"Leave her alone!" Maggie scrambled to her feet and would have rushed across the room if Hooker hadn't planted his hands on her shoulders and forced her to stay. She tried to shake free. His fingers bit harder into her flesh.

Gentle Wind struggled as Walden dragged her closer. Maggie held her breath and waited. Luke rose slowly to his feet and pressed farther back into the shadows. Walden stopped just inches from where she stood. Gentle Wind winced as the outlaw's fingers tightened around her slim arm.

"Now, I'm gonna ask one more time. Is Sunny trying to get a message to Grierson?"

Maggie swallowed. "If she is, I don't know anything about it."

"You're lyin' again, schoolteacher. His men are already camped outside of the canyon."

McGuire? Maggie wondered. "I don't know anything about a message. I was only taking the girl back to the fort."

Walden stared down at Gentle Wind, and Maggie suddenly wished she hadn't said anything to bring his attention back to the girl. "This the same girl Sunny wants to make an exchange of Gray Wolf and Swift Arrow for?"

How does he know that? Maggie hid the surprise from her face, but Gentle Wind's startled gasp was all the outlaw needed. Walden smiled, and turned to Hooker.

"Take the schoolteacher out back, tie her up with Swift Arrow."

The leer Hooker shot her made Maggie's skin crawl.

"You want me to search her, Jake, see if she's carrin' a message?" Hooker's eager voice spoke volumes of his intent and reminded Maggie of the other two outlaws who had tried to rape her. She shuddered.

"Not now," Jake growled. "You'll get your chance at her later . . . before we kill her."

Sunny opened her eyes just enough to see the dawn give its first peek of promising glory, then huddled farther under the blanket. Her backside settled against warm, hair-roughened muscles. Matt stirred, draped his arm over her waist, and pulled her closer. Sunny sighed her contentment, her pleasure. She had never slept in a man's arms before, never woken up feeling as safe and secure as she did this morning with him by her side. Yesterday, she had woken before him with the firm resolve this would not happen again. Today, she was just happy that it had, and wished she could wake up with him beside her every morning.

He kissed her cheek, and she rolled to her back, pleased to find him looking down at her with his gorgeous smile and hypnotizing midnight eyes.

"Morning, angel," he whispered. "Sleep good?"

She nodded, and smiled. "I wish there was no reason to get up."

"That makes two of us." He pressed his lips against hers in a brief kiss, then gently brushed the hair from her face with smooth, warm fingers. "Sunny, I—"

She pressed her finger to his lips, silencing his words. "Please," she whispered. "Don't say anything. I want this memory to stay like this forever."

He kissed the tip of her finger, then gently moved her hand. "We could make more memories together, angel."

"There isn't time," she whispered. "We need to leave."

Matt looked as though he wanted to say more, but only nodded. Sunny wondered if she had misunderstood his meaning about making memories. Had he meant something more than staying here and making love? Matt started to throw the blanket back from his body. She placed her hand over his.

"Wait."

He smiled, and looked expectantly at her. She swallowed her sudden nervousness.

"I . . ." She swallowed again. Should she tell him how she felt? Tell him about the love overflowing in her heart for him? Or would it only make things worse?

"Yes?" He cocked a brow.

"I . . . I'm going to miss you."

His smile faded, and sadness filled his gaze. "I'm going to miss you, too, angel."

He held her tenderly in his arms for a long time, neither of them saying anything. Sunny held back her tears, not wanting him to feel the moisture against his skin, not wanting him to know the depth of how bad her heart was breaking. She loved him so much, more than she had ever thought possible, and she realized she would always love him—forever. But she had to think of Running Bear and Gentle Wind. Her future was with them. Matt's future was in Wyoming, and he had made no mention of wanting them to join him there.

She sighed. "We must go," she whispered.

He hesitated, looked longingly at her one last time, then nodded.

He built the fire up and started coffee while she gathered her clothes and headed for the creek. By the time she returned, he was freshly shaved and dressed. He offered her a cup of coffee and the last of the dried fruit Jube had sent, along with some strips of hardtack. They ate in silence; then Matt readied the horses while she packed up the campsite and stowed their gear.

He brought the horses over, but instead of handing her Molly's lead rope, he dropped the reins of all three mounts and gathered her in his arms. Sunny clung to him, thinking of the danger waiting ahead, knowing when all this with Walden was over they would go their separate ways. She had known all along their parting was inevitable. And it was for the best, Sunny told herself. She understood his reluctance to forgive the death of his family. She would never ask him to look at her brother and sister and be reminded day in and day out. She would never ask him to accept what she couldn't change. The Comanches would always be a part of her life, a part of her heart.

He kissed her again with loving tenderness, and she held him tighter, grabbing every moment possible in his arms. All too soon, he set her from him, then stared into her eyes with his tortured midnight gaze. "I want you to know, I'll never forget you, angel."

She touched his smooth cheek with her palm and blinked back the tears welling in her eyes. "And I will never forget you, Matt. Ever."

He held her close for another moment, then stepped back. Sunny shivered at the cold which suddenly swept through her, and wondered if the rest of her life would always feel as empty as it did at this moment.

They rode out side by side, following the trail west that would take them to Outlaw Canyon, a heavy silence hanging between them for the first few miles. She saw Matt pull a cheroot from his pocket and light the end. A lazy smile formed on her lips as she watched the white smoke curl from between his lips. It reminded her of the other times she had watched in fascination at the way he blew the smoke rings into the air, reminded her of the feel of his lips on hers, on her body.

She smiled when he caught her looking, and he returned it with a broad one of his own. "Wanna see it again?" he asked teasingly, with a knowing look in his eyes.

"Definitely," she quipped.

Their shared laughter was like a balm to her aching emotions. Then silence fell between them again as they rode on for a ways.

"Can I ask you something, angel?" Matt softly inquired.

Her heart jumped with expectancy. She nodded.

"Why won't you talk about your father?"

Sunny drew her brows together in confusion. "I've told you much about Black Eagle."

Matt shook his head. "I'm talking about your real father. The man who sired you."

Sunny's heart stopped, gripped in a cold panic. The last thing she wanted to do was lie to Matt, not after everything they had shared. But how could she tell him the truth?

Chapter Fifteen

Matt caught the fear in her eyes before she turned away. His heart sank, though he couldn't have said if it was from her look, which spoke of a painful past, or the fact that he instantly felt her pull even farther from him. God, how would he live without her? How was he going to force himself to rise every morning, knowing he would face each day alone for the rest of his life? He knew he would never love another woman. He had waited all his life for her, but he sensed she was as much gone from him now as she would be when Walden was captured and the Indian brave returned to the fort.

"My father was not a nice man."

Her softly spoken words surprised him and drew his full attention. He stared at the taut lines in her face, the hatred suddenly burning in her eyes. A myriad of questions formed in his mind, but he asked none as he waited with hesitant expectancy for her to continue. Silence hung heavily for several long minutes, long enough for Matt to almost give up hope that she would tell him more.

"He used to beat my ma."

He guided Thunder closer and pulled her hand into his. "Did he ever hit you?"

She shook her head. "Only Mama. I used to wish he would hit me, though, instead of her . . . instead of the punishments."

He saw the tear slip from the corner of her eye and felt his heart rip in two. "What punishments?" he demanded softly, not wanting to frighten her with the intensity of his soaring temper at the faceless, cruel man who had fathered his beautiful little spitfire.

Sunny closed her eyes and shook her head. "There were many . . . but the snakes were the worst."

Matt sucked in a loud breath, reeling from the shock of her admission, then hatred unlike any he had ever known raged through his blood. He wanted to pull her from the mare, hold her in his arms, but he didn't. "Will you tell me about it?"

She opened her eyes, and he could see the painful remembrance hovering in her dulled blue stare. She sighed deeply. "I was eight the first time he did it. He was hurting Mama again. I tried to stop him, hit him with a broom. Made him so mad, he took me out to one of the stalls in the barn and strung me up with a rope so my toes would barely touch the floor. Then he left, and I thought surely Mama would come and cut me down like she always did before. But she never came. It got dark."

She lowered her head. Matt squeezed her hand tighter. "What happened?" he quietly urged, appalled at what she had been forced to endure, and hating to make her relive it now. But he strongly sensed her need to release the rest of this long-buried burden.

"*He* came back, carrying a large bag over his shoulder. He set it on the ground not far from my feet, opened the top, then left. When he closed the barn door, I couldn't see anything. I didn't know what all the hissing was, until the snakes came closer . . . and started to crawl up my legs."

Her tears fell harder. Matt stopped the horses, then did pull her over onto his lap, cradling her in his arms as she released the pent-up sobs which racked her body.

"God, I'm so sorry, angel," he whispered into her ear, knowing the words were inadequate, but at a loss as to what else to say.

A sickening tightness gripped his gut. He couldn't begin to understand what she had suffered. His own parents had been loving and kind to each other and their children. His pa hadn't been opposed to a good spanking when it was warranted, but Matt had never endured anything worse than a couple of licks with a hard switch.

He rocked her in his arms, held her close to his chest until her spent tears soaked his shirt and slowly began to subside. She turned her shimmering stare up at him.

Her chin quivered, and her fingers lightly touched the dampness on his shirtfront. "I'm sorry."

He took her hand and kissed her fingers. "No, angel, you have nothing to be sorry about." Matt felt as though he should be the one who was sorry. Sorry he had asked, and forced her to relive this memory. Sorry he hadn't been there for her, to protect her.

"I've . . . never told anyone before. Not even Maggie."

"I'm glad you told me, angel." He didn't know how long he sat there holding her. He didn't care. He would hold her for an eternity if she would let him. "What happened to your father, Sunny? Did the Comanches kill him when they took you and your ma?"

Sunny stiffened in his arms and slowly shook her head. "No, he was gone hunting the day Black Eagle led the raid on our rundown farm."

"How old were you?"

"Nine. Black Eagle told me later he took us captive because he felt sorry for us. He had seen the bruises on Mama's face, the fear and pain in my eyes despite the bold words which flew from my mouth. He later named me Morning Sky because he said my spirit was as bold and brilliant as the morning's first rays of sun.''

''He's right,'' Matt told her, smiling at her upturned face. He wished he had known Sunny as a young spitfire, wished he had been the one to take her away from the bastard who had fathered her and treated her so horribly.

''Black Eagle was kind to us, and soon fell in love with Mama. He was a good husband, a good father. We were happy and safe with the Comanches for a long time.''

Matt didn't want to, but he found himself wishing he had known Black Eagle. He would have liked to thank the man who had saved Sunny, the mistreated frightened girl, and given her courage and strength to become the stubborn, determined spitfire he loved. She felt so good in his arms, so right, that Matt had an overwhelming desire to tell her how much he cared, how much he loved her. But he remembered her words spoken just that morning. She had already told him goodbye, even though their time together was not yet over. She had let him know in no uncertain terms she would leave when this was over, and seek her happiness from now on with her brother and sister . . . with her family. He understood her commitment to the Comanches now, understood why she had never made any attempt to reunite with her real father after the raid, and more than anything, he wanted her to be happy again. At this moment, it mattered not at all that his own happiness would never be. He cared only about her, would always care about his little spitfire. He silently vowed to do everything within his power to keep her safe today, to help her find the happiness she sought—the happiness she so richly deserved with her family.

He kissed away the last of her tears and stroked the soft tendrils of hair from her face. She lifted her lips to his, and he couldn't have denied her if he had wanted. He captured her sweet mouth, faint with the taste of salt from her recent tears. He kissed her slowly, savoring every last second he could hold her in his arms, knowing all too soon it would end . . . forever.

Thunder snorted, breaking the silence which surrounded them on the prairie, then tossed his massive head. Reluctantly, Matt tore his lips from hers, tightened his arms for one last embrace, then pushed her slowly from him and looked into her eyes . . . eyes that he would remember every time he stepped outside his house and saw the skies over his ranch.

"We should get going."

She nodded, and he helped her slide down from his mount, then watched her with painful longing as she walked to where her mare had wandered off to graze. She swung herself onto the palomino's back and rejoined him.

He was glad to see the spark of determination returning in her eyes, and thrilled when she reached out and touched his arm with fingers that seared through his sleeve and warmed his skin. He wished now he had made a different suggestion, other than leaving.

"Thank you, Matt. For everything."

"You don't owe me any thanks, angel. I'd do anything for you."

Matt was puzzled at the way she quickly removed her hand, confused at the pained expression which tightened her face. She rode off before he could say anything. Matt followed, but didn't chase her. He realized she hurt as badly as he did over their certain parting. He wanted to believe it was because she loved him, but he didn't dare let himself think about it. To know she loved him—even half as much as he did her, which was with every breath in his body and every beat of his heart—would only make it that much harder to watch her walk away. And as it was, he was already certain he wasn't going to survive.

Matt watched Sunny get farther ahead, and he nudged Thunder just a little faster. The tightening in his gut grew worse, and he realized it was more than just heartache. He had been fighting the feeling all morning, but with every mile they covered, it had gotten a little worse. Something wasn't right. They were riding into more trouble than they were expecting. He sensed it, even before the hollow, scared feeling settled in the pit of his stomach.

The sun rode low in the waning afternoon sky. The lush grass and trees of the prairie were hours behind, and still all Sunny saw ahead was a sea of desert sand, rocks, and sparsely dotted scrubs. Where was the ravine Red Cloud told her about? Where was the damn canyon? She tucked her hat brim lower, shielding her eyes from the sun and the gust of heated, dust-coating wind that kicked up again.

Outlaw Canyon was a haven for thieves and murderers because of its remoteness. A place lawmen called ''no man's land,'' and with good reason, Sunny thought. A man could lose himself fast out here, and she had heard that the only law to make its way consistently to these parts was Judge Colt—The Gun. It was not a place she wanted to be lost in, but that was exactly what she was . . . and now she had to figure out a way to tell Matt.

''How much farther?'' He reined his horse a little closer, then grabbed his hat before it could blow off in another sudden gust of wind.

Sunny swallowed back her nervousness, then wished she hadn't as she choked on the dirt that was forever seeping into her mouth here and started coughing. Matt leaned over and took hold of Molly's lead rope, bringing both horses to a stop. Sunny accepted the canteen he offered, drank of the lukewarm liquid, then sighed her relief. Short-lived relief, she realized as she looked into Matt's hard, wind-chapped face. She had to tell him.

''Matt, I . . .'' She sighed, then tried again. ''I . . .''

His eyes narrowed. He placed one hand, palm downward, on top of his thigh and leaned slightly closer. ''I asked you how much farther we had to go, and now you're stalling again. I thought you knew the way to Outlaw Canyon.''

''I do . . . sort of.''

"What exactly do you mean, 'sort of'? Sort of like the law knows this place exists, but can't find it? Or sort of like we might be a mile or two off course?"

She didn't answer, and Matt blew out an exasperated breath. "Damnation, woman! Talk to me!"

"Oh, all right," she snapped. "Yes, I'm lost. Red Cloud mapped out the way to the canyon for me, but he thought I'd be riding in from the south, not from the north."

"Red Cloud? Who the hell is Red Cloud?"

She could see the burning suspicion in his midnight eyes, as well as a spark of anger that oddly reminded her of the jealous look she had seen whenever White Bear's name came up between them. If he wasn't so angry with her at the moment, she might have chuckled, since Red Cloud already had a wife and three children. But she doubted Matt would find any humor at his misguided jealousy.

"He's a friend. A Kiowa brave who's been helping me pass messages back and forth to Colonel Grierson. I was supposed to speak with him again the day of the stampede, but I missed our meeting."

Matt sat back in his saddle and stared at the unfriendly land around them. "So what will Red Cloud do now?"

"I'm not sure. He'll either be waiting at the south entrance to the canyon, or he may have gone back to the fort to inform Grierson I never showed up."

Matt shook his head. "I don't get it. If we're supposed to be coming from the south, then why aren't we?"

Sunny turned away from his probing stare. "Because Gentle Wind saw soldiers headed that way."

"And that's a bad thing?" Matt grated.

Sunny nodded. "Captain McGuire was leading the troops."

Matt's brow furrowed in puzzlement. "McGuire? Wasn't he the same captain with you when Walden attacked and killed Danny?"

"Yes."

Matt shook his head. "I don't understand, Sunny. Why are

we avoiding the army? Especially if Colonel Grierson's trying to help?''

Sunny met his flat, hard stare. Her shoulders slumped as much from the intense heat in his eyes as from her growing weariness of the troubles that had constantly plagued her over the last few weeks. ''I strongly suspect McGuire's working with Walden. The day of the ambush when Danny died, the captain was the only one besides Grierson who knew about the detour I took to Red Cloud's village to bring food. There was no other way for Walden to know where to find us. The payroll shipment was phony. It was all a setup. Walden was supposed to make his move several miles away where Colonel Grierson and his troops waited. Problem was, Walden knew that, too, and had his own plans. He wasn't expecting your brother and the cowhands to be there. McGuire was just as surprised. Nothing went right that day.''

Matt turned from her, and not just his sight. She saw the tension in his jaw, in the hands gripping the reins to his horse, and felt a fear unlike any she had ever known. He was angry because she had not told him the truth sooner. She was angry with herself for not trusting him before now. But she had done it hoping to keep him safe, wanting him to stay away from Walden, and all she had accomplished was to bring further trouble down on them.

Sunny tucked her head. ''I'm sorry. I know you have every reason to hate me, and I wouldn't blame you for riding away and leaving me out here.''

Matt's hand gently took hold of her chin and forced her to look up at him. ''I don't hate you, Sunny, you know that. But no more secrets, no more lies and half-truths. If McGuire's suspected of being in cahoots with Walden, why would Grierson send *him* up here?''

''I don't know. The last time I spoke with Red Cloud was the day you found me and Shorty, but at that time, he hadn't talked with Grierson for over a week. I wouldn't even know about McGuire's presence here if it weren't for Gentle Wind.''

Matt lowered his hand from her face and looked away. Sunny wanted to reach out and grab his hand back, beg him not to leave her, beg him to forgive her. But she knew that would be asking too much. She realized now that all she had accomplished by trying to keep him safe was to make their inevitable parting that much easier for him, and devastatingly harder for herself. Having his trust had made her feel good, complete. Losing it was like ripping her heart out. She felt the tear slip from her eye and quickly brushed it away.

There was a lethal calm in the gaze he turned back on her. "Far as I can see, there's only one thing to do."

Sunny held her breath, dug her nails into her palms to keep her hands from visibly shaking.

"We head south."

"But—"

"But nothing. It's the only way you know how to get into the canyon. We'll just have to keep a close eye out for McGuire and his men."

Sunny nodded, pleased and afraid. She wanted to throw herself into his arms, thank him for giving her another chance, thank him for not abandoning her. But she kept her seat. She knew enough about him now to know his tense stance and closed expression were signs of his controlled anger.

She made to nudge Molly forward, but Matt's hand on her arm stopped her. She looked up at him, wary and hurt at the suspicion lingering in his dark depths.

"Is there anything else you haven't told me?" His voice was low and gruff.

Sunny swallowed the sudden lump in her throat and shook her head, then quickly turned away before he could read the lie in her eyes.

Will reined the gray to a halt atop the small rise and tipped the brim of his hat, shielding his gaze against the late afternoon sun. Beyond the sparsely rooted trees and scrubs, he saw the soldiers camped beside a narrow stream, their horses grazing on small patches of grass sprouting through the dirt and rocks that covered the desert land this far north of the Indian Territory. He nudged the gray forward.

Two soldiers, rifles held at the ready, stood at the edge of their camp and greeted him as he approached. He reined the gray to a stop, then casually crossed his arms over the tall horn on his saddle.

"What can we do for you, mister?"

"Colonel Grierson said I could find Captain Roberts here."

The taller of the two blue-clad privates stepped forward and lowered his rifle. "Captain Roberts got hurt right before we left Fort Sill. Captain McGuire's in charge."

"I'd like to talk to Captain McGuire, then," Will told the young private.

"His tent's at the other end of camp," the soldier informed him, then turned to point the direction Will should head.

Will nodded his thanks and nudged the gray forward, staring at the dozen or so soldiers Grierson had told him should already be out looking for Sunny. Why weren't they? he wondered.

No one paid him much attention as he rode through camp toward the large white tent at the other end. Reining to a halt, he dismounted. When he turned to walk the rest of the way, he saw the Indian dressed in buckskin pants and shirt. His long black hair hung loose and dragged in the dirt. The brave lay on his side near the tent, his legs and arms bound tightly behind him, a shorter length of rope tying them together so he couldn't sit or stand.

The Indian stared at him with black, hate-filled eyes. Will narrowed his gaze and eyed him right back. There was a long gash crusted with dried blood running the length of his bronze cheek and a wide, purpling bruise above his right eye.

The front tent flap was thrown back, and a man who looked to Will to be barely over thirty stepped outside.

"Captain McGuire?" Will stepped forward and extended his hand.

"Who are you?" The pock-faced officer growled, ignoring Will's gesture.

Will took an instant dislike to the man, but it had more to do with the shifting look in his brown eyes than his rudeness. He lowered his hand back to his side. "Name's Will Hollister. Colonel Grierson suggested I stop here."

"Grierson? Why?" McGuire's eyes narrowed with suspicion, but Will was more concerned with why the man's face paled at the mention of the colonel.

Grierson seemed like a decent fella to him, going out of his way and all to help Sunny, not someone who would inspire fear. "I'm looking for my sister. Got it on good authority Jake Walden's taken her, and he's up here somewhere. Also looking for another woman headed up this way, leading a cattle drive."

"Su—" McGuire coughed, then hacked like he had something caught in his throat. Will wasn't the least bit fooled. The captain regained control of his composure, standing a little taller and his shoulders just a little more squared. "Sorry 'bout that, been weeks tryin' to get over this blamed cough. Also sorry to tell you, we haven't seen anybody up 'round here. Except for that Injun."

Will didn't look where the captain pointed. "Do you or any of your men know the way inside Outlaw Canyon?"

"Nope, 'fraid not."

The Indian grunted loudly.

McGuire spun around. "You keep quiet, Injun, or you'll get another beatin'."

"The man was only clearing his throat." Will spit the words out with contempt. "Just like you were doing."

"Look, Mr. Hollister." McGuire took a step forward and turned a cold eye on him. Will crossed his arms over his chest. "That Injun's a renegade, and this is army business, not yours. Now, I'm right sorry about your sister, but we can't help you. Even if we knew the way into that canyon, we're waitin' on a payroll shipment, and I can't spare any of my men."

Will slightly shifted his stare to the Indian. The brave's face showed nothing; but Will was good at reading eyes, and he could tell that the brave had something on his mind he wanted to share. He looked back at McGuire. "Then, we have a little problem, *Captain McGuire*, because I've got a signed piece of paper stating that any and all men under Colonel Grierson's command or responsibility are to be at my disposal as needed. Right here in my pocket." Will tapped his shirt pocket with one finger hard enough to rustle the paper inside and forced himself not to chuckle in the captain's blanched faced. He was impressed McGuire recovered as quickly as he did.

"So what is it you want, Mr. Hollister?" McGuire snapped.

"Well, what I'd like first is something to eat. Then I'd like a few words with that Indian."

"You can't, he's a prisoner."

Will tapped his pocket again. "I can. Grierson's orders."

McGuire jerked his chin up, shaking the short brown curls on his head. "Maybe I should just take a look at those orders."

"And maybe I'd be inclined to show them to you if you'd have been a little more cooperative. But instead, I think I'll just report you to the colonel." Will deepened his angry tone. "Now, point me in the direction of some grub. And I hope to hell it's not beans!"

McGuire huffed, told him to follow the rest of the men headed to dinner, then turned and walked back into his tent, closing the flap behind him. Will looked at the Indian, surprised to see a smile curling the corners of his mouth. Then he turned and slowly made as though to follow the other soldiers walking toward a tent in the middle of camp. He waited until most of the soldiers had gotten their plates and wandered off; then he dropped back and slipped out of sight.

Will sauntered along behind the row of army tents as though doing nothing more than taking an evening stroll. When McGuire's tent came into view, he widened his path and approached the Indian from the side. Will motioned for the brave's silence as he approached, then crouched beside the Indian.

"McGuire's gone," the brave said, nodding his head toward the tent. "Don't know how long."

Will nodded his understanding at their need to hurry. "Do you know something about my sister?"

"The schoolteacher?"

Will nodded, his heart pumping faster.

"Walden has her. And McGuire lied. He knows the way to the canyon, because he meets with Walden there."

Will narrowed his stare, cocked a cautious brow. "How do you know?" he grated lowly.

"I have followed him."

The brave's eyes spoke the truth, further confirming Will's already formed suspicions about the captain. The soldier wasn't to be trusted, and he had lied about Maggie and Sunny. Why?

"Why are you being held? What are your crimes?" Will asked.

"I have done nothing."

"Are you a renegade?"

"I do not live on the reservation."

Will wasn't sure if he should trust the brave or not. He needed to get into that canyon, but there was no guarantee this Comanche wouldn't kill him. Will glanced around the camp. No one came, but he knew time was running short. He needed to make a decision.

"Will you guide me into the canyon in exchange for your freedom?"

The Comanche brave nodded.

"All right, I'll be back after dark. I'll help you escape then."

The brave drew puzzled black brows together. "Escape? Why do you not use that paper you have from the colonel?"

Will took the slip from his pocket and unfolded it. "The only thing on this paper is a couple of possible names for my child who's about to be born. But Grierson did send me here, and once I get in the canyon, you're free to go. Now, you still want to help me?"

The brave nodded.

Will stood and walked back the way he had come. He took the plate of beans and biscuits the army cook offered up, and when he had his belly full, he retrieved his horse and then went looking for McGuire. He found the captain sitting in on a hand of poker with his men.

"Come to tell you, I've changed my mind."

McGuire looked up, perturbed. "About what?" he grumbled.

"Needing you, or your men. I'll give your regards to Grierson, Captain McGuire." Will shoved his hat on his head, mounted his horse and rode out of the camp just as the sun was starting to set.

Chapter Sixteen

Sunny wanted to cry with joy when the rocky ravine Red Cloud had described came into view on the dusky horizon, wanted to shout her relief that there had been no sign of McGuire or the soldiers. But both those desires paled in comparison to how much she wanted to throw her arms around Matt's neck and thank him for not giving up. She doubted he would welcome her touch, though, since he had said nothing as they traveled the last few hours, doubted that he would ever want anything to do with her again if he found out she had lied earlier.

Guilt ate at her for not telling Matt her secret—the secret she had kept hidden from everyone. She had told Matt so much about her life already, trusted him with more of her heart, her past, than she had with anyone—ever. But the time for truth had passed. Twice now she could have told him and knew he would have understood. Twice, she had held back. For so long she had tried to pretend it wasn't true and push it forever from her mind. Living with the Comanches, she had been able to do that . . . until everything had been taken away.

"Red Cloud said to keep to the right and head toward that

ravine,'' she told Matt, pointing to the steep-sided wall of the narrow desert valley. ''There should be a passage about halfway down that leads into the canyon.''

Matt nodded, and headed that way. Sunny followed, leading the bay.

She sighed, and chewed on her bottom lip. Was he ever going to speak to her again? Or was he so angry he could never forgive her? She couldn't stand this silence between them. They were about to ride into Outlaw Canyon, and although Sunny felt certain she would ride back out with Swift Arrow and Matt, there was still a nagging concern that *something* could go wrong.

Matt suddenly reined his mount to a halt. Had he been thinking the same thing? she wondered. Sunny halted her mare beside him and guided the bay around to her opposite side.

She looked up at him. The tender warmth in his gaze stole her breath. She blinked her surprise.

''Did you expect me to still be mad?'' He smiled.

She nodded. He took her hand in his, slipped her glove off, and gently kissed the backs of her fingers.

''Sunny, I understand everything you've done, you did for your brother and sister. And I never believed Danny's death was your fault.''

Cautious relief washed over her. There was something in his tone that frightened her, though she couldn't put a name to it. ''But . . . you've been so quiet all afternoon.''

''I admit I wasn't too happy when you finally told me about McGuire and the truth about the ambush. And getting lost in this godforsaken place was a challenge, but that's not what's kept me quiet.''

''Then, what?'' she asked softly, doubts hammering through her mind, panic seeping in to claim her heart. Surely he wouldn't leave her *now,* not when she needed him so much.

''Aw, Sunny,'' he sighed and shook his head. He tugged at her hand, pulling her close enough to slip his arm around her waist; then he lifted her from Molly's back and sat her in his lap. "Don't look so scared, angel, I'm not going anywhere." He removed her hat and held it at her back as he looped his arms around her, pulling her to his chest.

Sunny's heart soared at the familiar endearment, and she wound her arms behind his back. Pressing her cheek against his shirt, she closed her eyes and deeply inhaled his scent, knowing she would never forget how good he smelled, how passionate, and strong, and manly. His lips brushed against her hair.

"I've been quiet thinking about you," he whispered. "And before we walk into that canyon, there's something I want you to know. You're the best thing that's ever *fallen* into my life. I want you to be happy, angel, that's all I care about . . . and if you ever need for anything, anything at all, I'll be there." There was an undeniable tremor in his voice.

Sunny managed a trembling smile at his reminder of how they met, and bittersweet joy filled her heart. He might not love her, might not be able to accept her ties to her family and the Comanches; but she knew he cared a great deal for her . . . and she told herself that would have to be enough.

"I want you to be happy, too, Matt. And I hope the dream Danny wasn't able to finish with you to the end still comes true for you."

He was so still, she might have thought he had stopped breathing if his heart wasn't racing beneath her ear. Sunny tilted her head back and looked up at him, stunned at the shimmering moisture in the corners of his eyes. Before she could find her voice, Matt kissed her softly on the tip of her nose and placed her hat back on her head.

"It's almost dark. We best be going, angel."

Night fell, and the moon beamed its soft glow over the camp. Will cursed the lack of clouds in the black sky and the stars twinkling like a million torches. From where he stood beneath the shadowing tree, he could see the brave clearly in the damning moonlight. One soldier sat watch a few yards away from the Comanche. McGuire's tent was dark. Will could see the yellow glimmer of the campfires near the center of camp and heard enough muffled laughter and groans to determine some of the men at least were still engaged in playing poker. He hoped McGuire was one of them.

Will turned his sight back to the soldier on watch and smiled when he saw the guard's head start to nod. He waited until the soldier's head fell against his raised knees and stayed put for a good long while. Then he crouched low and hurried across the moonlit distance until he came up behind McGuire's tent. On silent steps he edged his way to the corner and peered around the canvas. The guard slept on. Will came up behind the soldier and knocked him in the head with the butt of the knife he carried; then he crouched down and cut loose the brave's bindings.

The brave jumped to his feet. Will turned and headed back behind the tent, motioning for the brave to follow. Crouching low again, he retraced his steps to the shadows beneath the trees, then ran to his tethered horse down the stream a short way. The Indian followed close behind.

Will mounted the gray and helped the brave jump onto the horse's back, then crossed the stream and rode hard for several miles before he stopped. Dismounting, he faced the Indian under the moon's light. Will smiled. The brave smiled back.

"That was almost *too* easy," Will commented.

The brave shook his head. "McGuire rode out soon after you. The soldiers get lazy when their leader is gone. I would guess the captain left to tell Walden of your visit."

Will nodded. "I expected as much. I made sure McGuire didn't know for certain whether I was going on to the canyon or back to Fort Sill. That means Walden will be cautious, but he won't know if or when we're coming."

"You are smart man, Mr. Hollister, or foolish. I have not decided."

Will chuckled. "Sometimes, I don't know either. And the name's Will." He extended his hand.

The brave shook it. "I am White Bear."

Will jerked his head back with a start. "White Bear?" He gripped the brave's hand just a little harder. "Are you from Black Eagle's tribe?"

The brave stared at him suspiciously. "How do you know me?"

Shocked, Will released the brave's hand and stepped back. How could that be? Was it possible Sunny had been wrong?

"I thought you were dead," he whispered incredulously.

"I am not. But why would you know this if it were true?" The brave's voice was low, challenging.

"Because that's what Morning Sky thought."

The brave's jaw clenched. He crossed his arms over his chest. "Morning Sky is dead. Do not speak her name."

Will stared into White Bear's cold, black eyes. "Morning Sky is just as much alive as you, White Bear. She is known as Sunny now."

"You lie, white man!"

Will shook his head. "I found her two years ago, near Bear Creek where the army raided a Comanche village. Chief Black Eagle's village. I took her to my ranch. My family and I took care of her, saved her life."

White Bear's narrowed gaze held disbelief and anger. "Where is she?" His voice was low, cautious.

Until they could get this settled, Will was glad the brave was unarmed and the only weapons at hand were the guns strapped around his own hips, and the knife in his boot. "Somewhere up here. She's headed to Outlaw Canyon."

White Bear lifted his square chin higher. "Why?"

"I'll explain on the way to the canyon." Will walked over to the gray and mounted. White Bear followed, then hesitated beside the horse. Will held his hand out. The brave looked at him with sharp, questioning eyes, then grabbed Will's forearm and swung himself onto the back of the mount.

* * *

Yellow light shone through the lone front window of the soddie, but Matt could see no movement inside. He saw nothing stirring in the moonlit gray shadows surrounding the hideout either, except two saddled horses ground tied out front. The constricting knot which had sat in his belly all afternoon tightened further. Something wasn't right; he sensed it in every taut nerve in his body as he stared down at the hideout from the rocky advantage. With four men and Swift Arrow—hell, even the kid if he was mean enough—Matt was concerned at the lack of activity and the absence of any posted guards.

He glanced at Sunny, stretched flat on her stomach beside him on the rock ledge, and even in the dim light of night, he could see the apprehension on her face. He knew she was as troubled as he about Walden's obvious neglect in safety. After entering the canyon, she had guided them with confidence along the outer edges of the ravine. They hid the horses a safe distance away and cautiously approached the spot where Red Cloud had said one of the outlaws should be on watch—the same outlaw they planned to disarm before proceeding—but no one was there. He questioned her then about this plan to ambush Walden on his nightly walk, wondering if the outlaw's routine would turn out to be another misassumption, and still curious how she knew about the habit in the first place. She brushed his concern aside, telling him not to worry, but he knew when he took her trembling hand in his that her steadfast calm was only a front, even before he had looked into her anxious eyes.

The front door of the soddie swung open. Sunny's hand came to rest on top of his as two men he had never seen before walked outside, one dressed in dark denims and shirt, the other wearing an officer's uniform.

"It's Captain McGuire," Sunny whispered in a low, condemning voice.

Matt stared at the officer as he mounted one of the horses.

A searing hatred seeped into his bloodstream. *That's the bastard responsible for Danny's death. Him and Walden.*

"Do you recognize the other man?"

"No."

Probably one of Walden's men. Maybe even the one they had expected to find on watch, he surmised as the two men reeled the horses around and rode away from the hideout. Matt started to push himself up, but Sunny's hand tightened over his, halting him.

"Let him go."

He glared down into her shadowed face. "Why the hell should I?" he grated.

She stared at him with knowing eyes. "Grierson will see he's punished."

"Yeah, well, he can have him when I'm through." Matt backed away from the edge of the rock, but Sunny refused to let go of his hand.

Her pleading eyes pierced the short distance between them. "Please . . . I need you."

The soft-spoken words stopped his heart, and he slowly settled himself back down beside her. The corners of her mouth lifted in a small, grateful smile. Matt sighed. She needed him. He wouldn't leave her. He couldn't.

Movement from the hideout grabbed his attention. He turned as Walden stepped out to the porch. Sunny drew in a sharp breath and squeezed his hand with surprising strength. The outlaw raised his arms over his head and stretched with the ease of a man who didn't have a care in the world; then he stepped off the porch.

Matt watched with amazement as Walden sauntered into the night, close below where they hid. His little spitfire was right again. The outlaw was taking a damn evening stroll!

"Let's go," she whispered beside him, releasing his hand.

Matt followed her down the narrow path, and when they reached the bottom, he stepped in front and took the lead. The hideout was soon a good distance behind them. Walden turned and strode through a small grove of thick trees. Sunny tapped his shoulder. Matt stopped and looked back. She motioned her intention to circle around in front of the outlaw, and for him to stay at the man's back. Matt nodded, then waited until she disappeared in the darkness before drawing up closer. Walden stood in a bright spot of moonlight filtering through the sparse foliage and casually puffed on a fresh-lit cheroot. Matt expected to hear Sunny call out to the outlaw any second, but he didn't expect her to suddenly appear in the moon's light with her gun drawn and pointed straight at Walden's face. His heart leapt into his throat. *What the hell is she doing?*

"I've been expectin' you, girlie." Walden didn't move, except to take another slow draw on the cigar.

"Before or after you shot Gray Wolf?"

Venom laced his little spitfire's words, but Matt didn't look at her face. He stayed focused on Walden's gun, strapped around the outlaw's wide hips, and gripped the handle of his six-shooter tighter.

"Just tryin' to help you out." Walden's sarcasm was heavy. "I thought you were dead, like your ma."

"I wish you were."

Walden grunted. "You gave it a damn good try, girlie."

Matt tensed when the outlaw lifted one hand up toward his face.

"And now I get a second chance."

"You gonna shoot my other eye out, or do the job right this time?"

Matt jerked back with a start. Why hadn't Sunny mentioned she had hit the outlaw when she had shot at him during the raid?

"Believe me," Sunny warned, her voice low. "I won't miss this time."

"You're not gonna shoot me, girlie." Walden chuckled, shaking his head. "You've come for Swift Arrow. You fire that gun, my men'll be down on you like flies on horseshit."

"Well, I've known you long enough to know how to deal with flies and horseshit."

Matt cocked a brow, confused as much by her tone as her revealing words. *Just how long has she known this man?* Remembering his concern about no more lies and half-truths between them—and her nodded agreement—he felt his temper rise a notch.

Walden laughed. "You always did have a cocky mouth on ya. If I remember right, it's what got you into trouble."

"Your memory's as lousy as you are."

"Oh, yeah." Walden's sneer was as clear as glass in his tone. "You were pretty good with brooms, too."

Shocked, Matt loudly sucked in his breath. He barely glimpsed Sunny's widened eyes and pale face before Walden spun around, gun drawn. Matt fired, knocking the revolver from the outlaw's hold. Walden yelled and grabbed at his hand. Sunny quickly ran and picked the gun up off the ground. Matt stepped forward within inches of the outlaw's face and stuck the barrel of his gun in the man's gut.

"Who are you?"

Matt saw no fear in the outlaw's eye.

"Who the hell are you?" Jake snarled.

With a start, Matt realized the outlaw's eye was the same shade of blue as Sunny's, which confirmed his already growing suspicion. *This man is her father.* Why hadn't she told him?

The burning question was but a spark to the anger raging through him at the memory of what he had done to Sunny as a child. A blinding light filled his vision. He grabbed Walden's shirtfront and jerked him closer. "You bastard."

Sunny's fingers settled tightly on his shoulder. "Matt, don't. We need to get out of here before someone comes."

He shrugged her hand away and stared at Walden. "You got any last words, 'cause you've got two seconds left to live. One."

Walden's lips formed a sinister smile. "I got some words for ya. Maggie Hollister and Gentle Wind."

Sunny gasped.

Matt narrowed his stare. "What about them?"

"Jake?"

Startled, Matt took a split second glance at the kid who came running through the trees, and Walden used that moment to react.

The outlaw grabbed the barrel of the gun, shoving it upward at the same time he plowed one fist into Matt's chest. The shot Matt fired went aimlessly into the air as he slammed back against a hard trunk. He grunted at the stunning impact that knocked the breath from him and shook his body. The gun slipped from his fingers. Walden charged him. Matt sucked in a quick breath and pushed away from the tree, blocking the first punch headed for his face, and ramming his fist into Walden's gut. The outlaw didn't even flinch, but sent his fist flying up and caught Matt under his chin. His head snapped back. Matt growled, ignoring the sharp pain, and lunged at Walden again. He got in two good blows to Walden's midsection before the outlaw landed a hard punch to his jaw and sent him staggering sideways.

"Hit him again, and I'll kill you," Sunny warned heatedly.

Matt gained his footing and raised his fists. Walden didn't come at him. He realized the man wasn't moving because Sunny had a gun to his back. Matt quickly swept his gaze over the surrounding area. *Damn! The kid's gone.*

Matt grabbed his gun and hat off the ground, holstered his six-shooter, then hurried over and took Walden's gun, which Sunny held on the outlaw. He stared briefly into her worried gaze, then turned away. He knew the look in her eyes wasn't for their current desperate situation, but for the truth that had been revealed. Even if there was time for him to ease her concern, he wasn't sure he could. She had lied to him, and the pain was still gnawing at him pretty hard. Would she never trust him?

"Come on, we need to get out of here." He took hold of

Sunny's arm, then shoved the gun hard into Walden's back. "Start moving, you piece of scum, and make it fast."

Walden took one step.

"Hold it right there, ya ain't going nowhere."

Matt's heart hammered against his ribs at the gruff command from behind. Sunny's muscles tensed beneath his grip.

"Now, drop those guns. All of 'em."

Walden spun around and grabbed the gun Matt held, then reached for the one in his holster. The outlaw pointed one gun at Matt's chest and the other at Sunny. Matt's pulse roared in his ears when she hesitated. Finally, she tossed her Colt to the ground. Seconds later, a tall, hawk-nosed man stepped forward and retrieved it.

"About damn time you showed up, Hooker."

"That blasted schoolteacher got loose. Jumped me. I was tusslin' with her."

Matt glanced sideways at Sunny. Her panicked, widened eyes matched his own concern. The outlaws had Maggie, and God only knew what they had done to her. Matt's anger mounted.

"Where's she now?" Walden demanded.

"I had to knock her out. Left her in the hideout with the girl. Luke's watchin' 'em."

Girl? Gentle Wind! Matt's fists bunched at his sides; then fear gripped him when, heedless of the gun aimed at her, Sunny stormed across the short distance and faced Walden at close range.

"What have you done?" She stood with hands on hips and glared up at the outlaw. Matt's heart pounded faster.

Walden curled his lips back. "Nothing yet. I knew you'd wanna watch."

Sunny let out a fierce cry Matt recognized as angered pain; then she spit in the outlaw's face. Walden backhanded her across the mouth. Matt growled, and lunged for the outlaw as Sunny went sprawling in the dirt. Walden stopped him with the gun pointed in his face.

"No!" Sunny screamed. She scrambled to her feet, started to rush the outlaw from the side, but Hooker grabbed her arm and halted her flight. Sunny struggled against the man's hold.

"Damn! She's a fighter, too," Hooker complained, jerking hard enough on Sunny's arm that Matt saw her wince.

Matt seethed inwardly, angry with Walden and with himself for not doing a better job of protecting Sunny.

Walden cocked a bushy pale brow. "Seems she don't want you to die. Why is that?"

Matt stood silently. Walden pressed the barrel of the gun against his nose. Matt didn't move.

"Leave him alone. It's me you want," Sunny snapped.

Matt wanted to groan at the caring note in her tone. He could tell by the glint in Walden's eye, he had heard it, too. Matt had no doubt the outlaw would use it against his little spitfire.

"Well hell, lady, if you're offerin' yourself up, I'll get in line for some of that." Hooker's voice was full of the leering stare Matt could imagine he was running over Sunny's body. His blood boiled.

"Watch it, Hooker," Walden warned, but his stare never left Matt's. "You don't know who that little girlie is."

"I know she's the one you been huntin' down all these weeks and won't tell anybody why," Hooker argued. "What makes her so special, Jake? I ain't known ya to go chasin' after a woman before, and you sure as hell never squawked at sharin' one."

"She's not gonna be shared with the likes of you, Hooker. Or *you,* mister. What's your name?" Walden pulled back on the hammer. Click. "The rest of your name, Matt."

"Lanier."

Walden took a deep breath and released it slowly. The patch over his eye shifted across his broad cheek when he drew his brows together. "Matt Lanier? Now, why's that name sound familiar? You wanted for something?"

"No."

"Ever rustle cattle down in Texas."

"No."

"Lanier?" Hooker mused. "Wasn't that ranger's name Lanier? You know the one I'm talking about, Jake. The one who pert near caught us a few years back, rustlin' cattle south of Fort Worth."

Matt's thoughts jumped back into the past. Oak Valley was south of Fort Worth. Matt thought about the two rustlers giving Will and the other ranchers trouble over five years ago. It was those rustlers who had brought Matt to the town, and Ashley into his life. He had come close to catching the outlaws, but not close enough to get a good look at them. It was one of the few cases he had never solved. But *those* two men were named Charlie Cutter and Harold Picket.

"You that ranger?" Walden asked, tilting his head slightly.

"No," Matt lied. No sense in giving the man information to use against him. Outlaws weren't fond of lawmen, even ex-lawmen.

"Name Charlie Cutter ring any bells?"

Matt didn't move, not even so much as to blink an eye. "Can't say that it does."

Walden lifted one corner of his mouth in a half smile and lowered the gun to Matt's chest. "You're lyin', Ranger, and now I'm gonna have to kill ya."

"No!" Sunny cried.

"Maggie? Maggie, are you all right."

Maggie heard the hushed, worried whispers and fought her way through the blackness. Closer. Closer.

"Maggie?"

She was almost there.

"Maggie, are you all right?"

The dull pounding in her head increased as she fought her way toward the voice. The foggy darkness began to lift. Maggie moaned.

"Maggie? Maggie, wake up."

The fear in Gentle Wind's voice roused her further. She had to get to the girl. She had to help her. Slowly, she opened one eye. The small bronze face hovering above wavered in watery lines. Pain sliced through her head. Maggie groaned and closed her eyes.

"Maggie, please wake up."

Maggie forced her eyes open again and stared at Gentle Wind through half-lowered lashes, then at the young boy kneeling beside the girl.

"Are you all right, ma'am?"

Maggie opened her mouth to speak and grimaced at the sharp agony in her jaw. Lifting a hand, she touched the sore flesh of her cheek and the corner of her oversized lip. Her fingers came away with blood.

"You shouldn't argue with Hooker, ma'am," the boy told her. "He don't like that."

"So . . . I no . . . noticed," she choked the words out.

"I brought you some water, ma'am. Feel like sittin' up?"

Maggie nodded, then placed her hands against the dirt floor on either side of her and, using her elbows, lifted her head and shoulders off the ground. The long hours on the horse, Walden's powerful blows to her face, and Hooker's hard fist hitting her after he had grabbed her breast earlier and she had reached down and bit him, all combined in one scorching blast of agony as she moved. She closed her eyes against the pain shooting through her body.

"Here, let me help you."

She felt the boy's hands against her back, felt him gently push her up. Maggie opened her eyes. Gentle Wind's anxious brown eyes stared out from her worried face. The girl knelt on the floor, her hands tied behind her.

"Maggie, are you all right?"

She nodded. "I'll be fine. What about you?"

"Luke has been kind to me. He gave me food."

Maggie tried to look behind her, but her sore neck refused to turn that far. As though sensing her dilemma, the boy stood and came around, then knelt and offered her the cup of water. She took it gratefully and sipped.

"Thank you," she whispered to the boy. "And thank you for taking care of Gentle Wind . . . Luke."

The boy nodded, and tucked his head shyly. "I don't like to see folks sufferin', ma'am. 'Specially if I can help."

Maggie saw him turn a quick smile toward Gentle Wind, which the girl returned, and sensed a tenderness in the boy that wasn't shared with the hard, cruel men around him.

"I got some fresh water and a clean cloth." He pointed toward the table. Maggie saw the bowl of water and neatly folded cloth beside the rifle. "If you'll let me, I'll clean that cut on your face. You don't want it to get infected."

"I'd be much obliged, Luke."

He stood and walked the short distance across the room, then returned with the basin of water, the cloth, and a length of rope she hadn't seen earlier. He knelt and set the bowl beside her. There was a sad, almost pained look in the warm, green eyes which stared at her from his round, boyish face.

"I'm right sorry, ma'am, but Hooker told me to tie you up. I didn't want to do it while you were unconscious. If he comes back, though, and I ain't done it, he's gonna be mad."

Maggie didn't want this boy hurt because of her and moved her sore, weary arms so that her hands met behind her back. "Go ahead. Do that first, just in case."

When he had finished tying her hands, Luke dabbed gently at the cut on her cheek and lip, and all the while Maggie noted that Gentle Wind knelt at his side. Judging by the silent looks that passed between them, and the way Luke chatted on like this was nothing more than a church social, Maggie realized that somehow through the nightmare that was their lives at the moment, these two young people had managed to become friends.

Chapter Seventeen

Sunny walked ahead of the outlaws, purposefully keeping her head held high and the tears from her eyes, but the deep mortification in her heart was threatening to kill her. Her father hadn't shot Matt; but now he had a good idea of the depth of her feelings for the rancher, and Sunny had no doubt he would use that knowledge to hurt her—by hurting Matt. She had wanted to keep him away from her father, away from the evil man's clutches. In wanting to keep Matt safe, she had succeeded in doing just the opposite. Matt's refusal to even look at her as he walked beside her, though, was the hardest of all to bear.

She should have told Matt the truth. Then he wouldn't have charged the outlaw in a blind fury after her father had mentioned the attack with the broom. She shouldn't have let her father goad her into the verbal sparring match with his taunting comments about the past, but she hadn't counted on her hatred for the man consuming her so completely, dislodging all rational thought. It was her fault. And now Matt hated her. She had seen the surprise in his eyes, the disbelief that she had lied to him again after promising there were no more secrets, no more half-truths. He would never forgive her. She would never forgive herself.

The soddie came into sight, yellow light spilling through the open doorway and mingling with midnight's pale white glow. Sunny knew Gentle Wind and Maggie were inside. Renewed fear washed through her. What had Walden done to them? What did he have planned?

Walden stopped them at the bottom of the steps. ''Hooker, go 'round and fetch Swift Arrow. We'll just get this whole damn reunion thing over with at one time . . . and move on to more fun.''

Sunny didn't attempt to try to look at her father. There was no need. She well remembered the haunting, evil gleam in his eyes and face associated with that tone—the same tone he had used the day he had brought the snakes. She did look at Matt, however, but his stoic expression hadn't changed. His stare remained fixed ahead. She wanted to cry.

''Move!'' Walden shoved Matt into motion, and he slowly climbed the porch steps. ''You, too, girlie.'' Her father came around, waving the gun close to her face.

Sunny followed Matt inside the soddie, then quickly scanned the small room, passing over the young boy sitting at the table. She couldn't stop her gasp when her gaze fell on Maggie and Gentle Wind tied and huddled together in one corner. Maggie's face was beaten and bruised, one side of her mouth swollen to twice its normal size. Her green eyes registered sadness and fear, but not defeat. Gentle Wind had a large, purpling bruise on one cheek and looked terribly frightened. The girl glanced up, and Sunny tried to warn her into silence with her eyes. It was too late.

''Morning Sky!'' Gentle Wind cried out with trembling lips.

Walden stalked across the room, grabbed the young girl up by the front of her dress, and hauled her to her feet. ''Her name's Sunny, you stupid half-breed.'' He slapped her across the face.

The boy jumped up from the table. Sunny rushed past him and

ran across the room. She raised her fists, prepared to pummel Walden, but at the last second, Matt's hand at her shoulder hauled her back.

"Why don't you pick on someone your own size, you bastard," Matt growled.

Walden pushed the girl to the floor, and it took all of Sunny's strength not to rush to Gentle Wind's side.

Walden spun around and shoved his cocked gun in Matt's gut. "I intend to get to you, don't worry. Get me some more rope, Luke," Walden snapped.

The boy hurried outside and returned at the same time Hooker pushed Swift Arrow through the door. The Indian stumbled and, with his hands tied behind his back, was unable to stop his fall. Sunny closed her eyes against the building tears and prayed for strength to get through this sudden nightmare, prayed for the wisdom and courage to do whatever she must to try to regain the freedom of her family and friends.

Hooker hauled Swift Arrow to his feet. His dark eyes met hers, but she could read nothing in their black depths. She also kept her gaze guarded. Walden already knew enough about her ties to the captives in the room, without learning the special place this Comanche held in her heart. Hooker motioned for Swift Arrow to sit along the same wall with Maggie and Gentle Wind. Walden finished tying Matt's hands behind him and forced him to sit beside the Indian. Sunny eyed the rifle lying across the table.

"Don't even think about it, girlie, or the first one to die will be this little gal who doesn't seem to know your name. Seems to me you've forgotten it, too. Or is there a reason you took your whoring mother's name when you finally left those filthy savages?"

She looked up and met her father's heated stare. "How would I know which one to use. You change your name as often as you change shirts. When did the army find out you weren't really an Indian scout named Sam Waterman?"

Walden took a step forward. "The same time they lied to me about your death during the raid."

"So you became Jake Walden then?" She crossed her arms, forced herself not to shake with fear at his narrowing gaze. As long as he focused on her, he couldn't hurt the others.

He nodded, then took another step closer. His smile was cold and calculating. "Been payin' 'em back ever since by helpin' myself to their payrolls. Course, they don't know that. They're too stupid to figure it out. Then I found out you weren't dead, and now my plans have changed again. Me and you, we're gonna head to California."

"I'm not going anywhere with you."

Walden moved to within arm's reach and glared down at her. "Sure ya are, girlie. You're gonna do exactly what I tell you."

"And if I don't?" she snapped, knowing the second the words left her mouth, she had let her temper get the better of her.

Walden backhanded her across the mouth and sent her sailing sideways over the table. Her hand landed on the rifle. At the same moment she gripped the stock, a single blast of gunfire resounded in the soddie. Gentle Wind screamed.

Sunny saw the hole in the mud wall inches above the girl's head and quickly removed her hand from the gun. She pushed herself off the table and stood to face her father, swallowing the trickle of blood which oozed from the inside cut on her lip.

"Ya gotta learn to watch that smart mouth of yours," he snarled. "Even if I have to beat the reminder into ya."

Sunny bit back the hot retort on her lips.

Quick, heavy footsteps sounded on the porch outside. "Hey, Jake, I found three horses tied up—"

Sunny turned toward the nasally, grating voice and saw the tall, brown-haired man who suddenly filled the doorway. A wide scar started just below his left eye and ran the full length of his cheek.

"Well, never mind, looks like you already know we got visitors."

"Did you bring the horses with ya, Stu?" Walden asked.

The man nodded. "I put 'em in the pen out back."

"Good. Come on in here." He waved the gun, gesturing for the outlaw to enter. "Now that everyone's gathered around, I'd like you boys to meet my daughter."

"Your daughter?" Hooker and Stu responded in stunned voices at the same time and turned widened eyes to Sunny.

Walden nodded.

Sunny briefly glanced at the shock on Maggie's face, then Gentle Wind's. Swift Arrow's eyes gleamed with surprise, but nothing else. Matt didn't even look up.

"You're kidding, right?" Hooker's craggy face tightened with suspicion as he stared from the outlaw to Sunny. Stu stood openmouthed.

"Nope. And if either one of you try to lay a hand on her, I'll kill ya. Ain't no one gonna touch my little girlie, less I say so." Walden turned slightly, and Sunny saw him glare at Matt. " 'Specially you, Ranger. I find out you've laid one finger on her, and there ain't none of her pleadin' gonna keep you alive. It's bad enough I gotta wonder how many savages she and her mama laid with to stay alive."

Matt stared back, his expression unreadable. "Is that why you killed your wife, and tried to kill Sunny, too? Because they stayed alive? Or because they preferred living with the Comanches instead of you."

Sunny knew by Matt's low tone that his temper was threatening to boil over. She tried to catch his eye to warn him into silence. He refused to look her way.

Walden fired another shot. The bullet slammed into the wall above Matt's head. Sunny's heart stopped, then leapt into her throat. Maggie and Gentle Wind gasped loudly. Matt didn't even flinch.

"Shut up, Ranger!" Walden turned and grabbed her arm

before Sunny could move. "And I've had enough out of you, too."

She pulled and twisted her arm, but was unable to free herself from his cruel, biting fingers. He started to pull her toward the doorway. Renewed panic fueled her fight. The memories rushed in. He had always made her leave their cabin when he aimed to hurt her, punish her. She dug her boot heels into the dirt and raised her fists. Walden looked over his shoulder at her.

"Don't do it, girlie, or it'll be that much worse."

Sunny's heart pounded wildly with fear. What was he going to do?

No, he wasn't going to do anything. She wasn't going to let him. Sunny swung her fist and connected hard with his jaw.

"You bitch!" Walden spun full around, released her arm, and rammed his fist into her stomach. Sunny doubled over from the powerful blow, but bit back her cry of pain.

"You sonofa—"

"Shut up, Ranger!" Walden yelled.

Sunny straightened, sucked in a quick breath and swung at him again, hitting him in the neck. Walden grabbed her fist in his large hand and twisted her arm behind her back until she thought it would snap. She forced herself not to cry out from the pain, knowing he would only take pleasure in hearing it.

"All right, I've had enough out of ya, girlie. Time to teach you some manners," he growled low in her ear.

"Let her go!" Matt shouted.

Her father came around to her front and looked her in the eye. A wicked smile formed on his lips. "Your ranger fella sounds worried." The smile faded. "He should be." Walden looked away. "Hooker, you and Stu make sure those men's feet are tied. I don't want 'em goin' anywhere. Then you boys meet me outside. We gotta decide what we're gonna do. Luke, you're on guard. Anything happens, it'll be your hide that does the payin'."

Walden jerked her arm, and Sunny winced from the stinging jolt it sent to her shoulder. Then he pushed her ahead of him as he walked outside and down the steps. A cold chill ran up her spine when he paused briefly beside the saddled horse the outlaw, Stu, had ridden, and snatched up the looped length of rope from around the saddle horn.

A cold dread washed through Matt. What was that bastard going to do to Sunny? He didn't want to think about the possibilities, but could think of nothing else. He had to get out of here! He had to save her. Matt twisted hard against the ropes binding his wrists.

"Forget it, Ranger." Matt stilled and looked up into Hooker's sneering, craggy face. "Ya ain't goin' nowhere."

The outlaw squatted and tied Matt's feet together, then moved over and did the same with the Indian's. With a stern warning to the boy to keep the rifle close at hand, Hooker followed Stu outside.

Matt watched the boy calmly walk over and close the door. Then he turned, dropped the rifle on the table, and rushed to Gentle Wind's side.

"Get away from her, boy!" Matt ground out.

"It's all right, Matt." Maggie leaned her head forward and looked around the Indian at him. "Luke's been helping us."

"Yeah, well thanks to him running back for help, Sunny's out there going through God knows what."

"I didn't run back to get help, mister. My brother was already on his way."

Matt glared at the boy's steady green stare. "Where'd you go?"

"He came back to help me, Matt." Maggie's voice came out harsh and raspy through her swollen lips. "When we heard the gunshot, Hooker was trying to . . . well, we were struggling. He sent Luke ahead while he showed his dislike of being bit by knocking me unconscious."

"You bit him?" the brave asked.

Matt drew his brows together at the faint smile Maggie gave the Indian.

She nodded. "I know you said don't fight, but—"

"You did good."

The underlying tone of pride in the Indian's voice confused Matt as much as Maggie's defense of the boy.

"What the hell's going on?" Matt grated. "How'd you get here, Maggie?"

He listened with grave interest as Maggie quickly explained. Then she told him about Luke watching after the girl, and her conversations with Swift Arrow. All the while she talked, Matt's questions mounted, but he had only one concern.

When she finished, Matt turned to Luke. "Would you mind looking out and telling me if you see Sunny?"

Luke got to his feet, walked over, and slowly opened the door. Matt was surprised when the boy slipped outside. He hadn't expected him to do anything more than look out the window. His heart hammered harder with each passing second Luke didn't return. No one spoke in the tense silence. Finally, Luke returned and quietly closed the door. Matt's blood pounded in his ears at the grim expression on the boy's round face.

"Walden tied her hands and ankles. He's got her hanging from a tree."

Matt barely registered Maggie's surprised gasp and Gentle Wind's startled cry. He closed his eyes and leaned his head back against the mud wall. *Dear God! The pain she must be reliving, the fear.* His body shook with anger. He took a deep breath, released it, then slowly opened his eyes.

"Untie me, Luke," he demanded in a low voice.

Luke shook his head. "Sorry, mister, I can't. Jake'll kill me. My own brother will kill me. Then they'll hurt the women."

"Untie me, boy. Now!"

"Luke is right." Swift Arrow's voice was deep, gruff, and fueled Matt's rising temper.

He looked at the brave, no longer able to control his anger

and worry. "You might not care what happens to Sunny, but I do," he snapped. "And I'm getting out of here one way or the other."

"I care very much about Morning Sky." Swift Arrow swept his stare over Matt. "Maybe not with the same depth of love as you."

Matt bristled at the brave's words and stare, but said nothing. The first time he spoke of his love for Sunny, it would be to his little spitfire, not this stranger.

"Walden will be watching her close," Swift Arrow continued. "If you go out there, you'll get yourself killed. And Luke is right, they will suffer." The brave nodded his head toward Maggie and Gentle Wind.

"So what are you saying? That we should just sit here and *wait* for that bastard to hurt her, then come in here and kill us?"

Swift Arrow shook his head. "Luke is not like his brother. He wants out, and he will help. But we must work together to save ourselves . . . not die trying to save only one."

Matt knew he couldn't let his fear for Sunny rule over rational thought, but hearing Swift Arrow reinforce it with words didn't lessen the feeling. Nauseating spurts of adrenaline coursed through his veins. He had told her he would always be there for her and vowed to keep her safe. They had barely ridden into the canyon, and already she was in the worst trouble of her life. All because he had let his temper take over when he learned Walden's identity. This was his fault.

"Matt, please." Maggie's plea broke the lengthening silence. "Swift Arrow is telling you the truth. We've been discussing a plan."

Matt glared at the brave. "Why should I trust you? You're riding with Walden."

Swift Arrow's firm jaw drew taut, and there was a slight twitch at the corner of his mouth. "I rode with Gray Wolf. I was wrong to stay with Walden. I did not know your Sunny was Morning Sky, but Walden did. And now, he uses me as bait because he knows she comes to take me to the reservation.''

Blood surged to his fists. ''*Will* you return when this is over?''

Swift Arrow narrowed his eyes and drew black brows together to form a single line. ''This I will discuss with Morning Sky, not you.''

Matt didn't like the brave's answer, but he kept silent, figuring it was fair, for the time being. Much as he hated to admit it, he knew Sunny shared a past with this Indian and considered him a friend. He would wait, and let the brave talk with her. Then, if Swift Arrow didn't make the right decision, Matt would make it for him. This Indian was going back to the reservation, one way or the other. His little spitfire *was* going to be with her brother and sister. She *was* going to be happy.

''All right, tell me about your plan.''

Suddenly, the door flew open, and Hooker sauntered inside, cutting off any further conversation.

''Morning Sky lives. This is hard to believe.''

Will heard the awe in White Bear's tone and felt the brave's breaths against the back of his shirt.

''Well, I can tell you she was alive when she started out on this mission to free Gentle Wind and Running Bear. I'm praying she and my sister both are still that way. Gentle Wind, too.''

''We will be at the canyon soon.''

Will nodded, and glanced at the moon halfway down on its descent toward morning. White Bear had suggested they take a longer route to avoid the possibility of an encounter with McGuire. Will wasn't thrilled about the hour-long delay, but couldn't argue with the necessity of it. He wanted to get this done, make sure everybody was safe, and get back home to Becky. He was worried sick about her. Was she all right? Was the baby?

''Why does Morning Sky come to Outlaw Canyon?''

"She comes to talk your brother into going back to the reservation."

"I do not believe you," the brave snapped in a low, harsh tone. "Morning Sky would not turn on her people."

"She hasn't, White Bear. Sunny's done a lot to help the Comanches."

"How does Morning Sky help, if she lives the white man's life as you say?"

Will set aside his concerned thoughts about his wife and concentrated on White Bear's question. "For almost a year now, Colonel Grierson has allowed her to live on the reservation with the other survivors from your village. Their camp is on Cache Creek, south of Fort Sill." He heard the brave suck in his breath at the news. "She's badgered the army to supply the government rations on time, and still managed to make friends with the post commander. She arranged a deal between your people and the army which freed a hundred and fifty Comanche prisoners. She's worked to teach your people the white man's ways and help them adjust. My sister's helped, too. Maggie wants to start a school for the Indian children."

"And why does Morning Sky drive the cattle for you?"

"To save money. She wants to buy land, start a new future with Running Bear and Gentle Wind. She'll move back to my ranch for a while after . . ." Will pondered whether he should tell the brave about the bargain, and decided not. White Bear would probably receive the news of his brother's pending fate better from Sunny. "Well, after all this is over."

White Bear said nothing. Will let the silence linger, knowing he had given the brave much to think about and wonder. But he had been wondering about something, as well, ever since he met the brave, and after a few minutes Will spoke up.

"You never did say what you were doing up here, White Bear, or why you've been tracking Walden." Will cocked his head and stared back with one eye at the brave.

"Revenge." His stoic face showed no remorse.

Will nodded, and turned his sight to the moonlit path ahead. "Kinda thought as much. Walden do something to you?"

"He called himself Sam Waterman, and led the army to our village."

Will sat up with a start. "Whoa, I wonder if Sunny knows that?"

"She will know when she sees him. He is the one who shot her."

Will's heart pounded with surprise. He furrowed his brow as he recalled Sunny's assurances that she could handle Jake Walden. Even Colonel Grierson had been curious about her certainty. But she had been adamant, and now Will knew why. She knew all about the outlaw's identity. Will's gut tightened. He suddenly had a strong feeling her mission up here had a large dose of revenge tied to it, as well.

"Did you know your brother was riding with Walden?"

"I thought my brother also died in the raid. I was shocked to see him in Walden's camp. Instead of striking quickly, I waited these past days in hopes of speaking with Swift Arrow. But I did not get the chance since Walden has been on the move, chasing after the woman driving cattle. And then you tell me that woman is Morning Sky." Will heard the chuckling wonderment in White Bear's voice. "I should not be surprised. My Morning Sky did not enjoy the woman chores around camp."

Will smiled. "She's not much good in the kitchen, I know that. My wife let her try to cook a rabbit one Sunday while we were at church. By the time we got back, Sunny had the house filled with smoke and nothing but a charred carcass to show for it."

White Bear laughed. "Yes, but she can run with the buffalo as well as any warrior."

Will nodded. "Probably did that the same way she runs after cattle, with no fear."

"That is my Morning Sky."

* * *

Sunny didn't know which was going to kill her first, the pain in her arms or the fear coursing through her blood with the speed of a swollen river. Her father had left her hanging in the darkened shadows under the tree for hours, and every second she had watched, expecting him to return, dreading what he would do—worse, what he would bring with him. He never came, but she knew he would.

She remembered the evil smiles on his face while he beat her mother, the chuckles at her own cries of agony at being tied this way as a child, her screams of panic with the snakes. But no more. She wouldn't let him do it anymore. He might have her bound, but she wouldn't watch him smile at her pain, not again. Never again.

Sunny dug the toes of her boots into the dirt as she had done innumerable times during the night, finding the perfect balance on the tips that would relieve the strain to her arms. for the few seconds she could hold the stance.

She stared at the moon hanging low in the sky, then began counting the stars again in hopes of keeping her mind off Walden's intentions, or the horrifying thoughts of what he might be doing to the others. She got to three, before glancing across the long distance to the side of the hideout washed in pale moonlight. *Great Spirit, please don't let him hurt them.*

Gentle Wind's frightened brown eyes swam across her vision. Then Maggie's swollen, bruised face, and Swift Arrow's familiar black stare, filled with awe at her presence and concern for their situation. And Matt, his loving, passionate eyes filled with desire for her, filled with angry fire in defense of her, and washed with disbelief and distrust when he learned the truth. How could she have hurt him so? Why hadn't she just told him the truth?

Sunny sighed. The time for truth was past. Matt would never forgive her, and she couldn't blame him.

"Hey, girlie, I'm back." She jumped at the low, venomous voice behind her. "And I brought you something."

Sunny stiffened, tilted her chin up. *A warrior does not show fear to his enemy.* White Bear's words rang in her ears. Walden was the enemy.

She remained silent as her father came around and forced herself not to spit at the grin on his lips. He held up one hand. Sunny stared at the cloth bag he swung back and forth, and clenched her teeth to halt the sudden tingling in her cheek. Gray shadows bounced off the odd, round shape that weighted the sack. Sunny swallowed.

"Wanna see?" Her father leered at her.

Sunny narrowed her gaze, but said nothing.

"No? Well, I'll tell ya about it first, then ya can decide." He stepped back and held his arm out straight so the bag was inches from her face.

Sunny stared at it, but didn't see anything moving.

"I took notice of your fondness for that ranger, so I thought ya might wanna have him with ya."

Sunny's heart stopped. No. She widened her eyes at the bag. No. Her father had once brought her the head of her favorite cat . . . in a bag. Said almost those very same words. No! Panic swelled through her limbs and rushed into her breast. Her heart suddenly raced. No!

He's lying! The thought screamed itself over the pounding in her head. *He won't let you see his face. He's lying.* Her mind raced with the rationale. *He's not boasting a smile. He only smiles when he knows I'm truly going to be frightened.*

Sunny breathed deeply through her nose. *A warrior does not show his fear to the enemy.* Her heartbeat slowed. Walden lowered the bag from her face. Sunny looked into the eye that was identical to her own. "You're lying." She smiled when his lips curled back in a scowl.

"I guess those Comanches toughened you up some."

Sunny let her smile fade. She may have been right this time, but she didn't trust this man at all, especially when he stepped closer.

"Well, you're right, I ain't killed your ranger fella yet. It's just a big rock in here." He shook the bag, and the smile she had been dreading began at the corners of his mouth. "But I did bring you a present. I hope you still like snakes. Only got one for ya this time. The poisonous ones are harder to catch. And this one's good and riled after having this rock sittin' on top of him." The evil grin spread across his lips. "Oh, I'm only funnin' ya, girlie. It's not really poisonous. I told ya I was takin' ya to California with me, didn't I?"

Sunny didn't care if it was poisonous or not. She couldn't stop the wave of panic which rushed through her. Her breath lodged. *Don't let him do this.* A shudder coursed up her legs, her belly, into her chest. *A warrior does not show fear to his enemy.* Sunny forced a breath into her lungs. Walden shook the bag close to her breasts. She grabbed the rope above between her hands.

"Ready, girlie?"

Sunny gripped the rope tighter, then in one quick movement bent her knees, swung her legs out, and planted the bottoms of her boots in Walden's groin. The outlaw staggered back, swearing visciously, then doubled over on the ground and dropped the bag. A long, brown snake slithered out from the opened end. Sunny raised her legs at the knees and closed her eyes as it crawled under her.

"You bitch!"

Her eyes flew open. Walden was up and staggering toward her as he reached for his gun. "I am gonna kill—"

A gunshot rang out. Walden spun around. Sunny looked in the direction of the cabin from where the shot came. Suddenly, there was more gunfire, and Hooker and Stu were jumping off the side of the porch, firing at someone behind them. Another round blasted the air. Hooker fell into the dirt face first and didn't move. Stu ran around the side toward the back. Sunny wondered if Matt had somehow gotten free. But how? The outlaws hadn't left the hideout that she had seen since her father brought her out here.

An Indian with long black hair down to his waist ran after Stu. Sunny screamed to get the stranger's attention, but Walden ran over and shoved his fist in her mouth, stifling her signal before she barely got it started. She kicked at Walden with her bound feet. Walden kicked her back, then bent and retrieved the bag, dumping the rock out before removing his fist and shoving one dirty end of the cloth into her mouth.

Another round of firing drew her attention. The strange Indian pressed himself against the side of the hideout and fired around the corner. The outlaw pulled the gate to the corral open as he fell. The frightened horses fled, trampling over Stu.

Her panic rose as the stranger turned and ran back to the front of the hideout, unaware of her predicament. Stepping out of reach of her legs, Walden pulled a knife from his boot and cut the rope above her hands. She fell to the ground and reached for the gag. Walden grabbed her tied wrists and dragged her over the dirt and rocks, farther into the darkness behind the tree. He made short order of retying her hands behind her back and securing the gag to her mouth; then he left.

Sunny squirmed, twisted, and inched herself along the ground. She had covered only a few short yards when Walden returned and quickly found her. He picked her up and threw her belly first onto a saddleless gray. Then he climbed on the horse and turned away from the hideout. Sunny lifted her head and peered around his leg at the fading soddie.

She prayed her sister, her friends . . . and Matt were all safe and unharmed. She knew Swift Arrow would follow and try to find her. Matt, she wasn't sure. He had cattle headed to Wyoming. He didn't have time to go chasing off toward California. *And why would he?* She started to cry. He was angry with her for not telling him the truth.

A new sudden fear gripped her. What if no one found her.

Walden knew how to disappear, start over. He had done it many times. Hot tears flowed fast and silent down her cheeks. A sharp sense of loss twisted her heart. Nauseating despair settled in her stomach. She hadn't gotten to say goodbye to anyone, not Gentle Wind and Swift Arrow, not Maggie . . . not Matt. Or to tell them how much she loved them . . . especially Matt.

"Where's Sunny?" Matt shouted at Will as he stepped through the door.

"I didn't see her."

"Get over here and untie me!" Matt tugged at the ropes around his wrists.

Will hurried over, pulling a knife from his belt as he came. "Maggie! Are you all right?"

"I'm fine."

"Hurry up. Walden's got Sunny tied up in a tree out there somewhere." Matt waited impatiently as Will sliced the ropes between his ankles, then twisted around and held out his wrists. He was on his feet as soon as the ropes gave way.

"Luke, come with me. Show me where you saw her." He ran outside and down the steps. "Come on, hurry. Which tree?" he yelled over his shoulder, then slowed his steps until the boy caught up.

Matt's heart raced with fear. He had to find her. *Dear God, please let her be alive. That was all that mattered.*

"Over here, off to the side more." Luke waved a hand and ran ahead.

Matt followed at a dead run, then slowed his steps when he saw the rope dangling from the tree limb. A chill ran up his spine. He stared down at the large rock on the ground below, and a cold panic tightened his gut.

"Sunny!" he shouted, looking around. He ran farther into

the darkened shadows of the trees, shouted her name again, and again. Nothing.

Damn! He had promised to keep her safe. How could he have let her down like this?

He had to find her. More importantly, he had to tell her how much he loved her, how much he wanted her in his life . . . forever. *Hang on, angel, I'm coming.* And when he found her, Jake Walden was a dead man. This time Matt didn't plan to screw around making it look like a dispute over a poker game, either.

Matt ran back to where Luke waited by the tree. ''Get the horses sad—'' He looked up as he spoke and saw the corral standing empty in the moonlight. *Damn!* ''See if you can find the horses, then we'll worry about getting them saddled.''

Luke nodded, and ran off. Matt hurried back to the hideout, jumped on the porch at one end, and ran inside. He stopped short at the sight of a strange Indian brave hugging Swift Arrow. But his concern for Sunny quickly overrode any curiosity.

Maggie rushed to his side, her eyes wide with alarm. ''Where's Sunny? Didn't you find her?''

Matt shook his head and turned to the girl standing beside Maggie. Gentle Wind's round, anxious eyes tore at his heart. Slowly, he lifted his hand to her bronze cheek and brushed away the tear sliding past the tiny freckles on her nose—little, pale brown freckles that reminded him of Sunny's. He kept his palm pressed against her face and stared into her worried gaze. ''Don't worry, I'm going to find her.''

Gentle Wind nodded, but he saw the spark of doubt glint in her eyes—the same spark he used to see in Danny's eyes after their folks died, after they had been on their own awhile and experienced tough times and disappointments. It got hard to believe in dreams. For Danny. For himself. It wasn't fair for a child not to have hope, not to dream. Any child.

He squatted to eye level with her. ''I'll find her, Gentle Wind. I won't come back until I do. I promise you.''

She hesitated, then nodded again.

He stood, and turned to face Maggie. "Will you take care of her?"

"Of course," Maggie rasped through swollen lips, then put her arm around Gentle Wind and drew the girl to her side.

Will stepped up. "I'll see they get back to the fort."

"Good." Matt turned toward the door, but Will's hand at his shoulder prevented him from taking that first step to finding Sunny.

"Do you have any idea where Walden's taken her?" Will inquired with concern.

Matt turned back. "No, but I'll pick up their tracks. He said something about heading out to California."

"He will head south first. To the mountains," Swift Arrow stated with certainty.

Matt glanced over Will's shoulder at the brave and furrowed his brow. "You sure?"

Swift Arrow pondered Matt's question for only a second, then nodded. "I will go with you."

Matt stiffened, and stared down his nose at the brave. Did he dare trust the Indian? Did he want to go riding around the countryside with this brave? He knew Swift Arrow was concerned about Sunny. He also knew pure evil ran through the outlaw's veins, and that Walden was cunning and mean enough to have sidestepped being captured by the law for a good number of years. There was no telling what the man would do to ensure his escape, or what he would do to Sunny. If this Indian knew where to find them, Matt had no choice. He nodded once at the brave. "I could use the help. Let's go."

"I will go as well."

Matt slipped his sight to the brave he had seen hugging Swift Arrow earlier and made a cursory examination of the man's square copper face, waist-length black hair, and broad build. "And you are?" Matt growled his impatience at the delay.

The brave crossed his arms over his large, buckskin-covered chest. "I am White Bear. Swift Arrow's brother."

Matt's breath lodged in his throat. A sharp prick of alarm

jabbed at his heart. "White Bear," he grated, stunned. "I thought you were dead."

The brave looked around at the others in the room with his expressionless face, then back at Matt. "So everyone keeps telling me."

Chapter Eighteen

By the time they finally found Walden's tracks, it was just after mid-morning, and the outlaw had a good six-hour lead. Walden had made a wide circle around the canyon, zigzagged his way several times, making it harder to find their southbound trail, and Matt was frantic over the delay. His worry for Sunny grew stronger with every passing minute. But he was thankful he hadn't let his concern overrule good sense and had listened to Swift Arrow. Matt had been ready to charge off toward California, where Walden had said he was planning to take Sunny.

He wanted to charge off now, as well, instead of riding at this slower pace; but the horses were tired, and the sun overhead was grueling in its intensity. He didn't want to think about the necessity of stopping soon, either. The only thing on his mind was finding Sunny—as fast as possible.

Matt shifted in the saddle and turned slightly to look at the brave riding beside him. Swift Arrow's black eyes met his. ''How did you know he'd head this way, Swift Arrow?''

''He goes to the mountains for the gold.''

Matt cocked his head and lifted one brow. "Gold? What gold? I thought the stolen payroll Will's taking back to the fort was all there was."

Swift Arrow shook his head. "Those shipments were the ones stolen after I joined Walden's gang. But I have heard the outlaw and McGuire speak of the gold they stole before that. Gold the others did not know about. It is hidden somewhere in the mountains north of the fort."

"And you think he's headed down there to get it before taking Sunny out west?"

Swift Arrow nodded. "He did not say, but I believe he was only waiting to capture Morning Sky and steal the money shipment coming from Fort Dodge this morning before leaving anyway." A glint of amusement flashed in the brave's black eyes. "I imagine the captain was surprised when there was no attack today."

Matt knew McGuire had more than that surprise waiting for him, especially after Will finished speaking with Colonel Grierson. And when Matt caught up with McGuire, he planned to rearrange the traitorous captain's face for putting his little spitfire in danger.

"Is there anything else you know that might help?"

Swift Arrow's face tightened gravely. "Only that Walden has no heart. I did not know Morning Sky was the woman he sought, or that she is his daughter."

"What do you say, my *moneta?*" White Bear's surprise was evident in his deep, harsh voice.

White Bear's hard copper face came into Matt's range of vision as the brave leaned forward on his dappled mount and stared at Swift Arrow from the opposite side. Matt turned his sight away and shut out Swift Arrow's explanation.

The thoughts he had pushed aside about White Bear since he learned the brave's identity in the hideout came rushing back to haunt him. Matt was torn between being sick with despair and crazed with anger at the brave's return.

Would his little spitfire welcome her Indian love back into

her life? Would she choose the man she once planned to wed over the love, the life, Matt wanted to offer her? Could he keep himself from killing the brave if she did?

Matt pulled the pack of cheroots from his shirt pocket, removed one long cigar, and offered one to Swift Arrow, which the brave declined. Matt made no gesture toward White Bear, continuing to ignore the brave just as he had done all morning.

"You do not like me, Matt Lanier, why is that?" White Bear asked in a dead, cold tone.

Matt heard the underlying challenge in White Bear's tone and, turning to look at the brave, swallowed back the urge to smash his broad, flat nose by way of explanation. "I don't know you, or what it is you're after."

"I seek Morning Sky's safe return, same as you. And revenge on the man who holds her."

"Walden's mine," Matt ground out. "If there's anything left when I'm done, *then* you can take your revenge." Matt turned away before he blurted out that Sunny was his, as well, and concentrated on lighting the end of the cheroot while he reined his temper to a more controllable level. But White Bear didn't give him the chance to finish the process.

"Do you have feelings for my Morning Sky?"

His Morning Sky! Matt felt the blood rush to his head and pound in his ears. He turned and glared at the brave now riding slightly ahead of his brother. "My feelings for Sunny are none of your damn business."

White Bear narrowed his black stare. "They are my business if you plan to stop Morning Sky from leaving with me."

Anger raged through his veins, tightening his muscles. He balled his fists around the leather reins in his gloved hands. "Sunny will go where she chooses," he fumed. And he wished like hell he knew what that choice would be.

His heart ripped at the thought that she would choose this brave. This man whom she once loved. This man who was so much a part of the past she longed for and, Matt knew, would give almost anything to have back. Uncertainty clouded his mind, and he looked away, but not before he saw the same hint of doubt flash across White Bear's eyes. Matt took small comfort in the knowledge the brave was not sure of Sunny's decision, either.

"Be prepared, white man, I know my Morning Sky's heart," White Bear warned, fueling Matt's temper.

He snapped his head around. "You've been gone a long time. It's possible you don't know her as well as you think anymore."

"And maybe you do not know her at all."

"And none of this will matter," Swift Arrow smoothly interjected, looking from one to other, "if we do not find her."

Matt stared at the trail ahead and took a long draw on the cheroot. Swift Arrow was right. Nothing would be settled until Sunny was found. But knowing it did nothing to ease the pain slicing his heart. He felt as though he was standing at that church altar again, waiting. Ashley had promised to marry him, and never showed up. Sunny had made him no promises, but he knew she cared. Reliving the depth of pain he had experienced riding into Outlaw Canyon, holding no hope of a future with his spitfire, he realized how much harder it would be if she walked away when he did tell her of his love. He knew it would tear him up a thousand times worse than Ashley's disappearance, and *that* had nearly destroyed him, both physically and emotionally.

Sunny sat astride Walden's bareback gray with her hands bound behind her and her mouth gagged as her father led the exhausted horse by the reins up the steep mountain incline. They had been riding for two days with little sleep, and Walden hadn't stopped to rest the mount since early afternoon. Sunny was surprised the horse was still on its feet now that darkness had settled nearly an hour ago. She knew they traveled through the Wichita Mountains northwest of the fort, but she had no idea why they were here. The outlaw had said almost nothing during the long hours, outside of a few words that consisted of, "get down," "mount up," or "be still."

Sunny ducked her head to avoid a low-hanging tree branch stretched across the narrow trail and stared at her father's wide, stiff back. Had he lied about going to California? she wondered. Had he only said that for Matt's benefit, and Swift Arrow's, in case something went wrong at the hideout . . . as it had? Was Swift Arrow even now headed west in search of her? Was Matt? No, she knew they were both good trackers. They would find Walden's trail, know he brought her south, but would they find her in the vast mountainous range?

The horse followed the path through the trees and brush up a long hillside. At the top, the ground leveled out flat for about thirty yards and was covered with small rocks and sparse patches of grass; then the mountain shot up again with a massive wall of large jutting rocks. Sunny stared at the darkened cave entrance at the bottom of the wall where Walden led them. He stopped out front, told her to get down, then placed his hand against the center of her back and shoved her inside when she hesitated at the opening.

Sunny stumbled into the pitch darkness and fell to her knees on the rock-hard floor. She heard Walden's boot heels sound against the smooth surface, saw his shadow come around her, then disappear. She listened to the ping and scrapes of metal and wood as he rummaged in something. Then she heard a match strike, and suddenly light filled her vision. Sunny blinked against the glare until her stare adjusted. Walden touched the flame to a candle he held in his hand, then blew out the match. Rocky walls surrounded the long, narrow confines inside the cool cave. Her father stood at the far end. Behind him she noticed a smaller, square entrance just large enough for a person to crawl through, and which lead into blackness. At his feet were two worn saddlebags. A small skillet, some canned goods, candles and matches spilled through the torn leather sides. Why had he brought her here? Sunny briefly considered jumping to her feet and making a run for the entrance, but she knew if she tried right now, Walden would shoot her, wounding her just enough to keep her from attempting to escape again. He had already threatened it more than once during the last two days.

"Here, girlie." He tossed a dead squirrel he had shot earlier. It landed with a soft thud and skidded to a stop inches from her knees. Then he raised a hand and pointed at a small stack of wood off to the side. "Start a fire and cook us somethin' to eat. I'm hungry."

Sunny smiled behind the gag in her mouth. *With pleasure.* Matt was always telling her a man could starve around her. She would see if she could prove him right. She rose to her feet. Walden strode over and untied the ropes which bound her wrists at her back.

An hour later, she sat against the damp rock wall near the rear, her hands and feet retied and the gag back in her mouth. Silently, she fumed as her father sat by the fire near the entrance and ate the best prepared meat she had ever cooked in her life. He had offered her nothing more than hardtack for her own nourishment while the squirrel cooked, and told her not to even think of sharing his meal. She watched his every bite with tense anticipation.

"Arrrggh!!!!!" His eye bore into hers. She smiled behind her gag as he pulled the bullet she had left in the carcass from his mouth. "You bitch!" He threw the remainder of the squirrel across the cave.

Sunny fell to the side and barely missed being hit as the meat slammed against the wall with a loud smack. She expected him to get up and come over, but he didn't. Instead, he pulled a cheroot from his pocket, lit the end in the fire, and turned his attention to the cave's entrance. Sunny scooted over a little and sat up. The remaining one-quarter of the cooked squirrel lay next to her hip. She smiled again. *If there's a next time, I won't bother to skin it.*

Hours passed, and still he sat watching the entrance, smoking, saying nothing. Sunny stayed alert, watching her father.

"Jake?" Someone whispered cautiously from outside the cave.

Sunny sat up straighter.

Walden jumped to his feet. "Get in here, Cyrus!" he whispered back harshly.

Sunny was only half-surprised when Captain McGuire strode through the entrance and stood in the light of the fire. He removed his dark blue helmet, then briefly glanced at her with disgust in his brown eyes, before turning his attention to Walden.

"What the hell happened?" McGuire asked. "First, you make me look the fool yellin' Indian attack when you're not even there to steal the payroll. Then I see that Hollister fella leadin' a whole damned parade out of the canyon. And two of 'em were bodies." His voice rose higher with each frustrated word.

Sunny's heart slammed against her breast. Hollister? Will had come to Outlaw Canyon? No, it couldn't be. That wasn't Will she had seen. It was an Indian.

"Yeah, he showed up with that renegade, just like you said they might. Somehow caught Hooker and Stu off guard. I barely got away."

Sunny wondered if the Indian she had seen kill Stu had been Red Cloud. But she quickly chased the thought away. Red Cloud was not a renegade. And she knew by the Indian's buckskins it had not been Swift Arrow.

"What happened to Swift Arrow? He wasn't with Hollister. And neither was that renegade."

Walden screwed his face up with sudden concern and slowly turned his blue stare on her. "That means they're lookin' for *her*. Probably got that ranger fella with 'em, too."

"Ranger?" McGuire snapped. "What ranger? Damnation, Jake." The captain raked his fingers through the brown locks on his head. "What the hell's goin' on?"

Sunny's heart stopped. *Was* Matt coming? Was that why McGuire hadn't seen him? Or had his anger at her lie, her lack of trust in him, driven him back to the herd, and Wyoming, leaving her to her own fate?

"There's no time to explain," Jake growled. "I need you to get us some horses. We'll need at least two to carry the gold so we can travel faster, and one for the girl. Couple of saddles, too. How soon can you get back?"

Gold? What gold? Sunny looked around the cave, then stopped at the smaller, dark hole facing her on the opposite side. *It must be in there,* she decided. At least now she knew why her father had come here.

"Shit, Jake, I'm gonna have to steal this stuff. I can't let Grierson see me. He may have already found out I'm the one that caused Captain Roberts' accident, and that I disobeyed orders. I didn't have any choice, though. Grierson didn't want my hide anywhere close to Outlaw Canyon."

"You never said anything about that." Walden planted his fists on his hips.

Sunny watched the two men square off. So, Grierson *hadn't* known McGuire's whereabouts. And she wouldn't have either, she realized, if it wasn't for Gentle Wind.

"Yeah, well, I knew it would just rile you. Besides, I didn't figure it would matter, since we were plannin' to leave tomorrow, anyway."

"Well, it does matter. We need some damn horses."

McGuire huffed. "We wouldn't if you hadn't gone chasing after this blame girl and got us into this mess." The captain waved in her direction, but didn't turn his sight from Walden.

"You let me worry about the girl. Now, how quick can you get back with those horses?" Walden shouted the last, his face inches from the captain's.

McGuire shook his head and blew out an exasperated breath. "Not before tomorrow night."

"Well, leave now, and see if you can make it quicker!" Walden bellowed.

The captain turned and stormed out of the cave, muttering under his breath.

Sunny closed her eyes and leaned her head back against the rock wall. Her thoughts turned again to Matt. Was he coming? Had he forgiven her? Did he care? She released a heavy sigh through her nose. She thought of his promise to help her meet the deadline, his word of assurances that he would protect her, his tenderness as he had made love to her. The memory helped to calm her fears and steady her heartbeat. She realized she trusted him to keep his word. He would come; she knew it in her heart. He wouldn't go back on his promise to keep her safe. Whether he forgave her or not, he would come.

Her eyes flew open as another thought sprang forth. If he was coming, then he was riding with Swift Arrow and the unknown renegade! Great Spirit! She prayed he didn't lose his temper and display his dislike of the Indians. She prayed they would find her before McGuire returned and Walden put them on the move again.

She prayed once they found her, she would be able to talk Swift Arrow into returning to the reservation. Her deadline was only two days away.

"Here! I found it!" White Bear called out.

Matt stood from where he squatted on the grass- and rock-littered slope and saw the brave waving his hand slowly over his head from a spot farther up the side of the mountain.

Thank God! They had lost Walden's trail at Cache Creek shortly after mid-afternoon and had been searching the mountains ever since.

Walden had definitely taken advantage of his head start. This was the fifth time they had lost the tracks, and the third time White Bear had been the one to find them again. Matt was more than a little impressed, but he would take that information to the grave with him. He wasn't the least bit interested in making friends with this brave.

Matt grabbed up Thunder's reins and worked his way up the mountain on foot toward White Bear. Swift Arrow came from the opposite direction. He watched the young brave approach, and was surprised to realize he rather liked *this* brave. Matt had to admit, he admired the way Swift Arrow had stayed calm and level-headed back at the cabin, not like his own panicked anger when he had yelled at Luke. He was grateful the brave had done what he could to keep Maggie safe. And he knew Swift Arrow was definitely a needed fixture between him and White Bear.

After two days and nights of constant word jabs and arguments about Sunny, it was obvious both men had deep feelings for her, and the tension between them tightened with every heated look and word. If Swift Arrow hadn't been here to intervene at the right times, Matt was sure he would have already come to blows with the brave.

Matt stopped in front of White Bear. "Which way? We've got less than an hour of daylight left."

White Bear crossed his arms over his buckskin shirt. "I am aware of the sun's passing."

Matt stared at the brave's clenched jaw, then at his narrowed black gaze. He didn't want to lose his little spitfire to this man, but he feared he could. And he knew it was that fear that drove his temper, but he had no power to stop it. "Then, why aren't you moving. Or don't you care if we find Sunny or not?"

"Yes, I care if we find my Morning Sky."

Matt growled low in his throat. If White Bear called her "my Morning Sky" one more time, he was going to—

"There's no time for this." Swift Arrow stepped between them. "Which way, White Bear?"

"Up the hill." He mounted his horse and rode up and over the top of the mountain.

Matt followed behind Swift Arrow and watched as the sun slowly eased farther behind the rolling range of mountain peaks in the distance. But his thoughts never strayed from his little spitfire. Matt prayed she was holding up. He scanned the vast range of the Wichitas washed in a burst of orange and pink streaks and tried not to think of all the places Walden could find to hide. He hoped they would find her soon now that they had the trail again. He didn't want to think of her having to spend another night alone with that man.

He followed White Bear and Swift Arrow down the opposite side of the hill. A scissortail flew over the brush- and tree-lined path. Other birds chirped their early evening tunes. Thunder stumbled on the uneven downward slope, and Matt loosened the reins, letting the mount take its lead as they headed toward a sharp curve in the path up ahead.

Matt heard the loud curse and a horse's startled neigh carry on the air from around the bend. White Bear and Swift Arrow came to a sudden halt and exchanged a quick look before heading off the path into the dense trees. Matt reined Thunder in behind them, then dismounted and walked quietly over to where the braves stood. White Bear nodded for them to follow, then crouched low and made his way through the woods.

Matt hid with the braves behind the heavy brush, peering through a parted section of the leafy scrub. Three saddled mounts stood grazing a ways down the trail, their reins secured to a thick bush. A man dressed in army blue half ran, half walked down the path and offered soothing words mingled with his curses as he chased after a bareback horse trailing its reins as it trotted away. Matt recognized the familiar build, knew it was the same soldier he and Sunny had watched ride from the hideout. McGuire. Matt's heart pounded. His blood boiled. He glanced at Swift Arrow, then White Bear, and knew they recognized the soldier and shared the same thought he did. McGuire could lead them to Walden . . . and to Sunny. But Matt's intentions were to beat the information from the man, and Swift Arrow must have read that in his eyes, because the brave placed a hand on his shirtsleeve and stopped him from rising.

"Let him lead us closer to her first," Swift Arrow whispered.

Matt hesitated, his hands clenched into fists. He saw the wisdom in Swift Arrow's words. Overpowering McGuire now wouldn't ensure he would tell the truth. He could waste the night running them all over the mountains. Matt nodded his agreement and was surprised at the look of approval he saw in White Bear's stare.

McGuire returned with the errant horse. They waited for him to get a good ways down the hill, then mounted their horses and followed his path. The sun slipped farther behind the mountains, and evening's gray shadow snaked its way up the hillside. Slowly, night settled around them. They followed McGuire through the mountains for a good two hours underneath the full moon before he started up another long, sloping hillside. Looking toward the top of the mountain, Matt spotted the faint glow of yellow light shining from the large rock formation and quickly pointed it out to Swift Arrow and White Bear. With nodded agreement at their prearranged plan, they separated and quickly rode up the hillside. Matt nudged Thunder into the moonlit path as the captain started to pass.

''Hold right there, Captain.'' Matt cocked his gun and aimed it at the startled officer.

''Who are you?'' McGuire slowly reached for the Colt strapped to his hip.

''The man who's going to kill you if you touch that gun. Now get your hands up.''

''What do you want?'' The captain drew his arms slowly out to the side, then up over his head.

''Some information.'' Matt rode closer, keeping the barrel of his gun aimed at McGuire's chest. He leaned over and snatched McGuire's gun from its holster.

''Get it somewhere else. I've got army business to tend to, and I'm in a hurry.''

Matt lifted one brow. ''Army business, you say?''

''That's right.''

''Since when did it become army business to steal gold and kidnap innocent women?''

McGuire narrowed his stare. ''Who are you, mister?''

Matt lifted his head and stared down his nose at the captain's thin, pocked face. ''Walden calls me Ranger, but the name's

Matt Lanier.'' He almost smiled at the fear which paled the soldier's face. ''Now, is anyone else up there besides Walden and Sunny?''

''Why should I tell you?'' McGuire snarled.

Matt clenched his jaw. Rage pounded in his head. He pulled his foot from the stirrup, raised his leg, and planted his boot in McGuire's side. The captain flew sideways off his horse and hit the ground. Matt jumped from Thunder's back and stood over the man as he sat up.

''I'm not in the mood for games.'' He stuck the end of the Colt closer to McGuire's face. ''I want answers. Or I'll just beat you now till you're almost dead. Then I'll turn you over to them to finish the job.'' Matt nodded where he knew Swift Arrow and White Bear would emerge from the shadows.

McGuire looked, and Matt saw the man's eyes widen, but the depth of the surprise in the captain's stare made Matt glance briefly, as well. Moonlight bounced off the long, curved knife Swift Arrow held between his hands.

McGuire swallowed, then turned his wary gaze up at Matt. ''Yeah, it's just Walden and the girl.''

''Walden expecting you?''

The captain nodded.

Matt glanced up at the distant mountain top, then back at McGuire. ''What's up there?''

McGuire huffed. ''I'm not telling you anything more. You're gonna kill me anyway.''

Matt straightened slightly, but didn't move his gun from the man's face. He cocked his head down at the officer. ''You don't have to die, McGuire. If your only crimes are stealing and disobeying orders, you can take your chances with the army. They'll send you to jail, but you'll be alive. That's if you do what I say. If you don't, you'll die whenever these braves get through carving you up.'' Matt lifted one corner of his mouth in a suggestive sneer. ''And whatever else they have planned.''

McGuire shifted his sight to the braves again. Matt saw the ripple in his throat as he swallowed hard.

"They're in a cave."

Matt bent and grabbed the captain's shirtfront, then hauled him to his feet and shoved him toward Swift Arrow. "Let's go. We'll leave the horses here. Less noise."

The brave took hold of the captain's arm, spun him around, and pushed a gun in his back.

Matt started to fall in behind as Swift Arrow forced the captain into step up the mountain, but White Bear's hand on his arm halted him. Matt was surprised he didn't see the familiar hatred burning in the brave's black stare.

"A warrior must focus his anger only on his enemy. To do less, is to invite a death arrow. For Morning Sky, we must fight together now, not against each other. Are we agreed, Matt Lanier?"

Matt bristled at his spitfire's Indian name on this man's lips, but he didn't hesitate with his answer. "Agreed." Whether or not he liked this brave, he knew White Bear spoke the truth—saving Sunny was all that mattered.

Sunny shifted her sore, bound limbs, and sat back against the hard wall. The rock's natural coolness seeped through the thin cotton of her shirt and brought a welcome relief to the tense muscles in her shoulders. Walden had let her up a few times to take care of necessities, move around and eat, but for the most part she had spent the long hours watching and waiting.

She nervously observed her father's mounting agitation as he paced about the cave, then every few seconds paused to glance at the entrance and the darkness outside. She had watched that same opening all day herself, hoping and praying Matt or Swift Arrow would come charging through, hoping and praying McGuire would get caught at the fort or fall off his horse and break his neck on the way back.

Walden stopped again and stared outside. "Where the hell is McGuire?" he grumbled for the hundredth time.

Sunny offered no comment, not because her father would have welcomed anything she had to say on the subject of McGuire's whereabouts, but because the gag was still stuffed in her mouth.

She glanced down to the eight saddlebags gathered in one back corner of the cave. Late this afternoon, she had watched him light a candle and crawl into the small entrance, only to scoot back out minutes later with the first of the saddlebags. He made two more trips before he had finished dragging all of the leather pouches into the cave. The contents were shut off from her sight, but Sunny knew by the way Walden tugged and pulled, they were weighted with the stolen gold.

Walden turned from the cave's entrance and looked down at her with his cold, blue stare. "That captain's about as worthless as your mama always was."

Sunny bristled at the comment and glared back at him.

"Should have just left that whore in the saloon where I found her." He strolled over and knelt in front of her, then ran one finger along her cheek. "Course, without your mama, I wouldn't have my little girlie, now would I?" His smile turned her stomach.

Sunny jerked away from his touch. Walden slapped her, and the impact twisted her head sharply to the side. He stood. "At least you don't whine and cry around like your mama always did. But don't anger me, girlie, or it'll be that much harder on ya."

Harder than what? she wondered, narrowing her eyes, not caring if he saw her hatred. Harder than what she had already lived through? Harder than what she saw her mama go through? Sunny knew about her mama's past, about leaving the saloon hoping for a better life, about the reality of walking out of one hell straight into another.

He started pacing again. On the third pass around the small

fire, he stopped and stared at the entrance, then smiled as the long-awaited call rang out.

"Jake?"

Sunny's heart and hope plummeted at the sound of McGuire's voice. She tried to stem the flow of panic slowly sweeping through her at the realization that Matt and Swift Arrow had not found her in time, and more than likely wouldn't find her now. She fought the despair that threatened to overwhelm her at the thought of never seeing Gentle Wind and Running Bear again, of never seeing Swift Arrow or Maggie . . . or Matt.

"About damn time, Cyrus," Walden bellowed, stepping closer to the entrance. "Get in here."

"Come out here, Jake. I need to tell you something."

Walden made no move forward, but cocked his head and shouted, "What? Did ya get the horses or not?"

"Yeah, I got the horses," McGuire yelled back. "Just come out here. I need to tell you something, and I don't want the girl to hear."

Sunny heard the high-pitched fear in McGuire's tone and stared at the solid blackness outside the cave entrance. What didn't the captain want her to know? She knew her father was wondering the same thing by the curious glance he shot her before pulling his gun from its holster and slowly stepping forward. Walden barely cleared the rock opening when a tall form suddenly sprang from the side and plowed into him, knocking him to the ground.

She instantly recognized the broad build and dark hair. Matt! Her heart soared at the sight of him, then pounded with fright as she watched him fight her father, struggling and rolling on the ground farther away from the cave into the darkness. She heard men shouting, heard fists connecting with flesh, and loud grunts and groans. Then a gun fired. Sunny's eyes widened, and she squirmed against the ropes holding her, desperate to know what was happening, desperate to know that Matt wasn't hurt.

Tears slid down her cheeks. *Great Spirit! Please don't let it be Matt, or Swift Arrow.*

Walden rushed into the cave, his gun still in his hand. He paused long enough to look at the saddlebags on the floor, then glanced over at her. He raised his gun, aiming it at her face.

"Drop it, Walden," Matt shouted from the entrance. Walden spun around and fired.

Sunny caught only a glimpse of the Indian standing beside Matt before Walden's bullet rammed into the brave's upper chest and sent him flying backward. Matt's gun went off. She heard Walden grunt, and turned in time to see the blood staining his shirtsleeve as he ran to the end of the cave, dropped to his knees, and crawled into the smaller passage. Matt fired at him again, but the bullet went wild and ricocheted off the rock walls. Sunny threw herself on the ground to avoid being hit. Then Matt was at her side.

He lifted her back to a sitting position with his strong hands and quickly ran his gloved fingers over her body. "God, Sunny. I'm sorry. Are you all right? Did you get hit?"

She shook her head, devouring his handsome face with her eyes, noting the bruises on his jaw from his previous fight with Walden and the fresh cut at the corner of his left eye. He untied the gag from her mouth. Her tears fell faster. Her heart pounded.

"I wasn't sure you'd come," she whispered past the knot in her throat as he undid the ropes that held her.

He pulled her to her feet and gathered her in his arms, then cradled her head against his shoulder. "Of course I'd come for you, angel."

He held her for only a brief moment, and Sunny tightened her arms around his neck when he tried to pull away. Matt gently pried her from him and stared at her with warm, but angry, blue eyes. "And I'll come back, after I find Walden."

"No, let him go," she begged, fearing for his life.

Matt shook his head. "He's not going to hurt you ever again. I'm going to see to that. Now, do you know where that passage he crawled through leads?" He cursed under his breath when she shook her head, then released her and walked across the cave.

Sunny followed and pulled at his arm. ''Please don't go, Matt.''

Matt stared down at her with loving tenderness in his midnight stare and lifted a finger to gently stroke her cheek. ''I have to, angel.''

Hands tied behind his back, and feet bound at the ankles, McGuire sat on the rock floor just inside the cave. She followed Matt as he strode across the cave and stopped in front of McGuire. ''Where's that passage lead to?'' he demanded.

''Morning Sky.''

Sunny turned at Swift Arrow's call and saw him leaning over the brave who had been shot. She never heard McGuire's answer as she stared at the man lying on the ground with blood rapidly staining the buckskin covering his chest. Her head pounded with the force of a herd of buffalo as shock washed over her and sent her heart racing.

''Whi . . . White Bear,'' she whispered incredulously, then flew to the brave's side. She knelt and touched his face. His eyes slowly opened, and she stared into his black gaze, which shimmered with surprise and relief at seeing her. ''Great Spirit, you . . . you've come back to me,'' she stammered.

White Bear nodded, and closed his eyes.

Chapter Nineteen

Matt ran, keeping close to the outside rock. He slowed, and followed the two-foot-wide ledge on the opposite side of the cave, searching for the spot where McGuire had told him the tunnel emptied.

Sunny's words rang in his ears, "You've come back to me," over and over.

Matt shook his head to clear his thoughts and scanned the side of the moonlit mountain. Up ahead a few feet, he saw where the ledge appeared to drop off, just like McGuire said. Around that corner, Matt knew, was the end of the tunnel. He inched his way along slowly and listened for sounds of Walden from around the side. But he heard nothing over the painful pounding in his chest.

Matt had known the very instant Sunny first recognized White Bear, known the very second she no longer even knew *he* was in the cave. He had felt an acute sense of loss when she ran to the brave's side, and the weight of that loss crushed him still. Grief like he had never known washed over him in icy waves.

He closed his eyes, took a deep breath, then released it and concentrated on the emptiness at the end of the ledge. Quietly, he stepped closer. Walden had to come this way. McGuire said it dead-ended around the corner. So where was he?

Matt faced the rock wall and sidestepped the last few feet to the end. Removing his hat, he leaned sideways and peered around the corner of the wall. Two shots rang out in rapid succession. Searing pain sliced the top of his right arm as the bullets zinged past. Matt jerked back.

"I've been waitin' for ya, Ranger. But I was hopin' ya'd come outta the hole," Walden shouted.

Matt said nothing. Warm blood oozed down the inside of his sleeve. He turned, pressing his back against the rough rock. On silent feet, he retraced his steps along the ledge until he reached a crevice in the side he had passed earlier and slipped into its darkened shadows.

"What's the matter, Ranger, did ya run off scared?" Walden taunted.

"Why don't you come find out, or are you not man enough?"

"I'm man enough, just not stupid enough to die over the damn girl. She ain't worth it."

Matt's hatred escalated at the outlaw's words. He would go to hell and back for his little spitfire, and she was definitely worth it. He stared at the end of the ledge. The wound throbbed in protest to his tensing muscles when he tightened his hold on his gun.

"You gonna sit there all night, Walden?"

Silence.

Matt furrowed his brow. "Walden?"

Nothing.

Damn! Had the outlaw crawled back into the hole? Was Swift Arrow watching the other side? With his brother wounded, Matt wasn't sure. He waited only a few more seconds, then withdrew from the shadows onto the ledge. Walden rounded the corner and fired. Matt jumped back behind the crevice, firing as he went. He heard the outlaw grunt, then a short scream, and seconds later a heavy thud from somewhere down below.

Matt eased his way to the end of the ledge and looked down. Walden's body lay twisted against the large rocks several yards below and showed no signs of movement in the moon's pale light. Matt stared at the dark stain covering the man's chest, then turned and left.

He stood outside the cave entrance and took several deep breaths. Matt felt no remorse for killing Walden, but he was dying inside knowing the woman he loved was going to walk out of his life forever. He told himself he had known this all along. They had made no promises to each other. She wasn't *his* betrothed. Hell, he hadn't even told her how much he cared, how much he loved her, and he wouldn't now. White Bear shared a past with her, and they would already be man and wife if the army hadn't raided that village.

Her words echoed again in his head, "You've come back to me." Sunny had made her decision. Now he would have to find a way to live with her choice.

Matt took a deep breath and released it slowly. He stepped into the cave and stopped just inside. His gaze went immediately to Sunny. She knelt beside White Bear's inert form and wiped the blood from his naked chest as Swift Arrow used a red-hot knife to remove the bullet from just below the brave's right shoulder. She didn't look up. Matt doubted she even knew he was here. But he could see the tears on her cheeks. The worry on her face. His heart ripped in two at the sight. He wanted her so much.

Why hadn't he told her before they rode into Outlaw Canyon? Why hadn't he told her how he felt when she had given herself so freely to him, made sweet, passionate love to him. But would that have made it any easier now? No. Sunny cared about him, he knew that, and she wouldn't want to hurt him. At least this way she would never know his feelings, and she could be with White Bear with no guilt or sadness at his great pain.

She could be happy. Matt realized that was more important

than his own deep heartache, more important than his own lonely life which loomed in his future. His little spitfire had known too much pain in her life already, and she deserved happiness. By not telling her how he felt, he could take comfort in knowing he played a part in giving her that happiness; then he could remind himself every day for the rest of his life, and that small comfort would have to be enough.

Matt spared a glance at McGuire, still tied up, and sitting with his eyes closed against the back wall now. He lowered his sight back to Sunny. Her words came rushing back, "You've come back to me." Matt quietly backed out of the cave.

Sunny finished bandaging the hole in White Bear's upper chest and pressed her palm against his forehead. He was warm, but not feverish. She offered up a prayer of thanks and another prayer for his quick recovery. She glanced at Swift Arrow sitting by the fire wiping his brother's blood from his knife, then shifted her stare around the cave.

The gold was still on the floor. The captain was tied and asleep against the wall. Her gaze lowered to the brave at her side. She stared in awe at White Bear's face, still unable to believe he was alive. Here. Where had he been these past two years? What was he doing here now? Had he truly come for her?

Her heart filled with a sudden sadness she didn't understand; then a strange sense of loss overwhelmed her.

She looked up and swept her gaze over the cave again. Something wasn't right. Something was missing. Her eyes widened. Matt! Where was Matt? Her heart pounded.

"Swift Arrow," her voice croaked with sudden worry. "Where's Matt?"

Swift Arrow's black stare was filled with concern and added to her rising fear. "He has not returned since all the gunfire, after he went to find Walden."

"What gunfire?"

He stared, puzzled. "Before I removed the bullet. You did not hear?"

Sunny shook her head. She hadn't heard anything. Nothing at all since . . . she glanced down, since the shock of seeing White Bear. She remembered begging Matt not to go after her father, remembered him telling her he had to, but she hadn't seen Matt leave the cave. And now Swift Arrow was telling her there had been gunfire. Her stomach knotted with worry; the powerful feeling of loss increased.

She quickly snapped her head back up to look at Swift Arrow. "We must find him."

"I was about to do just that." Swift Arrow stood.

"There's no need. I'm fine."

Sunny sucked in a loud breath as Matt strode into the cave, and stared at his bruised, swollen jaw, then lower to the blood which soaked the top of his right shirtsleeve. "You're hurt." Jumping to her feet, she rushed to his side and reached up to touch his arm.

He grabbed her hand. "It's just a graze."

"Let me see," she insisted, trying to pull her hand free, but he held firm. She looked up into warm midnight eyes, and froze. There was something different in the way he looked at her which caused her heart to stop, then beat frantically with fear.

"How's White Bear?"

Sunny glanced back at the Indian and sighed. The sight of her brave still surprised her, and confused her. She pushed away the pressing rush of emotion. "He's bad, but he will live."

"Good, I . . . I'm glad."

"May I see to your wound now?" she asked softly, staring back up at him.

"I already took care of it . . . but thanks." A flash of warmth sparked in the blue depths of his gaze, then died and was replaced with a sadness that made a part of her feel as though it just died.

"Where is Walden?" Swift Arrow asked from where he stood beside the fire.

Matt glanced briefly at the brave, then turned his sight to her and squeezed her hand tighter. "He's dead."

Relief washed through her at the news; then a binding weight lifted from her heart. She felt no grief, no remorse, for the man's passing, only a sense of long-awaited freedom and deep gratitude to Matt for giving her that freedom. He had promised he would keep her safe, promised he wouldn't let Walden hurt her ever again, and because of him she could now be at peace with that part of her past. Because of Matt, she no longer had to live in fear of her father's return. "Thank you," she whispered.

He nodded, then squeezed her hand again and ran his thumb lightly along her palm. "Sunny, can I talk to you? Alone?"

She wondered at the hesitancy in his eyes, at the sadness in his tone. It frightened her, but she tried not to let it show. "Of course."

Holding her hand, he led her from the cave out into the moonlit darkness. He said nothing as they walked for a good distance, and Sunny's anxiety increased with every silent step they took. Matt was being unusually quiet, distant, and her mind searched for an explanation. She could think of only one. Matt hadn't forgiven her for the lie about her father.

"Matt, I'm sorry I didn't tell you the truth about Walden."

He stopped, and turned to look down at her. "I wish you *had* trusted me enough, but I think I understand."

"I do trust yo—"

He touched her lips with his finger, silencing her protest. "I didn't bring you out here to talk about Walden."

He looked at her with such painful longing, it nearly made her cry. When he suddenly pulled her into his arms, pressing her close against his chest, she couldn't stop the tears from falling. He held her for a long while and gently stroked her hair. It felt so good to have his arms around her, so right to be held and comforted by him, but yet, she felt something different in his touch, almost as though he were pulling away from her. Before she could ponder the fearful feeling of losing him, he *was* physically pulling back, then lifted her chin with his finger.

"It's almost morning. You'll need to leave soon."

She furrowed her brow. "Leave?"

"Your deadline, angel. It's today."

Sunny reeled with shock. How could she have forgotten? Gentle Wind and Running Bear were waiting for her, depending on her. She had been so worried about Matt, then shocked at seeing White Bear alive, and concerned he *would* die this time, she had completely forgotten the date.

Matt stepped back and placed his hands on her shoulders. "You need time to talk with Swift Arrow. Tell him why he must return."

She wiped the tears from her eyes and nodded. Then she tilted her head up with a start as another realization crossed her thoughts. "White Bear can't be moved."

"I'll stay with White Bear."

Sunny's eyes widened. "You would do this for me? For him?"

"I'd do anything for you, angel. Don't you know that yet?"

She knew he had said it to her before, but until this moment she hadn't realized the extent of the sacrifice he was willing to make. His kindness made her love for him swell to near overflowing.

"Besides, White Bear's not such a bad fella. I'd say we've gotten to know each other pretty well over the last couple days."

Sunny was speechless at the admiration for the brave she heard in Matt's voice. Her heart filled with a love deeper than she had ever known. She reached up and touched his face. He pulled her hand to his mouth and kissed her palm. His tenderness, his caring, tugged at her heart, and she wanted to tell him how she felt, tell him how much she loved him.

"Matt, I—"

"Sshh, don't say anything, angel." He searched her face

intently; then he lowered his lips gently to hers in a brief, but sweet kiss. All too quickly, it ended, and Matt was leading her by the hand again back to the cave.

Great Spirit! How she wanted to tell this man of her love for him. And she would have if the warmth hadn't gone from his eyes when the kiss ended, if the strange, invisible barrier hadn't fallen between them again, if she didn't feel as though she had just lost Matt . . . forever.

He released her hand before they entered the cave, then told her he would take McGuire and put the captain to work helping him fetch water from the creek and ready the horses while she spoke with Swift Arrow.

She watched Matt follow the disgruntled captain outside, then knelt beside White Bear, grateful his breathing was still shallow and even, and his skin cool to her touch.

Swift Arrow came and sat down beside her. "I still cannot believe he is alive."

"I know," she whispered softly. "Did he tell you how he survived? Where he's been?"

Swift Arrow nodded. "He was wounded, as so many of us were, but managed to escape as I did." He reached over and took hold of her hand. "He took refuge with a Nokoni tribe until he was well. Then he set out to find the man who led the raid on our village and take his revenge for your death, and mine. But you did not die, either. How is that, Morning Sky?"

She told him about Will and his family.

"This is the same Hollister who stormed the hideout with White Bear? Maggie's brother?"

Sunny nodded.

"White Bear says he is a good man, and that you drive the cattle for him."

"He has been very kind to me. So has Maggie."

"She is a good woman, brave. She was very concerned about Gentle Wind."

"Maggie has a soft spot in her heart for children. She has

helped our people greatly. She wants to start a school for the Indian children.''

''That is good.'' Swift Arrow nodded, and regarded her closely with his black stare. ''And you, Morning Sky, what do you want?''

Sunny sighed, and glanced briefly at White Bear's face. What did she want? All she had ever wanted was a safe home for herself, for Gentle Wind and Running Bear. She had planned her future with them and had given no thought beyond that . . . until Matt came into her life. And now White Bear was back. This brave who was part of her tribe, part of her life. But Matt was a part of her life, as well. The rancher had touched her heart in ways she had never known were possible. White Bear was the man she had planned to marry, though, and she realized she still had strong feelings for the brave.

''You are troubled, Morning Sky?'' Swift Arrow's deep, concerned voice pulled her from her musing.

She looked at Swift Arrow's square, bronze face and pushed aside her thoughts of Matt and White Bear, concentrating on the one thing that hadn't changed in her life these past two weeks—her siblings' freedom.

''Yes. The fate of our people has troubled me for a long time, just as it did Black Eagle.''

''Black Eagle spoke of peace between the Comanches and the white man.''

''Black Eagle spoke the truth, though we didn't want to see it. And unfortunately, peace will be a long time in coming, but we must start somewhere.''

Swift Arrow released her hand and crossed his arms over his chest. ''And you wish to start this peace process with my return to the reservation?'' His tone took on a sharp edge.

''*That* was not my choice.'' She explained of her search for Running Bear and Gentle Wind and her success in having them sent to the reservation. Then she told him about Agent Taylor's bargain and her concerns if Gray Wolf should die.

"I heard Hollister tell his sister he found Gray Wolf and a man named Pete. They were still alive."

Sunny was relieved. She had wondered about the two men's fate when she had first learned Walden had kidnapped Maggie and Gentle Wind. And even though she knew Gray Wolf would hang, dying anyway, she was thankful he could do so as a proud warrior for all to see.

"And if I return, this agent will release Running Bear and Gentle Wind, and you will leave the reservation. Then what happens? I hang with Gray Wolf, even though I did not ride with him when those settlers were killed? You abandon our people?"

Sunny shook her head. "Since you aren't guilty, I can speak to Colonel Grierson and plead your case. He will listen to me. And I have not abandoned our people. I never will." There was a sharpness in her voice when she spoke the last.

Swift Arrow narrowed his stare at her. "But you intend to leave. You cannot take us all with you."

Sunny nodded. "I am leaving so that Gentle Wind and Running Bear can live free on land that will belong to us."

"Land that the government cannot take from you, because no matter your heart, you are a white woman."

"Land that will show our people there is hope, if we are willing to *work* for it. We can't go on fighting the white man, Swift Arrow." She sighed, and touched his arm lightly with her hand. "Too many of our people have already died and others are dying. We must stop the fighting, or there will be none of our people left. No children to grow up and carry on our traditions, even if it is only in their hearts. As long as we fight, there will never be peace. And without peace, Swift Arrow, we can't have freedom. Freedom must come first here." She tapped one fist over her heart. "Then in the land. The white man can take many things with their government power and their guns. But they can't take what is in our hearts."

"In our hearts we are hunters. But you want us to work at being farmers."

"I want our people to be survivors," she firmly stated. "I can't read the future, but I can see the past. We can't stop the white man. We can't stop the changes they bring. But we can stop our people from dying by their guns. And we don't always have to be farmers. Matt Lanier raises horses. Sells them to the army. The Comanches are good with horses. We could raise horses."

"And who would buy *our* horses?"

"I would. Will Hollister would, and I will find others."

"But you won't be around."

Sunny sighed. "Because I *am* white, the army will not let me stay on the reservation forever. I must have a way to take care of Running Bear and Gentle Wind. I won't leave them behind. I can't. Surely, you can understand that," she pleaded, and saw his slight nod. "And no matter where I settle, I will always help our people. I'll continue as I do now, with my complaints to the army and my letters to the white man's government. I will negotiate more agreements for our people as the army allows."

Swift Arrow lifted his chin and stared down at her. "White Bear told me the things he learned from Hollister that you have done."

"And do you believe I will always help our people?"

Swift Arrow hesitated. "I believe you will try."

"Do you believe enough to help me? Will you go back so that our chief can walk through the afterlife knowing his children live in peace as he wanted, as he tried to tell our people?"

Swift Arrow cocked his head to one side. "White Bear has asked me to go north with him. Cross into Canada, where we can live free."

Sunny arched one brow. "You would go and abandon our people to their fate here?" she challenged.

Swift Arrow sat back and stared at her with surprise in his black eyes.

"She is right."

Sunny turned at the deeply whispered words and looked

down to find White Bear staring up at her through hooded eyes. "You have been awake? Listening?"

White Bear nodded slightly, then tried to smile, but it was a weak effort filled with pain that instantly tightened the muscles along his smooth, square jaw. His tired stare slid to Swift Arrow. "You must go."

"You *want* me to go to the reservation, *moneta?*"

White Bear nodded. "For our people. For our chief." White Bear lifted his hand, and Swift Arrow gripped it.

"Will I see you again, my *moneta?*" Swift Arrow asked.

White Bear only nodded, then closed his eyes. Sunny could tell by the even rise and fall of his chest, he had slipped back into unconsciousness.

Swift Arrow stood, then crossed his arms and stared down at her. "When do we leave, Morning Sky?"

Sunny got to her feet and placed her hand gently on his crossed arms. "Thank you."

"I do this for White Bear, as well as for you. And I do this for our people."

Sunny nodded her understanding, then shifted her sight toward the cave's entrance. Light gray shadows began to chase away the night. Birds chirped their welcoming morning songs. She looked back up at Swift Arrow. "We will leave when the sun rises full."

"And what about White Bear? He cannot travel." The brave glanced briefly at his brother.

"Matt has said he will stay with him until I can return."

"Matt Lanier is a good man." Swift Arrow tilted his head back and stared down at her with a strange look she didn't understand. "So is my *moneta.*"

Sunny stared at Swift Arrow's back as he walked from the cave, and pondered his parting comment. Did the brave know what had happened between her and Matt? Did he guess the depth of her feelings for the rancher? Probably. She hadn't hidden them well as she clung to Matt when he first arrived to save her, nor when she had fretted over his absence when he didn't return from following after Walden. For the first time, Sunny wondered what the three men had talked about as they had traveled together to find her. Had Matt and White Bear discussed their feelings for her? And what were their feelings? More importantly, what were hers now?

She looked down at White Bear's resting form. She was overjoyed he had not died. She was sad she couldn't stay with him now and make sure he recovered. But what did she feel in her heart for this brave she almost married? Sunny chewed on her bottom lip. White Bear had done so much for her as a young girl. He had gone against Black Eagle's wishes, listened to her mother's pleadings, because he cared for her. And she had loved him once, still did, but not with the same intensity and desire she felt for Matt. She wanted to take care of White Bear, make him whole and well as he had done for her by teaching her the skills from which she drew strength and courage. But Matt was the man she wanted to be with. He was the one who owned her heart now. And he was the man she couldn't have. The man who didn't love her, and didn't want her.

They had made no promises. He had not asked her to go to Wyoming with him. But that didn't stop her from loving Matt, or from knowing he would live in her heart forever. And she would not wrong White Bear by going to him when she would always love another.

Matt finished tying down the last of the saddlebags filled with the stolen gold and glanced up as Sunny walked out from the cave into the bright morning light. He swallowed when she continued coming straight his way. He tried not to notice how the sun shined upon her hair in glistening wonder, but one glimpse and the memory was burned into his mind forever. He tried not to think about saying goodbye, but his already splintered heart continued to break into tiny pieces with every crushing step she took closer.

As she stopped beside him, his pulse raced. Matt blew out a short breath, then turned to look at her.

"Horses are all set," he told her, trying not to get lost in her sky blue eyes. "All I've got to do is get McGuire tied up on one, and you can leave whenever you're ready."

She nodded, then lifted a hand and pressed it against his cheek. Matt closed his eyes at the feel of her warm, soft flesh. He couldn't stop himself from taking her hand in his and gliding her palm to his lips. He kissed her smooth skin.

"I want to thank you for everything you've done."

He opened his eyes in time to see her move closer and watch her arms disappear behind his neck. Matt pulled her into his embrace and melted into blazing, painful heat at the feel of her in his arms again. Tears welled in his eyes. He blinked them back. "You don't owe me any thanks, angel." His voice cracked. "How many times do I have to tell you, I'd do anything for you." *Including watch you walk away to White Bear and not beg you to stay.*

Sunny leaned back and looked up at him. Matt could see the tears swimming in her eyes. "Any doubts I had of that were chased away the minute you offered to stay with White Bear. I can't thank you enough for your kindness."

Matt brushed his hand along her cheek. "Your happiness is all I want, angel, whatever it takes. You need to be with Gentle Wind and Running Bear." *And me.*

She reached up and kissed his mouth. Matt pressed his lips closer against her sweet skin, but forced himself not to deepen the kiss, for fear he wouldn't be able to let her go. Then he set her from him and made himself drop his hands back to his sides. She looked up at him with shining eyes, her skin slightly flushed, and he saw her lip tremble.

"Matt, I—"

He waited. Her mouth moved, but no words came out. She twisted her hands together and scuffed one boot against the rocks.

"What is it? And why are you fidgeting again?"

"I . . . I . . ." She released a heavy sigh. "I wanted . . . to tell . . ." She closed her eyes, then promptly opened them and sighed again. "I'll be back in two days."

Matt furrowed his brow and nodded his head slowly. "Okay," he drawled out. *That doesn't seem like such a hard thing to say, so why is she having so much trouble?* Then he froze. Was she trying to tell him that was when she also planned to begin her life with White Bear? "You've come back to me." The haunting words returned.

She turned, and walked back toward the cave. Matt followed her with his eyes, watching the sway of her hips, and remembering the satiny feel of her as they made love, remembering how perfect her body fit against his. That was a memory he planned to cherish forever. And he knew it would be the only thing to get him through the many lonely nights ahead on his ranch. The Rocking L. The dream. Matt snorted through his nose and crossed his arms over his chest. Well, he was through with dreams. He had the land, and he had the house, but it just didn't seem to be in the cards for him to have a family to share it with.

Matt shook his thoughts aside as Swift Arrow emerged with McGuire. The captain's hands were still tied behind his back, and Matt held the horse's head as McGuire mounted the roan. Then Swift Arrow tied the officer's feet with a rope stretched under the mare's belly. When he finished, the brave straightened and walked over to Matt.

"You're doing the right thing, Swift Arrow. Sunny deserves to be with those children."

The brave nodded. "Morning Sky is a strong woman. Chief Black Eagle would be proud of his daughter."

"I think your chief would be proud of you, as well. After all we've been through these past few days, I know I would be honored to call you my friend." Matt held his hand out.

Swift Arrow lifted his chin and shook Matt's hand. "And I would call you friend, as well, Matt Lanier."

"If there's ever anything I can do for you, just get word to me up in Cheyenne."

Swift Arrow nodded once. "I will remember those words." The brave turned and mounted his saddleless spotted pony. After a long, silent minute, Swift Arrow glanced at the riderless palomino beside him, then down at Matt. "Would you see what keeps Morning Sky?"

Matt nodded reluctantly, then made his way slowly to the cave. He paused just inside the entrance when he saw Sunny kneeling beside White Bear. She brushed the brave's hair back from his face with one of her slender hands. Then she brought one finger to her lips, kissed it, and lowered the slim digit down to the brave's mouth. Matt swallowed, then clenched his jaw and strode farther into the cave. Sunny looked up, then without a word rose to her feet and walked over to him.

"Swift Arrow is ready?"

Matt nodded. To his surprise, she slipped her hand into his and led him back outside. She stopped beside her horse, then looked up at him.

"I will miss you," she whispered. Then before he could say anything, she took her hand from his and swung her leg over the palomino's back.

Matt shaded his eyes from the morning sun and watched them ride down the hill. Sunny looked back once, and waved. He lifted his hand in return, grateful she was too far away to see how badly it shook without his effort. When they were gone from sight, he turned and walked back to the cave.

Matt placed another log on the fire and checked to see if the tea Sunny had made from the cottonwood leaves he had gathered for her earlier was ready. Then he poured himself a cup of coffee. From his spot beside the small fire, he looked over to see if White Bear was awake yet.

The brave stared back at him with hooded black eyes. "They . . . are gone?"

Matt nodded. "You feel like trying to drink something?"

The brave shook his head. "Why do you do this for me?"

"I'm doing it for Sunny, and because you care enough about her to risk your life to save her."

"So do you."

"Yes, White Bear, I do."

The brave nodded, then closed his eyes. "You are a good man, Matt Lanier."

If he was such a good man, then why did he wish White Bear was well so he could get up and punch his nose for coming back and taking Sunny away.

Chapter Twenty

It was still early afternoon when Sunny first saw the fort, a large, square compound neatly spread out atop the small dirt rise in the distance. She knew there would be trouble. The guards would wonder about her riding in with Swift Arrow untied and guiding his own horse, while McGuire rode with limbs bound and the brave holding the reins to the captain's roan. As they traveled along the road leading to the fort, Sunny pulled her gun from its holster and rested it in front of her.

She heard the rifles cock and, even without looking up at the guards, knew the soldiers had their weapons trained on them as they rode up the slanting hill to the fort.

"Stop right there!"

Sunny reined Molly to a halt several feet away from the lanky, blue-clad private standing between two other average-size soldiers, all with their rifles aimed at her and Swift Arrow. She recognized none of the men. "I'm here to see Colonel Grierson," she informed the private.

"He expecting you?"

"Yes."

lead ropes to the two saddleless horses and reached for the reins to the three saddled pack mounts Sunny held in her hands.

"Leave these, I'll take them to Grierson," she told the private.

Johnson led the horses away, and Carter followed behind leading McGuire, who was still seated on his roan.

"Let's go." Matthews turned on one black boot heel. Sunny fell into step beside the lieutenant. Swift Arrow walked close to her other side.

"What's the problem, Lieutenant?" she asked as they approached the grassy quadrangle centering the outside square of buildings housed the officers and enlisted men. On the east side of the courtyard sat four long buildings, and she stared at the one second from the left—the post commander's headquarters.

"When I left, Miss Hollister was screeching at the top of her lungs in a shouting match with Agent Taylor, and the colonel was about to have them both thrown in the ice house to cool them off."

Sunny furrowed her brow. Her stomach tightened into a hard knot. "Why was Maggie yelling?"

"Agent Taylor was trying to take Gentle Wind and Running Bear, but she wasn't about to let go of those children."

Sunny quickened her pace at the mention of her siblings, leaving Matthews and Swift Arrow to catch up with her. Tying the reins around the hitching post out front, Sunny climbed the two steps up to the porch of the commander's headquarters and went inside. The colonel's office door was partially opened.

"Taylor, you *will* wait until this evening!" The commander's deep bellow penetrated the walls, and Sunny fairly ran across the small outer office and past Lieutenant Matthews' desk.

She pushed against the heavy wooden door and stepped into the colonel's spacious quarters. Gentle Wind was the first to see her.

"Morning Sky!"

The young girl pulled from Maggie's hold and ran across the hardwood floor, straight into Sunny's arms. Running Bear followed. Sunny gathered them both into her embrace, then kissed them both on the cheeks. She looked from one to the other, smiling into their round, bronze faces. Outside of a small bruise on Gentle Wind's cheek, she saw no visible signs of her ordeal with Walden. The girl looked fresh and clean in a new green dress with black stockings and shoes, and there was a shine of happiness in her brown eyes that warmed Sunny's heart. Running Bear stared at her with shimmering hazel eyes—their mother's eyes.

Sunny swept her gaze over the long-sleeved white shirt and black pants and boots covering his boyish frame. He looked a little thinner. "You are well?"

Running Bear nodded. "Colonel Grierson let me stay in his house," the boy told her with wide-eyed wonder.

Sunny released a heavy sigh of relief, and smiled. "So I heard."

"Thank God you're here." Maggie lifted the hem of her dove gray skirt and walked over to stand behind the children.

Keeping one arm snugly around each sibling, Sunny looked into her friend's still slightly bruised and swollen face, then slid her gaze to Grierson, seated behind his desk, and Agent Taylor, standing on the opposite side.

Grierson stood, his formidable, uniformed presence commanding as much attention as the aggravation etched on his darkly bearded face. "Cut it pretty close, didn't you, Sunny."

She lifted one corner of her mouth in a half smile. "Ran into some trouble."

Grierson arched one thick, black brow. "McGuire?"

"Him, too."

"Did you get the Indian?" Agent Taylor demanded, drawing her attention.

Sunny stared at the short, squat agent dressed in his usual attire of black pants and coat with a white shirt buttoned to his thick throat. His head was free of the black hat he usually wore, exposing his partially bald head. She looked into his brown button eyes. "Yes, Swift Arrow has returned with me."

"Where is he?" Taylor asked.

Sunny lowered her arms from her siblings' shoulders and turned, surprised that Swift Arrow was not standing behind her. She saw him waiting in the outer office with Lieutenant Matthews and waved at him to enter. Running Bear and Gentle Wind threw their arms around him in a fierce hug as he came to stand beside her.

Grierson smiled beneath his mustache and turned to the agent. "Well, Taylor, that's the end of that. Gray Wolf is in custody and recovering, and Swift Arrow is here."

Sunny looked at Maggie when Grierson mentioned Gray Wolf and saw her friend smile and mouth the words, "Will found him."

"There's still another matter to contend with first," Taylor stated in a gruff, uncooperative tone.

Sunny stiffened, and frowned. The knot in her stomach constricted into a hard ball. She glanced quickly at Gentle Wind, then back at the colonel.

Grierson's brows drew together and formed a line above his narrowed, deep-set stare. "And what matter is that?"

Agent Taylor crossed his arms above his protruding belly. "The horse that young girl stole when she ran away." He pointed a short, wide finger at Gentle Wind.

Grierson never turned his attention from the agent. He straightened into a stiff military stance. "You're mistaken, Taylor. I don't know anything about this girl stealing a horse."

Sunny swallowed the gasp which threatened and glanced at Maggie, whose widened green gaze showed she was just as surprised.

"She left the reservation without permission," Taylor argued.

"She left without *your* permission, and she returned. Now, you've put these folks through enough. I want those release papers for Running Bear and Gentle Wind on my desk by the supper hour."

Sunny could tell by the scowl on Taylor's face that the agent was not pleased. A slow wave of panic began to build. Would the agent come up with another way to delay her siblings' freedom?

''What about the Indian?''

Sunny tensed. Her pulse pounded in her ears.

''The Indian's crimes are an army matter, and one I will deal with. You got what you wanted, now it's time to fill out those papers.'' Grierson's deep tone strongly hinted at his irritation with the conversation.

The agent uncrossed his arms and slumped his shoulders in defeat. ''Very well,'' he snapped. Crossing the room, he paused and looked hard at Sunny for a second, then proceeded out of Colonel Grierson's office.

Sunny released a long, heavy sigh and looked at the colonel still standing behind his desk. ''Thank you.''

Grierson smiled, nodded once.

''Does that mean we can go with you now, Morning Sky?'' Running Bear asked in an awed, childish voice.

Sunny smiled and ruffled the top of his thick black hair with her fingers as she looked into his happy, wide-eyed stare. ''That's exactly what it means.''

Running Bear clapped his small hands together, and Gentle Wind squealed her delight, then ran around the room hugging everyone, including the colonel and Lieutenant Matthews, who had stepped inside behind Swift Arrow.

When the initial excitement began to wear down, Sunny asked Maggie to take the children so that she could speak with Grierson alone. The colonel ordered Lieutenant Matthews to lock Swift Arrow up with the other Indian prisoners being temporarily contained in the ice house. Sunny was grateful when Grierson also ordered that the brave not be tied. When everyone was gone, she crossed the distance to Grierson's wide oak desk and sat down in the chair opposite. Grierson took his seat and leaned forward, placing his elbows on the polished wood and steepling his tapping fingers. There was no smile on his face now.

''I'm sorry about McGuire. I had to ride out for a reconnaissance with Colonel McKenzie. While I was gone, he left the fort strictly against my orders. I think he may have been involved in Captain Roberts' accident, too.''

Sunny nodded. ''He was. I was there when he told Walden about it. Red Cloud missed you, too, when he came for the supplies.''

Grierson smiled. ''Those rations finally came in. I had some of the men take the allotment out to your friends at the camp. Rode along with them, that's why I was gone.''

Sunny reeled with astonishment at Grierson's actions. The Indians were supposed to come into the fort to receive their allotment. ''Thank you, Colonel.''

He shrugged, and smiled. ''Didn't want you in here hounding me again.''

Sunny cocked her head. ''I can't promise that won't happen,'' she warned.

''I didn't think you would.'' Grierson chuckled. ''Red Cloud was worried when you missed that last meeting. He returned to the fort, told me about it. By then I knew about McGuire and sent more troops up to the canyon, but they ran into Will and Maggie and came on back.'' The corners of Grierson's mouth lifted in the beginnings of a smile. ''Guess I should thank you on behalf of the army for finding those payroll shipments. I had a feeling Walden was involved. Just no proof.''

Sunny leaned back farther in the chair and rested her hands on the wooden arms. ''Swift Arrow showed us where it was hidden.''

Grierson nodded. ''Will told me that.'' He sat back and crossed his arms over his chest. ''Now, I'd like to hear the rest of what happened from you.''

Sunny told the colonel everything, even about Matt showing up, and White Bear. He didn't interrupt with a single question, but when she got to the part about Swift Arrow helping to track Walden and knowing the outlaw would go after the gold McGuire had helped steal, his thick eyebrows shot up. Sunny wasn't sure if the reaction was because of Swift Arrow's help or the gold and McGuire's involvement. She detected a smile beneath his black beard when she told him about Walden's death. She ended by telling him of her strong belief that Swift Arrow was telling the truth about not riding with Gray Wolf when the settlers were killed, and asked the colonel if the army would consider dropping the charges against him.

Grierson blew out a weighty sigh. "That's quite a story, Sunny. To be honest, I wasn't sure you were going to be able to bring these braves back. I'm glad you did, though, and I'm glad you understand that Gray Wolf will hang. As for Swift Arrow, his involvement was always in question, and there shouldn't be any problem getting the charges dropped, especially with the return of the payroll and gold. I'd say the government owes you a debt of gratitude, your cohorts in all this, too."

Sunny leaned forward and, arching one brow, stared hard at the colonel. "Then, maybe the government would consider granting me a request."

Grierson eyed her suspiciously, but there was a smile on his face. "And what is your request, young lady?"

It was near evening when Sunny finally made her way across the courtyard toward the housing quarters Grierson had provided for Maggie, Will, and the children.

She had spent a good deal of the afternoon talking with the colonel; then she had gone over to the army hospital and visited with Pete. She was pleased to see the cowhand sitting up and well enough to plan on returning to the Circle H with Will the following day. She ran into Will as she left the hospital and told him about White Bear's injury and Walden's death. He went with her to see Swift Arrow in the ice house, and they were still there when Grierson's order came for the brave to be released. Swift Arrow's surprise was evident in his eyes, and Sunny thought he was going to crush her in his arms when he pulled her into a grateful hug. He wasn't even the least bothered that the orders also stated the brave couldn't leave the fort for a day or two, until the paperwork was all cleared up. Sunny knew the real reason for Grierson's order, but she remained silent. Will asked Swift Arrow to come with him while he checked on his horses and readied the wagon for the trip home, and the two planned to stop by Grierson's office so Swift Arrow could thank the colonel personally for his release.

Sunny barely crossed the threshold of the quarters before Gentle Wind came running from a small parlor off to the left and grabbed hold of her arm.

"Where is Mr. Lanier?" the young girl asked.

Sunny sighed at the anxious look in her sister's eyes, knowing she would have to explain about White Bear. She removed her hat and saw Maggie standing in the doorway of the room with Running Bear at her side. Her friend's green stare was as concerned as Gentle Wind's. Running Bear's look was one of confusion.

"Who is Mr. Lanier?" the boy asked.

Sunny smiled. "A very kind man who went out of his way to help make sure I could be with you."

Gentle Wind planted her hands on her hips and sent her brother a look of annoyance, then rolled her eyes. "He's the white man I told you about. The one who made that promise to me, remember?"

Running Bear nodded and, when Gentle Wind turned away, stuck his tongue out at the girl. Sunny cocked her head at the boy and gave him a disapproving stare, but she couldn't stop the smile which formed on her lips. It didn't help that Maggie was chuckling behind her hand.

"What promise?" Sunny asked.

Gentle Wind's face grew serious. Her eyes widened slightly. "He promised he would find you. He said he would not come back until he did."

Sunny straightened with a start. Matt had said that! Her heart soared, then plummeted back to the painful ache she had carried all day. Great Spirit, how she missed him. How would she ever manage to get through the days without him? The years?

"I believed his promise, and he did not let me down."

Sudden tears welled in Sunny's eyes. She blinked them back and swallowed. "Matt would never let you down."

"I'd do anything for you, angel," his words echoed in her head. His promise to Gentle Wind touched her heart, and only increased the overflowing love she felt for the rancher. Sunny suddenly wanted to rush back to the cave, tonight. She longed to tell Matt what he had stopped her from saying after his offer to tend White Bear, and what she had been too afraid to say before she left.

"Where is Matt, Sunny?" Maggie's concerned voice pulled Sunny's attention.

She saw the worry in her friend's stare. "He's fine," she quickly assured. "Why don't we sit down."

Sunny took hold of Gentle Wind's arm and followed Maggie and Running Bear into the small sitting room. Sunny sat on the blue, high-backed sofa with Gentle Wind and Running Bear seated one on either side. Maggie chose one of the red rose-patterned chairs opposite. When they were settled, Sunny started her explanation with an apology, then told them about Walden being her real father and how she hated the cruel, evil man so much she wanted to forget that fact, and hadn't wanted anyone else to know the truth. Then she told them what had happened at the cave. Gentle Wind cried at the news of White Bear's injury, and though Running Bear tried to be brave, Sunny saw his bottom lip tremble.

She told them about Matt's kind offer to stay and how she planned to return and take care of White Bear until he was well.

"You will leave the children here at the fort with me, won't you?" Maggie asked.

"If you don't mind?" Sunny smiled her thanks when Maggie shook her head.

"I want to go," Gentle Wind protested. "I want to see Mr.

Lanier, so I can thank him for finding you . . . and for the candy.''

Sunny sighed at the reminder of Matt's kindness to her sister. Pain twisted her heart. ''Matt is going back to his herd, Gentle Wind, then to Wyoming.''

'' But—''

She silenced her sister's protest with a stern look, then sighed at the tears welling in her brown eyes and covered Gentle Wind's hand with her own. ''I will ask Matt if he has time to stop by the fort before he goes.''

Gentle Wind smiled.

''He's not going to stay with you?'' Maggie arched one brow quizzically.

Sunny shook her head and turned away before her friend could see the tears filling her eyes. She was thankful Maggie didn't pursue the subject any further.

The front door opened, and heavy footsteps sounded on the hardwood floor in the small foyer. Seconds later, Will and Swift Arrow filed into the small sitting room.

Will removed his hat. ''The colonel has invited us to dine with him and his wife this evening.'' He turned to Swift Arrow and lifted his mouth in a slow smile. ''All of us.'' Then Will chuckled and shifted his gaze back to Sunny. ''But he said for you and Swift Arrow to clean up. Mrs. Grierson has a firm rule about no one sitting down at her table if they're wearing more trail dust than the trail itself.''

Sunny looked down at her filthy pants and blue shirt. Her boots were coated with a heavy layer of brown dirt. She laughed. ''I suppose he'd like me to wear a dress, too.''

Will cocked his head, and smiled. ''He said it would be nice, but he didn't insist.''

An hour later, Sunny was freshly bathed and dressed in Maggie's yellow skirt and white, long-sleeved blouse. She had planned to wear the blue dress she bought in Dodge, but it was dirt-smudged around the skirt and, she realized, reminded her too much of Matt and the last night they had made love. Swift

Arrow entered the sitting room, his hair still wet, but braided neatly down his back, and looked slightly uncomfortable in the new black boots and pants and white shirt he told her Will had purchased for him earlier.

As they proceeded out the door and across the grassy courtyard toward Grierson's house, Will caught Sunny by the arm and held her back a few steps behind the others.

"Sunny, I don't know what you discussed with Grierson concerning White Bear, but I promised that brave he could go free if he led me into Outlaw Canyon."

Sunny placed her hand lightly on Will's arm and looked up. "White Bear will be free, do not worry."

He nodded and said nothing more, but Sunny could see the questions burning in his eyes. The same questions she had seen in Maggie's eyes. The same question she suddenly recalled seeing in Matt's eyes, though at the time she had not understood. But now she did. They all wanted to know if she planned to stay with White Bear. Was that what Matt thought? That she would choose White Bear? Was that why he had seemed so distant at the cave?

They arrived at Colonel Grierson's two-story house, and Sunny was forced to push her plaguing thoughts aside. Dinner was a lively affair with plenty of good food, conversation, and laughter. Sunny was glad when Swift Arrow finally stopped looking so nervous and joined in the talk around the table.

It was dark and growing late by the time they left and headed back across the courtyard. Running Bear and Gentle Wind both could barely keep their eyes open and dragged their feet the whole way. Maggie helped her get the children into their night clothes and snugly tucked into bed. They were asleep before Sunny closed the bedroom door. Swift Arrow and Will sat in the sitting room, talking, and didn't even look up as Sunny walked past. Quietly, she opened the front door and stepped out onto the narrow porch.

The full moon rode high in the black velvet sky. Sunny wondered if Matt was staring at that same moon and thinking of her as she was him. The door opened behind her. Heels clicked across the wood porch. Sunny smelled Maggie's light, flowery perfume.

"Thinking about White Bear?" Maggie softly inquired as she came to stand beside Sunny. "Or Matt?"

"Both," Sunny admitted.

"Will you make your future with White Bear as you once planned?"

Sunny sighed, and shook her head. "White Bear will always hold a special place in my heart, but things are different now."

Maggie's hand rested lightly on her shoulder. "Different because of Matt?"

Sunny moved away from Maggie's hold and walked down the steps toward the courtyard. She wasn't surprised when her friend followed.

"Are you in love with Matt?"

Sunny stopped beside the flagpole in the center of the grassy quadrangle and gripped the warm metal with shaking fingers. Silent tears slid down her cheeks as she finally looked at her friend and nodded in response to Maggie's question.

"Have you told Matt how you feel?"

"No, he doesn't . . . want to hear it." Sunny choked on the sob caught in her throat.

"Why wouldn't he want to hear it? The man's crazy in love with you." There was a gentle scolding in Maggie's voice.

Sunny turned and looked at her friend. "I make him crazy, all right. Crazy with anger and distrust, but he does not love me."

"Then, why did he insist on going with you to find Walden? Why did he shout the roof off at the hideout with worry about you? Why did he make that promise to Gentle Wind and push aside his own feelings for the Indians to ride with Swift Arrow and White Bear to find you?"

"Because he is a kind man."

Maggie pursed her lips and shook her head. "Thanks to you

he has found the kindness in his heart again. But it's more than that, Sunny.''

Sunny wanted so much to believe Maggie's words, believe that Matt did love her. *I'd do anything for you, angel.* His words pounded in her head.

''He has never said anything,'' Sunny argued weakly.

''And neither have you.'' Maggie raised a finger and gently wiped the tears from Sunny's cheek, then took her by the hand and led her across the moonlit grass. Sunny reluctantly followed.

They walked in silence for a long time, past the enlisted men's barracks and several soldiers taking in the night air on their porch. Moonlight washed their path as they walked aimlessly toward the cavalry stables at one end of the spread-out fort.

''Sunny, I think Matt's afraid to say anything about his feelings.''

Sunny lifted her head with a start. ''Matt's not afraid of anything.''

''Matt's afraid of very little, that's true. But he's afraid of his temper, and he's afraid of being hurt.''

''Matt knows I would never hurt him,'' Sunny defended. ''He knows I care. We have—'' She stopped, realizing she had almost blurted out about their lovemaking.

Maggie's arched brows and steady gaze told Sunny her friend knew exactly what she had been about to say. ''He thought Ashley cared also.'' Maggie stopped, and turned to face her. ''I think you should know what happened back then. Maybe it will help you to understand why Matt has closed his heart all these years.''

Sunny narrowed her gaze with puzzled curiosity, but said nothing. Maggie started to walk again, and she fell into step beside her.

''That morning when I arrived at the church and told him Ashley ran off with the cowhand, Matt got furious. He started breaking furniture, kicked the front door off its hinges, and before I could stop him, he punched the reverend in the face. He was threatening to ride after Ashley and kill the cowhand, but he ended up sitting in jail instead. I figured he was safer there, and waited until the next morning to bail him out. He felt so bad about what he had done. He apologized to the reverend and paid to replace everything he had broken. He had to stay in Oak Valley on Ranger business, but he spent more time getting drunk than he did on work. We talked a lot during those days, and got to know each other pretty well."

Sunny nodded, and looked at her friend. "I could tell you two are very close. I even wondered if there had been more between you at one time," she confessed.

Maggie shook her head. "I admit I developed a small crush on him, but Matt never felt anything more than friendship, and guilt."

"Guilt?" Sunny arched one brow, puzzled.

Maggie nodded. "You see, I was in love with that cowhand Ashley ran off with, so Matt and I had a lot in common."

Sunny's eyes widened at her friend's revelation. She had had no idea. As far as she had known, Maggie had never glanced twice at any man. Was this cowhand the reason?

"Then one day I got a letter from that man, telling me he had had a change of heart about Ashley and wanted me to come to him. I wasn't planning on going, but I made the mistake of showing Matt the letter. As soon as he saw it, and knew where the cowhand was, he took off, intending to go after them. I chased after him on horseback. The horse took a sudden jump over a large stump, and I fell. Matt saw the accident and came back."

"Were you hurt?"

Maggie nodded. "I lost the baby I was carrying."

Sunny reeled back with shock, as surprised by the news of a baby as she was by the blank, tearless stare in Maggie's eyes.

"Matt blamed himself. I never did. He took care of me, brought Elethea to tend me. And he kept my secret. To this day no one knows, except for Elethea and Matt, and now you."

Sunny sighed and shook her head, still trying to absorb everything Maggie had told her.

"The day Matt left Texas for good, he promised not to hunt the cowhand down and kill him because of Ashley, and he vowed never to fall in love again. But that didn't happen. He fell in love with you, and if he thinks you still have feelings for White Bear, I'd guess he's hurting pretty bad. And I'd also guess he's fighting his temper mighty hard. The fact that he offered to stay behind tells me just how much he cares about you. But I knew that already. He never looked at Ashley the way he looks at you. And I think it was more his pride than his heart that got hurt that day at the church."

Sunny looked away, glancing up at the moon again, and wondered what Matt was doing right then. Was he thinking of her, wondering if she indeed had chosen White Bear over him in her heart? She had thought he didn't profess his love because of her ties with the Comanches, because of her siblings. Was she wrong? She remembered the distant look in his eyes at the cave, remembered the way he had seemed to pull away from her. And she recalled the change had taken place in him *after* she had run to White Bear's side.

I'd do anything for you, angel. His words came rushing back.

"I must go to him." Sunny turned, but only managed one step before Maggie's hand touched her arm.

"You can't go tonight, it's late."

Sunny sighed, and hung her head, remembering she couldn't go at all, not until Grierson received an answer to her request. Two days. In two days she would see him again, and she vowed that as soon as she returned to the cave, she would not waste a single minute telling him how much she loved him.

Sunny turned back to her friend. "Thank you," she whispered. "Thank you for telling me, and for helping me to know Matt's heart, and my own."

"Oh, Sunny." Maggie shook her head slightly. "Anyone that sees the two of you together knows you belong with each other. I'm just glad I could help."

Sunny smiled, and started to chuckle.

Maggie furrowed her brow. "What's so funny?"

"I owe Jube a hundred dollars."

"What on earth for?"

"He started this bet with the men that Matt and I would fall in love."

Maggie arched her brows high. "And you bet against him?"

Sunny nodded. "Double or nothing."

Maggie shook her head and laughed under her breath. "You know better than to bet against Jube."

The first thing Sunny noticed as she approached the cave beneath the hot afternoon sun two days later was that Matt's black gelding was nowhere in sight. A lone, spotted pony she had never seen before was ground tied outside the cave entrance. She turned to Swift Arrow, who rode beside her and led White Bear's horse, which the army troops who had captured him returned when they had come back to the fort. She could see the confusion and wariness in the brave's dark eyes and knew it mirrored her own.

Low light spilled through the cave's entrance from the small fire she could see burning just inside. Smells of brewing tea and a meat stew wafted through the air. They stopped in front of the cave, and Sunny swung herself down from Molly's back. Swift Arrow came around and stood beside her. As they slowly approached the lighted entrance, a young Comanche woman with short-cropped black hair and a pretty, round face emerged. She stopped and waited for them to walk closer.

"You must be Morning Sky," she said with a smile.

Sunny slowly nodded her head. "And who are you?"

"My name is Desert Flower. I am friend of White Bear."

At the mention of the brave's name, Sunny peered past the woman into the cave.

"He has been waiting for you," Desert Flower told her. Her

chocolate brown eyes darted to Swift Arrow, then back to Sunny. "He wishes to speak with you alone."

Sunny glanced at Swift Arrow and saw him wave her on inside. As she walked into the cave, she heard Swift Arrow and Desert Flower speaking in low voices that soon faded away. Sunny looked around the cave and gave a small start of surprise to see White Bear sitting on a buffalo robe and leaning back against one side of the cave wall. He smiled at her.

She smiled back, walked over, and sat down beside him. "You are doing well?"

He nodded. "I have had good care. And you, Morning Sky, you are also well? You now have Running Bear and Gentle Wind with you?"

"Yes, but I didn't bring them with me. I did bring Swift Arrow."

White Bear narrowed his curious stare. "How is it my brother is allowed to come to me? Why do they not hold him?"

"Swift Arrow is free of all charges because of his innocence. He's also freed in the Indian Territory. He doesn't have to live at the fort, only on Indian land. He will stay free as long as he doesn't partake in any renegade raids."

White Bear's eyes widened. "How do you do this?"

Sunny smiled. "Colonel Grierson is a good friend." She had been surprised to learn he had already started the paperwork for the two braves' release shortly after Will and Maggie returned to the fort. She had gone ahead and waited the two days she told Matt she would be gone, so that everything could be finalized and she could bring White Bear the news. "The army is grateful for the return of the payroll and gold. Grateful enough that you are no longer considered an escaped renegade, either. You've been granted the same freedom status as Swift Arrow."

White Bear shook his head in disbelief, then smiled slowly. "You have much power with the white man. I feel in my heart you will accomplish many things for our people."

Sunny clutched her fist over her heart. ''That's because they are my people, too. In here.''

White Bear nodded. ''So where is my brother?''

Sunny lowered her hand to her lap. ''He's outside, with Desert Flower.'' She cocked her head. ''Is she your woman?''

White Bear narrowed his gaze. His lips curled down slightly. ''No. Her family fled north after their village was raided. I am helping her to find them. But would it matter to you if she was, Morning Sky?''

She took a deep breath, then released it slowly and stared into the brave's dark eyes. She lifted her chin. ''I would be happy for you, my *moneta.*''

White Bear's frown deepened. ''You call me brother. Has your heart changed for me?''

Sunny nodded. ''I will always walk the way of our people, and you will always hold a special place in my heart, *moneta,* but my love belongs to Matt Lanier. And I have come to tell him that.''

''He is not here.''

''What!'' He was gone! He had left! Tremors ran through her veins. Her heart pounded.

''I am sorry, Morning Sky. He left yesterday, after Desert Flower came.''

''Why?'' Her lip trembled. She blinked back the tears.

''He did not say, but I believe he thought your heart still belonged to me.'' White Bear's eyes darkened with sadness. ''And so had I. When you said, 'You've come back to me,' I had hope that we could begin a life together as we once planned.''

Sunny gasped. Had Matt heard her say that? She didn't remember saying the words, but she had been so shocked at seeing White Bear again, she might have said anything. Was that why Matt had turned from her? Grown so distant? That had to be it. She had to find him and tell him the truth.

The rest of White Bear's words slowly sank in. Her heart ached at the knowledge that he still cared deeply for her and would suffer pain because of her choice. "I am sorry I have hurt you, White Bear. I was so . . . surprised to see you, and then so worried you *would* die. I didn't know what I was feeling then. I—"

White Bear gently placed one finger against her lips, silencing her. "I knew in my heart, Morning Sky, you were gone from me. I just did not want to accept it. But I have. Matt Lanier is a good man. You have made a good choice . . . my friend."

Sunny pulled his finger from her mouth, then leaned over and hugged him, careful of his wound. "Thank you, my friend, for understanding," she whispered as a single tear slipped from her eye.

Chapter Twenty-One

"What if Matt is not happy to see me?"

Maggie smiled, and grabbed Sunny's hands away from the ropes which held the supplies on the packhorse.

"You've checked those ropes four times. Stop being so nervous. Matt is going to welcome you with open arms, as soon as he knows how you feel."

Sunny sighed. She hadn't stopped being nervous since she rode back to the fort three days ago. The decision to pack up their belongings and bring her siblings along to catch up with the herd—and Matt—had felt right in her heart. But now that it was time to leave, she was having grave doubts. What if Matt had given up? Forgotten her already? What if he really didn't love her as Maggie believed? And Great Spirit, what would he say about Gentle Wind and Running Bear?

"Come on, Morning Sky, let's go." Gentle Wind stared down from atop the saddleless bay mare, her eager brown eyes aglow with excitement. "We have to find Mr. Lanier." The girl had talked of little else, and Sunny prayed she would not be disappointed.

Running Bear sat on the horse behind his sister and looked just as excited, but since he had never met Matt, Sunny knew his eyes sparkled because of the peppermint stick he was sucking on, and the one in his pocket he was saving for later.

Sunny knew her doubts would plague her the entire trip, but they wouldn't keep her from going. This was right. She knew it in her heart. She loved Matt. And now it was time to go to him.

She turned to Maggie. Tears flowed down her cheeks. Sunny's eyes welled.

"I'm going to miss you, Sunny."

"And I will miss you, my friend."

She stepped forward at the same time Maggie did, and they held each other in a tight hug.

"We will meet again, my friend," Sunny whispered. "I'll be coming back to the fort. And you can come north."

Maggie nodded. "You take care. And don't worry, Matt loves you."

Sunny wiped her tears away and swung herself up onto Molly's back. Gentle Wind and Running Bear rode beside her. Sunny held the rope to the packhorse trailing behind as they followed the road leading away from the fort. Sunny looked back once and waved at Maggie; then she tilted her chin, faced front, and turned to the north.

Matt dumped out his half-eaten plate of food and deposited the tin plate on Jube's wagon.

"Where ya headin' off to, Bronco?"

"Just taking a walk." Matt didn't bother to look back over his shoulder as he answered. What was there to see?

Jube joking with the cowhands. The men relaxing after a long day in the saddle, finishing up a filling meal of fried meat and beans. The same thing he had seen every night since rejoining the herd north of Dodge a little over a week ago.

The one person he wanted to see sitting around that fire

wasn't there. She wasn't even in the same territory as he anymore. Matt wondered if his heart would ever catch up with him, or if it would spend the rest of its beating life wandering the Indian Territory, worrying and wondering where she was, or if she was happy.

Her Indian love had come back to her. Matt sighed and let his shoulders slump. She was happy.

He followed the narrow path through the trees and short brush, stopping along the creek's edge. He watched the sun disappear on the horizon, and wondered if she watched the same sunset and thought of him. Matt closed his eyes. Why would she think of him? She was with the people she loved, with the man she wanted. He couldn't help but wonder how White Bear was faring. No matter his feelings about the brave, he had never wanted the man to die. White Bear had risked his life for Sunny. Matt took small comfort in knowing she would at least be with a man who loved her and could protect her.

Were they still at the cave? Or had they moved on to begin their life together? Matt knew he would know that answer if he had stayed. He would have stayed with White Bear until Sunny returned. But when that Indian woman came, he thought about how Sunny had stammered around trying to tell him when she would come back, and couldn't help but think she had sent the woman so he *wouldn't* be there. And what good would it have done for him to wait, only to watch his little spitfire walk into the arms of another man. *You've come back to me.* A heart could only break so hard, and his had crumbled into pieces at those words. She had made her choice. And that choice wasn't him.

Matt opened his eyes and took a deep breath. He took in the solitude around him—the darkness, the soft moonlight, the sound of flowing water, the birds singing. So peaceful. So lonely. Would he ever get used to the loneliness? His family was gone. Sunny was gone. There were no more dreams, no more hopes, only emptiness.

God, how he missed her. Matt wiped the single tear sliding down along his nose. He stared at the silvery reflection in the water and saw her pretty eyes, her beautiful golden face, her soft, flowing hair. Another tear silently fell. Matt brushed it away and took another deep breath.

Loud whoops and hollers from the men sounded on the air and carried through the trees down to the creek. Matt listened, and wondered what the cowhands were getting so excited about. He frowned. Whatever it was, they better keep it down before they started a damn stampede. The thought of a stampede reminded him of Sunny, seeing her take charge, watching her ride her little palomino bareback and scaring the hell out of him, admiring her quick thinking. Her laughter.

Her laughter? Matt drew his brows together, cocked his head, and listened. Muffled male voices. More laughter. A feminine, melodious chuckle. Sunny? Matt shook his head. No, it couldn't be. Sunny wasn't here. Sunny wasn't coming.

Matt spun around at the sound of approaching footsteps. Web came sauntering through the trees.

"Hey, boss. Jube sent me down here to fetch ya."

Matt wondered at the smile on Web's face. If this had something to do with a damn bet or another attempt to draw him into a poker game, he wasn't in the mood. "Why?" he ground out harshly.

Web's smile got bigger. "He thought you might wanna come see who just rode into camp."

Before Matt could tell the cowhand he wasn't interested, Web spun on his heel and hurried off. Matt grumbled under his breath as he slowly followed the path back to camp. Emerging from the trees, he looked up. His heart stopped at the sight of her sitting by the fire surrounded by the cowhands. He closed his eyes and shook his head, thinking he was going crazy. Not only was he hearing her voice, now he was even seeing her. God, he didn't know a heartache could hurt so bad.

"Mr. Lanier!"

Matt's eyes flew open at the childish voice shouting his

name. He barely had time to see the young girl dressed in pants and blue shirt before Gentle Wind launched herself into his arms. She knocked his hat off when her arms looped around his neck and then hugged him fiercely.

"Thank you," she cried. "Thank you for keeping your promise and finding Morning Sky."

Matt couldn't move, couldn't find his voice. He held the young girl in his embrace as she buried her face against his shoulder and hugged him tighter. He looked past the men seated around the fire and met Sunny's sky blue stare. His heart slammed against his ribs. She was here! She smiled, and Matt choked on his next breath. What was she doing here? He looked around expecting to see White Bear standing off to the side somewhere. He didn't see him. Sunny was still smiling. Matt's confusion mounted. He tried to still the rapid beating of his heart, and failed. Why had she come? Hadn't she hurt him enough by choosing White Bear? What could she possibly hope to gain by coming here? At least Ashley had the decency not to rub his nose in her choice by coming back to see him after she had made it. Slow anger began to build. What did she want?

Matt eased Gentle Wind's arms from his neck, and he set her gently away from him, then looked down into her round, bronze face. Her brown eyes shimmered with unshed tears of joy. "I believed you would not let me down, and you didn't," she told him. "Thank you."

Matt ran his hand along her smooth cheek, surprised to see his fingers shaking. "You don't owe me any thanks," he whispered, smiling slightly. "I was glad to do it."

"Hey, Bronco?"

Matt looked up and saw Jube waving one of his long wooden spoons in the air, motioning for him to come over.

"Miz Sunny's come back to finish the drive," Jube hollered out, a wide grin spreading on his face.

Finish the drive? What the hell was she doing that for? His

anger grew a little more. And where in tarnation was White Bear?

Matt retrieved his hat, then put his arm around Gentle Wind's slender shoulders and walked toward the fire. For the most part he kept his gaze on Sunny's smiling face, but he glanced once to the young boy sitting at her side, his light eyes rounded with curiosity.

Sunny stood as he came closer, and Gentle Wind ran from him to join her. Matt stopped several feet away.

"What are you doing here?" His demanding tone caught him by surprise, and everyone else as well. The men's laughter and good humor died. Sunny's smile faded. Gentle Wind stared openmouthed at him, and the boy glared at him with a fierceness that reminded him of Sunny.

The hurt he thought he detected in Sunny's eyes was quickly replaced by a spark of temper he recognized. He jerked his head up and braced for battle. He wasn't going to let her come in here and tear his heart up any more. There was nothing left to rip and break. Damnation, what was she trying to do to him?

"You heard Jube," she snapped, planting her fists on her hips. "I came back to finish the drive, just like I promised Danny."

"And I told you there wasn't any reason to keep that promise. Besides, I'm in charge now, remember."

"And in case you've forgotten, *Mr. Lanier,* I'm still the one who paid these men to drive your herd."

Matt blew out an exasperated breath and grumbled a string of curses. Sunny narrowed her heated gaze.

"Hey, ya two," Jube interjected. "What are ya gettin' all heated up over? Why don't ya both just boss the drive, together."

"Shut up, Jube!" They said the words in unison, then glared harder at each other.

Matt turned and stormed off back toward the creek. His heart pounded, and his blood raced hotly through his veins. God, how he wanted her, his anguished thoughts cried. But more than anything at the moment, he wished she would just go away, before he broke down and made a real fool of himself begging her to stay.

Sunny sat beside the creek with Running Bear and Gentle Wind and tried not to let them see her tears which had started to fall the minute Matt walked off, and hadn't stopped. He didn't want her. Maggie had been wrong. A dull, empty ache gnawed at her heart, her soul. She clenched her trembling lips together.

"Why did Mr. Lanier get so mad?" Gentle Wind asked as she tossed a small pebble into the moonlit creek.

"I don't like him," Running Bear stated in a firm, childish tone.

Sunny didn't know what to say. She didn't understand either. Matt hadn't given her a chance to say anything. Why had he been so mad? If this had to do with White Bear, she could explain. She wanted to explain. A cold fist closed over her heart. But Matt didn't want to hear it. She knew now he hadn't said he loved her because he didn't. He was furious she had come.

"I thought Maggie said he would be glad to see you?" Gentle Wind threw another rock into the water.

Running Bear picked up a handful and tossed them in all at once, making a loud splash, then turned his frown up to Sunny. "Why would you love that man, Morning Sky? He's mean."

"He's not always mean," Gentle Wind quickly defended. "Remember when I told you he gave me the peppermint."

"Well, he's not getting the one I brought for him, not after yelling at Morning Sky." Running Bear lifted his small rounded chin and pursed his lips.

"What are we . . . going to do now?" Gentle Wind's voice cracked on her low sob.

Sunny sighed and put one arm around Gentle Wind's shoulders. "Don't fret, little one. We can always go to the Circle

H like we planned. We can buy our own land and build our own house. We'll be fine.'' *And the two of you can grow up happy and loved, and I will somehow try to survive this heartache.* ''We'll leave tomorrow.''

Dear God! What had he done? Matt raked his fingers through his hair, then peered around the tree again and stared at Sunny's and Gentle Wind's sad faces, and the angry glare on the boy's. He hadn't meant to walk up and overhear their conversation. Hell, he hadn't even known they were there. But they were, and he had heard, and now he was feeling as low as the snake-bellied varmint Sunny had called him when they first met.

Running Bear had brought him peppermint, but now hated him and didn't want to give it to him. Gentle Wind had jumped into his arms, hugged him, thanked him, even defended him a moment ago, and now she was crying and confused because of him. And Sunny. God, his beautiful little spitfire looked devastated. But the one thing that stuck in his head the most was Running Bear's words, ''Why would you love that man?''

Was it true? Did Sunny love him? Is that why she had come? His heart pounded with anticipation. Did he dare to hope?

''Do you still love Mr. Lanier, Morning Sky?'' Gentle Wind asked.

''Very much, little one.''

Matt's heart soared. She loved him. His breathing came in short gasps. She loved him.

''I don't want to leave,'' Gentle Wind whined.

''We must. We are not wanted here,'' Sunny insisted.

Matt's gut tightened. They couldn't leave. He wouldn't let them.

''You're wrong, angel.'' Matt stepped from behind the tree as three startled faces turned to look at him. ''You're very much wanted here. All of you.''

''Go away!'' Running Bear shouted, jumping to his feet. He ran over and kicked Matt in the leg.

Sunny jumped to her feet and rushed over. ''Running Bear, that's enough.''

Matt held out his hand for her to stop and hid the smile which almost formed at the boy's actions. He liked the way the boy came to his sister's defense. It reminded him a lot of himself years ago.

"He has a right to be angry." Matt stepped closer and knelt down in front of Running Bear. "I shouldn't have yelled like I did. I'm sorry." He lifted his stare to Sunny as he said the last. Her shimmering gaze pricked at his conscience.

Gentle Wind stepped forward and crossed her thin arms. "Morning Sky said we must give you time. That your heart still grieves for your family as ours do. Is that why you are mad we came?"

Matt swept his stare over Gentle Wind's thin frame dressed in tan pants and a long-sleeved blue shirt tucked in at her narrow waist. Her long black hair was fixed into a thick braid, and tiny curls framed her round bronze face. He pictured Sunny at this age. His little spitfire learning to be a warrior, learning to fight for her own survival and that of the people she cared so much about. These two children had Sunny's same tough spirit. The same spirit he loved and admired.

"I'm not mad you came, Gentle Wind." Matt stood and, placing his hand on Running Bear's shoulder, drew the boy with him as he moved closer to Gentle Wind. He stood the children in front of him, then knelt on one knee to their smaller level. "My heart will always grieve for my family, as yours will. But I don't blame you, or your people, for what happened anymore. Your sister," he paused and looked up at Sunny. She stood with her arms crossed and chewed on her bottom lip. His heart twisted at the look of apprehension in her blue stare. He turned back to the children. "Morning Sky has taught me many things about your people, and I am proud to call Swift Arrow my friend . . . and White Bear."

Sunny gasped. Matt was surprised himself that White Bear's name rolled so easily from his tongue.

"I would like to be your friend, too." He looked first at Gentle Wind's anxious brown stare, then at Running Bear's cautious hazel glare. "I didn't yell at your sister because I was mad, but because I was afraid."

Running Bear swept his stare over him in disbelief.

Gentle Wind's eyes widened. "But Morning Sky says you are not afraid of anything."

Matt sighed. "Your sister is wrong. I'm very much afraid she won't forgive me and *will* leave tomorrow, taking my heart with her again."

Running Bear cocked his small head to one side and eyed him closely. "What does this mean, take your heart? Morning Sky does not use her warrior skills to kill."

Matt smiled slightly. "It means that I will hurt inside again if she goes away."

Running Bear narrowed his stare as though in deep thought, then slowly nodded his head. "I did not like it when Morning Sky was gone from us. It did hurt inside." The boy touched a small fist to his heart; then a small smile lifted the corners of his mouth. "Morning Sky says you own land. That you have a big ranch with lots of horses."

Matt nodded. "Would you like to come and see my horses?"

Running Bear nodded, then tilted his chin. "I like horses."

"And what about you, Gentle Wind? Would you like to come to Wyoming?"

"Oh, yes," she answered eagerly, then paused and darted her gaze past him. "Can we still go, Morning Sky?"

Matt didn't turn around, but held his breath and waited.

"I think we'll talk about this in the morning. Right now, it's late and time for you two to be in bed."

Matt's heart sank at her less than encouraging words. Choking back the sudden knot in his throat, he stood.

The children protested as Sunny stepped forward and started to urge them along. Matt thought she was going to walk off without even looking at him, but before they had taken two steps, she turned. Her small smile sent his heart soaring.

"Will you wait for me to come back?" she quietly asked.

Matt smiled, hoping she couldn't see how badly he shook inside. ''Always,'' he whispered.

Forty-five minutes later, Sunny hurried back down the narrow path to the creek, her heart pounding in anticipation. Would Matt still be there as he said? She smiled, remembering his words to Gentle Wind and Running Bear about not wanting her to leave, about taking his heart with her. He would be there.

She emerged from the trees and stopped in the soft moonlight-washed path. Matt stood with his back to her, staring out across the small stream. She devoured his tall, muscular form with her eyes. Love swelled in her heart to near overflowing.

Slowly, he turned as though sensing her presence, and his gaze swept over her, sending tingling heat shooting through her. He smiled.

''You changed.''

Sunny nodded and looked down at the blue dress, suddenly feeling foolish for putting it on, but she had wanted to wear it for Matt. He had told her she was beautiful the one time he saw her in it, then he had made sweet, passionate love to her. The dress held good memories for her, and for Matt, she hoped.

''You look beautiful, angel.''

Sunny's heart tripped. ''I was hoping you'd think so.''

Matt's smiled deepened, and he stepped toward her. Sunny met him halfway.

He raised a hand and touched her cheek with gentle fingers, then stared into her eyes with his desirous, midnight blue gaze that melted her insides to a warm pool. He sighed heavily. ''God, how I missed you, angel. I thought I'd never see you again.''

Maggie's words echoed in her head, *Tell him how you feel.* Sunny swallowed. ''Matt, I . . . I wasn't sure you wanted to see me again. When I went back to the cave, you were gone.''

Matt's smile faded. His hand fell to his side. ''I was sure you'd chosen White Bear. I—''

Sunny pressed a finger to his lips, silencing him. ''White Bear will always have a place in my heart, with all my Comanche friends and family. But my love belongs to you, Matt Lanier. It has from the moment you pulled me from that tree and looked into my eyes. I'm sorry I didn't trust you sooner. I'm sorry I didn't tell you about my father. And I promise you, there are no more secrets, no more lies or half-truths in my life. I will never keep anything from you again."

Matt captured her hand with his, kissed her finger, then removed it from his lips. There was no smile on his face, and Sunny's heart pounded with sudden fear. Her lips trembled; then tremors shook her body as he stood there staring down at her.

"Don't look so scared, angel. I've wanted nothing more than to hear you say those words, and God knows, I love you. But there's something I haven't been honest about, and you've got a right to know."

Sunny furrowed her brow. Her stomach constricted into a hard knot. She tried not to panic and clung to his admission of love for her.

"You asked me once if I'd ever killed a man, and I never answered. But I'm going to tell you now, because I don't want any secrets between us anymore, either. I've killed before, in self-defense. But there's one man I killed because I let my temper get the best of me. I swore it would never happen again, and I promise you it won't."

Sunny sighed her relief. She had been so afraid he was going to turn her away. Cupping his smooth, taut cheeks in her hands, she gazed into his tortured stare. "The cowhand who left Maggie?"

Matt's eyes widened. "She told you about him?"

Sunny nodded. "At the fort. But she didn't tell me what you did."

"And how do you feel about what I did?"

"I feel that you are a good man, and you wouldn't do anything without good reason." She raised up on her toes and brought her lips to his.

He crushed her to him in a tight embrace and kissed her

hungrily with a passion that sent heat swirling in her stomach. Sunny wound her arms around his neck and savored each heat-stroking touch of his lips, his tongue, his hands, roving over her body. Then his lips left hers, but he still held her and looked down at her with such love in his eyes, Sunny couldn't stop the tears from welling in her own.

"I love you, Sunny. I've wanted to tell you that since the first time I kissed you. You're the best thing that's ever come into my life, and I've got to warn you, now that you're here, I'm not ever letting you go."

"There's no place else I want to be. I love you, Matt. The Comanches are my people, but you are my destiny. Always and forever."

He kissed her again, crushing her breasts against his chest and pressing her hips closer to his. She felt the full evidence of his desire between them, and waves of delicious heat swept through her veins. She moaned when he pulled his mouth from hers and leaned back.

"Have I told you how beautiful you look in that dress?"

She nodded, smiling.

He smiled back, and cocked one brow. "Have I told you how much I'd like to slip it from your body and make love to you under the stars tonight?"

She nodded.

Matt frowned slightly. "When?"

"Just now," she whispered.

"So I did." He smiled, then swept her into his arms and carried her to a shadowed spot underneath one of the trees, where he laid her gently on a blanket spread beneath.

She raised one brow teasingly as he started to unfasten the buttons down her dress. "Where did you get the blanket?"

His fingers stilled. "From camp, while you were putting the children to bed. And I told Jube to keep the men away from the creek the rest of the night."

She smiled. "So you planned this."

His lips curled up at the corners, and he stared at her with such longing her heart skipped its next beat. "No, angel, I only had hope."

Matt woke as the first light of day began to work its way above the horizon. Sunny stirred in his arms, then snuggled her warm body closer to his. He stared into her pretty, sleeping face and smiled. It hadn't been a dream. She was here, and she had promised to stay with him forever. His heart swelled with love. He wanted to rouse her, make love to her again; but sounds of the men stirring around the camp reached his ears, and he worried that Gentle Wind and Running Bear would come looking for them.

He trailed his finger down her smooth, golden cheek, then leaned over and kissed her lips. She responded to his touch, and he had to force himself to pull back before he threw caution to the wind and took her anyway, regardless of the people in camp.

"Time to get up, angel."

She slowly opened her eyes and gazed up at him. Her lips parted in a small, sexy smile. "Do we have to?"

He nodded. Then, as though in confirmation, there was a loud clang of pots banging together which carried on the air through the small stand of trees separating them from the camp. She groaned.

They dressed quickly, and Matt bent to retrieve the blanket, then walked over to the creek where Sunny knelt and splashed water on her face. She dried the moisture with the hem of her dress, then turned and looked up at him. There was no smile on her face, and a sudden apprehension gripped his heart.

"What's wrong, angel?"

She stood and faced him. "Nothing. I was wondering about that dream Danny talked about. The one he was sorry he couldn't finish with you. Will you tell me about it?"

The dream. Matt sighed, then smiled and touched his palm to her cheek. "The dream was about owning land, building a ranch, having a legacy that we could share as a family and pass down to our children. It was a hope, a dream my pa started, and that I thought died forever with Danny. But you came into my life, angel, and now I realize those dreams aren't gone. They're right here, with you, and Gentle Wind and Running Bear . . . and maybe someday our children.''

Matt took her hands in his, then dropped to one knee and looked up at her hesitant blue stare. ''I can have those dreams, Sunny, if you'll do me the honor of becoming my wife.''

Tears flowed down her cheeks, but the smile on her lips when she nodded told him of her happiness. He stood and gathered her into his arms and couldn't remember a single time he had ever felt so at peace, so happy . . . so complete. She was the only thing he needed. *She* was his dream.

The noises around camp grew louder, and reluctantly he stepped back, but kept one arm around her shoulders as they walked along the narrow path. They emerged from the trees to a bustle of activity around Jube's large cook fire. Several of the men were already sitting around the fire waiting for Jube to finish breakfast. Web and Hank were entertaining Gentle Wind and Running Bear with card tricks. Matt dropped his arm from Sunny's shoulders, but captured her hand in his as they approached.

Jube looked up. ''Well, well, lookee who's here, boys.'' His wide grin spread across his face. The murmurs and laughter died around the fire as all eyes turned to them. ''So what's new, Bronco? How's life treatin' ya?''

Matt smiled. ''Life's treating me just fine.'' He turned and looked down at Sunny's glowing, happy face. His heart swelled with love and pride. ''Sunny and I are getting married.''

The men cheered and offered their congratulations. Running Bear and Gentle Wind rushed over and hugged them. After a few minutes when things started to settle down some, Jube banged his wooden spoon against his large Dutch oven, drawing everyone's attention.

''All right, boys, time to pay up.'' The cook turned and

looked straight at Sunny, his smile spreading across his narrow black face. ''And you're the first one I'm collectin' from, Miz Sunny. I believe that's a hundred bucks you owe me.''

Matt furrowed his brow, confused. He looked at Sunny.

She shook her head and rolled her eyes, then quickly told him about the bet Jube had started over them falling in love.

He cocked a brow. ''You bet against us?''

She shook her head. ''My stubbornness bet against us. My heart already knew I lost the bet.''

''You didn't lose, angel. We both won.'' He smiled, then kissed her in front of everyone, mindless of the cheers that started up around them again.

Epilogue

September 1873

Sunny stepped out onto the porch of the two-story, white clapboard house and pulled her wrap tighter around her shoulders against the cool afternoon breeze. White, puffy clouds dotted the rich azure sky and floated by lazily. She looked to the large corral in the distance and saw Gentle Wind riding the saddleless mare Matt had given the girl as a birthday present a few weeks earlier. The young horse was only partially tamed, and Matt held the long lead rope in the center of the corral while Gentle Wind rode the black horse in a circle. Running Bear sat on the top fence rail, watching. Sunny smiled, then walked over to one of the two white chairs and, using one hand to brace herself on the wooden arm, lowered her cumbersome body down onto the seat, then arranged her skirt around her bulky form.

Great Spirit, she would be glad when this baby was born.

''Why you got Captain McGuire all tied up instead of that Indian?'' The soldier eyed her warily.

''Arrest these two,'' McGuire shouted out.

Sunny raised her gun as the soldiers stepped forward, and turned the revolver on the captain. ''Shut up, McGuire. You've caused enough trouble.'' Then she shifted her attention to the soldier. ''This is a matter for the colonel's ears, not yours.''

''Well, I'm afraid I can't let you go any farther, not with that Indian, or that gun.''

Sunny sighed and holstered her gun; then she tipped the brim of her hat and leaned forward slightly over Molly's neck. ''I'm not here looking for trouble. I'm here to see the colonel. Now, is he at headquarters or his house?'' She didn't bother to hide the irritation in her voice.

''Let her through, men!'' The deep, military tone cut across the air.

Sunny looked up at the shouted order, surprised to see Lieutenant Matthews, Grierson's adjutant, sauntering forward at a quickened pace. He stopped beside the three guards and glared at them until they lowered their rifles. Then he turned his sight to Sunny.

He nodded his head. ''Good to see you again, Miss Donovan. The colonel sent me down here to see if there was any sign of you yet. He'll be glad to know you're here.''

Sunny stared at the lieutenant's tightened, angular face and sensed there was some kind of problem associated with the urgency in his tone. ''Where is he, Lieutenant?''

''In his office, ma'am. And we need to hurry.'' Lieutenant Matthews turned slightly and faced the guards. ''Johnson, see to their horses. Carter, for the time being, take McGuire and put him in the basement of the cavalry barracks with the rest of the prisoners.''

The guards' eyes widened with shock, but no one said a word. Sunny dismounted and motioned for Swift Arrow to do the same. The soldier, Johnson, stepped forward and took the

Matt had refused to let her ride for months now, and she missed being able to race with the wind on Molly. He hadn't let her travel either, not since her trip to the reservation in late spring when they had shipped a good number of the thriving longhorns to market, and she had led a small drive of two hundred and fifty head down to the reservation for the Indians. She had been pleased to find the rations arriving on time. But the government had come, surveying the reservation lands, and there was unrest among many of the Comanches and Kiowas concerned that their land was about to be divided for settlers. She feared peace was still a long time in coming. Colonel Grierson had agreed. Maggie's small school was going well, but even with the arrival of the new Quaker Indian Agent, there was still discord concerning the children's education.

Sunny was concerned about the upcoming winter months, and Matt had been kind enough to send one of the ranch hands on the day-and-a-half ride to Cheyenne to post her letter to Washington in hopes of securing better, warmer clothing for the Indians this year. The ranch hand had returned just this afternoon, bringing with him a letter from Will. She pulled the small envelope from her pocket and opened it.

Matt's rich laughter rang out, mingled with the children's, and Sunny looked up. He sauntered toward the house with Running Bear and Gentle Wind tugging at his arms, and she could tell he was purposefully slowing his steps to tease them. Her heart swelled with love. He was such a good man, so kind and gentle with her and the children. She couldn't imagine her life without him, didn't even want to try.

The children bounded up the steps first, then eyed her skeptically when she told them there were cookies and lemonade waiting on the table. They only rushed into the house after she told them she hadn't burned the sweet treat this time.

Matt strolled over to where she sat, his smile warming her insides. He leaned over and kissed her full on the mouth, sending a rush of desire coursing through her veins. Great Spirit, she would be glad when this baby was born and they could make love again.

"What's that?" Matt nodded down at the letter in her hand.

"It's from Will."

"Good news, I hope." He lowered his tall, muscular frame into the empty chair beside her.

Sunny nodded and smiled. "Swift Arrow has been granted 'protected status' to travel from the reservation to Oak Valley. He's going to work for Will and learn about driving cattle."

"That's great. Now he can give *Will's* cattle away to the Indians." His voice was full of lighthearted teasing, and Sunny playfully swatted at his arm.

"Any news of White Bear?" he asked after a moment.

Sunny smiled. "You'll be happy to know White Bear and Desert Flower got married two months ago. Will gave them horses as a wedding present. They plan to settle on the reservation and raise their own stock, and try farming."

Matt nodded. "That is good news."

Sunny cocked one brow. "Which part?"

"The part about him being married, of course." Matt's dark blue gaze hinted at a jealousy she knew he hadn't quite gotten over. "What else did Will have to say?"

Sunny chuckled. "He said to tell you he's still upset about missing the birth of his first child because of me and Maggie, and he hopes you get caught in a snowstorm when it's my time."

Matt laughed. "No chance of that, angel."

Sunny's smile faded as a sharp pain suddenly ripped across her lower belly. She gasped, dropped Will's letter, then clutched at her stomach."

Matt was instantly on his feet and at her side. "What's wrong?"

Another pain tore at her insides. Sunny groaned and reached

for the medicine bag hanging around her neck. She looked up at her husband. "Nothing's wrong. I think it's time."

Matt knelt, his eyes wide with sudden alarm. "Time? Time for what? The baby's not due yet."

Sunny gritted her teeth as another pain came, then passed. She smiled. "It's a few weeks early, but it looks like there's about to be another addition to our dreams."